ANOTHER ZIONISM, ANOTHER JUDAISM

ALSO BY GÖRAN ROSENBERG

A Brief Stop on the Road from Auschwitz: A Memoir

ANOTHER ZIONISM,

The Unrequited Love of Rabbi Marcus Ehrenpreis

ANOTHER JUDAISM

Göran Rosenberg

OTHER PRESS
NEW YORK

Originally published in Swedish as *Rabbi Marcus Ehrenpreis obesvarade kärlek* by Albert Bonniers Förlag, Stockholm, in 2021

Chaim Nachman Bialik poems on pp. 11, 161, 320, and 357 translated by the author from Ehrenpreis's translations into Swedish. Nelly Sachs's poem "An euch, die das neue Haus bauen" on page 346 translated from the original German by the author.

Production editor: Yvonne E. Cárdenas
Text designer: Jennifer Daddio
This book was set in Trajan and Bembo by
Alpha Design & Composition of Pittsfield, NH

1 3 5 7 9 10 8 6 4 2

 Printed in the United States of America on acid-free paper. For information write to Other Press LLC, 267 Fifth Avenue, 6th Floor, New York, NY 10016.
Or visit our Web site: www.otherpress.com

Library of Congress Cataloging-in-Publication Data
Names: Rosenberg, Göran, 1948- author.
Title: Another Zionism, another Judaism : the unrequited love of Rabbi Marcus Ehrenpreis / Göran Rosenberg.
Other titles: Rabbi Marcus Ehrenpreis obesvarade kärlek. English
Description: New York : Other Press, [2025] | Includes bibliographical references and index.
Identifiers: LCCN 2024009616 (print) | LCCN 2024009617 (ebook) | ISBN 9781635423549 (hardcover) | ISBN 9781635423556 (ebook)
Subjects: LCSH: Ehrenpreis, Marcus, 1869-1951. | Rabbis—Sweden—Biography.
Classification: LCC BM755.E39 R6713 2025 (print) | LCC BM755.E39 (ebook) | DDC 296.092 [B]—dc23/eng/20240829
LC record available at https://lccn.loc.gov/2024009616
LC ebook record available at https://lccn.loc.gov/2024009617

CONTENTS

ANOTHER ZIONISM, ANOTHER JUDAISM

PREFACE TO THE ENGLISH-LANGUAGE EDITION

A premise of this book is that the losers of history may have just as interesting a story to tell as the winners, who are usually the ones telling it. The story of Marcus Ehrenpreis (1869–1951) is indeed, on the face of it, the story of a loser. His vision for a Zionism aiming at the spiritual and cultural renaissance of Judaism lost out to a Zionism aimed at making the Jews a nation like all others, with a state like all others. His vision of the Jews as an emblematic and exemplary minority, living as a nation amid nations, heralding a world in which minorities and majorities would learn to coexist in peace and prosperity, was rendered tragic, if not naive, by murderous antisemitism and the destruction of European Jewry. And not least, his vision of Judaism as a nonnational force for universal peace and brotherhood was irrevocably challenged by the emergence of a fiercely nationalist and messianic-territorialist interpretation of Judaism, made historically possible by the re-emergence of a Jewish nation-state in Palestine.

Undeniably, then, to enter the world of Marcus Ehrenpreis is to revisit ideas and visions that have been deemed unviable by the court of history. And to meet with a generation of thinkers, writers, rabbis, and activists who saw a future for Jews and Judaism that is no longer for us to see, and who, to the pressing Jewish questions of the time, provided answers that were shown to be illusory.

Nevertheless, the questions they hoped to answer are back to haunt us, as are the human forces that gave rise to them. Wars and conflicts are again ripping our societies apart, authoritarianism, nationalism, xenophobia, and antisemitism are again on the rise, ethnic cleansing is again à la mode, and what Marcus Ehrenpreis termed "the question of Israel" remains as pressing as ever. Not only has its national answer, a Jewish nation-state in Palestine, failed to deliver on its main promise, to solve "the Jewish problem" once and for all, but it has arguably contributed to a plethora of new Jewish conundrums and challenges.

When grappling with "the question of Israel" in an essay written in 1943, knowing full well that "the entire people of Israel" was about to be "swept from the face of the earth," Marcus Ehrenpreis concluded that if there were ever to be a solution to "the Jewish problem," it must go hand in hand with a solution to the wider human problem he had had to confront as a European-Jewish leader in a time of aggressive nationalism, malignant antisemitism, and incessant ethno-national wars. "Peace must be made, not only between the world and the Jews," he wrote, "but more widely, between the weak and the strong, between minorities and majorities, between the oppressed and the oppressors. [...] The strengthening and cementing of minority rights is a sine qua non for a lasting peace, and an imperative requirement for both Jews and other minorities."

Where others saw a new Jewish answer to the question of Israel appearing, Marcus Ehrenpreis saw an ancient question remaining.

This book began with a gift from a friend, a series of neatly bound volumes of a Swedish-Jewish monthly magazine, *Judisk Tidskrift,* covering the period from 1928 to 1951. As I began to peruse its yellowing pages, volume by volume, I found myself entering a Jewish universe brimming with ideas and visions, essays and poetry, sermons and lectures, reviews and reports, discussions and reflections, and, not least, hope. Not unbridled hope, of course—this was a time when the European skies were darkening, and antisemitism was poisoning the air, and a Jewish disaster was looming—but nevertheless a time when a multitude of Jewish venues still seemed open, and Judaism in its many manifestations still seemed to have a European future.

The founder and editor of the magazine was Marcus Ehrenpreis, and as I ventured further into his life and work I got sight of a European-Jewish personality of a larger stature than I had imagined, having played a more significant role in European-Jewish life than I had known, having been more instrumental in the efforts to aid and rescue the Jews of Nazi-ruled Europe than I had been led to believe. In fact, his memory and legacy had been tarnished by malign allegations that he had not done what he could have done to save Jewish lives that could have been saved.

At this time, I had just finished writing my childhood memoir, *A Brief Stop on the Road from Auschwitz*, a book about me and my father and the shadows of the Holocaust in my life. In a previous book I had woven together a history of Zionism and Israel with my years as a teenage pioneer in the young Jewish state, which was a book that began where my childhood ended, with the death of my father and our *aliyah* to Israel in 1962. And thus, the idea came to me that I would continue my writing journey backward in time, into the vanished European-Jewish world from which I had been born, setting out to explore a Jewish heritage that had become mine by contingency and history, hoping to find a Jewish heritage that I could make mine by choice and affection.

From what I had learned about Marcus Ehrenpreis, he promised to be the Virgil I would need for such a journey. Not only had he lived a remarkable life and played a significant role in shaping the European-Jewish world from which I came, but he had done so by bringing forth a Jewish heritage, a line of traditions and values, that appealed to me. I knew full well that with my choice of Virgil I would be guided by a loser of history, but as I came to see the world through the eyes of Marcus Ehrenpreis, I was struck by the continued relevance of the questions he had raised and the answers he had hoped to inspire.

This became even more striking to me at the shocking turn of history on 7 October 2023, in the wake of the Hamas-instigated massacre and hostage-taking in Israel, and the unhinged Israeli response of mass killing and mass devastation, leading to yet another round of displacement and ethnic cleansing, and thereby to the final collapse, morally and politically, of a "winning" answer to the question of Israel. The Zionism that in 1948 had promised to create a Jewish state based "on freedom, justice and peace as envisaged by the prophets of

Israel" had not only produced an ethno-national fortress based on suppression, injustice, and war, but had also failed on its existential promise, to provide a safe haven for the Jews of the world. Paradoxically, the least safe place for Jews to be in at this juncture of history might be Israel itself.

The young Marcus Ehrenpreis had played a central role in the planning of the First Zionist Congress in Basel in 1897, writing and cosigning the Hebrew invitation together with Theodor Herzl (the charismatic leader of the nascent movement), appearing on the stage of the congress to introduce a discussion on the cultural aims of Zionism.

However, the Zionism of Marcus Ehrenpreis would soon turn out to be of another kind than Herzl's, and Ehrenpreis's apprehensions about a Zionism aimed at making the Jews a nation like all others, in a state like all others, would remain strong even as it seemed to realize its aims. At the heart of Ehrenpreis's Zionism was instead the strengthening of Jewish life everywhere by creating a Jewish cultural and spiritual center in Palestine, and at the heart of his Judaism was the conviction that it had a significant contribution to make in the struggle to save the threatened spirit of humanity in humankind.

Or, as he wrote in 1934, as he witnessed the spirit of humanity being extinguished all around him, in words that sound eerily familiar today:

> A wave of hatred wells through the countries, and not only against the Jews. A world order built on the foundations of humanity has been shaken. Terrible forces are set in motion to break the unity of the human race. Confused and anxious, we stand before the ruins of a world that was our common home.

And here we are again, confused and anxious, in yet another momentous turn in Jewish history. Although it's too early to gauge the full significance of the calamitous events following 7 October, they mark the end of the State of Israel as a unifying symbol for Jews and Judaism. They also bring into sharp light the inherent conflict between Zion and Diaspora, between Jews as a national community dwelling in a Jewish nation-state and Jews as a historical, cultural, and spiritual community dwelling among the nations. This conflict, which was all-pervasive in the time of Marcus Ehrenpreis, appeared for a while to have been resolved in my time, albeit tragically, by the near-annihilation of the Jewish Diaspora in Europe and the founding of a Jewish nation-state in Palestine. In the course of Israel's existence, however, it has become increasingly apparent that the ideal of a state based on ethnic-religious dominance must be at variance with the ideal of a state based on ethnic, religious, and cultural diversity. To Marcus Ehrenpreis, the latter was an ideal based on the sources of Judaism itself, and the sine qua non for Jewish spiritual and cultural life to develop and flourish.

At a time when this ideal is again being derided and maligned, and the "never agains" of the postwar era are fading into oblivion, we may contemplate the somber words of Marcus Ehrenpreis, written in 1946, after the near-destruction not only of the European-Jewish world whence he came, but of the larger European world of cross-cultural diversity and creativity which he had strived toward:

> The question was then—and still is today—and will become even more pertinent tomorrow: Can the world be reordered so that ethnic and territorial borders will be made to coincide? And if this cannot be

> done—and hardly anyone in his right mind believes that it can—should any country have the right by divine and human law to deprive the minorities living within its borders, or within provinces conquered by war—peoples of a different historical origin and of a different faith from that of the ruling majority—of their freedom and life opportunities?

Needless to say, the question remains as pertinent today as in 1946, although had Ehrenpreis posed it today it would also have been perceived as a criticism of present-day Israel. However, Ehrenpreis could not imagine that Jews in a Jewish state would become a majority oppressing a minority, and even less that the tenets of Judaism would be used to justify it.

The Zionism and Judaism of Marcus Ehrenpreis were indeed of another kind, and although both of them may be deemed losers of history, this book is written in the conviction that the losers of history need not necessarily have been in the wrong.

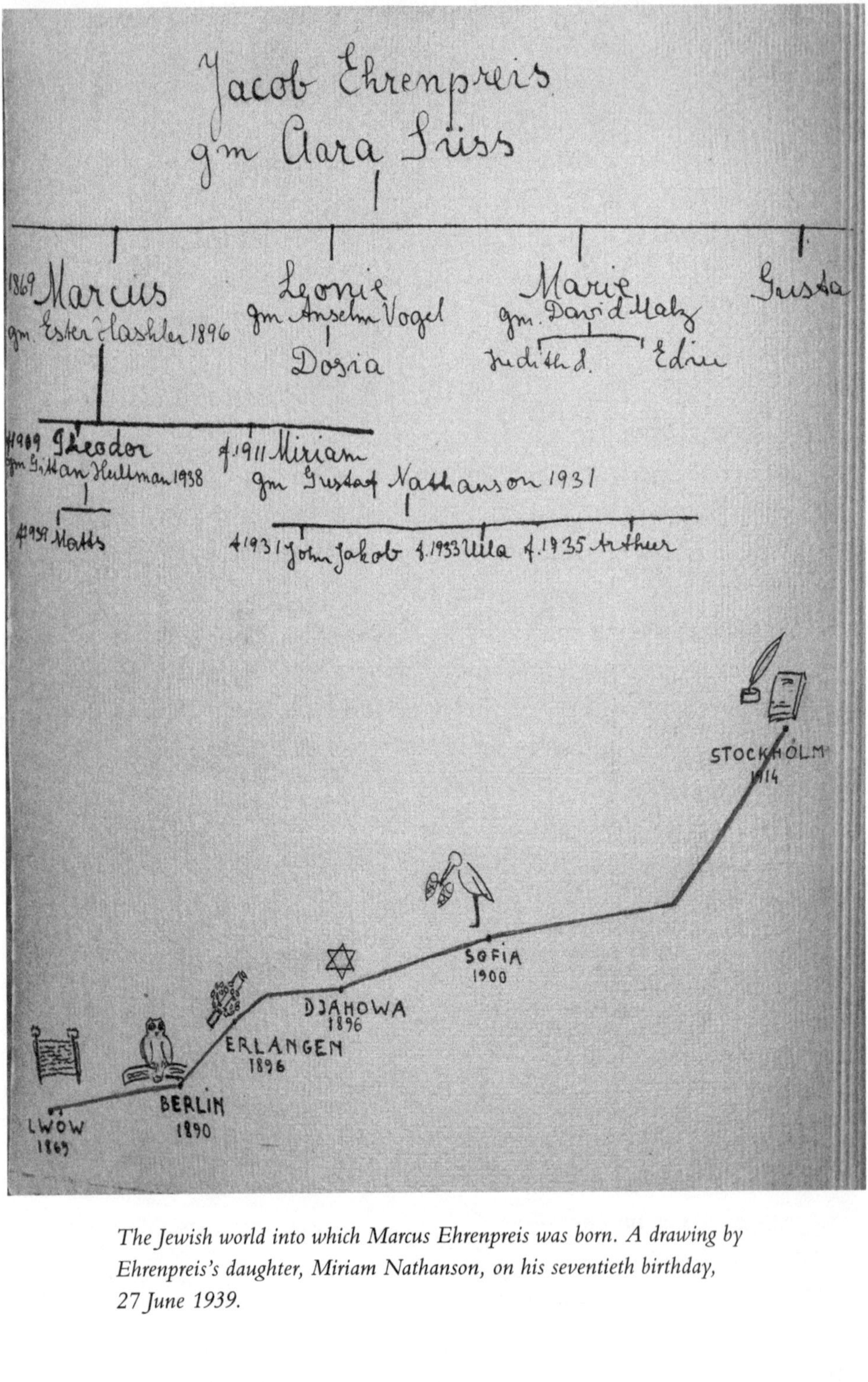

The Jewish world into which Marcus Ehrenpreis was born. A drawing by Ehrenpreis's daughter, Miriam Nathanson, on his seventieth birthday, 27 June 1939.

1.

BEING JEWISH. A PROLOGUE

A chronicler who recites events without distinguishing between major and minor ones acts in accordance with the following truth: nothing that has ever happened should be regarded as lost for history.

—Walter Benjamin, 1940

The year I was born, Rabbi Marcus Ehrenpreis gave his farewell sermon in the Great Synagogue in Stockholm. Three years later he was dead, and there was little reason to expect that I would ever take an interest in his life and work. Even less so, as his name was soon to be tarnished by suspicion and recrimination, and his particular brand of Judaism, envisioning a Jewish spiritual and cultural renaissance, would seem to have little relevance in post-Holocaust Europe.

I was born a stateless Jew in Sweden in 1948, son to survivors of Auschwitz, at a time when it could be asked whether being a Jew in Europe was even possible anymore. Instead, there was a nascent Jewish nation-state with its promise of a reborn Jewish nation and a safe haven for the Jews of the world to fill the existential void in our midst. As a young teenager, "ascending" to the Promised Land in the spring of 1962, I would explore the promise to the fullest. First as an all-embracing Zionist pioneer enthusiastically devoted "to build and be built by Eretz Israel," as our song went, and thereafter as an increasingly bewildered observer of occupation, expulsion, and settlement in the wake of the 1967 war, leaving me with a sense of embarrassment and bereavement. Embarrassed at having known so little about the land I had learned to love and cherish. Bereaved of my unflinching trust in its ideals and promises. It was a shattering experience that would lead to a painful reexamination of my Zionist beliefs.[1] It would also reopen the question in my life of what it meant to be a Jew, since to my generation of children of survivors, remaining a Jew was not an option but an obligation. Remaining a Jew was to deny Hitler a posthumous victory. Remaining a Jew was to give meaning to survival. Remaining a Jew was to share a fate that had been intended for us as well. In my case, remaining a Jew would assume many forms, and at times look like something else, but to deny or hide it was never a consideration of mine.

One form it would assume was a literary endeavor to bring my father back to life. Or more precisely, to understand why he took his life when I was eleven years old. And thereby, I now believe, to better understand the impact of the Holocaust on my own life—and on what it meant to being a Jew.[2]

As the offer of being a national Jew in a Jewish nation-state had proven to be an unsatisfactory answer to my—admittedly high-strung—demands on Jewish meaning, so was the prospect of remaining a Jew in defiance of Hitler. A Jewish existence determined and sustained by the millennial hatred of Jews could have little Jewish meaning in itself, since it was a meaning forced from the outside of Judaism and not emerging from within it. Being born a Jew was certainly not a choice, but wishing to remain so should preferably be. And if it had to be an obligation nevertheless, it should preferably be to something that you could develop an affinity to, and perhaps even learn to love.

Thus, remaining to explore in my haphazard search for the meaning of being Jewish was Judaism itself: that peculiar spiritual and cultural heritage with which I had been born and which had managed to sustain and transform itself over thousands of years, surviving and even flourishing under the most excruciating of circumstances, providing Jews with meaning and purpose in the darkest of times.

As, for example, in the dark fall of 1943, when Marcus Ehrenpreis, the aging chief rabbi in one of the still-unscathed Jewish communities in Nazi-ruled Europe, standing before the densely packed pews in the Great Synagogue of Stockholm on the Day of Atonement, tried to give meaning and purpose to a disaster that was about "to sweep the entire people of Israel from the face of the earth" and whose instigators and perpetrators were hard at work "burning, poisoning, and gassing millions of Jews and tossing them into mass graves in Poland."[3] This was the ultimate test, he preached to his congregation, the final battle between the Sword and the Spirit, the mighty struggle through which the God of Israel, by inscrutable ways, would bring "final victory to the spiritual powers upon which life itself depends." With the Psalmist he invoked a God who in his provocative absence was still among them:

> Save me, O God!
> For the waters have come up to my neck.
> I sink in deep mire,
> Where there is no standing;
> I have come into deep waters,

Where the floods overflow me.
I am weary with my crying;
My throat is dry;
My eyes fail while I wait for my God.
Those who hate me without a cause
Are more than the hairs of my head;
They are mighty who would destroy me,
Being my enemies wrongfully;
Though I have stolen nothing,
I still must restore it.
O God, He knows my foolishness;
And my sins are not hidden from Him.
Let not those who wait for Him, O Lord God of hosts,
be ashamed because of me; Let not those who seek Him
be confounded because of me, O God of Israel.[4]

No, not even in this the darkest of hours would Marcus Ehrenpreis bring shame and dishonor upon the God who had given purpose and meaning to his life.

It is true that for the greater part of his life, now stretching over seventy-four years, from Lemberg in 1869 to Stockholm in 1943, finding purpose and meaning in being Jewish had arguably been easier; easier to imagine a Jewish path from darkness to light, from irresolution to certitude, from humiliation to vindication, from despair to hope. Or, to speak the language of young Ehrenpreis, from the renaissance of Judaism to the redemption of the world, which was a very Jewish path indeed.

But when I was born and Ehrenpreis had only a few years left, and there was no Jewish path without Auschwitz, it was harder to imagine the renaissance of Judaism, let alone the redemption of the world, and thus harder to imagine the continued meaning of being Jewish at all.

One meaning remained, of course, and Ehrenpreis would live to see it replace all others, as being Jewish was reduced to "race," and Jews were reduced to targets for extermination, and Jewish meaning was reduced to the physical survival of Jews. But for Marcus Ehrenpreis there could be no Jewish meaning in survival only. Being Jewish could only have a meaning if the Jewish covenant with God survived, which would compel him to find a Jewish meaning in Auschwitz as well. "Those who will survive these catastrophic times, who will emerge unscathed from the shattered ruins, will take part in the building of a better and happier world with clear vision, pure hearts, and undiminished faith," he wrote in December 1943, when the Jews of Europe were being annihilated and physical survival was all that mattered.

But what else could he do?

Throw the God of Israel on the dustheap of history?

Retract everything he had said and written and believed in?

Tell his flock in the Stockholm synagogue that he, too, had lost faith in the God of Israel?

No, that he could not do.

So there he was, the rabbi in Stockholm with a Jewish light on the horizon in the darkest of times, waiting to be my Virgil into the largely destroyed Jewish world from which I was soon to be born, guiding me to see and understand what being Jewish had meant to him, and what it possibly could still mean to me.

Largely forgotten, Marcus Ehrenpreis entered my life by coincidence. A friend one day took me out to the barn of his country house, where he stored parts of his extensive library, and showed me a beautifully bound collection of *Judisk*

Tidskrift, a Swedish-Jewish cultural journal founded in 1928 and edited by Ehrenpreis until his death in 1951. When asked if I wanted to have them, I accepted with gratitude, and after a few years, as I began to peruse the yellowing pages, I discovered a vibrant Jewish universe brimming with ideas and visions, plans and prospects, polemics and poetry, doubts and disappointments, and yes, a Jewish light on the horizon in the darkest of times.

I knew then, it was the light of Marcus Ehrenpreis I wanted to see.

It may seem futile to search for a light that has been so effectively dimmed by the shadows of Auschwitz. And yet, without a light on the horizon it is hard to be human. At least if by human we mean a being who, seduced by the fruit of knowledge and cast out of paradise, is condemned to seek their place in the world and find meaning in it and take responsibility for their actions in it, which is what I believe being Jewish is ultimately all about.

On the light rests our hope, and on hope rests our humanity.

That's how I see it.

As I also see it, my time needs that light every bit as much as his, which is why I take the liberty to address him from one time to another. Also, to address him as a friend and a kindred spirit, dispensing with the formalities. By that I mean his titles, which are many and at times exotic sounding. In his new country he is addressed as Mr. Chief Rabbi or Doctor Ehrenpreis, singly or in combination, and the letters that come to him from every corner of the Jewish world, written in all its languages, excel in formal greetings—His Eminence, His Excellence, His Most Esteemed, His Most Honorable—in pitches ranging from the respectful and deferential to the entreating.

Increasingly entreating, as time goes by.

Also, in the letters written in Hebrew, the age-old Jewish greetings from the world that he was born into, and that are assumed to be so familiar to him that he is expected to decipher the long-winded Hebrew acronyms in which they come.

May he live in good times, Amen.

May God protect him and keep him safe.

May a good health stand him by.

Well, I will let no bygone titles or formalities stand in the way of the most audacious of liberties that I intend to take—the liberty toward history. Or rather, the liberty toward the verdict of history, which is the verdict handed down by the winners of history, who consign all closed venues, shattered ideas, failed plans, thwarted dreams, extinguished lights, not to mention wasted sufferings and lives, to the dustheap of history.

I will not accept the verdict of history. That which happens to have happened cannot be allowed to determine what was once possible or impossible, let alone what was right or wrong. A defeated idea need not have been a bad idea, a shattered dream not an impossible one. Of course, it might be said that much of what never came to be was neither possible nor desirable, and that what came to be was for the best, but as I see it, the dustheap of history is a treasure trove of unfulfilled possibilities.

That history is not the final arbiter of human actions, that what happened to have happened is not necessarily what ought to have happened, is also a very Jewish view of things. As I see it, the idea that humans are created in God's image means that they have been created to take the step from what *is* to what *ought to be*, and by so doing have been given the capacity to fulfill the creation of God. Jews have made a specific commitment to do so by following the Commandments of God and not the verdict of history, which is what the much-maligned notion of chosenness is all about.

"All that the Lord hath spoken we will do," the children of Israel commit themselves at Sinai, which is the meaning of chosenness and the origin of Judaism.

It is also the horizon of Judaism. The Covenant at Sinai gave the children of Israel the fulfillment of God's creation to live for, and the redemption of the world to look forward to. In the light of history, this may seem a dauntingly distant horizon to look forward to, and not surprisingly the children of Israel have from time to time lost their patience and glimpsed the dawn of redemption in ever-new historical events and individuals.

But the horizon of Judaism, as I understand it, cannot be perceived in the light of history. History can only bring light to that which is, whereas the horizon of Judaism can only be perceived in the light of that which ought to be, that is, in the light of Sinai.

If the verdict of history is that the Jews are losers, the Jews have a horizon against which the losers of history are not necessarily in the wrong.

Marcus Ehrenpreis was undeniably a loser of history, as was his entire generation of Jewish philosophers, rabbis, writers, poets, prophets, and activists, who at a time when their world was about to be annihilated, could still believe that there was a Jewish horizon to be set against the horizon of history. But it is not in the light of history that I wish to see him, since I refuse to grant history the right to judge between right and wrong, or good and evil, or even between the possible and the impossible. The hope for a better world is the hope in a possibility that my time needs as much as his, whatever history has to say on the matter.

Saving the remnants of a possible future from the mounting dustheap of history is what being Jewish ultimately has been all about, I believe. Making no distinction between the winners and losers of history, actually caring more about the losers than the winners, is thus a very Jewish tradition that I gladly join.

Especially at a time when the skies are darkening again, and the winners of history seem to have no other future to offer than economic necessity and technological inevitability, and the horizon seems endless and empty, and the moral wilderness is spreading.

"Light is sown for the righteous, and gladness for the upright in heart," sings the Psalmist (97:11) and he explains in a single verse why Jews stubbornly (obstinately, pigheadedly, provocatively, as the anti-Jewish rhetoric would have it) have refused to submit to the verdict of history.

With Marcus Ehrenpreis I shall explore a Jewish path of light and hope—from his time to mine.

Two Jewish worlds. Father and son, Jacob and Mordechai (Marcus) Ehrenpreis, Lemberg, 1906.

2.

PREMONITIONS OF SPRING

Welcome back, my singing bird,
From countries that radiate warmth—
The lingering winter, how I longed,
my soul, the homeless, the poor.

—Chaim Nachman Bialik

Perhaps I should start from the beginning, with his birth and all that, but I believe that the early years of Marcus Ehrenpreis's life are better viewed from that height where he at twenty-eight can see his past and his future seamlessly stretch backward and forward in time, with all that has already happened pointing to all that is still to come.

I have been at such a height myself and I know how clear the view can be in both directions.

Deceptively clear, to be sure, but the deception is part of the view.

This height in Marcus Ehrenpreis's life was a rabbi's house tucked in among chickens, ducks, and a vegetable garden in the provincial town of Djakovar (now Đakovo) in the region of Croatia known as Slavonia, which at the time of Marcus

Ehrenpreis's arrival in August 1896 belonged to the Austro-Hungarian dual monarchy.

At his first sighting of "this godforsaken den" a few months earlier, Marcus Ehrenpreis had wished that the position would pass him by. But as a young rabbi engaged to be married, he needed a job, and since there had been thirty applicants even to "this little South Slavic corner," it was not a time to be picky.[1] Soon enough, however, he learned to appreciate what the house had to offer: the opportunity to have his sense of nature nurtured by "the living, bounteous earth in its constant self-renewal," and not by Psalm 104 alone.

Nor could he complain about his reception. Celebrating his arrival, the shops on the main street had closed and white-dressed schoolgirls had formed a line, and a few days later, on Emperor Franz Joseph's birthday (18 August), at a religious service honoring the occasion, he was invited to deliver a sermon before the dignitaries of Djakovar.

With the most prominent among them, the eighty-year-old Catholic bishop Joseph Strossmayer, a central figure in the nascent movement for a South Slavic cultural renaissance (Illyrianism), the newly married Marcus and Esther Ehrenpreis would soon become friends and be given access to the private park of the bishop's residence, where Esther liked to take her walks and Bishop Strossmayer liked to see her. In the bright twilight of early summer, the young couple would dwell on the steps of the small synagogue listening to the evensong of the frogs and contemplating the silence beyond the walls of the white nunnery across the street, enjoying the stillness of the place, and perhaps for a while imagining that everything was peace and quiet.

Which in fact very little was. As in most of the Balkans, Djakovar was a smoldering powder keg of nationalist conflicts.

The Croats hated the ruling Hungarians, feared the domineering Serbs, and cultivated their own aggressive nationalism. The few Jews of Djakovar had a hard time figuring out with whom to associate so as to not get into trouble. Strossmayer, a comparatively broad-minded cultural nationalist, nevertheless expressed his dissatisfaction that the Jews of Djakovar preferred to speak German and Hungarian rather than Croatian, and thus had not wholeheartedly committed themselves to the South Slavic cause.

"You Jews always make the mistake of siding with the strong," Strossmayer told the new rabbi.

When, a year later, Marcus Ehrenpreis, in fluent Croatian, delivered a tribute from the Jews of Djakovar celebrating Strossmayer's fifty years in office, Strossmayer's eyes glimmered, and a few days later the Croatian speech of Rabbi Marcus Ehrenpreis was published in the official organ of the bishop's seat in Zagreb.[2]

The fact that the height with the clear view happened to be Djakovar had little to do with Djakovar itself. "How small you are, Herr Doktor," the *preses* (chairman) of the congregation had let slip when he greeted the newcomer to his general store on Djakovar's main street. However, the preses and his congregation made a similar impression on Herr Doktor. He described them as friendly and decent; most of them were craftsmen and small merchants, some were physicians and lawyers, "but there was no intellectual level to speak of." Nor did he take much notice of Strossmayer's brand-new cathedral, which rose above Djakovar like a giant in Lilliput, and in those years seemed to mark Djakovar to be a higher place on earth than the small people living in its shadow really understood.

Marcus Ehrenpreis was not a tall man, as the preses had correctly observed, but neither was he remarkably short, only slightly under the average height for men of his time. The information about his ascending prominence preceding him, however, might have created expectations of a more imposing figure than the dapper young man who had entered the preses's general store. Moreover, Marcus Ehrenpreis's beard was better groomed, his mustache more neatly trimmed, and his clothes more worldly than would have been expected of a rabbi in the eastern regions of Europe. Gone were the traditional attributes—the hat, the caftan, the sidelocks, and the prayer shawl tassels—but also the Orthodox view of Jewish life and customs.

Yet the Jews of Djakovar must have known that Marcus Ehrenpreis was a rabbi of a new kind, and that by choosing him they seemed to have opted for a compromise between Orthodoxy and Reform, tradition and enlightenment. If so, they seemed to have made the right choice—although the word "compromise" was not frequent in Rabbi Ehrenpreis's vocabulary at the time.

"I do not expect to grow anymore," Ehrenpreis had humbly responded to the greeting remarks of the preses, but that wasn't quite true. Marcus Ehrenpreis expected to grow considerably more. There was little to be done about the body, that was true, but for the spirit there was growth to be expected as far as the eye could see. Ever-new waves of spiritual and cultural awakenings were sweeping the Jewish world, and on the crest of the most inspiring and promising of them rode the young man who had just arrived in Djakovar and who had already made a name for himself in four languages, in Berlin, Vienna, Lemberg, Warsaw, and wherever new generations of frustrated and restless European Jews hungered for change. To Djakovar he had brought the manuscript of a manifesto, soon to be published in both German and Hebrew, calling for nothing less than a Jewish-Hebrew literary renaissance in Europe.

"There are Young Hebrews!" *Es gibt Junghebräer!* Ehrenpreis would proclaim in the very first sentence. "They are the first full-blooded Europeans in Hebrew literature. They are all dissatisfied and hungry. The crushed human soul [rises] in these late-born ghetto children and [yearns] for liberation. [...] The great longing for Europe has awakened in them. [...] A ravenous hunger for Europeanness, for *Europäerthum*, for culture, for science, for art—for the vitality and magnificence in that which [Europe's] outstanding spirits have shaped and created."[3]

Ehrenpreis's generation was not the first to have sensed new and fresh winds penetrating the murky walls of the Jewish study-house, nor the first to have hidden books of a different kind beneath their Talmud folios. But perhaps it was the first to become disillusioned by the Jewish Enlightenment, the Haskalah, which had held out the promise of a Jewish path to civic belonging and acceptance in Europe based on reason (*Vernunft*) and education (*Bildung*), but had failed to make the case for the continued relevance of Jews and Judaism to Europe. They had been told that the gateway to Europe was enlightenment, but they soon discovered that the only people in Europe who were considered in need of enlightenment were the Jews. By which was usually meant that they should become enlightened enough to leave Judaism behind.

For the young Ehrenpreis and his circle of "late-born ghetto children," that was too high a price to pay: in such a Europe they would never be at home. "Their heart was still in the Jewish street," the manifesto continued. "Judaism was their destiny even as they railed against it. [...] Amid their airy dreams, they understood the painful cry of the tormented Jewish people and saw a new world emerging from the ruins [of the Russian pogroms]. The quiet Jewish quarter had taken on new life, the cowardly had gained courage, the weak had gained strength, a promise flashed in their tear-filled eyes. Finally, these life-yearning young people knew what they wanted."[4]

It had already become clear to them that enlightenment, whatever that meant, would not mean the end of Jew-hatred, but, on the contrary, the beginning of a Jew-hatred from which there was no escape by any amount of enlightenment and assimilation. In fact, it was a Jew-hatred that seemed fueled by enlightenment and assimilation. Enlightenment had provided Jew-hatred with a new, racist "scientificity" (and a "scientific" name, antisemitism), and assimilation had provided it with ever-new "evidence" of secret Jewish conspiracies. In a Paris beset by Jew-hatred (1894), Captain Alfred Dreyfus's crime was not that he was too much a Jew, but that he was a Jew who wanted too much to be a good French officer.

The Enlightenment had inspired a generation of young Jews to make the journey from the Jewish learning houses of Galicia to the academic lecture halls of Berlin and Vienna, confident that a world of tolerance and respect would open to them. Only to discover that they had ended up in a no-man's-land between the world they had left behind and the world they longed to be a part of. And that it was not European enlightenment that was lacking in them, but Jewish self-esteem. Particularly so in a Europe where the terms of belonging were increasingly draped in the words of nation, culture, language, and race. In such a Europe, the Jews would find their rightful place only if they knew how to become more Jewish, not less; if they knew how to affirm and develop their cultural and spiritual distinctiveness instead of suppressing and watering it down; if they knew how to create, in their inherited language, Hebrew, a literature and poetry that would express the "soul" of the Jewish people and touch the hearts of the world.

Weren't the first voices already heard? The first writers and poets breathing new Hebrew life into the words of the Psalmists and the Prophets.

Or as Ehrenpreis had proclaimed in his manifesto:

> To us, there is a new world crying out to be expressed! The new life of our people! The new goals! The new hopes! We are Jews, but we are European Jews. The Jewish culture we strive for must be both Jewish and European. We shun national assimilation because it is both impossible and unnatural, but we want to belong to the European spirit, we want to be part of the community of cultured humankind. To us, a petrified Jewish culture must not be perpetuated forever. To us, culture must be forceful and dynamic. To us, there are Jews of here and now, vigorous, sensitive, creating and destroying values. Like a fresh well it will burst forth; invigorating and fortifying—the literature of the Young Hebrews.[5]

Clearly then, the new rabbi of Djakovar was not a man of compromise. He was a Jewish radical, who besides having a congregation to lead had a cultural revolution to prepare. Among the "dwarfish books of unholy texts" hidden beneath the Talmud folios of his childhood were Darwin and Nietzsche, and in his manifesto's tribute to the vitality of the Jewish people, and to the willpower of the Young Hebrews, one could trace the influence of both. Nor was it difficult to trace the influence of Gottfried Herder, the German philosopher who had postulated that every people had a distinct soul, *Volksseele*, and that language and literature were the means by which it came to light. In Herder's view, national and cultural distinctions were an intrinsic feature of human existence, and not a passing historical phase to which Enlightenment and Progress would put an end. Cultural and national difference must therefore be the very starting point for any idea of human brotherhood and understanding. The more a people could understand itself the more it could understand other peoples, and a people could primarily understand itself by means of its own language and literature.

Maybe it was not the exact words of Herder that echoed through Ehrenpreis's manifesto, but the idea that language and literature were the key to the soul of the Jewish people and the gateway to a place in the world was what permeated it. Only by breathing new life into their own language, Hebrew, could the Jews breathe new life into their spiritual and cultural heritage, and regain their spiritual and cultural self-esteem.

On reflection, it was more than Djakovar that united Ehrenpreis with Bishop Strossmayer. What Strossmayer wanted to do with the Croats—awaken them to national consciousness through language and literature—Ehrenpreis wanted to do with the Jews. Strossmayer had founded a publishing house for young Croatian literature and poetry, and detailed plans for a publishing house devoted to new Hebrew literature and poetry were now being concocted by Ehrenpreis in Djakovar.

All over Europe there were the shackled souls of people longing to be released by language and literature: Croats, Serbs, Poles, Bulgarians, Romanians.

So why not the Jews?

In the spring of 1897, a close friend and soulmate moved in with the Ehrenpreis couple in Djakovar. There he was to recover from a period of illness, work on a short story, assist

Ehrenpreis in planning the new publishing house, and otherwise prepare for the Hebrew cultural revolution. His name was Micha Josef Berdyczewski, and his presence is clearly felt in the tone and text of Ehrenpreis's manifesto, which was being published in Hebrew and would soon be published in German. It was during "a constant exchange of ideas" with Berdyczewski that the text had taken shape, and it was after "a lively exchange of letters" that the visit to Djakovar had come about.

Berdyczewski had grown up in the same intense Jewish environment as Ehrenpreis, in yet another spiritual and cultural hub of eastern European Jewry, Medzhybizh, in a part of western Ukraine that had once been Polish and was now Russian, and which in the eighteenth century had become the birthplace of the charismatic movement in Judaism known as Hasidism. Berdyczewski had been born into Hasidism, and like Ehrenpreis, had spent his childhood and adolescence in houses of Jewish learning and seminars of Talmudic studies, and like Ehrenpreis, had found himself in a spiritual prison. However, his yearning for another life, another Jewish life, had found far more uncompromising expressions in both his personal life and in his writing.

Berdyczewski was a restless spirit, one could say, which could not be said of Ehrenpreis at the time. Before his visit to Djakovar, Berdyczewski had already broken up two marriages by making himself religiously and socially intolerable to the families of the brides, and in his feverish writings he had exposed a traumatic relationship to the Jewish world.[6] A young wine that had stopped fermenting, Ehrenpreis would write of Berdyczewski only a few years later (1901), a thinker who had put his "muscular radicalism" on display, and who angered far too many with his "unwarranted paradoxes."

"I cannot forgive him for this," Ehrenpreis wrote.[7]

They had met a few years earlier in Berlin, at a gathering organized by the Russian-Jewish students, and in the noisy environment Ehrenpreis had immediately noticed the stubbornly silent Berdyczewski, who with his "strangely un-Jewish" head, defiant expression, and light-blond mustache, seemed very "Aryan." Ehrenpreis had read him without being impressed, "he wrote badly and all over the place," and had found most remarkable the deadly contempt with which the young Berdyczewski in his articles (and in his life) burned his bridges to the Jewish world.[8]

Ehrenpreis didn't want to burn any bridges, but the small association of Jewish students in Berlin where the two of them had met yearned for Jewish renewal. Berdyczewski may not have written well, but his radicalism was in the air and "his whole personality, his rebelliousness, his hunger for life, his ethical pathos" made a strong impression. "In the midst of our clamoring Jewish world, I could hear the bold cry from a fiery spirit calling us to awaken," Ehrenpreis later wrote, explaining what had drawn him to Berdyczewski; a short-lived attraction between "two combative dreamers, dissatisfied with the world and with themselves."[9]

> Everything within us suffered from Judaism, from its inner degradation more than its outer. The eighties, with its Russian pogroms, its Western European antisemitism, its forced migrations of Jews, weighed on our young minds. The inner spirit of Jewish life seemed to us hopelessly weakened. [...] We wanted a clean house, a new start, rebuilding a living Judaism from the ground up.[10]

For a few years they would stand together on the barricades of the Hebrew-language revolution, then they would part ways. Berdyczewski would become the self-tormented Hebrew bard of Jewish ambiguity, anxiety, and burned bridges, while Ehrenpreis would climb down from the barricades and look back upon his years of "youthful exuberance" with self-deprecation and forbearance.

In the summer of 1897, however, the view from Djakovar was perfectly clear, and the Jewish spiritual and cultural revolution seemed imminent, and at the end of August, when the wheat fields surrounding Djakovar had been harvested, representatives of the Jews of the world were to assemble in Basel, Switzerland, to discuss in earnest the possibility of a Jewish state in Palestine.

Convening the congress in Basel and spearheading the idea of a territorial solution to "the Jewish problem" was a tall, thirty-seven-year-old man with sharp features, a visionary gaze, and a feverish faith in himself and his cause that made some see him a madman and others a prophet. In the late autumn of 1895, Marcus Ehrenpreis and his Jewish circle in Berlin had read an excerpt from a forthcoming book by Theodor Herzl titled *Der Judenstaat*, The State of the Jews, and they soon saw him as a prophet. Not so much because of what he had said in his book, they had all already said and thought something similar, and perhaps even done so in a more profound way, but because it was he who had done it. Theodor Herzl, of all people! The famous journalist and playwright, whom they had all read and admired for his elegant reflections on everything between heaven and earth, "those rare fine little works of art, at once profound and clear, melancholic and cheerful, elegantly structured and finely chiseled."[11] Theodor Herzl was born into a Jewish family in Austro-Hungarian Budapest, but few who read him in *Neue Freie Presse* or saw his plays on the stages of Vienna's theaters associated him with anything Jewish. He might have described himself as a person of Jewish origin writing in German, but the Jewish world alienated him, and the influx to Vienna of Yiddish-speaking "ghetto Jews" from Ehrenpreis's Galicia horrified him.

That this very Theodor Herzl should come out as a full-blooded Jew, wholly dedicating himself to the Jewish cause, was a conversion on par with Paul on the road to Damascus, and to Ehrenpreis and his circle he was a revelation. "That is how many of us imagined King David, the embodiment of the ancient Hebrew in his strength and perfection," he would later write, recalling the rousing impact of Herzl's appearance on the Jewish scene, the embodiment of the new, free, upright, liberated Jew, "as he lived in our fantasies and yearnings."[12]

Six months after the publication of *Der Judenstaat*, in August 1896, Ehrenpreis sent a message to Herzl in Vienna, wishing him a prosperous Jewish New Year and invoking God's blessing on his work for a solution to the Jewish problem. The young rabbi's modesty, or was it the limitations of the greeting format, forbade him from pointing out that ten years earlier, he had himself founded a student association called Zion in his hometown of Lemberg, with a program that in some respects resembled Herzl's. He could also have mentioned, albeit modestly, that he had played a not-insignificant role in convening a congress in Lemberg in April 1893 that had brought together representatives of the "Zionist movement in Galicia" with a total of thirty-six associations and four thousand members, and which in both form (congress) and name (Zionism) could be said to have preceded Herzl.

Perhaps Herzl would also have benefited from learning something about the World Zionist Congress that Ehrenpreis and his circle were laying plans for in 1893, with ambitions that might well have matched those of Herzl: a Zionist party was to be formed, the colonization of Palestine to be organized, and Hebrew to become a modern language.[13] In early September 1893, a preparatory meeting was held at the home of the writer Nathan Birnbaum in Vienna. Seven people were present, Ehrenpreis took the minutes, and it was unanimously decided that the world congress should be held in Berlin in the spring of 1894 and last for three days, and after some discussion, that the proceedings should be conducted in Hebrew, German, and French (not Yiddish!), and sympathetic personalities be invited to attend.

No, no adversaries! They had had enough of adversaries.

The plans of 1893 came to nothing. There was a Herzl missing, Ehrenpreis might have told Herzl if he had been asked about it. From Herzl's response to Djakovar on 13 September 1896, it was evident that he knew nothing about any of this. Instead, he deplored the continuing lack of understanding among "our rabbis" and warmly welcomed the supposedly new convert Marcus Ehrenpreis to the Zionist cause.[14]

A few months later, Ehrenpreis received a letter from his childhood friend in Lemberg and fellow student in Berlin, Osias Thon, inviting him to a meeting with Herzl in Vienna. What Herzl mainly wanted to discuss was the founding of a German-language Zionist newspaper. What Ehrenpreis mainly wanted to discuss was a resumption of the plans from

1893 for a world Zionist congress. To the meeting, which took place on 5 March 1896 among a small circle of invitees, Ehrenpreis had brought his handwritten minutes from the meeting in 1893, but as soon as he got sight of Herzl he knew the minutes would make no difference. The first sight was overwhelming: the prophetic gaze, the stately posture, the rare combination of unbound imagination and cunning calculation.[15]

Henceforth, Herzl would make all the difference.

At the meeting Herzl listened attentively, took careful notes, and probably learned a thing or two about Judaism, but at the same time made perfectly clear that he had little time to waste. The plans for a Zionist daily resulted in a Zionist weekly, *Die Welt*, to appear two months later, in May 1897, and the 1893 plans for a world Zionist congress became the 1897 plans, to be realized at a feverish pace in August the same year. Letters and telegrams were to be written, opponents dealt with, venues scouted, delegates appointed, invitations formulated, and mailing lists compiled.

From Herzl in Vienna a restless flow of directives, warnings, and appeals. On 24 July 1897, a letter to Ehrenpreis in Djakovar demanding him to immediately, *sofort*, compile and print an invitation in Hebrew, and without delay, *unverzüglich*, have it sent to the most prominent Zionists in Russia:

> Emphasize in the most energetic manner, *in der energischesten Weise*, that the congress must unconditionally, *unbedingt*, be a success and that it is therefore absolutely necessary, *unerlässlich*, that the Russians [representatives of the Russian Jews] attend in large numbers. The invitation shall be signed by you as a member of the Preparatory Committee with the title "secretary" (whatever Hebrew word you can find for this) and by

me as chairman of the Preparatory Committee. I trust, Dr. Ehrenpreis, that you will do this with immediate effect and with the utmost energy. Time is short and I am weighed down with work and I must be able to rely on my colleagues. Please let me know as soon as possible that everything has been done. Best regards from yours truly, Th. Herzl.[16]

On 28 July yet another letter: "I have reserved for you the introduction of Hebrew and cultural issues. Munich must be abandoned. We will go to Basel. As you know, a terrible campaign against the congress has been launched, and we must all make sure that the first time is a success."[17]

Among the many things that didn't exist in Djakovar was a Hebrew printer. What did exist was Max Bruck's book and paper shop, which had a small press for printing invitations, business cards, posters, and local brochures. As it turned out, it also housed a case of Hebrew types for announcing Jewish weddings and funerals. The number of types didn't suffice to print much more than that. Neither did the skills of Hebrew in Max Bruck's book and paper shop. If there were to be a Hebrew invitation, Ehrenpreis would have to type and print it himself. Which he did with a skill that must have surprised and impressed not only the shop owner in Djakovar but the visiting Berdyczewski as well, who had to tear himself away from his writing desk to serve as a printer's assistant.

To solve the problem of too few types, the invitation had to be printed in two rounds, half an invitation at a time, so that the types used in the first round could be reused for the second. Words for which there were not sufficient types had to be excluded. On the finished invitation, which barely filled a page, there was no visible gap between the two rounds of printing, and the printed Hebrew text flowed seamlessly from right to left.

Dear Sir! it opened, *Adon nichbad!* Then the date and place of the conference, and a few words about its significance and importance. In accordance with Herzl's instructions, a special plea to the "Russians," who had a pogrom-prone government to consider and must be given assurances that their attendance would not provoke it. Also, on this one and only page, slander must be refuted, and criticism must be preempted. There must also be space left to mention that the congress will be the beginning of a new era and that Hebrew will be one of its official languages.

Right there and then, on a makeshift press for Hebrew typesetting and printing in Max Bruck's book and paper shop in Djakovar, the high-flying visions hit the ground and became a printed invitation to a specific congress at a specific date in a specific place. Finally, in Basel, all the aberrant Jewish paths of the world would converge in a broad thoroughfare, leading toward one and the same goal. The only-yesterday, all-important conflict—between those who dreamed of a spiritual-cultural renaissance and those who dreamed of a national-political awakening—seemed suddenly irrelevant. After all, didn't they all want "to breathe new life into Israel's withered bones"?[18]

Consequently, Ehrenpreis's radical manifesto could be published both in the newly launched Hebrew monthly *Ha'shiloach*, which dreamed of the spiritual-cultural renaissance, and in a newly launched German-language weekly, which dreamed of the national-political awakening. The latter was Herzl's *Die Welt*, in which the manifesto was given the laconic title "The Young Hebrew Literature," *Die junghebräische Literatur.* In the Hebrew magazine, which was closer to Ehrenpreis in every

Commission d. Zionisten-Congresses
Wien,
II, Rembrandtstr. 11.

אדון נכבד!

ביום א׳ ב׳ וג׳ אלול ש״ז יתאספו חו״צ בכל הארצות לקונגרס־הציוני
בבאזל (בשווייץ). והיום ההוא, שבו יתאחדו אחינו המפוזרים בדעה אחת,
יהיה יום נצחון לתחית לאומנו. האספה בבאזל תהיה התחלת תקופה
חדשה בהתפתחות תנועתנו.

שם יספרו לנו אחינו מכל פנות הארץ ע״ד מצבם ומגמותיהם, שם יתברר
מה התנועה הציונית דורשת ממעריציה, שם תתרכז ותתאחד פעולתנו,
שהיתה קרועה לכמה גזרים, ע״י הנהגה כוללת לכל סניפי העבודה. שם
תראינה עינינו קבוץ־גליות, שיאחד כל הכחות לפעולה אחת, גדולה וכבירה.

הקונגרס שואף למטרות קרובות ואפשריות. כל הידיעות האחרות
על אודותיו קלוטות מן האויר. כל מעשי הקונגרס יהיו בפרסום גמור.
בכוחו והחלטותיו לא תהיה שום התנגדות לחוקי איזה ארץ ולחובותינו
האזרחיים. ביחוד אנחנו ערבים בזה, שכל מעשי האספה יהיו באופן
מקובל ומרוצה לחו״צ ברוסיא ולממשלתם הרוממה.

בזה נבקש אותך, אדון נכבד, ואת חבריך שבחוגך, שתואילו לבא לבזל
ולהשתתף באספתנו. הקונגרס הראשון שלנו הוא החל שהכל פונים אליו.
אוהבים ואויבים מחכים לו בעינים כלות. ולכן עלינו להראות לכל כי הפצנו
ברור ויכלתנו גדולה. אם לא ימלא הקונגרס את תפקידו, אז תבא ע״כ נסיגה
לאחור בתנועתנו לזמן רב. והכל תלוי רק בהשתתפות מרובה של
אחינו ברוסיא, ששם רוב מנינו.

אנו מקוים, שתדעו את חובתכם ותבאו לאספתנו. באספה אפשר יהיה
לדבר עברית. בבאזל יש אכסניא כשרה.

דבר בואך מהר נא להודיענו עפ״י הכתבת הנ״ל.

בשם הועד להכנת הקונגרס הציוני:

Dr. Marcus Ehrenpreis
המזכיר

Dr. Theodor Herzl
ראש־הועד

The Hebrew invitation to the First Zionist Congress in Basel, written, typeset, and printed by Marcus Ehrenpreis in Djakovar in August 1897. With a dedication from Theodor Herzl to "Dr. Ehrenpreis."

respect, and of which he was the literary editor, the title was a more combative "Whither!?" *Lean!?*

The Hebrew periodical had been named, somewhat contradictorily, after the slow-moving river Shiloh, which in Isaiah (8:6) is made to symbolize the patient trust in God that the children of Israel must adopt. Patience might have been a characteristic of the magazine's founder, Ascher Ginsberg, better known as Ahad Ha'am, "one of the people," but hardly of his young followers, including Ehrenpreis, who wanted to see the Jewish Renaissance "break forth like a mighty river, fertilizing and path-breaking."[19] Nor did the young firebrands hesitate to take issue with their patient mentor on the all-crucial question whether the new Hebrew literature should be for Jews or for the world. The Young Hebrews wanted it to be a literature for the world, and Ehrenpreis, in the Hebrew version of his manifesto, took the matter to its revolutionary extreme: "The history of human culture has taught us that only great goals can unleash great forces. We must not move slowly, there must be a revolution, a revolution of the spirit, *mahapecha baroach*."[20]

Ahad Ha'am let the impatient Young Hebrews rummage about in his magazine, which was a wise thing to do, since they would soon discover that larger issues were at stake and larger conflicts awaited, and that in the larger conflicts they were on the same side. Still, Ahad Ha'am had to make clear who was ultimately the editor. When Ehrenpreis suggested that he could send his manuscripts directly to the printer in Berlin without a detour to Ahad Ha'am in Odessa, Ahad Ha'am replied acidly: "I always find it necessary to add comments to your chronicles, and our diverging opinions on a number of issues will probably make this necessary in the future as well."[21]

Soon Ehrenpreis would look back on his disputes with Ahad Ha'am with embarrassment. At the end of the day, they were children of the same eastern European–Jewish milieu, with the same frustrations at what they saw as Jewish decline and irrelevance and with the same dreams of a coming Jewish spiritual and cultural golden age. While Herzl's national-political project aimed to save the Jews from persecution and humiliation by securing a sovereign territory in Palestine (or somewhere else), Ehrenpreis, like Ahad Ha'am, wanted to save the Jews from spiritual and cultural decay by creating in Palestine (not somewhere else!) a spiritual center "from which cultural impulses would radiate all over the Jewish Diaspora."[22] Or as Ehrenpreis would later put the difference between one Zionism and another: "While Herzl wanted to save the house of Jacob, we wanted to save the indispensable treasures contained in it."[23]

In the clear view from Djakovar all Jewish roads were now converging on Basel. Harsh conflicts about ends and means had mellowed into friendly discussions about nuances and emphases, and certainly Ehrenpreis had no intention of using his promised spot on the congress floor to stir up a fight.

On 2 August, a letter from Herzl to Ehrenpreis thanking him for his swift completion of the mission and urging him to be on his guard—as if the whole thing could still collapse: "Please keep an eye on the Hebrew press in Russia, demand clarifications and corrections if necessary."[24]

On 16 August: "Do not send an invitation to Mr. Bambus. An offer to subscribe to *Techija* [the Hebrew publishing house planned by Ehrenpreis and Berdyczewski] will be published in the next issue [of *Die Welt*]."[25]

Mission completed. The Hebrew invitations sent out. The Hebrew revolution prepared. Herzl seemingly on board. Two weeks to Basel.

Never again would the Jewish horizon of Marcus Ehrenpreis appear as bright as in the summer of 1897, and never again would his life journey seem as straightforward. Without the childhood in a printer's house in Lemberg, there could be no rabbi in Djakovar with the surprising ability to compose, typeset, and print a Hebrew text in two rounds.

Time, then, to say something about his birth and childhood.

Mordechai Ehrenpreis was born on 27 June 1869 in Lemberg. He had learned the art of typesetting Hebrew texts in his maternal grandfather's publishing and printing house, on the ground floor of an inconspicuous two-story house on Zulkiewska Street, where Mordechai, or Marcus, as he would be called, spent a great part of his childhood. It was not uncommon for newly married Jewish couples to be housed in one of the parental homes, as they usually married very young, or rather were brought to marry.

Clara (Chaje) Deborah Süss was thirteen years old when she was brought to marry Jacob Ehrenpreis, who was sixteen. Clara's father and Marcus's maternal grandfather was Abraham Nissan Süss, remembered by Marcus as "a noble prophet figure [suffused] by a piety that was genuine and deep."[26] During the day he ran a demanding business as a publisher and printer of Jewish books and writings, while at night he studied and prayed. At street level, a wine merchant kept his stock of oak barrels, which were rolled in and out of the house through a wide portico, emitting a scent of alcohol that percolated up to the second floor, where Reb Süss lived with his wife and nine children, and eventually with his first grandson, Marcus. Two rooms served as book storage, but discarded proof sheets also found their way to the nursery, where they were soon to be transformed from toys to reading material. Even before Marcus, at the age of four, was put in a Jewish school, a *heder*, he spelled his way through the books produced by his grandfather's printing house. Prayer books at first, but soon enough rabbinic expositions, Hasidic sayings, and all sorts of ritual precepts. An abridged ritual code, *Kitzur Shulchan Aruch*, was a bestseller of the publishing house and sold tens of thousands of copies all over Jewish eastern Europe.[27]

Grandfather Süss understandably gave his most attentive care to his first grandson, promptly impregnating his fertile mind with appropriate parts of the Torah, as well as the prayers and the blessings. Marcus would describe his grandfather as his first and foremost tutor, and the love with which he would later describe the Jewish world in which he was formed, "the home of my soul," was clearly rooted in memories from his stay in Grandfather's house.[28]

At first the house was the home of his parents too, and the publishing house became the responsibility of his father as well. When the business became temporarily insolvent, and the separate home that his parents had managed to create for themselves had to be temporarily dissolved, some of that responsibility fell on the shoulders of Marcus, not yet thirteen years old. As his mother, Clara, had to move in with a sister in the countryside, and his father, Jacob, had to set off to work in a bookstore in Moldavia, Marcus had to move back in with his grandfather to help him manage the remainder of the business. This meant registering new orders from the dwindling book stock and carrying heavy book parcels to the post office, all while ignoring the anti-Jewish slurs from the delivery boys in line.[29]

By the time the business was back on track again and the parental home was reinstated, Marcus Ehrenpreis not only knew how to run (or not run) a publishing house, but at the age of thirteen had written his first literary opus, a Yiddish account of the 1882 antisemitic ritual murder trial in Tiszaeszlár, Hungary, in which a thirteen-year-old son had been induced to give false testimony against his father. Shortly afterward

Marcus wrote a biography of Napoleon, also in Yiddish, and a few years later a biography of the British-Jewish philanthropist Moses Montefiore, whose centenary (1884) was celebrated in the Jewish world. The latter became a minor bestseller, and after a while a letter arrived for the young writer in Lemberg from the still-living centenarian in London with a one-pound note attached.

To the early literary debut of young Marcus Ehrenpreis, his father might have served as a source of inspiration. Jacob Ehrenpreis was not only a publisher and a printer but an author in his own right. He penned articles in both Yiddish and Hebrew for the local Jewish press, and he was himself the author of several booklets on Jewish topics that were printed and sold by the publishing house. "The Jewish Hartleben," he would later be dubbed by his granddaughter, the poet and essayist Debora Vogel, Marcus's niece.[30] Otto Erich Hartleben was a German writer who in the 1890s had become known for his outspoken reflections on contemporary mores and morality, and although the comparison was fundamentally misleading—Jacob Ehrenpreis was not a moral critic—it went to show that in the family at least, he was remembered as a free-spirited observer of his place and time. In the way he lived and dressed, he remained an inseparable part of the Jewish world of his father and father-in-law, but in his way of seeing the world he was a generation closer to the Jewish-Hebrew revolution that Marcus would soon be dreaming of. The love of Hebrew was already there, as was the sensitivity to the new Jewish ideas spreading in Lemberg and shaking its Orthodox hegemony.

Right next to Grandfather's house, on the old town square where there had been a fish market, a wealthy group of reform-minded Jews had built a temple that in its appearance had little in common with Grandfather's houses of prayer. With its enormous dome, its organ and choir, its German-language sermon, it looked more like a church, and by Lemberg's overwhelmingly Orthodox majority was perceived as such—and as a provocation at that. Its first rabbi was poisoned under unclear circumstances, and the frequent protests against the heretics in the temple "gave a foretaste of the thunderstorm that was about to sweep the peaceful Jewish street."[31]

Jacob Ehrenpreis never set foot in the new temple, and never changed his way of praying and dressing, and from his outer appearance no one would suspect that he had opened the door of his house to literature from another world, and thereby a door for Marcus to exit into a world different from that of his father and maternal grandfather.

And of his paternal grandfather.

Mordechai Zeev Ehrenpreis died in 1865, four years before Marcus (Mordechai) was born, allowing him to bear his paternal grandfather's name. After a living grandparent, a Jewish child could not be named. Thus, if Mordechai the younger could have no personal memories of Mordechai the elder, the latter would nevertheless leave him with a personal document, which in its dry and factual way would cast yet another light of love and clarity on the Jewish world into which Marcus had been born.

The document, which was to accompany Marcus Ehrenpreis from his parental home in Lemberg to his library in Stockholm, was a folio-sized ledger containing a meticulous accounting of the tithe (in Hebrew, *ma'asar ksafim*) that Mordechai Zeev had set aside each year between 1837 and 1849 from his initially modest business income, to be used for righteous purposes. In the ledger, each week's earnings were carefully recorded, along with the amount set aside for tithing and what it had been spent on. Most often it had gone to poor and needy people, several times to one and the same person, but also to synagogues and prayer houses and the purchase of religious books outside of what a pious Jew was required to have. Mordechai Zeev also gave a deeply personal account of why he had chosen to express his piety in this way. Tithing was certainly an existing Jewish tradition, but it was not a religious commandment, nor was it a particularly widespread practice. Mordechai Zeev was a bookkeeper and a private lawyer (*Winkelschreiber*, a village scribe) by profession, and his mind was more that of a businessman than of a bookish scholar. And perhaps it was precisely the business aspect of this form of religious practice that appealed to him. In Mordechai Zeev's comments in the ledger one can certainly find expressions of hope that God will reward him for his tithe, but what is to be found above all, in the meticulously arranged columns of names, numbers, and notes, is a world in which God is present in every detail of life, from cradle to grave. "Ever since the day I first went to the market, You have never abandoned me, and You have always shown me the right path," Mordechai Zeev writes in his ledger. "Oh, I thank You, my God and the God of my ancestors, for the care You have shown me and will show me in the future, and for having sown in my heart the will to set aside for You a tenth of my earnings."[32]

Both on his father's and mother's side, then, Marcus Ehrenpreis had been nourished by a love of Jewish tradition, Jewish life, and the Jewish God who would suffuse his vision for a Jewish renewal. He had also acquired a taste for a literature other than that of the Jewish school and the Talmudic seminar, and for this he owed much to the women of his home.

Some words, then, about the women of the world into which Marcus Ehrenpreis was born. A few words only, unfortunately, since not much is recorded or preserved about them, neither by Ehrenpreis nor by anyone else. From the words that do exist, however, it is fully possible to imagine their central role in sustaining the family, materially and spiritually. His mother, the early married Clara Süss, would be remembered by Ehrenpreis in the words of the Proverbs: a diligent wife whose deft hands worked with joy and whose lamp never went out at night. But he would also remember her tears and "her longing for inner liberation, new horizons, and beauty."[33]

The few words also tell us that Clara Süss had learned to read German, and that she subscribed to the family magazine *Die Gartenlaube* (The garden pavilion) and the book series *Das Buch für Alle*, and that Schiller's dramas and poems occupied an important place in her literary universe. In a sketch for a short story in Yiddish, "Two Worlds," the still very young Marcus describes how, on a quiet Sabbath evening, a grandmother reads the week's Bible passages while the granddaughter immerses herself in a short story by Maupassant.[34] It was perhaps no coincidence that a daughter of Marcus's younger sister Lea, Debora Vogel, would become a noted poet and essayist in interwar Poland. Within its traditional Jewish setting, the home of the Ehrenpreis family was an open and intellectual environment, and the door to the literature of the world was very much left ajar by its women.

Perhaps a few words, too, about the subsequent stops on the journey to the height in Djakovar. At the age of fifteen,

Marcus Ehrenpreis left the Talmudic studies in the Jewish seminar to enter the German-speaking Imperial and Royal Gymnasium in Lemberg. In this endeavor, he seems to have been more encouraged by his mother Clara than by his father Jacob, who rather wished he would learn a genuine profession, such as bookkeeping. In any case, this was a big step to take for a young man from the Jewish quarter of Lemberg, and it would take two years of diligent preparatory studies.

The transition from "Talmudism to World Culture," as Ehrenpreis would call it, was made possible by a newly formed Jewish educational society, Mikra Kodesh, in which a German-speaking Reform rabbi from Bamberg, Joseph Kobak, "a rabbinical figure out of Rembrandt,"[35] and some self-taught Jewish enlighteners in Lemberg had taken on the task of plugging the secular holes in the traditional Jewish education. It was here that Marcus had his first lessons in the German language, and his first encounter with German literature, and his first knowledge of the many subjects that were not included in the curriculum of the Talmud seminar but were included in the curriculum of the Imperial and Royal Gymnasium. He also learned to read the Bible with somewhat new eyes. A contemporary witness to the activities in Mikra Kodesh noted in particular a slender, highly mobile, alert boy, a brilliant Hebraist, a contributor to several Hebrew newspapers, a brilliant agitator, the greatest political talent of the society's members, a writer of surprising dimensions.

Under the impact of rising Jewish frustrations (this was the time of rampant pogroms in Russia) and rising Jewish expectations (this was the time of romantic national awakenings in Europe), the young men in Mikra Kodesh (no women in sight) were rapidly radicalized. In October 1888, the aging Joseph Kobak was induced to resign, Mikra Kodesh was reconstituted as the Association of Zion, and the Jewish renewal took on a distinctly national-cultural orientation. To the idea of Hebrew as the language of the Jewish nation was added the idea of Zion-Palestine as the home of the Jewish nation, and to the need for Jewish enlightenment was added the need for Jewish self-awareness and self-esteem.[36]

When Ehrenpreis arrived in the Prussian capital of Berlin on a cloudy October day in 1890 after completing his studies at the Imperial and Royal Gymnasium in Lemberg, the path to Djakovar was beginning to stake itself out. On board the train to Berlin were not only his close friends and fellow students from Lemberg, Osias Thon and Markus Braude, but their shared dreams and plans as well. The Association of Zion in Lemberg became the Jung Israel Association in Berlin, and Marcus Ehrenpreis became its president. In Jung Israel, it was said, Galician "Eastern Jews" would make common cause with German-born "Western Jews."

However, this was easier said than done. The German Jews saw themselves as culturally superior to the Eastern Jews, and as more connected to German culture than to Jewish culture. At their common gatherings, the "Germans" sang the German national anthem, "Deutschland, Deutschland über alles," which to Ehrenpreis had something jittery about it, "as if to compensate for a lackluster inner uncertainty."[37] When Ehrenpreis and his friends enrolled at the "German" rabbinical seminary in Berlin, the Hochschule für die Wissenschaft des Judentums, the principal informed them that their Eastern accent would not be to their advantage, neither at the seminary nor in the job market for newly graduated rabbis—and for a moment Ehrenpreis felt a strong urge to buy a return ticket to Lemberg.[38]

Once the urge had been overcome and Ehrenpreis had embarked on his dual study track, rabbinical studies at the seminary and philosophical studies at the University of Berlin, the cultural shock from the meeting with Western Jewish students abated, and some of them were to become close friends.

After all, the West was a world of breathtaking horizons—of science, philosophy, and culture—and the parents back home in Lemberg were soon to be provided with enthusiastic accounts of personalities that he had met, lectures he had attended, books he had read, and theatrical performances he had seen. In the "enormous bright hall" of the Royal Library in Berlin he was surrounded by "the best works of the human soul," and could feel the presence of "the genius of the world spirit," and even sense "a whiff of the immortal."[39] At the same time, he was keen to link his impressions to current Jewish issues, so that those at home would not think that he had forgotten where he came from and why he had gone away.

He wrote in German with Hebrew letters, just as Moses Mendelssohn had done when translating the Hebrew Bible into German—and for the same reason: bridging the gap between ghetto and Europe required a transcribing hand.

Mother Clara kept his letters like a treasure, Marcus noted.

Did he thereby hint at an answer to a question that was hanging in the air: How did he pay for his studies?

"After difficult financial and other preparations, [Osias Thon and I] ended up at Bahnhof Friedrichstrasse in Berlin"[40] was all he had to say about the material foundations of his years as a student at both the seminary and the university. The question seemed no less unanswered by the fact that he devoted much of his student years to extracurricular Jewish activities, which were certainly enriching in many ways, but which did not necessarily pay for food and rent.

However, there would soon be fees forthcoming for articles he wrote for the German-language weekly *Allgemeine Zeitung des Judentums* and the Hebrew-language weekly *Ha'magid*, as well as from Nathan Birnbaum's weekly *Jüdische Volkzeitung* in Vienna, and maybe this was the answer after all: a talented student in 1890s Berlin could finance his studies by writing articles.

But then, what were the difficult preparations mentioned? Most likely, efforts by the Ehrenpreis family to support him. The family was not wealthy, but as it realized that Marcus was destined for something other than bookkeeping, it decided to make the necessary savings and sacrifices. When the letters from Berlin began pouring in, confirming that their son had found his way and the family had put its savings to good use, it was then perhaps no surprise that Mother Clara kept the letters "like a treasure."

Found his way? Not quite yet. The rabbinical seminary pointed in one direction, the university in another. The rabbinical route was the more expected and foreseeable, while the way of the university was uncertain, both in direction and objective. At the university he attended the lectures of several prominent thinkers of his time, among them the philosopher Georg Simmel, with whom he came into personal contact. Simmel was born into a Jewish family in Berlin, but his work had little to do with Judaism. His lectures were on Kant and Schopenhauer, and on Rembrandt and Goethe, and on sociology, the newborn science for the study of human society to which Simmel would make some pioneering and groundbreaking contributions.

It remains unclear what Ehrenpreis wanted to accomplish with his university studies; he wanted a taste of everything and was attracted by many vocations, not least literature, and at times he seemed to doubt his rabbinical vocation. The subordinate position of the rabbi in modern Jewish congregations appeared ill-suited to his understanding of the vocation of a rabbi, and his beginning success as a writer seemed to make other venues possible. When he confided his rabbinical misgivings and literary dreams to the un-Jewish Simmel, perhaps expecting to be encouraged to follow his literary inclinations, he was advised to stick to the rabbinical path.

"Literature is not a profession," Simmel said.

"But what about the rabbi's subordinate position?" Ehrenpreis asked.

"My friend," Simmel replied, "the position of the rabbi does not depend on the congregation. It depends on the rabbi. So just go on, it will be fine."[41]

Whether Simmel's words were as significant as Ehrenpreis later made them to be ("thanks to him I found my way early on"[42]), the academic venue eventually came to coincide with the rabbinical. The topic for his doctoral dissertation had very little to do with Kant or Goethe, but all the more with Jewish learning and thinking.

In the autumn of 1894 Ehrenpreis left teeming Berlin for tranquil Erlangen, Bavaria, to write a thesis on the doctrine of emanation in the Kabbalah, the Jewish mystical tradition.[43] Few outside the Jewish world had yet heard of the Kabbalah, let alone explored it, but to Ehrenpreis, in his quest of spiritual sources for a Jewish renaissance, the Kabbalah was a treasure trove waiting to be rediscovered. The fifty-page dissertation was completed in seven months, and on 11 March 1895 Marcus Ehrenpreis was promoted to doctor of philosophy at the annual ceremony in the university's banquet hall.[44]

"The science about the evolution of Jewish spiritual life has hitherto been neglected, or treated as something absurd, not to be taken seriously," he wrote in the preface to the printed edition, published in late autumn of that year and dedicated to "my dear parents." The preface is dated Rome, October 1895, as Ehrenpreis was then working in the library of the Vatican, gathering material for a sequel to his thesis. The newly printed edition had the heading "Kabbalistic Studies I," and the world was now waiting for Kabbalistic Studies II and perhaps III, and for Marcus Ehrenpreis to make a name for himself as the great contemporary explorer and interpreter of Jewish mysticism. Nor could there be any doubt that Ehrenpreis viewed his exploration of the Kabbalah as a contribution to the spiritual renaissance of Judaism, and to a Jewish mode of thinking that was not grounded in a "philosophy of facts."

Ehrenpreis was not alone in seeking sources for a Jewish renaissance in seemingly obsolete Jewish traditions and ways of life. Just a few years later, Martin Buber would seek it in Hasidism, the charismatic Jewish movement that had captured the ghettos of eastern Europe in the eighteenth century and had opened the door to a more intuitive and emotional expression of Jewish faith. What Ehrenpreis sought in kabbalistic manuscripts, Buber would seek in Hasidic legends and myths. Their paths soon crossed, and the dream of the Jewish Renaissance would bind them together in a lifelong friendship. When, a few years later, Buber wrote about the awakening of the soul of the Jewish people and its role in the spiritual renewal of the world, he very much reflected ideas that Ehrenpreis had already expressed in his neo-Hebrew manifesto. In this, they reflected the spirit of the times: the rooting for the souls and destinies of different people did not necessarily herald an era of conflicts and wars but could just as well herald an era of brotherhood and peace.

"Only when each and every people is allowed to express its true being can we realize Goethe's dream of a world literature," Buber wrote.[45]

In delving into the manuscripts kept in the libraries of Rome and Florence, Ehrenpreis had set out to show the connection between the Kabbalah and Hasidism, thus underscoring that Ehrenpreis and Buber were looking for the same: sources to a more authentic and vibrant Judaism. Buber, though born in Vienna, had spent much of his childhood in the Lemberg home of his learned Jewish grandfather, and like Ehrenpreis he was deeply critical of what Judaism had become, and deeply hopeful of what Judaism might become again.

Buber was to choose the path of philosophy and become one of the most important Jewish writers and thinkers of the twentieth century, but when Ehrenpreis in January 1896 applied for the position of rabbi in Djakovar, his choice between philosophy and pulpit was made, and "Kabbalistic Studies II" was to remain unfinished.

Instead, engagement and marriage.

Esther Tynia Haskler was a second cousin of Marcus Ehrenpreis—Marcus's maternal grandfather and Esther's paternal grandfather were brothers—and they had known each other since childhood. Esther was seventeen and Marcus was twenty-five, and during a family vacation in a village in the northern Carpathians in 1894, a romance developed. "Mordechai and Esther" was a biblically charged name constellation, which they were to be reminded of at the engagement ceremony in Lemberg in the spring of 1895.[46] What Marcus also was reminded of was the urgent

Mordechai and Esther, a biblical constellation of names, on their honeymoon in Zagreb, November 1896.

need to wrap up his studies and prepare for a more family-friendly career.

On 18 October 1896, two months after taking up his post in Djakovar, Marcus "Mordechai" Ehrenpreis returned to Lemberg to marry Esther in the disputed temple with the large dome next to his grandfather's house. On their wedding trip to Zagreb in November, the young couple had their photograph taken, Esther in a black dress and white blouse with a black-embroidered cape over her shoulders and a neatly arranged scarf around her neck, her dark hair loosely pulled back from her soft features and dreamy eyes. And we may understand why Marcus Ehrenpreis never completed "Kabbalistic Studies II" and why Bishop Strossmayer invited the young rabbi's wife to stroll at will in the private park outside the bishop's residence in Djakovar.

On the morning of 29 August 1897, the first World Zionist Congress opened in the large concert hall of the City Casino in Basel. The Ehrenpreises had arrived a few days earlier, to attend a preparatory meeting, to walk along the Rhine, to watch the delegates pour in, and to feel the excitement rise. Herzl had, after all, promised Marcus a spot of his own on the agenda, and thus an opportunity to convince the delegates (Herzl not least) to make the cultural renaissance a central goal of the Zionist movement, making clear that Herzl's idea of a state for the Jews made no sense unless there were a Jewish people worthy of the name, with its own language, literature, and culture. It was certainly true that the Jews were not a people like any other, nor should they be, but a people without cultural self-awareness and self-esteem was not a people at all.

When Ehrenpreis discovered that his promised spot on the agenda, introducing the "cultural question," had been placed as the very last item on the third and last day of the congress, he openly voiced his disappointment. Why had such an important issue been relegated to the "twelfth hour"?[47] How could he possibly do it justice in the short time he had been allotted? How to explain the necessity of an all-embracing Hebrew-Jewish school system, for example? Having to explain it in German and not Hebrew at a Zionist congress went to show, if nothing else, how urgent the issue was.

In addition to initiating a Jewish-Hebrew school system, Ehrenpreis wanted the Congress to appoint a literary commission to found Hebrew newspapers and magazines, subsidize the publication of Hebrew works, and support Hebrew authors. He also raised the idea of founding a Hebrew university in Jaffa or Jerusalem, to which the minutes of the Congress registered "thunderous approval." When he added that such a university could only be founded when there was a system of Hebrew high schools, the minutes registered nothing. The proposal for a literary commission was passed by acclamation, and Ehrenpreis was elected one of its members, as were Ahad Ha'am and Eliezer Ben-Yehuda. Ben-Yehuda was the author of a new Hebrew dictionary and would go down in history as the father of modern Hebrew.[48]

Ehrenpreis's efforts to make the Jewish cultural renaissance a central goal of the Zionist movement would result in more words than deeds. The cultural radicalism of the Young Hebrews remained a minority position in the Jewish world, and it soon became clear that the Jews were not only a people unlike all other people, but in many respects not a people at all. Even to convene the literary commission proved to be an overwhelming task. Ehrenpreis was in Djakovar, Ahad Ha'am in Odessa, Ben-Yehuda in Jerusalem, two other members in Warsaw and Prague. There was no budget for travel expenses, much less a budget to organize and finance even a fraction of the cultural initiatives that Ehrenpreis had proposed, and which all had to be tailored to widely different political and social circumstances and therefore had to be organized and financed in widely different ways.

The cultural question would return at the next congress, and at the next again, and Ehrenpreis would continue to introduce it until the eighth congress (The Hague, 1907), which would be his last. Already at the second congress in 1898, again in Basel, his ideas and proposals met with active opposition, primarily from the small minority of Orthodox Jews who had not distanced themselves from Zionism, but who now distanced themselves all the more strongly from Ehrenpreis and his *Kulturisten*; their cultural renaissance would secularize Judaism, their Hebrew would profane the sacred language, and their Jewish education would bring about the disintegration of Jewish life in Europe. To fight for a Jewish homeland, like Herzl, was one thing, to fight for a new Hebrew-Jewish culture, like Ehrenpreis, was quite another—and downright threatening.

It was beginning to dawn on Ehrenpreis that the cause of cultural Zionism was perhaps not as simple as it had once seemed to him. In the aftermath of Basel, Ahad Ha'am wrote an article in which he criticized the one-sided focus of the congress on territory and state-building, insisting that spiritual and cultural goals must take precedence over the political ones. Ehrenpreis, on the other hand, no longer seemed so sure. In a surprisingly polemical commentary in Herzl's *Die Welt*, he criticized Ahad Ha'am for underestimating the significance of the political-national mobilization for the spiritual-cultural renaissance. Ahad Ha'am was certainly an inspiring thinker, but he did not take sufficient account of the complex reality in which the Jews of Europe lived.

For example, the reality facing a newly appointed rabbi of a Jewish congregation in a corner of the Balkans where nationalist sentiments were fermenting and where he had had a personal experience of the charged political environment in which cultural Zionism had to operate.

In the spring of 1903, when some leading cultural Zionists, including Martin Buber and Chaim Weizmann (who would become the leader of the Zionist movement and the first president of the State of Israel), asked Ehrenpreis to participate in a joint statement defending Ahad Ha'am against an attack by Herzl's closest associate, Max Nordau, Ehrenpreis made it a condition that no "notorious opponents" of Herzl and "Congress Zionism" be among the signatories.[49]

The joint statement was never published, and twenty years later Ehrenpreis himself would emerge as a strong opponent of Congress Zionism, which he thought had lost its raison d'être. In an article in Martin Buber's journal *Der Jude*, addressed to the thirteenth Zionist Congress in Karlsbad 1923, he harshly criticized those who had "doggedly, hypnotically, and mechanically" pushed ahead with the Jewish land, *das Judenland*, and left Judaism, *das Judentum*, behind. With the unifying power of Herzl gone, Ehrenpreis argued, all that remained of Congress Zionism were petty politics and unrealistic fictions.

Not least the fiction that a Jewish state in Palestine would be "the answer to the Jewish question," and that the Jewish Diaspora had played out its role. Every clear-thinking person must realize that this is not feasible, Ehrenpreis wrote. Parallel to establishing in Palestine a spiritual-cultural center for Judaism, the Zionist movement must invest in a continued Jewish existence in the Diaspora and there seek new forms of coexistence, modi vivendi, with "our neighboring peoples."[50]

It is hardly possible to understand the "congress speech" of 1923, with its emphasis on the continued significance of the Diaspora in Jewish life, without understanding how fourteen years as Grand Rabbi of Bulgaria, and by this time nine years as chief rabbi of Stockholm had come to shape Marcus Ehrenpreis's view of the Jews and the world.

Bulgaria and Stockholm. In due course.

Ehrenpreis would remember the summer of 1897 as the richest and brightest of his life, with the journey to Basel as its unforgettable climax. A trampled people had at last "risen from the ground, shaken off the dust of centuries, and resolutely set out on a new path."[51]

But not its women. Not this first summer. Two hundred and four delegates from seventeen countries had come to the congress in Basel—but only seventeen women. Some of the women had been invited in their own capacity, some in the capacity of companions to male delegates, but in no capacity had they been given the right to vote. At the end of the congress, one of the accompanying women asked her husband to tell Herzl how deeply hurtful this was (to approach him directly was apparently unthinkable). Herzl, in turn, asked the husband to let him meet the wife. The meeting resulted in "Frau Dr. Ehrenpreis" receiving a dedicated portrait of Herzl "in memory of the days in Basel" and Herzl being given some food for thought. By the second Zionist Congress in Basel the following year, female delegates had been given the right to vote, and from then on their number would steadily increase.

The young couple were in no hurry to get home. In Schaffhausen they stopped to view the Rhine Falls, in Innsbruck and Zell am Zee they stayed overnight to enjoy the clear air and the breathtaking Alpine scenery, and in the company of other hotel guests discover that the congress was a highly viable topic of conversation.

It is today hard to imagine what an impression the congress had made around Europe, Ehrenpreis noted much later. With reports and comments in all major newspapers, Zionism had overnight become a word on everybody's lips, and as Marcus and Esther Ehrenpreis made their way home, many people were eager to hear what they had to say about the future of the Jews.

From there on, the road went downhill.

No, from there on, the view was dimmed.

No, not yet, from there on, another road altogether.

Marcus Ehrenpreis inaugurates "his" synagogue in Sofia in 1909, in the presence of King Ferdinand of Bulgaria.

3.

A TASTE OF ADVENTURE

Ruschuk, on the lower Danube, where I came into the world, was a marvellous city for a child, and if I say that Ruschuk is in Bulgaria, then I am giving an inadequate picture of it. For people of the most varied backgrounds lived there, on any day you could hear seven or eight languages. Aside from the Bulgarians, who often came from the countryside, there were many Turks, who lived in their own neighborhood, and next to it was the neighborhood of the Sephardim, the Spanish Jews—our neighborhood.

—ELIAS CANETTI[1]

In the spring of 1899, Marcus Ehrenpreis traveled to Gothenburg to apply for another position. The elderly rabbi of Gothenburg's Mosaic Congregation, Moritz Wolff, was retiring, and the rabbi of Djakovar was ready to break his "Slavonic isolation." The ducks and the chickens were getting on his nerves, and he longed for a "more enticing cultural environment." He probably knew that he would not find it in Gothenburg, but a journey toward an "unknown destination" with "a taste of adventure" was a hard-to-resist temptation.[2] Ehrenpreis liked to journey and to write about his journeys, and in his literary production journeys were to play an important role.

Adding to the taste of adventure was the opportunity to seek out the Danish-Jewish writer and literary critic Georg

Brandes in Copenhagen. To Ehrenpreis and his Young Hebrews, Brandes had become a symbol of the free human and the free community of culture of which they all dreamed. With his Jewish origins, his Nordic roots, and his European identity, Brandes was not only the name of a man, but the name of an ideology, Brandesianism, that signified much of what the Young Hebrews were fighting for. "His struggle for Europeanism up there in small Denmark, bound by its firm ties to Grundtvigianism, seemed in some measure similar to our struggle against medieval rabbinism. He opened the gates of Europe to the Danish people. We wanted to do the same for the Jewish people."[3] Ehrenpreis had translated some of Brandes's essays from German to Hebrew and was now hoping for the great man's blessings on his pioneering neo-Hebraic work.

Brandes received Ehrenpreis at his residence in Nyhavn, but he was sick and weary and showed no enthusiasm for either the visit or the pioneering neo-Hebraic work. In fact, he had never heard of the attempts to make Hebrew a modern literary language, let alone of the Young Hebrews. He emphatically disapproved of the attempt to translate his texts from German rather than Danish, and he had very little interest in Zionism. Or in Judaism. "I am Danish," Brandes stressed, as if to shield himself from the sudden intrusion of Ehrenpreis's world into his own. "I have worked all my life for the freedom and progress of Denmark, and I shall not cease to do so until my last breath."[4]

As Ehrenpreis walked out into the bright Copenhagen spring, he thought he had met a tragic figure: "This Danish Jew was at home in all the cultures of the world, but he was seen as a stranger in Denmark, and he was a stranger in Judaism [...]. He who had the rare ability to empathize with the innermost feelings of foreign peoples remained uncomprehending and indifferent to the historical fate of Israel."[5]

Worse still, when some years later Ehrenpreis published an article in *Die Welt* about his meeting with Brandes,[6] and the article was cited by a journalist meeting Brandes in Paris, Brandes said he had never met anyone by the name of Ehrenpreis. Brandes's disparaging comment got traction in the Jewish press, sarcastic comments were made, and Ehrenpreis was advised to write to Brandes and if possible refresh his memory. Brandes replied by return mail that he now remembered both the visit and the conversation, giving as an excuse that he was visited daily by so many people from so many countries that he could not possibly remember every name and conversation offhand. In case the matter persisted, he added, Ehrenpreis should feel free to cite his letter.

Perhaps Ehrenpreis had not made much of an impression on Brandes.

Perhaps he had made an impression that Brandes would rather not remember.

No, Gothenburg did not have what Marcus Ehrenpreis was yearning for. It was just another "idyllic, quiet small town, where only the harbor quarter bore signs of commotion and industry." The congregation, too, seemed more lifeless than he had expected. It had also declared its intentions to limit the authority of the new rabbi.[7]

Ehrenpreis lost the rabbinical election by four votes.

Perhaps it was due to a bout of hoarseness.

Perhaps his lack of enthusiasm was showing.

The most lasting consequence of the trip to Gothenburg would be his contact with the outgoing rabbi and his family.

When, fifteen years later, the time came to appoint a new rabbi in Stockholm, it was one of Rabbi Wolff's successful and well-assimilated sons, Admiral Henrik Wolff, who first brought up the name of Marcus Ehrenpreis.

Stockholm. Not yet.

First, a journey eastward, with a strong taste of adventure.

In the central part of Sofia, the capital of Bulgaria, stands one of the largest synagogues remaining in Europe after World War II. If at the time of its inauguration in 1909 it was criticized for being too large and lavish, it is today large enough to accommodate the entire Jewish population of Bulgaria, a few thousand at most. Even at major Jewish holidays, the pews are mostly empty. To the extent that morning and Shabbat services are held in the synagogue, they are held in a smaller room that seats fifty people at most. Such a small congregation cannot maintain and sustain such a large synagogue, and the extensive exterior and interior restorations that took place before the centenary celebrations in 2009 were financed through other means. Today, its splendor has been restored. The domes and facades have been repaired and painted. The golden candelabras (said to be the largest in the Balkans) standing in front of the Torah ark shine as never before, and the mosaic on the Venetian marble pillars carrying the balconies has been restored to its oriental glory. On the wall in the high-vaulted entrance, a stone plaque commemorates the people who built it.

On the top, in Cyrillic letters, I read Marcus Ehrenpreis.

Exiting to the street, I get a glimpse of Rabbi Marcus Ehrenpreis's vision for the Jews of Bulgaria. It's not just the building itself, with its soaring arches and heavy domes, that speaks to me. It's also its location, in the middle of central Sofia, surrounded by markets and cathedrals, a stone's throw from the Great Mosque, built in 1566, when Bulgaria was an Ottoman province. With the construction of the Great Synagogue of Sofia, Marcus Ehrenpreis, in his ninth year as the Grand Rabbi of Bulgaria, not only wanted to give the Jews of Bulgaria a unifying symbol. He also wanted to give them status as a fully recognized minority in a newly created nation-state based on diversity and tolerance.

On 9 September 1909, it looked as if he had succeeded on both accounts. At the inauguration of the synagogue on Exarch Joseph's Street, the highest levels of Bulgaria's political and religious leadership were represented. There was King Ferdinand with his newly wed Queen Eleanor, there was the Bulgarian government, headed by Prime Minister Aleksandar Malinov, there were the leaders of Bulgaria's religious communities, headed by the metropolitan Partenii of Sofia, there were Bulgarian generals in their shining uniforms, distinguished representatives of Bulgarian science and culture, and, of course, representatives of Bulgaria's Jewish communities, and no one would at this moment have risen to say that the new synagogue was too big or too extravagant. Moreover, no royal visit had ever before taken place in a Bulgarian synagogue. Nor in a Bulgarian Orthodox church for that matter. As the Catholic king Ferdinand (of Saxe-Coburg and Gotha) was soon to be reminded.

It was the king, sometimes referred to as the tsar, who formally inaugurated the synagogue by cutting a silk cord in front of the altar podium, and it was Marcus Ehrenpreis who, after a short ritual in Hebrew, delivered its first sermon in Bulgarian.

"Thanks to the complete freedom of faith that prevails in this beautiful country, and thanks to the friendly feelings of the Bulgarian people who, fighting for their freedom from foreign oppression, also have defended the freedom of a historical minority in this country, this house of prayer has been raised to God," the Grand Rabbi said to the king and the queen, and the ministers and the military, and the metropolitan of Sofia.

"I want you to know that I have strong feelings for our Jewish population and that I will work to strengthen its position in Bulgaria," King Ferdinand said to the Grand Rabbi before leaving the synagogue. "Through this solemn ceremony you have done an invaluable service to civil coexistence in this country. Thanks to your initiative, the people of Bulgaria will learn to appreciate Jews as human beings and citizens."[8]

At least, this is what Ehrenpreis remembered the king saying to him, and this is clearly what he had hoped to achieve with his symbol-laden inauguration of the Great Synagogue in Sofia. Or as Prime Minister Malinov explained to the king, "Dr. Ehrenpreis spoke of Bulgaria's tolerance of minorities as a fact, though he really meant it as a wish."[9]

Four years later, the synagogue would again be filled with high-ranking Bulgarian representatives, providing the setting for another solemn ceremony intended to symbolize and affirm the value of Jews as human beings and citizens of Bulgaria.

Four years later. In due course.

First, something must be said about how the Young Hebrew revolutionary in Djakovar became the Grand Rabbi of Bulgaria, and the official representative of the Bulgarian Jews, and the emissary of the Bulgarian government, and the friend of kings, ministers, and metropolitans.

As noted, Ehrenpreis had grown tired of Djakovar. He had been offered the post as chief rabbi in the neighboring and larger Osijek, the capital of Slavonia, and with it a newly built rabbinical residence in a somewhat more urban setting. But when the telegram came in the afternoon of 13 April 1900, just before the Sabbath, he did not hesitate long. In a few terse sentences in French he was informed that the representatives of the Bulgarian-Jewish congregations gathered at a conference in Sofia had unanimously elected Marcus Ehrenpreis to be Bulgaria's next Grand Rabbi. The congress was to remain in session until Sunday to await his response.

Marcus Ehrenpreis had not applied for the post in Bulgaria. It would probably not have occurred to him to do so even if he had known about it, since the majority of Jews in Bulgaria belonged to the Sephardic, "Spanish," branch of Jewry, while he belonged to the Ashkenazi, "German," branch. Apart from the many differences between the two branches of Judaism, they did not always take kindly to each other. The Sephardim liked to see themselves as genealogically nobler than the Ashkenazim, and the Ashkenazim liked to see the Sephardim as culturally and spiritually stagnant. If it was not natural for a Sephardic Jew to marry off his daughter to an Ashkenazi, even a broad-minded Ashkenazi like Ehrenpreis could not help but be concerned about the spiritual life of the Sephardic Jew.

Since the days of Maimonides and the great Hebrew poets of Spain, Sephardic Jews "had made no significant contribution to the spiritual development of Judaism," Ehrenpreis noted in his impressions of the Orient, as he preferred to call it.[10]

Ehrenpreis's view of the Orient was typical of his time; on the one hand a daunting inability to develop socially and culturally, on the other an inspiring ability to keep inherited traditions and resist the lure of Western materialism. "Between East and West" was not only part of the title of Ehrenpreis's memoirs later in life, but the Jewish position that he wanted to claim for himself, between Western rationality and Eastern spirituality. As a Swedish writer, Ehrenpreis would return time and again to the Orient, each time being both appalled and seduced by it. "A hitherto unknown world of richness opened up to me, and irresistibly attracted me, and would never let go of me. This was an experience that would steer me onto a new path and shape my life as a mature man."[11]

Swedish writer, in due course.

No, Marcus Ehrenpreis had not applied for the post of Grand Rabbi of Bulgaria; it was the post that had applied for him. In early 1899, the Central Organization of Jewish Congregations in Sofia, the Central Consistory, had contacted a select group of rabbis in Europe who were considered to meet their requirements: age no more than thirty-five, higher academic and rabbinical education, at least five years' experience as chief rabbi. Further limiting the list was the expectation that the new rabbi should open the eyes and hearts of Bulgarian Jews to Judaism and raise their status in Bulgarian society.[12]

The five hundred years of Ottoman, or "Turkish," rule in Bulgaria were only thirty years in the past, and the forty-five thousand Bulgarian Jews, scattered over some thirty congregations, lived up to most of Ehrenpreis's notions of the stagnant Orient: low levels of education, widespread poverty, and an archaic patriarchal system of justice in matrimonial matters and family disputes. "The woman was generally little more than the man's shadow, in the worst case his slave," Ehrenpreis observed.[13]

There was yet another expectation of the new rabbi, not explicitly stated in the letter from the Central Consistory: he must have an understanding of the Zionist cause, which had grown strong in Bulgaria, and whose representatives had just scared away a prospective Grand Rabbi from France who did not please them. Nor did the letter inform the prospective applicants that the Zionists were clashing with the established Sephardic families, the notabilities, and that the notabilities were clashing with the French-Jewish movement for the civilization of Sephardic Jews, the Alliance Israélite Universelle,[14] and that the incoming Grand Rabbi must be able to unite and lead them all. Under these circumstances, if the most suitable applicant turned out to be an Ashkenazi rabbi from Galicia, so be it. Ehrenpreis had willingly responded to the letter and announced that he was prepared to consider an offer. Thereafter, no word from Sofia in more than a year, and the preparations for the move to Osijek were well advanced.

Nevertheless, he accepted the offer by return telegram, and nine days later, on 22 April 1900, he traveled with Esther to Sofia to get a glimpse of the new city and settle the terms of his new position. On 1 August, the new rabbi and his wife were welcomed at the Sofia railway station by members of the congregation, and the very same day Marcus Ehrenpreis was approved as Bulgaria's Grand Rabbi by the Bulgarian Ministry of Religious Affairs. If not before, he must then have become aware that he had not only been elected the chief rabbi of the Bulgarian Jews but of the Bulgarian state as well. It was the state that would sanction and regulate his office by law, and it was the Ministry of Religious Affairs that would finance it in its annual budget.

All this was a remnant of the Ottoman Empire, where religious and ethnic groups had enjoyed a large measure of autonomy (the *millet* system) and where the representative of the Jewish *millet* to the sultan had been the Grand Rabbi, *hachambashi*, in Constantinople. Similarly, the Grand Rabbi in Sofia was the representative of the Jewish minority to the king and the Bulgarian government. This gave Ehrenpreis an official position that he would soon be tempted to use to push through the reforms of Jewish life that he considered necessary: raising the education level of rabbis and Jewish teachers, establishing a Jewish school system in congruence with the Bulgarian curriculum, instituting a central rabbinical court to ensure legal competence and equal treatment in matters under the jurisdiction of the local rabbis, having marriages be performed in public, requiring that marriage contracts be approved by the Grand Rabbinate in Sofia, and establishing central marriage regulations that would "put an end to many unpleasant conditions in marital relations."[15]

Marcus Ehrenpreis had come not only as an alien Ashkenazi to the world of the Sephardim, with all the suspicion and dislike that this might entail, but also as a determined Jewish reformer to Jewish congregations that did not always want to be reformed. The schools of the French Alliance had already aroused bad blood with their demand for French as the language of instruction and their French civilizing mission. The traditionalist Sephardim regarded l'Alliance as a cultural insult, the radical Zionists as an ideological opponent and contender.

Neither did Ehrenpreis have much regard for the French Alliance, since he thought it produced a Jewish youth with "a superficial veneer of French culture, which gave them an air of Levantine rootlessness." But his most bitter conflict was to be with the Zionists.[16] They had perhaps rightly expected an ideological ally, but they soon discovered that the new Grand Rabbi didn't always side with them. As when, in the autumn of 1903, he banned Zionist organizations from using synagogues for their meetings. Or when, in the spring of 1904, he opposed Zionist demonstrations on the streets of Sofia. Or

Marcus Ehrenpreis at the Jewish Teachers' Congress in Bulgaria, August 1902, in the process of implementing his Jewish reform program: raising the level of knowledge of Jewish teachers and adapting the Jewish school system to Bulgarian curricula.

when he decided that the delegates to the national congress of Jewish congregations in Sofia in February 1905 should be elected by the boards of the congregations and not directly by the members, which by the Zionists was seen as a support for the conservative and anti-Zionist "notabilities" dominating the boards.

Ehrenpreis soon made clear that he was not going to let himself be paralyzed by the internal conflicts of the Bulgarian Jews. However, as he began pushing through his reforms in opposition to one Jewish interest or another, his legitimacy was questioned, and not only by the Zionists. Articles in the Jewish press accused him of having established one-man rule, and throughout the country there were calls for his resignation.[17] In addition, the promised new law that would regulate the authority of the Grand Rabbi and the rights of the congregations was never ratified by the Bulgarian government. When push came to shove, Bulgaria did not dare to give the Jewish *millet* a legal status that it was not prepared to give to the far more numerous and politically stronger Muslims. Thus, each faction of the Jewish community was free to interpret the non-ratified paragraphs of the law as they saw fit, and if necessary to hit their interpretation on the head of their opponent, mostly on the head of Ehrenpreis:

> Why doesn't the rabbi stick to paragraph X, cried the party wanting to use the paragraph to bolster its own cause. Upon which the opposing party shouted just as loudly: The rabbi may not invoke paragraph X, since it is explicitly stated that the law does not come into force until it is ratified by the government.[18]

What Bulgaria's Zionists expected from Marcus Ehrenpreis is unclear. He claimed to be a Zionist still, and at the meetings of the World Zionist Congress he continued to play a visible role, but in his role as Bulgaria's *hachambashi* it became increasingly evident that his Zionism was of another kind than theirs. To Ehrenpreis, the striving for a Jewish future in Palestine was not opposed to the striving for a Jewish future in Europe. Zion and the Diaspora were to mutually inspire and enrich each other. Jewish life in Bulgaria was not only possible but desirable.

Ehrenpreis was convinced of the Bulgarian possibility early on. Bulgaria was a young nation with a relatively small

Jewish population, a not-too-noticeable anti-Jewish past, and a king and government that proved friendly to the new Grand Rabbi and his Jewish minority. With King Ferdinand, a German-speaking Catholic and thus himself somewhat of a stranger in the land of the Bulgars, Ehrenpreis developed a lasting friendship. In his very first audience, in the winter of 1901, the king told Ehrenpreis of his "extensive travels in the Orient" and of his encounters with Sephardic Jews and his conversations with them in their own language. Whereafter the king of Bulgaria continued their conversation in Judeo-Spanish, "which he had fully mastered," and which Ehrenpreis, after six months in the world of the Sephardim, had mastered well enough to respond.[19] When just a few months later, at the Torah-giving festival of Shavuot at the end of May, the Ashkenazi rabbi delivered his first sermon in Judeo-Spanish, he was greeted by outbursts of surprise and enthusiasm: *El Rabbino es judio! El rabbino habla giudesmo!* "The rabbi is a Jew! The rabbi speaks Jewish!"[20]

The most immediate hurdle in the relationship with the Bulgarian Jews, the language, had thus been overcome. Soon enough Ehrenpreis would initiate and edit a Judeo-Spanish weekly, *La Luz* (The light), after some time with a literary supplement, *Raljos* (Rays). If Bulgarian Jews were amazed that the rabbi could speak *giudesmo*, they would soon find out that the rabbi could write too—and write well. Neither would it take Ehrenpreis long to deliver his first speech in Bulgarian, and to make fluent conversation in French, which was the language of the diplomatic and political circles in Sofia, where the cultured and socially gifted Grand Rabbi soon became a sought-after guest.

He also became close friends with the leading literary and cultural figures of Bulgaria at the time, most closely with the acclaimed writer and poet Pentjo Slavejkov and his lifelong companion, the poet Mara Beltjeva. In the Beltjev family house in central Sofia the Grand Rabbinate had its offices, the Ehrenpreis family its private quarters, and Mara Beltjeva a small apartment of her own. The step to Bulgaria's cultural elite was literally short. A threshold away lived the playwright Petko Todorov, who would translate some of Ehrenpreis's literary essays from Hebrew into Bulgarian. The translations were intended for literary readings only, but some were printed in the literary journal *Mysl.* To Ehrenpreis, with his strong belief in the unifying power of language and literature, this was yet another confirmation of the Bulgarian-Jewish possibility, and when in December of 1901 he was preparing his speech to the Fifth Zionist Congress, to be held in Basel at the end of the month, he intended once again to stress the importance of the Hebrew language to the Zionist cause.

"A voiceless people cannot begin a new life," he wanted to begin.

"The Hebrew writers and poets are our new prophets, our new heroes, our new conquerors," he wanted to continue.

"The day when this congress will hold its proceedings in the language of the Jews, the rebirth of the Jewish people will be a fait accompli!" he aimed to conclude.[21]

This firm belief in the nation-building power of language Ehrenpreis shared with many of his contemporaries, including his Bulgarian friends, and ultimately with that entire national romantic movement that regarded language, literature, and art as expressions of a people's soul. In this sense, all over Europe, people's souls were dissected, people's roots were excavated, common destinies were evoked, national characteristics were defined, and national writers, poets, and artists were celebrated. The nation was the natural building block of the world order, with each nation having its specific contribution to make, not least a spiritually and culturally reborn Jewish nation.

On the second day of the Fifth Zionist Congress, Martin Buber spoke on art. If art had not been allowed to reflect the Jewish soul before (the prohibition against depicting humans), it was free to do so now. "Our art will be a powerful herald of a resurrected Judaism," Buber proclaimed. "It will awaken slumbering hearts and, in a storm wind, bring forth the songs of a nascent Zion."

"Strong applause," the minutes noted.[22]

Ehrenpreis was scheduled to speak before Buber, but he had fallen ill at the last minute and did not travel to Basel to give his speech. Instead, his manuscript was added to the records.[23]

This would be the last manifestation of Ehrenpreis's struggle for the rebirth of Hebrew. Partly because he had come to realize that the struggle was over; the new Hebrew literature was a fact, and the importance of Hebrew to the Zionist movement was undisputed. But partly, too, because of Bulgaria, where, if not before, he was having second thoughts. He would not put them in writing until much later, in yet another country, in yet another language, but it is in Bulgaria that his vision of a new relationship between "Israel and the nations" is born, and it is in his position as the leader of the Bulgarian-Jewish "nation" that Ehrenpreis sees a chance to test it out. In the meeting between a reborn "Israel" in Bulgaria and a newly awakened Bulgarian nation in Europe, mutual respect and understanding would arise, and mutual cultural flourishing would follow, he imagined.

This is the perspective in which I wish to understand Marcus Ehrenpreis's early and strong identification with the vexed cause of the newly awakened Bulgarian nation.

The vexed cause in brief: the new Bulgaria, born out of the Ottoman Empire's defeat in the war against Russia in 1877–1878, was an unstable creation with uncertain and unclear borders. The same was true of other newly created nations from the crumbling Ottoman Empire. Their populations had long been ethnically and religiously intertwined, and the wrong people kept ending up on the wrong side of newly redrawn borders. The Bulgarians felt, perhaps with some justification, that too many Bulgarians had ended up on the wrong side of the current Bulgarian border. In the autumn of 1912, Bulgaria saw its chance, in alliance with other disaffected Balkan nations (Serbia, Montenegro, and Greece), to conquer the European remnants of the Ottoman Empire and divide the spoils among each other along national lines. For a few months Bulgaria looked like a winner, subduing large parts of Thrace and Macedonia, where there were not only ethnic Bulgarians to incorporate into Bulgaria but also some hundred thousand Jews, twenty-five thousand in the city of Adrianople (Edirne), one of the oldest congregations in what was then called the Near East.

Ehrenpreis sided wholeheartedly and enthusiastically with the Bulgarians. "I saw before me a small people fighting with admirable heroism and relentless strength for their national liberation, their language, their Christian faith [...]. In this time of national awakening, when all, as one man, were prepared to sacrifice themselves for the cause of the people, the Bulgarians awoke in me a sense of awe. I was carried away by a pathos of intense fervor and unmistakable authenticity [...]. The Bulgarians went from victory to victory, and I rejoiced with all the jubilant people."

He even sensed a pang of envy, even shame, at the sight of "these splendid lads" driven by "genuine love for their country and their people [...] going to war as if to a dance." Should not the Jewish people also have such heroes in their struggle for freedom, he asked himself.

> We had had our Maccabees, who staked their lives to free the desecrated holy city. But that was a long time ago. Now I saw before me Bulgarian Maccabees. *Our* heroism was of a more passive nature. We were the heroes of suffering and perseverance, capable of enduring torment and humiliation like no one else. We stood steadfast in our place and did not yield. [But now] I felt the longing for new Jewish Maccabees, like those who marched before my eyes on the boulevards of Sofia.[24]

The years in Bulgaria would further confirm the link between Ehrenpreis's cultural Zionism and the world of romantic nationalism: the nation as the manifestation of a people's soul, the national awakenings of Europe as movements for political freedom, cultural flourishing, and universal brotherhood. The Jewish awakening was in this perspective not different from the Bulgarian, and in the all-ennobling light of romantic nationalism the soldiers in the streets of Sofia could be seen as marching toward a world in which the Jewish nation, too, would find its rightful place and fulfill its—to Ehrenpreis all-important—spiritual and cultural mission.

Nationalism and universal brotherhood did not have to be a contradiction in terms.

Not in October 1912.

It was no coincidence that other leading cultural Zionists at the time were captivated by the same national romantic ideas. At the outbreak of the First World War, Martin Buber enthusiastically hailed Germany's marching soldiers as fighters for a new and better world.

Buber would soon change his mind, and so would Ehrenpreis, but not until the Bulgarian adventure was over, which it wasn't yet.

During Bulgaria's brief time as a victorious nation in the winter and spring of 1913, Marcus Ehrenpreis had taken it upon himself to organize emergency relief for the fifty or so new Jewish congregations for which he had suddenly become the spiritual head, all of whom had been badly hurt by all sorts of soldiers marching their way. In a rapid tour to visit Jewish community leaders and relief organizations in Belgrade, Budapest, Vienna, Berlin, Frankfurt, Brussels, and Paris, he succeeded in forming an international relief committee for the suffering Jews of Thrace and Macedonia, based in Sofia and chaired by himself.

That Ehrenpreis was acting in full agreement with the Bulgarian government and King Ferdinand became evident in mid-January 1913, when a visiting delegation from the Jewish relief committees in England and Germany was immediately granted a royal audience. "My government will give you all the support you need, and if there are problems, we have our Chief Rabbi here; he knows that my door is always open to him," the king told the amazed guests, and none of them could fail to note the familiar rapport between the king and Ehrenpreis. Least of all after the king had taken a key out of his waistcoat pocket and opened a mahogany cabinet next to his desk, proudly displaying what was hidden inside, a gift from the Jewish communities in Bulgaria to celebrate the king's twenty-five years on the throne.

It was a magnificent Torah scroll, embellished with the traditional silver accessories; the crown, the shield, and the pointing hand, richly ornamented with ritual symbols and inscriptions in Bulgarian and Hebrew.

"You see what a wonderful work of art this is in every respect," Ferdinand said to the wide-eyed guests. "This Torah is indeed the most precious thing my Jewish citizens could give me on my day of celebration. After all, it is the common ground of us all, the ground on which you Jews, we Christians, and even the Mohammedans stand."[25]

Thus spoke King Ferdinand to the delegation for the relief of the distressed Jews of Thrace and Macedonia, and though the words may not have come exactly as Marcus Ehrenpreis would remember them, there was no doubting his deep faith in the king's benevolence toward the Jews of Bulgaria, and thus toward the Jews of Thrace and Macedonia, who, by means of the marching soldiers of Bulgaria, had now been incorporated into his spiritual domain.

Perhaps that is why Ehrenpreis did not seem particularly upset when the king told his visiting guests that he had had the silvered pointing hand turned into a gold-tipped pen with which he had signed the Bulgarian declaration of war on 5 October 1912 and proclaimed it to be a war of the Cross against the Crescent.

"What a remarkable circumstance His Majesty is revealing to us," Ehrenpreis commented on the fate of the Jewish royal gift, although the word remarkable was hardly sufficient to characterize a circumstance in which a Christian war against Islam had been proclaimed with a pointer from a Jewish Torah.[26]

In any case, these were the circumstances in which Ehrenpreis took it upon himself to meet with Jewish communities who overnight had been uprooted from centuries of Ottoman rule to assure them that they had nothing to fear from Bulgaria. At the end of March 1913, Ehrenpreis traveled to Adrianople with a military escort to provide supplies to the Jewish inhabitants of the conquered city. He soon realized that neither the Jews nor any other inhabitants saw the Bulgarians as liberators. Many had starved to death during the nearly five-month Bulgarian siege, and the people he met in his temporary headquarters in the office of the Turkish grand rabbi, Bedjaranus, had horror stories to tell. He was also aware that this was a tragic moment for Jewish congregations who "for generations had lived in complete freedom under Turkey's mild rule of the Jews."[27]

Yet not for a moment did he seem to hesitate in his self-imposed task of reconciling them with the cause of Bulgaria. Putting his trust in the power of symbolic ceremonies, he arranged for a closed synagogue to be reopened and for a public Shabbat service to be held. By "public" he meant that not only the Jews of the city would be invited to attend, but also representatives of the Bulgarian army and Jewish prisoners of war from the Turkish army. Up front, Adrianople's Bulgarian conqueror General Georgi Vazov with his uniformed staff were seated, and behind them Adrianople's frightened Jews, and from the pulpit Ehrenpreis had to summon all his homiletic and diplomatic talents to thread the line between "two camps that until yesterday had been enemies":

> You are leaving a country that has been a loving mother to you, where for four hundred years you have been free and respected citizens. What has happened now is God's will, but you are not coming to a stepmother either. In your new homeland you will find the same benevolence, the same esteem, and the same freedom that have been yours for generations. At this grim moment, let me assure you that we, the Jewish citizens of Bulgaria, see

> ourselves as free citizens of a free country, and that we have affectionate feelings for the land of Bulgaria and its broad-minded, tolerant ruler.[28]

Ehrenpreis had chosen to deliver his sermon in Judeo-Spanish to emphasize the unity between the Jews of Bulgaria and Turkey, and at the end of the service the chief rabbi of the defeated Turkey walked up to the chief rabbi of the victorious Bulgaria and embraced him "with tears streaming down his cheeks, while the moved congregation stood in motionless silence."

At least that's how Marcus Ehrenpreis wanted to remember the public Sabbath service in Adrianople on 29 March 1913.[29]

To the extent that Ehrenpreis had succeeded in sowing a Bulgarian seed of confidence and faith among the Jews of Adrianople, it was not given much time to grow. Only three months later, Bulgaria clashed with its allies Serbia and Greece over the conquered Ottoman territories. Serbia and Greece made it clear that they intended to retain conquered areas of Macedonia to which Bulgaria laid claim, prompting Ehrenpreis's friend and protector, King Ferdinand, to launch a new war.

In the light of history, he should not have done that. In a short span of time Bulgaria lost not only the war against Serbia and Greece over the disputed territories in Macedonia but also the war against Romania and a resurgent Turkey, which had both seized the opportunity to reconquer what they believed belonged to them. Romanian forces annexed the Bulgarian region of Dobrudzja south of the Danube, including the town of Silistra, and then marched all the way to Sofia. Ottoman forces retook eastern Thrace, including Adrianople, and did not halt until well into Bulgaria. It was all over in a month, and Bulgaria had gone from heroic victor to humiliated loser. The breakup of the Ottoman Empire had given new territories to all the Balkan states, but Bulgaria was the state that had claimed the most, and initially had gained the most, only to lose it all soon thereafter.

Ehrenpreis's support for the Bulgarian cause did not end with the Bulgarian defeat. On the contrary, in the hour of defeat he discovered a new and greater cause to make common with Bulgaria. The rapidly shifting lines and borders of the Balkan wars had as rapidly turned minorities into majorities, and majorities into minorities, and minorities in one country into minorities in another. The Jews of Adrianople went from being a minority in the Ottoman Empire to being a minority in Bulgaria to being an Ottoman minority again within six months, and the small Jewish community of Silistra that Ehrenpreis had regularly visited in his capacity as Grand Rabbi of Bulgaria was suddenly under Romanian rule.

And so it went across the Balkans; a patchwork of ethnic and religious minorities that had been stitched together under centuries of Ottoman rule was now being torn apart overnight, without the slightest regard for where the seams had previously run, or how relations between different communities had previously been regulated. Where the line would be drawn tomorrow, no one knew, nor what the consequences would be for those who ended up on the wrong side. The nation-state sought ethnic and religious unity, not an Ottoman patchwork of ethnic and religious communities.

In Silistra, the question was brought to a head early on. What Romania had in store for its few hundred Jews was something quite different from what they had been accustomed to as citizens of Bulgaria. Romania was notorious for the treatment of its Jews, classifying them as foreigners, denying them citizen rights, subjecting them to persecutions and pogroms, driving them to waves of suicide and emigration. Romania had consistently and flagrantly violated the requirements of religious freedom and civil rights that were made conditions for its independence in the Berlin Treaty of 1878, but as time went by the signatory powers had stopped paying attention.[30] Although the United States had raised the alarm about Romanian-Jewish immigration rising to spectacular proportions, the situation of Romanian Jews had, if anything, worsened by the time Romania annexed Dobrudzja and Silistra eleven years later. If the Jews of Silistra were to trade Bulgaria for Romania, they would also trade citizenship for lawlessness. The tragedy of the torn patchwork could not be more clearly illustrated. Millions of people were running the risk of becoming minorities in countries that did not want them.

The cause of the Jews was not only the cause of the Jews.

That the Jews of Silistra became the starting point for a campaign to protect the ethnic and religious minorities in the Balkans was due in no small part to Marcus Ehrenpreis's continued ability to unite his cause with Bulgaria's. Bulgaria's cause was to win international support for its claim to Dobrudzja and Silistra. Ehrenpreis's cause was to put Romania's treatment of its Jews on the international agenda. He was eager to link the problem of the Jews of Silistra to the larger minority problem created by the Balkan wars, since he knew that a problem being seen to affect Jews only could all too easily be seen to affect no one. Or, as Ehrenpreis put it, the struggle for minority rights had to be protected from being poisoned by Jew-hatred.[31]

In February 1913, with the tacit blessings of the Bulgarian government, Ehrenpreis submitted a memorandum to the Sofia representatives of the signatories to the Berlin Treaty, demanding guarantees for the Jews of Silistra. Memoranda were also sent to Jewish organizations in Europe and North America.

The international response was quicker and greater than Ehrenpreis and the Bulgarian government had probably expected. Perhaps most noticeable, a fiery appeal "to European diplomacy" by Italy's former prime minister Luigi Luzzatti, in the Italian newspaper *Corriere della Sera*, just a week after receiving the memorandum. Luzzatti was of Jewish descent and might have been suspected of having a Jewish bias, but his lifelong struggle for religious tolerance was well known and his moral authority was well established.

Although it soon became apparent that Romania would continue to treat its Jews as it wished, the question of the protection of ethnic and religious minorities in a Europe torn by ethnic-national wars had been put on the European agenda and would remain there as millions of Europeans lost their footing and a major European war drew closer.

This is the background against which Ehrenpreis's continued commitment to the Bulgarian cause in the late summer and autumn of 1913 must be seen. Or rather, a commitment to what he chose to define as Bulgaria's cause. Perhaps he already saw what was at stake, not only for the Jews of Europe but for Europe as a whole. Thirty-three years later, after Europe had all but destroyed both its Jews and itself, he saw it very clearly:

> The question was then—and is still today—and will become even more pertinent tomorrow: Can the world be reordered so that ethnic and territorial borders will be made to coincide? And if this cannot be

> done—and hardly anyone in his right mind believes that it can—should any country have the right by divine and human law to deprive the minorities living within its borders, or within provinces conquered by war—peoples of a different historical origin and of a different faith from that of the ruling majority—of their freedom and life opportunities?[32]

In the summer of 1913, political unreason was on the rise, but the question of war or peace in Europe was still open. As Ehrenpreis saw it, there were states and politicians who heralded a Europe of tolerance and ethno-religious diversity, just as there were states and politicians who heralded a war of all against all. The Treaty of Bucharest of 10 August 1913 sealed Bulgaria's military defeat, and Marcus Ehrenpreis accepted an unofficial diplomatic mission from King Ferdinand and his government to make the cause of the Balkan minorities the cause of Bulgaria. On 20 August 1913 he wrote a second memorandum demanding that the Treaty of Bucharest be supplemented with a clause for the protection of minority rights, and on the morning of 23 August he embarked on a European journey in the dual role of Bulgaria's Grand Rabbi and its diplomatic envoy.

The second role was demonstrated by the fact that the Bulgarian foreign minister had come to the central station in Sofia to wish him good luck. As his first stop was to be the lion's den, Bucharest, it was not a gesture of courtesy only. "You are a hated man in Romania," Ehrenpreis had been warned, and his meeting with representatives of the Romanian Jews had to be arranged in a secluded spot in a peripheral part of Bucharest. If it became known that the Jews in Romania were fraternizing with the "enemy," the visit to Bucharest could have ended badly.

It all went well, and Ehrenpreis was able to inform himself about the situation of the Romanian Jews and have them know that he represented their cause. He was again careful to emphasize that their cause was best served by being linked to the cause of all minorities. In a newspaper interview he detailed the minority situation in the Balkans after the Bucharest Treaty; half a million Macedonian Bulgarians in Serbia, a quarter of a million Greeks in Bulgaria, half a million Romanians (Kutzo-Vlachs) in Serbia, Greece, and Bulgaria, over a hundred thousand Turkish Jews in Greece, and over a million Turkish Muslims in "Christian" nation-states. "These millions of innocent Balkan inhabitants must not be left to the whims of administrative tyranny: the constitutions so readily invoked in these cases do not offer sufficient protection. It must be the foremost duty of the signatory powers of the Peace Treaty to settle this issue."[33]

At the beginning of September 1913, Marcus Ehrenpreis took his diplomatic mission to Italy. Here he found not only Luigi Luzzatti but also King Victor Emmanuel, who was considered sympathetic to the Jewish cause. In addition, Italy was a country "without antisemitism," or at least a country where Jews could freely "occupy the places to which they were entitled by virtue of their abilities," and thus a country that, like King Ferdinand's Bulgaria, portended the possibility of ethno-religious coexistence in a Europe of shifting front lines and borders.[34]

Joining him on the train to Italy were Esther and the children Theodor and Miriam, aged four and two. They were to disembark at the resort of Abbazia (at the time in Austria-Hungary, now Opatija in Croatia), to spend a mild late September week on the Adriatic Sea awaiting his return from the Italian mission.

In Rome Luigi Luzzatti awaited him with an open door, and from there new doors were opened to him, as Luzzatti sat down at his desk to pen one introductory letter after another.

To King Victor Emmanuel's first aide-de-camp: "This concerns the defense of that most sacred of liberties, the freedom of conscience."

To the Italian foreign minister di San Giuliano: "I would be grateful if you would receive with the greatest kindness the Chief Rabbi E., whose case concerns the defense of the most sacred of freedoms, freedom of religion. I would also be grateful if you would introduce him to His Excellency Giolitti [the prime minister]."

To former (and future) French prime minister Georges Clemenceau in Paris: "I ask you to receive M. Ehrenpreis, Grand Rabbi of Bulgaria, who wishes to present and defend before you a cause concerning the struggle for the great principle of fundamental justice and religious liberty."[35]

King Victor Emmanuel received him at his summer residence outside Pisa. Ehrenpreis had been advised by the adjutant that the king was small in stature and was standing to the left of the entrance, lest he accidentally start looking around for someone taller. The audience lasted forty-five minutes, and the king indeed showed strong sympathies with the Jewish cause, as well as a good knowledge of Judaism, and although his constitutional role did not permit him to make political statements, he made it clear that he fully agreed with the message Ehrenpreis had received from Prime Minister Giolitti at their meeting a few days earlier at the resort of Fiuggi outside Rome. There Ehrenpreis had been instructed to contact the Italian chargé d'affaires in London and on behalf of Giolitti communicate that if the British government were to take an initiative to supplement the Bucharest Treaty, the Italian government would support it.

"I felt that I had achieved the first positive result on my mission," Ehrenpreis noted.[36]

The meeting with Georges Clemenceau in Paris raised hopes for more. Count on me, *comptez sur moi*, Clemenceau declared, and ended their two-hour conversation by writing a letter of introduction to a "certain English statesman in London," and on 29 October 1913 the British government announced that it would not recognize the new borders in the Balkans until the minority rights inscribed in the Berlin Treaty of 1878 were guaranteed.[37]

Whatever Ehrenpreis had imagined might be the outcome of his mission, this was probably as much success as he could have hoped for.

Ehrenpreis made his last contribution to the cause of King Ferdinand's Bulgaria on 24 February 1914, during a visit to the German foreign minister Gottlieb von Jagow in Berlin, "the most unpleasant gentleman I have met in all my meetings with diplomats." The question raised by Ehrenpreis was whether Germany would consider giving the war-torn Bulgaria a loan in exchange for Bulgaria joining the Triple Alliance of Germany, Austria-Hungary, and Italy, a question that infuriated the German foreign minister. "Your king has been bowing to France long enough and he can continue to do so," shouted von Jagow, who, to make matters worse, was small and stooped and blustered as he spoke. As for the protection of minorities in the Balkans, "that's for the British. They want to play the role of the protectors of humanity in Europe. We are tired of the Balkans. *Wir sind Balkanmüde*."[38]

Marcus Ehrenpreis on his diplomatic mission in the service of Bulgaria to raise the issue of minority protection. Here he is seen in Fiuggi, near Rome, in September 1913, accompanied by Italy's foreign minister, Antonino Paternò Castello, the Marquis di San Giuliano (with cane); and Bulgaria's minister in Rome, Dimitar Rizov.

Had Marcus Ehrenpreis also tired of the Balkans? Did he fear a third Balkan war? Did he foresee that what awaited him in Bulgaria was a life of continued strife?

For whatever reason, as he got off the train in Berlin to meet Germany's screaming and blustering foreign minister, and the Bulgarian cause must have seemed particularly hopeless, he was literally on his way to explore another venue.

The meetings with Luigi Luzzatti, Victor Emmanuel, and Georges Clemenceau in the late summer of 1913, and the seemingly successful one-man diplomatic mission to Rome, Paris, London, Vienna, and Berlin, would have constituted a high-water mark in any man's life, but the day after the unpleasant meeting in Berlin, Marcus Ehrenpreis boarded the train to Stockholm to explore yet another life.

In November 1913 Marcus Ehrenpreis had organized and presided over the symbolically most charged of events during his reign as Bulgaria's Grand Rabbi: a public funeral service in the Great Synagogue in Sofia in memory of the Bulgarian-Jewish soldiers killed in the two Balkan wars. As at the inauguration in 1909, the front pews were filled with high-ranking representatives of official Bulgaria: Prime Minister Vasil Radoslavov, generals from the army, officials from the court, leading representatives of civil society and cultural life. And last but not least, on the altar podium, across from Ehrenpreis, the president of the highest body of the Bulgarian Orthodox Church, the Holy Synod, Metropolitan Vasily of Ruschuk, in full priestly regalia. From there, the metropolitan had a full view of the packed synagogue, and from there, in the words of Ehrenpreis, he was looking at "a shattering picture of sorrow and despair: a perplexed mass of people, black in black, with a muted question on their lips—why has this befallen us, why have our sons been taken from us, our husbands, the fathers of our defenseless infants?"[39]

For Ehrenpreis, however, this was not only an opportunity to manifest the sacrificial commitment of Bulgaria's Jews to the cause of Bulgaria in an hour of sorrow and distress, but an opportunity as well to take the sting out of the vicious antisemitic conspiracy theories that had begun to spread. By 1905, the Russian forgery *The Protocols of the Elders of Zion* had seen the light of day, and its inciting effect on anti-Jewish opinions and movements throughout Europe was palpable. In 1911, a Ukrainian Jew, Mendel Beilis, had been arrested in Kiev on suspicion of killing a Christian boy to use his blood for baking matzo. The longer Beilis was in custody and the longer the investigation dragged on (for more than two years), the more it looked as if a medieval ritual murder fantasy had been taken seriously. In the late summer of 1912, Ehrenpreis received a letter from the Anglo-Jewish journalist and historian Lucien Wolf, who, on behalf of the Board of Deputies of the English Jews, asked if Ehrenpreis could obtain a statement of protest from the Holy Synod of the Bulgarian Orthodox Church. The Russian Orthodox Synod was not to be reckoned with, as it neither wanted nor dared to take issue with the Russian government, which had contributed to the fueling of anti-Jewish sentiments across the country.

So maybe the Bulgarian Orthodox Synod?

A few days before the planned service, Ehrenpreis went to Ruschuk, on the banks of the Danube, to present his case to Metropolitan Vasily, whom he had come to know as a broad-minded church official with friendly connections to the city's Jewish community (which included the family of the writer and future Nobel Prize winner Elias Canetti). Vasily listened attentively and admitted to the absurdity of the blood libel, but he said he would not be able to make a statement on the issue. "You know the fragility of our relationship with Russia, our liberator, which is becoming even more fragile at this moment of our misfortune," Vasily explained to Ehrenpreis. "It pains me to say, but I dare not." To which Ehrenpreis made a diplomatic suggestion: "If you cannot speak out loudly, would you perhaps agree to testify for us in silence?"[40]

Which is what Metropolitan Vasily of Ruschuk, president of the Holy Synod of the Bulgarian Orthodox Church, had promised to do when, on 2 November 1913, he had himself placed opposite the Grand Rabbi on the altar platform of the

Great Synagogue in Sofia to hear Marcus Ehrenpreis say in Bulgarian:

> I call upon the spirits of the Jewish soldiers who fell for their fatherland to be witnesses against the offensive accusations now being leveled against the Jewish people. Dare anyone say that the religion that invites us to shed our blood for the fatherland would invite us to use the blood of others for our religious purposes? The Holy Synod of Bulgaria, whose highest representative sits among us, has in the past most emphatically rejected this unworthy and false legend. The current president of the Holy Synod confirms with his presence the previous declarations of the synod. He is here to show the esteem and sympathy of the Bulgarian Church for the offended Jewish people.[41]

As the service ended, Metropolitan Vasily silently agreed with what Ehrenpreis had said by walking up to him and embracing him with visible warmth. The following day, several European newspapers published a telegram saying that "the dignified protest against the events in Kiev made a strong impression on all present."[42] Bulgaria's Jews thus had not only been celebrated and honored as full citizens and patriots but had also been witnesses to a silent but clear statement by Bulgaria's highest political and ecclesiastical authorities against anti-Jewish propaganda.

So why leave now? The official Bulgarian goodwill toward Ehrenpreis and the Bulgarian Jews seemed to know no limits, especially since it must have been clear what a diplomatic asset Ehrenpreis was in Bulgaria's efforts to gain outside sympathy and support. It must also have been clear that during the rabbinical reign of Ehrenpreis the Jews of Bulgaria had experienced a period of recognition and well-being. They had seen their schools improve, their statutes coordinated, and their links with Bulgarian society strengthened. And although the constitutional law that had been promised to Ehrenpreis on his accession, formally recognizing and regulating the autonomy of the Jewish minority, was never adopted, the position and standing of the Jews in Bulgaria had visibly strengthened under Ehrenpreis.

Yet he remained a stranger, even among his own people, not only intellectually and culturally but also politically. Among those who opposed his reforms and distrusted his intentions and called for his resignation were also those who were concerned about his involvement in the politics of the nation. The Grand Rabbi's role under Ottoman rule had been to safeguard the interests of the Jewish minority and keep it out of domestic politics as much as possible. Domestic conflicts had rarely augured well for the Jews. Actively siding with Bulgaria in the battles for Adrianople, Silistra, and Salonika may have made Ehrenpreis a good Bulgarian patriot in the eyes of the Bulgarians, but not necessarily a good Jewish leader in the eyes of the Bulgarian Jews. The diplomatic and political efforts on behalf of Balkan Jews and other minorities, which Ehrenpreis himself would remember as his most important endeavors during his years in Bulgaria, may in fact have been what strengthened the opposition against him in the turmoil after the war defeat.[43]

Among the critics were not least the Zionists, who had become increasingly disenchanted with Ehrenpreis's cultural Zionism. Was he even a Zionist anymore? Was he not fighting more for the Bulgarian nation than for the Jewish nation, more for the rights of the Jews as a minority than for the right of the Jews to a nation of their own? And although this was a somewhat misleading characterization—in Ehrenpreis's cultural Zionism, the Jewish return to Palestine continued to play an important role—it was apparent that Ehrenpreis's diplomatic talents had not been sufficient to gain him the undivided support and love of Bulgarian Jewry.

That Ehrenpreis still had support within the Jewish community, perhaps stronger than he had realized, would soon be apparent. On 16 March 1914, Ehrenpreis summoned the highest body of the Bulgarian congregations, the Central Consistory, and handed in his letter of resignation. "I don't remember ever being so moved as when I slowly and in a subdued voice read out my letter to the members of the consistory, who were taken by complete surprise," he would later reminisce.[44]

The surprise must have been all the greater, as the Ehrenpreis family had already begun moving into the beautifully situated two-story house that the Bulgarian government had commissioned for them. It had everything they could wish for, spacious working and reception rooms on the ground floor and a private residence upstairs, from which they could look out over the snow-covered Vitosha massif to the south, with large balconies providing "a veritable paradise for our two little ones." When the telegram from Stockholm arrived on 9 March 1914, Marcus and Esther stood in the balmy spring air overseeing the delivery of furniture and fittings for their new home. "Elected by an overwhelming majority. Wholehearted congratulations," they read on the very doorstep to a "long-held dream."[45]

They could still have stepped back from the move to Stockholm instead of stepping back from their dream house, and a campaign was immediately launched to have them do so.

Esther Ehrenpreis's portrait of Marcus, painted during their early years in Bulgaria.

Delegations were sent, demonstrations were organized, a pamphlet in Judeo-Spanish in defense of Ehrenpreis was published, and the Central Consistory convened an extraordinary congress for the purpose of persuading Ehrenpreis to change his mind.

But the opponents of Ehrenpreis also made themselves heard. In May 1914, the main organ of the Zionist movement in Vienna, *Die Welt*, founded by Herzl, carried an anonymous article steeped in contempt for Ehrenpreis sycophancy. "For whom is Dr. Ehrenpreis really indispensable?" the anonymous writer asked and answered himself: "Well, for the few notables who need a leader to suppress the democratic and nationalist currents within Zionism." The article further insinuated that Ehrenpreis's reason for handing in his resignation was his discontent with his salary and pension, and that his wealthy backers were now prepared to take from the poor and give to Ehrenpreis in order to make him stay.[46] And we may perhaps understand why even the view of the Vitosha massif couldn't make him stay.

At the farewell service on Friday evening, 28 August 1914, the synagogue in Sofia was filled to its last row.

"I have served you for fourteen years," said Marcus Ehrenpreis as he looked out over his congregation for the last time.

And no one could misunderstand what story of the Bible he was invoking.

Everyone also knew the continuation of Jacob's parting words to Laban:

"By day I was consumed by heat, by night by cold, and sleep escaped my eyes."[47]

Three days later, the Ehrenpreis family left Bulgaria on trains packed with soldiers on their way to the battlefields of Europe. During an overnight stopover in Vienna they met horrified refugees from Lemberg, describing how the Russians had entered the city. A few days later, they learned that Ehrenpreis's mother and the families of two sisters had managed to catch the last train to Vienna, while his father and a third sister had been left behind in the turmoil at the Lemberg station.

Marcus Ehrenpreis's parents would never see each other again.

Jacob Ehrenpreis would die in Lemberg 1918.

Clara Süss-Ehrenpreis would die in Stockholm four years later.

On the morning of 14 September 1914, after two weeks of arduous travel, the Ehrenpreis family arrived in Stockholm. On the front page of one of the major newspapers, *Svenska Dagbladet*, a war-style headline across seven columns proclaimed, "Austria Admits Defeat at Lemberg," and underneath it a map of Lemberg and its environs, and Marcus Ehrenpreis didn't have to understand Swedish to understand that something momentous had happened to the world of his childhood.

"The New Rabbi Arrives. Shares His Impressions from Bulgaria," read a one-column headline in the same newspaper the next morning.[48]

Some weeks earlier, *Svenska Dagbladet* had reported on Ehrenpreis's departure from Sofia and on the "stately address" handed to him by "the Israelite congregations in Bulgaria."[49] Ehrenpreis could now confirm that he had brought the stately address with him, as well as an order of merit from the king, as well as a jewel brooch for Esther Ehrenpreis in gratitude for her contributions to the queen's charities, as well as many letters and telegrams of thanks.

To those reading the interview, it must have seemed a mystery why Ehrenpreis would have left such a regal position for

The synagogue that Marcus Ehrenpreis built.

a small Jewish congregation in Stockholm. Had they read the stately address, the mystery might have seemed even greater. Richly ornamented and elaborately hand-lettered on parchment, with a medallion portrait of Ehrenpreis in the pulpit, richly signed by representatives of Jewish Bulgaria, it concluded with the following words:

"We will never forget that you chose to spend the best years of your life among us, that you devoted to us the vitality and activity of your youth. Keep us in generous memory! May God be with you!"[50]

Not a trace of long days of heat and sleepless nights of cold. Possibly an undertone of unease.

What would happen to Bulgaria's Jews after Marcus Ehrenpreis?

Fifteen years later there was no Grand Rabbi in Bulgaria, and an observer painted a grim picture of the state of the Jews:

> The congregations have once again fallen into disrepair and show few signs of life, the synagogues are empty and deserted. The Sephardic Jewry is dying. Whenever an antisemitic organization is attacking the Jews, one can hear a deep sigh from the disheartened Bulgarian Jewry: "Alas, if only we had had Dr. Ehrenpreis with us."[51]

Fourteen years as the Grand Rabbi of Bulgaria could have been the high point in any man's life, but in the life of Marcus Ehrenpreis it would turn out to be just another journey with a taste of adventure.

What remained was yet another life.

Marcus Ehrenpreis and Ragnar Josephson (left) with family and friends at the time of their joint Swedish translation of neo-Hebrew poetry. In the resort town of Båstad in the summer of 1919.

4.

A NEW CHILDHOOD

Wondrously the tale weds the far and the near
the cedars of Lebanon and the junipers of snowy forests
weaving them together with shimmering bands,
the whispers of palms and pines,
the melancholy of West and the fire of East.
I am the West, and I am the East.

—Oscar Levertin[1]

In December 1920, a book of new Hebrew poetry in Swedish translation was published by an established publishing house in Stockholm and presented to the Swedish readers as a testimony to the rebirth of the Jewish soul.

> What is being offered here are but a few sparks of a distant burning fire, which, as they have reached us, may bear testimony to its ardor and ever-increasing strength.

The author of the Swedish introduction was Marcus Ehrenpreis. It was also Marcus Ehrenpreis who, together with the Swedish-Jewish writer and art historian Ragnar Josephson, had transmitted the fervor of the Hebrew renaissance to the

Swedish language, which thus became one of the first languages in which a new generation of Hebrew poets could be read in translation.

"In these poems, the violated Eastern Jewish soul takes its tormentors and slanderers to task, articulating its new youth and redeemed power in jubilant tones, saturated with life and light, nurtured from the rich springs of our ancient history," Marcus Ehrenpreis wrote of Chaim Nachman Bialik, the undisputed master of the new Hebrew poetry.[2] And in an essay on Hebrew literature through the millennia, in a book published six months earlier by the same publisher, it was as if the revolutionary glow from his days on the barricades of the Young Hebrews had never been extinguished—with the difference that the glow was now emanating from a language that had never "spoken Hebrew" before.[3]

After six years in Sweden, Marcus Ehrenpreis had not only mastered a language in which he had undertaken to deliver his sermons, but a language in which he was now beginning to write essays, pen articles, and deliver lectures. When, after yet another six years, he made his debut as a Swedish author and was interviewed on the front page of *Svenska Dagbladet*, he declared that he had fallen in love:

> It is precisely in your Swedish language that I have found the strong masculine seriousness and solemn brilliance which lend themselves to the thoughts and tones with which I have felt the need to express my feelings. [...] When I came here as Chief Rabbi of the Mosaic Congregation of Stockholm, I was over forty-five years old and had not heard or read a word of Swedish. [...] Nor did I think at the time that I could learn your language other than sufficiently enough to

fulfill the tasks of my office, but then I came to love it more and more.[4]

The article was entitled "Foreigner a Swedish Stylist of the First Rank," and the journalist compared Ehrenpreis to Joseph Conrad. "It must be quite remarkable," it said, "that a foreigner, and one of a race completely different from our own, should present himself in our own mother tongue not only as a thoughtful and captivating writer but as a first-rate stylist as well."

Debut as a Swedish author. In due course.

High time, however, for the obsession with race, since it was prominent already in the reception of the book on new Hebrew poetry. In a lengthy review in *Svenska Dagbladet* the poet Anders Österling, a newly elected member of the Swedish Academy, wrote about the remarkable vitality of Hebrew as a poetic language, and about Bialik as a world-class poet, but he could not let go of the Jewish race. Or rather the Jewish "racelessness," by which Österling meant "the unrestrained internationalism, the all-too-prevalent urge to conform, and the predisposition for ingenious imitation that characterizes the path of Jewish influence [...]. No antisemitism is pleasant, not even literary antisemitism, but if one looks at the terrible confusion that prevails in the German literary world at present, it is very difficult to rejoice in the contribution of the Jews. One almost gets the impression that the literary German Jews, by speculating in the dissolution of form, want to take revenge on Western civilization."[5]

And the subject of race again, in the review in *Dagens Nyheter*: "Despite the highly distinctive poetic individualities that meet us in this poetry [...] it is above all its general features, its racial characteristics, that stay in your mind when you put down the book. [...] Above all, the tribal feeling emanating from it, that wounded, trampled, but indelible Jew-feeling. However individualistic the poet wishes to appear, however European, it is to this he returns." Which again did not prevent the reviewer from naming Bialik "a poet of the highest rank in modern poetry, a poet of world literary importance."[6]

Thinking about race was normal at the time. Everyone thought about race. Race and tribe. The characteristics of races and the quality of tribes. Lower races and higher. Race also had an aura of science about it. In 1922, the Swedish State Institute for Racial Biology was founded with broad political support, the first such institute in the world. In fact, it was hardly possible to speak of Jews without mentioning the Jewish race and its characteristics. Even in seemingly universal poems about nature, the reviewer in *Dagens Nyheter* could find racial characteristics. Not necessarily because he saw Jewish poetry or the Jews as inferior—on the contrary, there was both admiration and compassion in his review—but because there was still something relatively innocent about the concept of race. People talked about race and racial differences without necessarily making it the foundation of a political ideology, let alone of oppression and persecution.

That the new Hebrew poetry was perceived as distinctively Jewish was after all neither surprising nor controversial. Ehrenpreis, too, saw it that way. The fire from afar glowing from its lines was a distinctively Jewish fire: "Through the new [poetry] shines forth, brightly and victoriously, the ancient Israelite vision, the psalmists' sense of eternity and the prophets' universalist ideals of the future."[7]

In the language of the Psalmists and Prophets, the Jewish soul would speak to the souls of the world and dispel centuries of anti-Jewish darkness.

This is what Marcus Ehrenpreis was dreaming.

Alongside the review of new Hebrew poetry in *Dagens Nyheter*, a report from a lecture that Marcus Ehrenpreis had delivered the night before, in which he had argued that the Jews of world literature mostly were portrayed as stereotypes, not as real people, and that this was due to the fact that "for long periods of time the Jews had lived in isolation and by themselves, so that poets and writers could not acquire any personal knowledge of them." With the reappearance of Hebrew on the stage of world literature, this was to change, Ehrenpreis predicted.[8]

The lecture was well attended and warmly applauded, and a major newspaper saw it worthy of front-page attention. After six years in Sweden, Marcus Ehrenpreis had become a cultural personality, with a Jewish path of his own to stake out in the Swedish cultural landscape.

To the flow of Jewish texts in Swedish translation that year (1921), Ehrenpreis added a collection of selected essays "by contemporary Jewish thinkers" about "Israel's present and future." If nothing else, it made perfectly clear that the Jewish paths were many and conflicting, and that the world of Jewish thought was in a state of chaos and creativity. Only a few years later, Martin Buber's book on Jewish mysticism, *The Legend of the Baal-Shem*, and *History of the Jews after the Fall of the Jewish State*, by the German-Jewish rabbi and historian Ismar Elbogen, were published in Swedish translation.

And there would be more.

Behind the increasing flow of books in Swedish on Jewish themes was an association formed in the spring of 1919, the Jewish Literary Society, with Ehrenpreis as its initiator and front figure. During his sermon in the synagogue on the Day of Atonement in 1917, he had appealed to the members of the congregation for their support in promoting "Jewish education in our midst," and when he returned home a few hours later, a letter from a member of the congregation was waiting with a check for ten thousand kronor (equivalent to $40,000 at the time of this writing), which became the foundation stone of Ehrenpreis's Swedish-Jewish education project.[9]

The formation of the society was also reported in the press. "It is our belief," the initiators declared, "that the Jewish Literary Society, through its publications, will be able to awaken in the wider public a sense of the best in the Jewish character, and provide it with a living source to the understanding of the contribution of the Jewish people to world culture and the value of its distinctive character."[10]

Weren't there already signs of success? In a lengthy review of the books by Buber and Elbogen, the influential literary critic and newly elected member of the Swedish Academy, Fredrik Böök, wrote that the books had an important mission to fulfill and deserved to be read "even outside the circle of a tribal community." He also wrote that "the soul of the Jewish people has penetrated the marrow of all tribes of Europe, our whole culture is imbued with it, our past has drawn strength from it, and our future cannot be detached from it."[11]

It remained unsaid whether Fredrik Böök thought this was for the good or for the bad. From his examples of contemporary expressions of the Jewish soul (homelessness, rootlessness, the Russian Revolution), it was easy to suspect the latter.[12] Böök had certainly become a warm friend of Zionism and of Jewish nation-building in Palestine, and in a few years' time he would travel with Ehrenpreis to the inauguration of the Hebrew University of Jerusalem, but to the extent that the book series of the Jewish Literary Society was intended to awaken interest in the contribution of the Jewish soul to Swedish society as well, it seemed not to have succeeded with Fredrik Böök. Nor would it succeed any better as time went by.

Fredrik Böök and the Jews. In due course.

Better success, then, with Ellen Key, one of Sweden's most famous cultural figures at the time, who wrote: "[T]hese books [should] give our people at least an idea of one of the great movements of our time, soon to become a mighty river, connected to the conscience of mankind by both subterranean and visible streams, which will not be stilled until they have reached their sea."[13]

However, not even Ellen Key had rid herself of anti-Jewish stereotypes. The "spiritual type" among the Jews, represented by the Rothschild banking family, had "a huge guilt in the World War," she wrote, and the type represented by the poet Heinrich Heine, "a no lesser guilt through its power in the world press and literature." The spiritual type she pinned her hopes on was the one represented by the Prophets and Jesus, which she thought still lived on in Judaism, and which "in our time may again have a major message to convey to a humanity in distress."[14]

All in all, Ehrenpreis should have been satisfied. In a country where hardly anyone had read the Pentateuch and the Prophets other than through the anti-Jewish lenses of the Christian tradition and liturgy, let alone had made contact with any postbiblical Jewish thinkers and poets, the works of Martin Buber and Chaim Nachman Bialik were now being published in Swedish, and so would soon the works of Marcus Ehrenpreis.

As in Bulgaria, Ehrenpreis had quickly gained access to the cultural elite of his new country. At an introductory literary dinner arranged for him, one of his earliest friends, the professor of literature Karl Warburg, had expressed hopes that the new chief rabbi would be making a contribution to Swedish culture as well. Ehrenpreis, who could still barely utter a flawless sentence in Swedish, had been somewhat embarrassed by Warburg's expectations, but his playful response in untranslatable German indicated that Warburg was onto something: *Schweden kann schwerlich mein Vaterland werden, aber ich hoffe dass es mein Kinderland werden.*[15]

Kinderland? The land of a new childhood? A land where a forty-five-year-old rabbi would acquire a new mother tongue, and in this tongue would henceforth begin to think, dream, and write the bulk of his life's work?

Perhaps Warburg had not expected that much, and perhaps Ehrenpreis had not intended that much with his answer at the introductory literary dinner in Stockholm in the autumn of 1914.

But that's how it would be.

Karl Warburg had seen and heard Ehrenpreis already during his brief visit to Stockholm in the spring of 1914, when the visiting chief rabbi from Sofia had given two well-attended lectures in German in the Great Synagogue on Wahrendorff Street. The first on Saturday afternoon, 28 February, on the essence of Judaism, the second on Sunday morning, on the psychology of Judaism in the nineteenth century. After the second lecture, "a middle-aged gentleman with a reddish-blond beard and animated gestures" had come up to Ehrenpreis to express his appreciation of the lecture and to offer him a tour of "our National Museum." Ehrenpreis would still make his dinner appointment at Rabbi Gottlieb Klein's snow-covered villa in the suburb of Djursholm, Warburg assured him.[16]

Karl Warburg proved to know not only "our National Museum" but also a large part of Stockholm's cultural and literary world, and when the Ehrenpreis family arrived in Stockholm in September, many open doors already awaited them. Warburg came from an established and well-assimilated Jewish family in Gothenburg, but his interest in Judaism had so far been small. Warburg's wife Betty (née Drucker) had noted to Ehrenpreis's credit that he spoke German without the slightest Jewish accent and hardly looked like a Jew either.[17] To the extent that Ehrenpreis had feared that Jewish issues would not be top of mind for the Jews of his new country, he had reason to worry. To the extent that he had feared that he would suffer from a lack of cultural interaction and inspiration in the Jewish periphery of Europe, he had reason to feel reassured.

In any case, there was not much time to contemplate the situation. A week after his arrival, the season of the Jewish High Holidays was due, and Marcus Ehrenpreis was to deliver his inaugural sermon on the eve of Rosh Hashanah, the Jewish New Year, and yet another sermon the next morning. He delivered his sermons in German, which was the foreign language that most of the congregation understood, but soon enough, and much earlier than stipulated by his contract, he would deliver his first sermon in Swedish.

He knew from experience that language was a key to acceptance and success. It was his Croatian that had made Bishop Strossmayer's eyes shine in Djakovar, and it was his Judeo-Spanish that had made Sofia's Sephardic Jews embrace him. "When you come to a foreign country and speak its language, doors and hearts open for you, but as long as you don't, people seem as if they want to shield themselves from the newcomer. There's no real warmth in the relationship unless you master the language of the country."[18]

He also understood the significance of pronunciation: a person with a strong accent would run the risk of being taken less seriously. His teacher in Swedish pronunciation and intonation was the best possible, the opera singer and opera director Sven Nyblom, who had the task of teaching foreign guest singers to pronounce the shibboleths of the Swedish language, among them the *u* sound, which they should make by forming their mouth into a trumpet and adding to the *u* sound a barely audible *b*, which he now trumpeted to Ehrenpreis as well. When another of his language teachers, the Jewish educator and philanthropist Axel Hirsch, tried to explain to him that this or that could not be said in Swedish, Ehrenpreis insisted on saying it anyway. "[Hirsch] didn't want me to violate the Swedish language, and I didn't want to suppress my train of thought," he wrote.[19]

Ragnar Josephson, who had been working with Ehrenpreis on the Swedish translation of new Hebrew poetry, would later write that "a Swedish-born could here learn about the possibilities of the Swedish language from a foreigner, who when the possibilities seemed exhausted, fearlessly created new ones."[20]

Those who are forced to wrestle with a language can sometimes get closer to it than those who have received it for free, and so it was with Ehrenpreis. He was forced to wrestle with the Swedish language, and he would eventually get closer to it than most Swedish-born.

Already during their dramatic journey to Stockholm, Marcus and Esther Ehrenpreis could sense that the new war in Europe was about to end the world into which they had been born. In Vienna they had already heard about the Russian conquest of Lemberg, and in Stockholm they had barely unpacked before the reports of persecutions and expulsions in the wake of the war began pouring in.

Also beginning to pour in were desperate letters from people looking for missing relatives. Hundreds of thousands of Jews had been uprooted from their homes and separated from each other, and word spread, perhaps via war-torn Lemberg, that in neutral Stockholm there was a famous rabbi from Galicia who might be able to help.

Soon the letters were delivered in bundles to the rabbinical office on Wahrendorff Street. "A pack of veritable tragedies came with the postman every morning, a sea of human distress, of physical and mental suffering, of nameless despair," Ehrenpreis noted. There were non-Jews writing as well, among them a Polish lady from a well-known noble family, suddenly cut off from families and homes by a front line or two.[21]

Thus the periphery had become the center, and Ehrenpreis would have use for every language he had wrestled with to fulfill his new role as "the postman of all Israel," and to exercise his demonstrated skills as a diplomat and opinion-maker.[22] The latter could not wait for his wrestling with the Swedish language. In April 1915, at a fundraising event for "Jews suffering from the war," Ehrenpreis lectured in German about the *Der Weltkrieg und die Juden*, The World War and the Jews, and according to a newspaper report of the event, he had no problems being understood. "Not for a long time had the auditorium of the Academy of Science gathered such a large assembly within its dilapidated walls," wrote *Dagens Nyheter.* "This appeal to our sense of human togetherness had attracted not only a large and representative part of the Israelite world in Stockholm, and a polyglot assembly from its international community, but a large number of other interested people as well. And they got full value for their money."[23]

The lectures and the fundraising events were to follow one another, and in the spring of 1916 a selection of the letters of distress received by Ehrenpreis were published in Swedish translation.[24] "The impact of the war on the civilian population is here brought forth in intimate, often moving letters [...] providing highly interesting information about their plight and undeserved suffering," a reviewer wrote.[25]

The extent of the Jewish catastrophe in eastern Europe was described by Ehrenpreis himself in an article in the Swedish review *Svensk Tidskrift*:

> An unfortunate fate initially brought the all-destructive war precisely to the most Jewish provinces of Europe: Poland, Lithuania, Volyn, East Prussia, Galicia, north-eastern Hungary, and finally Romania and Siebenburgen [Transylvania]. The densely populated Jewish communities in these provinces, home to approximately six million people, which for centuries had been the main centers of Jewish tradition and culture, were fundamentally destroyed, in some places literally swept off the face of the earth. [...] From the [Russian] governorates of Kovno and Courland [in present-day Lithuania and Latvia] alone, 280,000 Jews were expelled with incredible cruelty within 30 to 45 hours, precisely during the 1915 Jewish Feast of the Weeks, Shavuot. Compare this with the expulsion of the Jews from Spain—and this was in the dark Middle Ages [1492]—at which they were given four months in which to arrange their property and family affairs.[26]

The Eastern Jewish disaster of the First World War would eventually fade in comparison with the Nazi extermination project of the Second, but at the time it was disaster enough to prompt United States president Woodrow Wilson to proclaim 27 January 1916 as National Relief Day for the stricken Jewish people.[27] A year later, Ehrenpreis gave the opening address at a Scandinavian relief conference in Stockholm, describing the persecution of the Jews in eastern Europe as "the most perilous time that Judaism has yet gone through."[28]

Ehrenpreis may have sought the periphery in the hope of escaping the conflicts of the center, but the war drew him inexorably back. On 20 November 1917, on its front page, *Svenska Dagbladet* published an open letter from Marcus Ehrenpreis to Georges Clemenceau, the former French prime minister who had so graciously received him in Paris in September 1913, and who had just become prime minister again. Ehrenpreis reminded Clemenceau of his wholehearted support at that time for international guarantees to the Jews of Romania: "Now you are at the head of the French government, and the situation of the Romanian Jews is worse than ever, and most importantly—Romania is an ally of yours, an ally whose inhuman acts cast a shadow on the great democracies with which it is allied."[29]

The Jewish disaster in eastern Europe would also have consequences for Jewish life in Sweden. Already before the war, Jews from pogrom-ridden Russia had sought refuge in Sweden, a few thousand at most, but many enough to noticeably change the composition of a Jewish population that as late as 1850 numbered only 960.[30] Before the war, there were no formal restrictions on entry to Sweden; it was possible even for penniless Jews from eastern European shtetls, Jewish villages, to settle anywhere in the country and find a livelihood wherever they could. Like every culturally cohesive immigrant group, they sought each other out, especially those who sought to live an Orthodox Jewish life, and in a few neighborhoods in the cities of Stockholm and Lund there emerged for a time Swedish shtetls of a sort, with a relatively cohesive Eastern Jewish population.

With the Jewish immigration from eastern Europe, there were tensions arising, not only in relation to the non-Jewish community, but to the established Swedish-Jewish community as well. The cultural and social divisions were palpable: Swedish versus Yiddish, Reform versus Orthodox, assimilation versus nationalism, anti-Zionism versus Zionism, liberalism versus socialism, the magnificent organ-decorated synagogue on Wahrendorff Street in central Stockholm versus the Spartan shul of the Orthodox Jews on St. Paul Street, in the poorer, southern part of the city.

As early as 1851, members of the Stockholm congregation had expressed fears that the incipient eastern Jewish immigration would damage the position of the Jewish community in Sweden by "introducing and spreading haggling in its most disgusting and pernicious form."[31] In 1882 the congregation made Swedish citizenship a condition for membership, which effectively excluded a majority of the Eastern Jews.[32] In 1890, a leading representative of the congregation could speak of the Eastern Jews as "our half-Asiatic colony wandering out there in the desert of ignorance and superstition."[33]

These were tensions and conflicts that would long impinge on Jewish life in Stockholm and repeatedly challenge Ehrenpreis's rabbinical authority, but in the face of a war that seemed to threaten the very existence of Jewish life in eastern Europe, the ranks were closing.

Under the ominous headline "The Invasion of the Russian Jews," a leading newspaper noted that the events of the war seemed to have "a unifying effect on a dispersed people, which daily is suffering from deep-seated inner conflicts."[34]

There was no invasion of Russian Jews, of course. With the outbreak of the war, Sweden had introduced passport requirements and visa restrictions that made it considerably more difficult for poor Jews from the East to enter the country. During the decade of the war, 1910–1920, Sweden's Jewish population increased by only two hundred and fifty people, compared to two thousand the decade before. The same article that in one sentence had proclaimed the existence of a Jewish invasion would in the next sentence proclaim something else: "If earlier we could rejoice in the arrival of simple workmen and wandering peddlers ['the lesser apples from the tree of Judah'], we may now bow in admiration of veritable war merchants and financial wizards [. . .], wholly without experience in small business but with plenty of experience in million-dollar profits."

Phrases like these, published in a leading liberal Swedish newspaper, testified to the existence of the low-intensity background noise of anti-Jewish notions and stereotypes, even in a country on the periphery of Jewish life. Ehrenpreis did soon find out that not only would he have to contend with people who knew nothing about Jews and Judaism, but perhaps more so with people who thought they knew all they needed to know—about the Jewish race, religion, and character.[35] The anti-Jewish stereotypes were there before the Jews and applied not only to the newly arrived Eastern Jews but to the "old" Swedish Jews as well. The Jews were all irretrievably trapped in their Jewish race, in their Oriental souls, in all the evil roles that the Church had cast them in over the centuries, in all the repulsive qualities that modern antisemitism had ascribed to them, and which did not require any living Jews to keep alive.

With the new Jewish immigration Sweden had certainly had an influx of living Jews, who with their visibly distinctive culture and lifestyle might provide real-life material for already existing anti-Jewish attitudes and stereotypes, but antisemitism in Sweden made no distinction between Jews and Jews. In the Swedish humor press, all Jews were curly-haired, hook-nosed, pot-bellied, bandy-legged, arrogant, and pushy, and they all spoke a ridiculous Jew-Swedish, even highly cultured and long-assimilated Swedish Jews. Ehrenpreis's enthusiastic museum guide and introducer to Swedish literary circles, Karl Warburg, had plenty of experience with this kind of antisemitism. For instance, being recriminated for having the "Jewish" audacity to appear more Swedish than the Swedes themselves. "Nowadays a Swedish man can hardly utter a word of praise about Sweden, or even about Swedish nationalism, without the Semitic professor Karl Warburg jumping to the fore, eagerly gesticulating, reminiscent of the black figure in a children's toy called the 'the devil in the bottle,'" the writer Bengt Lidforss, an unabashed antisemite, would blurt out.[36] It is not hard to imagine what Lidforss would have thought of Warburg in his meeting with Ehrenpreis calling the National Museum in Stockholm "our" museum.

Very soon it must have become clear to Ehrenpreis that even seemingly successful and well-established Jews were living in a bubble of anxiety and uncertainty. They tried as best they could to steel themselves against the antisemitic noise surrounding them, to keep a low profile, to foster the image of themselves as well-behaving loyal Swedes "of the Mosaic creed." In that perspective, their fear of being associated with the "un-Swedish" Eastern Jews was perhaps explicable but hardly rational; antisemitism in Sweden did not need Eastern Jews to propagate and flourish.

The anxious efforts by members of the Stockholm congregation to distance themselves from the Eastern Jews must have created a dilemma for Ehrenpreis. After all, the Eastern Jewish world was the world he had been shaped by and was still emotionally connected to. Considering where he came from, he would presumably have more in common with the Yiddish-speaking, culturally self-aware Jewish newcomers than with the well-established Swedish Jews, whom he characterized as "detached" from their Jewishness.[37]

Yet it was among these Jews that he would feel most welcome. Many of them were certainly outspoken opponents of the Zionism with which he continued to be associated, not least among them his predecessor Gottlieb Klein, who only a year before their meeting in the snow-covered villa in Djursholm, claiming to speak for the majority of the congregation in Stockholm, had published an article strongly critical of Zionism: "Zionism is an apostasy from the highest ideal of Judaism, [...] from the central call in the history of Israel: preserve religion, not nationality." In addition, Zionism had nothing to offer the Jews of Sweden, "since here we are lacking the root cause of why Jews elsewhere might be attracted to Zionism, namely antisemitism. Nothing here forces us to an unnatural disengagement from society and awakens in us the chauvinistic instincts by which the propaganda [of the Zionists] is driven."[38]

Klein's article was prompted by the convening in Stockholm of a congress for the formation of a Scandinavian Zionist League. The scene of a public lecture under the auspices of the organizers seemed to bear out his view: "The majority of the audience filling the banquet hall of the Hotel Kronprinsen consisted of people from the camp of newly arrived Russian

Jews, who mostly seemed enthusiastically supportive of Zionism. The Swedish Jews, members of the Mosaic Congregation, were in an absolute minority."[39]

With Marcus Ehrenpreis's cultural interpretation of Zionism, however, neither Gottlieb Klein nor like-minded members of the Stockholm congregation had any problems. His name would certainly remain associated with the history and rise of the Zionist movement, but his early criticism of political-national Zionism had rather been strengthened during his years in Bulgaria. The notion that the Swedish Jews should strive for a nation-state of their own seemed to him both alien and unrealistic. To Ehrenpreis, the revitalization of Jewish life in the Diaspora was and remained an inseparable part of the Zionist idea.

With such a Zionism, Swedish Jews could very well approve of the Jewish settlement project in Palestine, and rejoice in its success, and lend their support to it. What they objected to was a movement that they feared would drive a wedge between Sweden and its Jews. Notwithstanding Gottlieb Klein's assurances that Swedish Jews had no problems with antisemitism, their anti-Zionism was a response to antisemitism as well, albeit a different response than Zionism. The reluctance to stand out, the fear of "provoking," was certainly rooted in the experience of a less malevolent antisemitism than that which had driven hundreds of thousands of Jews from their homes in Russia and eastern Europe, but Sweden's pervasive background noise of antisemitic caricatures and insults had left its mark. In face of the all-too-common accusation of having dual loyalties, many Jews might have felt it necessary to demonstrate their undivided loyalty to Sweden by proclaiming their rejection of Zionism and Jewish nationalism. And eventually, as in the case of Ehrenpreis's friend and co-translator Ragnar Josephson, to demonstrate an indivisible loyalty to a Sweden that in the 1930s would close its borders to Germany's fleeing Jews.

Ragnar Josephson and the dual loyalty, soon enough.

Fearing that Gottlieb Klein's successor would be yet another dedicated anti-Zionist, the organized Zionists in Stockholm had supported the choice of Ehrenpreis. In a letter in Yiddish to the members of the congregation, they had pleaded, without naming candidates, for a rabbi who, unlike his predecessor, would affirm and strengthen "the intimate connection between our nationalism and our religion."[40] And like the Zionists in Bulgaria, they had good reason to believe that Ehrenpreis, with his prominent role in the early Zionist movement and his commitment to a Hebrew renaissance, would be their rabbi.

Already by December 1914, however, an incident occurred that signaled otherwise. On the Jewish festival of Hanukkah (commemorating the Maccabean uprising), the Zionist Society in Stockholm had organized an evening in which children would perform songs in Hebrew and put on a play in Hebrew, with the purpose of promoting the Hebrew afternoon school that was to start in the spring, and which seemed to be fully in line with Ehrenpreis's Hebrew ideals. It must therefore have come as a shock when "their" rabbi declined an invitation to honor the event. The event that Ehrenpreis instead chose to honor that same evening was the annual ceremonial gathering of the Swedish Academy.

Nor would he show much enthusiasm for the planned Hebrew afternoon school, which went by the name Ivriah (from the Hebrew word for Hebrew, Ivrit), since he suspected, with some justification, that it had a nationalist political agenda. "Jews in Stockholm!" began an appeal from the school's initiators.

"See how other peoples—the Belgians, the Serbs, the Poles, even small peoples like the Montenegrins—are fighting for their national rights. Should we be inferior to them?"[41] When Ehrenpreis was asked if he would consider taking on the role of supervisor, or something to that effect, he either failed to answer or declined. In any case, his name quickly disappeared.[42] Nor did the congregation show any interest in the school project, and after only a few months, Ivriah had to close—for lack of students, money, and organizational capacity.

Ehrenpreis's latter successor in Stockholm, Morton Narrowe, would partly attribute Ehrenpreis's taciturn relationship with the organized Zionists in Sweden to personal motives: the new rabbi simply felt more at home among the Swedish Jews, with their Western culture, than among the Eastern Jews, who mostly had low levels of education and who formed the core of the Zionist movement in Stockholm. And to some extent this was probably true. Ehrenpreis may have come from the Jewish quarter of Lemberg, but his educational journey had taken him far from there. Socially and culturally, he was naturally at home with the elites in every society, and his Swedish *Kinderland* was soon to be populated with Swedish writers, artists, publishers, professors, academics, and bishops. And it soon became clear that he was to be less a rabbi for the already convinced than for the "detached" Swedish Jews, whom he saw as the potential bearers of a Jewish renaissance in Sweden.

From the very beginning of his Swedish undertaking, however, Ehrenpreis was actively and wholeheartedly committed to the Zionist settlement project in Palestine. As when the Swedish Zionist Association on 19 March 1916 organized an evening on "the old and new Palestine" and Ehrenpreis spoke "of the important place Palestine has always occupied in the feelings of the Israelites."[43] It was most likely also Ehrenpreis who had chosen the program for the evening's poetry reading: works by the medieval Spanish-Jewish poet Yehuda Halevi and the Swedish-Jewish poet Oscar Levertin. In any case, the program clearly reflected the objectives of Ehrenpreis: to demonstrate the potential fruitfulness in the tension between Zion and Diaspora, East and West, Longing and Fulfillment. "My heart is in the East, myself at the edge of the West," Yehuda Halevi had written in Toledo in the twelfth century. "I am East and West," Oscar Levertin had written in Stockholm eight hundred years later.[44]

On the twentieth anniversary of the death of Oscar Levertin in November 1926, Ehrenpreis spoke at his grave in Stockholm's Jewish cemetery. "To the great Swedish Jew Oscar Levertin," it said on one of the wreaths laid at the tombstone, and in Levertin's life and work Ehrenpreis saw a flourishing Swedish-Jewish future:

> Stronger than any of your contemporaries, you sensed the liberating force flowing from that which is inherited, and your words came from two sources, the mother tongue and the tongue of the ancestral heritage. [...] Thus you personified the synthesis of the old and the new, of the inherited culture and the newly acquired. [...] To our pondering youth, anguished by doubts and torments of the soul, feeling connected to Sweden and its culture but at the same time trying to find their way back to their own heritage, your song and your life speak with the words of the Ecclesiastes: hold fast to the one, but do not let go of the other—be Jews and Swedes at the same time.[45]

In Oscar Levertin, Ehrenpreis thought that he had found the perfect model for his Swedish-Jewish vision. Levertin had been at once very Swedish (belonging to one of Sweden's oldest Jewish families) and very Jewish, and the combination of the two had in his case not only been attainable but also culturally fruitful and widely appreciated. Levertin's close friend, the leading Swedish poet Verner von Heidenstam, speaking at his funeral twenty years earlier, had emphasized the importance of Levertin's Jewishness to his Swedishness: "No one could create more Swedish characters than you." And in an obituary in *Svenska Dagbladet*, the writer and journalist Gustaf Stridsberg wrote: "No Swede has loved more warmly, explored more wisely, nurtured more faithfully, proclaimed more devotedly, the heritage of Swedish culture than he [the stranger of Judah]."[46]

Oscar Levertin had had his fair share of antisemitic slurs and indignities as well, but if an Oscar Levertin was possible, then much might seem possible. In any case, Ehrenpreis soon realized that the "detachment" of the Swedish Jews from their Jewish heritage was largely the product of a European-Jewish success story. In the span of just a hundred years, Jews had not only been allowed to settle in Sweden (1775) but had been granted full civil rights (1873), and despite their small numbers (one per thousand of the Swedish population) had made their mark in art, science, literature, and politics. As the Swedish Jews saw themselves, they were now an inseparable part of Sweden, deeply connected to Swedish nature and culture and wholeheartedly involved in Swedish social life. It was perhaps true that some of them, out of affection for the country that had taken them in, might sometimes appear to be more Swedish than the Swedes themselves, but a person who had just gained his position in society might understandably value it more than a person who had never lost it. Swedish Jews had good reason to feel loyalty to the country that had allowed them to be both Jews and Swedes, and had good reason to reject a Jewish nationalism that sought to force them to choose.

At the same time, even in a country like Sweden, it was not easy to be both. The Jewish population was small and scattered, the foundations for the maintenance of a vibrant Jewish culture were fragile, while the surrounding national Swedish culture seemed vigorous and welcoming. Many Swedish Jews perceived themselves to be more Swedish than Jewish, and the liberal Reform Judaism that they mostly associated themselves with—inserting into the liturgical order prayers in Swedish, taking out prayers emphasizing the distinction "between Israel and the nations"—was perceived by Orthodox (mostly Eastern) Jews as an unprincipled accommodation to the demands and anticipations of their non-Jewish environment.

And perhaps this was what the "detachment" of the Swedish Jews was all about: wanting to be both but not really knowing how, and perhaps not even why. As the social and cultural significance of being Jewish weakened, the social and cultural contexts in which their Jewishness had acquired its meaning did as well. To be both Jewish and Swedish arguably required that being Jewish could be given a meaning alongside being Swedish. In a Sweden imbued with antisemitic background noise, there was a constant need to explain and defend the meaning of being both Jewish and Swedish, not only to Swedes who saw "dual loyalties" everywhere but also to Jews who no longer saw what being Jewish had to do with them.

The outgoing rabbi Gottlieb Klein might have done his best, but his Reform Judaism, steeped in nineteenth-century rationalism, had a hard time providing a coherent answer to the great existential question facing the Jews of Sweden: how and why to be a Jew in the intensifying cross fire between the promise of citizenship, the lure of secularism, the rise of nationalism, and the threat of antisemitism. Neither did he know how to navigate the growing divide between Orthodoxy and Reform, between Eastern Jews and Western Jews, between Zionists and anti-Zionists, between Jews who saw themselves as Jews and Jews who saw themselves as Swedes.

Against this backdrop, the choice of Marcus Ehrenpreis would have seemed a stroke of genius: a Zionist pioneer who could speak to both Zionists and non-Zionists. A European-Jewish personality who could speak to the need of the "detached" Swedish Jews for self-knowledge and self-esteem. A learned Jewish thinker and visionary who could speak to the concerns and conflicts besetting the Jews of Europe.

Occasionally the internal Jewish conflicts came out in the open, as when a young Swedish Jew, Daniel Brick, in the fall of 1924, in the Scandinavian-Jewish journal *Israeliten*, The Israelite, published a flaming indictment of his parents' generation for alienating their children from Judaism: "What have the old done to awaken in the young a love for all the beautiful values with which Judaism is so filled, and which would make the lives of the young so much better and richer? Virtually nothing."[47]

And a few issues later, in the summer of 1925, a new accusation, this time in the form of an explicit *j'accuse*, from Olof Valentin, one of the Swedish Jews whom Ehrenpreis would probably have put in the category of "detached" and who defined himself as a modern and a skeptic, but who nevertheless thought it scandalous to "be a Jew and know nothing about customs and traditions," and for this he blamed Jewish religious education, which he considered not designed for "modern-thinking children."[48]

And in the following issue, an outraged counteraccusation from Leon Fried, son of the congregation's recently deceased religion teacher, Moses Fried:

> What good can a first-class Jewish religious education do, if the Jewish congregants disregard their teachers, their synagogue, their congregational library, the Jewish associations that wish to disseminate knowledge of Jewish customs and practices? Certainly, in the way the Swedish Jews now are living, not even Moshe Rabenu [our teacher Moses] could achieve anything. I, too, *accuse*, Mr. Valentin. I accuse the Swedish Jews of indolence. I accuse the Swedish-Jewish parents who consider it unwise for their children to mingle with other Jews. I accuse Swedish-Jewish cowardice.[49]

In the same issue of *Israeliten*, yet another *j'accuse*, a separate appendix of forty (!) pages entitled "Troubled Situation in Sweden's Jewish Congregations." The author was Hirsch Nissalowitz, a representative of the Orthodox minority in Stockholm, and on page after page he enumerated the sins of the Reform-Liberal congregational leadership, first and foremost the persistent and unforgivable sin of alienating Jews from Judaism by the erosion and abolition of inherited customs and practices, and thereby contributing to their assimilation and disappearance from history.

"Now is the time for the liberal, so-called modern Jews, those holding power in the Mosaic Congregations of Stockholm and Gothenburg, ... [to] repent," Nissalowitz thundered on the very first page, and then launched a barb directed at the liberal Jew, the modern Jew, at "our reformist and assimilationist enthusiasts [whose] minds are numbed by the temporary gratifications of wealth and power. They are only aware of the superficial pleasures of life but not of its reality, its meaning, its purpose in the world. They do not think clearly and soundly: that all things are perishable, and that the only asset that will eternally endure is the preservation for the posterity of their ancestral faith and doctrine. [...] *You Israelites, who are standing on the threshold of liberalism and assimilation, beware!*"[50]

Hirsch Nissalowitz did not name any of the sinners in the Stockholm congregation, but Marcus Ehrenpreis had by now been its chief rabbi for eleven years and was the public face of the Swedish Jews, and there can hardly have been any doubt that Ehrenpreis was one of the targets. At the same time, after eleven years it should have been clear to both Nissalowitz and the readers of *Israeliten* that whatever you could say about Ehrenpreis, an advocate of Jewish adaptation and assimilation he was not. He was certainly no friend of the form of Orthodox Judaism that Nissalowitz represented, but in his many lectures, sermons, and articles he had made it abundantly clear that he was deeply worried about both adaptation and assimilation. He just had a different view of the cause of the problem, and what needed to be done about it. In his sermon on Rosh Hashanah, in the fall of 1924, he phrased the problem as a question: "Does our Judaism still have anything to say to us in this time of bewilderment and distress, and through us, to the human race as a whole?"[51]

"The question of Israel," he called it, but as he saw it this was no longer a question for Israel only, since it stemmed from something far more universal than the shortcomings of Jewish religious education. Ultimately, from the disappearance of God from the hearts of men, Jews and non-Jews alike, from what Nietzsche had called the death of God and Max Weber had called the disenchantment of the world, and which Ehrenpreis time and again would call the triumph of matter over spirit.

Thus, a decisive influence on the Judaism of Marcus Ehrenpreis was the ailment of the time as he saw it, a time when "life falls apart and loses its unifying and fortifying center," and "people begin to doubt the presence of God and with the Israelites in the desert are asking: 'Is the Lord still in our midst or not?'"[52]

However critical Ehrenpreis may have been of Orthodox Judaism and political Zionism, and however coldly their representatives in Sweden may have felt that he related to them, there can be little doubt that he shared their concern about the state and future of Judaism and that he was determined to deal with the matter in his own way.

"What we now must do," he continued his New Year sermon of 1924,

> is not so much to answer a question as to focus on a goal, to take a stand, to make a decision. We must reawaken in us the faith in Judaism, the will to Judaism. When we ask ourselves *hajesch adonoi bekirbenu*?—Is the power of God alive in our midst?—do we still have faith in our own vitality and possibilities of life? If we want to secure our existence in the future, then the answer must be plain and decisive: yes—or no. Not yes *and* no, not yes two days a year and no all other days, not yes here in the synagogue and no in daily life on the outside.[53]

Ehrenpreis did not only raise questions, he answered them too. Only his answers were not what his Orthodox critics attributed to him, and not what his Zionist supporters expected of him. Neither of them could have failed to notice the many Jewish cultural and educational activities that he had brought to life, and which, whatever they thought of it, could hardly be interpreted as a lack of commitment to the survival of Judaism.

In addition to the Jewish Literary Society, with its high-profile book publishing, a Jewish Academic Club was formed in 1918, with a rapidly expanding range of public lectures and discussions, and in 1926 a Hebrew Club on the initiative of Swedish Jews, "most of them merchants, strictly occupied by their daily work."[54] The Hebrew Club gathered once a week in the classroom of the Jewish Religious School, and its didactic idea was to learn Hebrew by plunging headlong into Hebrew literature and thereby getting a glimpse of the Jewish soul. It started off with Ehrenpreis lecturing in Hebrew on Hebrew poetry "from Deborah to Bialik." It wasn't easy at first, he admitted to the members of the club on its fifth anniversary: "But during these years you showed a spiritual bravery, which each time I had to admire anew. [...] Rarely have I felt such a deep communion of spirit as during these Hebrew evenings."[55]

His ambition to make Zionism a matter of Jewish cultural and spiritual renewal won the support of non-Zionist Swedish Jews as well, and his ambition to communicate the spirit of Judaism to a broader Swedish public seemed to be appreciated. Writers and publishers, publicists and professors, bishops and priests, were all impressed by his learning and language, and attracted by the vitality of his activities, not least by the Jewish monthly journal he founded in 1928, *Judisk Tidskrift*, and which in immaculate Swedish brought a Jewish universe of learning, literature, and ideas to the European-Jewish periphery.

Yet it was clear that "the question of Israel," as Ehrenpreis had phrased it, spoke more to "detached" Jews, who were still pondering the answer, than to Jews who with the certainty of faith already knew it, sometimes all too well. In the aftermath of the Jewish disaster of the First World War, the Jewish world had become a hotbed for certainties of faith. To each certainty there was an answer, and to each answer there was a solution. The answer varied from certainty to certainty, and with it the solution. When in a few decades the ground collapsed under much of the Jewish world, the step from bewilderment to certainty could be short. Zionists and assimilationists; Orthodox Jews and liberal Jews; nationalists, socialists, and communists: in the Jewish world certainty of faith was increasingly born from desperation and longing.

Ehrenpreis had had his share of religious certainty and was now more a rabbi for the doubters than for the assured, and thus in practice more a rabbi for the Swedish Jews than for the Eastern Jews. His detractors would portray this as taking a stance for conformity and assimilation and, by extension, for Jewish self-extermination, and even worse, as a pursuit of personal gain and comfort. It was an enticing but grossly unfair portrayal of Ehrenpreis. As Ehrenpreis had come to see it, there was no external solution to the question of Israel, or "the Jewish problem," as it increasingly and ominously was being labeled. Political Zionism certainly promised such a solution, but to Ehrenpreis, spiritual bewilderment was a greater existential threat to the Jews than national homelessness. Ehrenpreis had fought on the barricades of the Young Hebrews, and campaigned at Zionist congresses, and explored the Bulgarian-Jewish possibility, and was now exploring the Swedish-Jewish possibility, and it might seem that at every stage of his life he was exploring a new answer to the question of Israel. But the answers were not as dissimilar as they might appear, and the question remained steadfastly the same.

What had changed were the times. As Ehrenpreis saw it, the horizon had darkened not only for the Jews but for humankind as a whole, and in his answers to the question of Israel a messianic impulse becomes increasingly explicit: a renaissance of Judaism must be a renaissance for the prophetic vision of universal peace and brotherhood. The continued threat of war and the moral bewilderment of humankind called for the creation of a League of Religions, he argued in 1923. "Perhaps this would be the proper path to the universal peace we all desire." Wasn't it true that all world religions had a core of absolute values that united them: "faith in God, love of neighbor, some form of messianism"? A sphere of relative values certainly separated them from each other, values formed by "heritage, experiences, memories, traditions, customs, tempers; immeasurable religious imponderabilia that may render comfort and strength only to the bearers and heirs of a particular creed." These values did not necessarily stand in conflict with each other.

"When our prophets [...] herald a time when all peoples on earth will be united by the faith in one God, it does not mean that they will all worship God in one and the same temple, and in one and the same way," Marcus Ehrenpreis proclaimed two years before Nathan Söderblom, the Archbishop of Sweden, convened the first ecumenical world conference in Stockholm in August 1925. With the difference that Ehrenpreis had claimed a place also for Judaism at the ecumenical table, or at least in that League of Religions that he believed must precede and prepare for the formation of "a real and viable League of Nations."[56]

When by chance Ehrenpreis bumped into Nathan Söderblom at the Munich Central Station in April 1925—Söderblom on his way home from Lausanne, Ehrenpreis on his way home from the inauguration of the Hebrew University of Jerusalem—Ehrenpreis told Söderblom that the ecumenical idea that Söderblom was advocating originated with the prophet Micah.

"One faith, several creeds—this seems to me to be the ecumenical idea of Micah," Ehrenpreis had said.

"That's very interesting," Söderblom had replied, "but is it really Micah saying that, or is it Dr. Ehrenpreis?"

"The speech of Micah was not written down in shorthand, but I can find no other meaning in that statement," Ehrenpreis had answered.[57]

Regardless of exactly what was said by whom that night, the episode, as remembered by Ehrenpreis, testified to his wide-ranging Swedish connections and his far-reaching Jewish ambitions.

"Dr. Ehrenpreis's remark about Jewish participation in the ecumenical movement is entirely appropriate," Söderblom had added before they separately boarded the train for Stockholm.[58]

The choice of Ehrenpreis was a stroke of genius indeed, but perhaps not as it had been imagined at first, as a brilliant compromise between adaptation and renewal, Eastern Jews and Western Jews, Zionism and anti-Zionism. Instead, the stroke of genius turned out to be the recruitment of a high-profile European-Jewish personality with the ability and authority to speak up for Jews and Judaism at a time when, increasingly, the surrounding world was speaking against them, and the Swedish-Jewish periphery would become a center of sorts for the dwindling remnants of Jewish life in Europe.

The congregational leadership in Stockholm would soon find out that Ehrenpreis was not the man of compromise that perhaps they had expected, just as it soon must have dawned on Ehrenpreis that the divisive conflicts in the Jewish world he had left behind would pursue him in Sweden as well. As in Bulgaria, he was reluctant to associate himself with one Jewish group against another, ending up not being too closely associated with any one of them. Ever since his transformative journey from Lemberg's Jewish quarter to Berlin's boulevards, Ehrenpreis had followed a Jewish path of his own, and he showed no signs of wanting to change his ways now.

His Jewish path was perhaps not entirely his own; Europe was crisscrossed by Jewish paths and visions, more or less their own, but the path of Ehrenpreis was sufficiently remote from the main intra-Jewish battle lines to create uncertainty and suspicion about where he stood and belonged. On matters of Jewish rituals and regulations, he was decidedly liberal and reform-minded, not even seeing the proliferation of mixed marriages necessarily as a threat to Judaism.[59] On matters of Judaism's spiritual destiny and significance, on the other hand, its theology or concept of God if you will, he was conservative and uncompromising. Without a renaissance of the Jewish heritage from the Torah and the Prophets, Judaism had no future. Nor without a radical change in the Jews' relationship to the world—and in the world's relationship to the Jews.

The latter explained much, such as his embrace of the Swedish language and his rabbinical ambitions to show "our true face," not only to the detached Swedish Jews but to the non-Jewish Swedes as well, indeed, ultimately to the entire non-Jewish world—which was not an obvious ambition for a rabbi, neither in Stockholm nor elsewhere. Judaism was a non-proselytizing and mainly inherited community of liturgically traded texts, beliefs, and rules of life—shaped by a sometimes-hostile environment. A rabbi's task was to maintain the Jewish community, not to edify the world. Marcus Ehrenpreis, on the other hand, saw himself as living in a time when the survival of the Jewish community and the edification of the world had become dependent on each other. Indeed, in a time when Judaism might have something significant to contribute to the edification of the world.

"Through its way of life and its beliefs, the people of Israel occupy a place in the world in which they serve as a living testimony to the ideal of peace," he preached to his congregation in the winter of 1930.[60]

In his main literary work, a three-volume series of tales of prophets and sages, saints and heroes, poets and visionaries "who had built Israel," Ehrenpreis would return time and again to the importance of Israel to the world, and of the world to Israel, and in doing so he would not hesitate to put his own words in the mouths of the Prophets. As when he transforms the prophecy of Amos about a coming famine on earth, "not a famine of food, nor a thirst for water, but of hearing the words of the Lord" (Amos 8:11), into an exhortation to the spiritually lost and morally bewildered human race of his own time:

> To a distant generation I will speak, to a happier generation, which will have bread to eat and water to drink, which will be blessed with the bounties of the earth, and will possess all that the heart desires. But this happy race will wake up one day with a tearing emptiness in its soul, desireless and joyless, dissatisfied with itself and with life, and will seek what it cannot find and cannot even name. To this hungry and thirsty race I shall speak long after my death.[61]

When the renowned biblical scholar Josef Klausner, professor at the newly opened Hebrew University of Jerusalem, criticized him for using the Prophets to promote his own vision of Israel as a spiritual "diasporic" nation, and maintained that the Prophets had spoken mainly to Israel's yearning for political and national liberation, he responded with a quote from the mentor of his youth, Ahad Ha'am:

> Today there is a tendency to sacrifice on the altar of rebirth our prophets and our teachings, for which our people has lived and suffered, and for which only it is worthwhile for us to become a people in the land of our fathers. For without them—my God!—what are we? And what land would that be, that we should make such immeasurable sacrifices for? To create in some corner of the Orient another little people of new Levantines, who will compete with the already existing Levantines in all the bad customs that are the substance of their life—[bloodthirstiness, vengefulness, and discord]?[62]

At the end of March 1925, Marcus Ehrenpreis traveled from Stockholm to the corner of the Orient that was still called Palestine, that was still ruled by Britain on a mandate from the League of Nations, and that the British government had promised as a "national home for the Jewish people."[63] At the First Zionist Congress in Basel in 1897, when the young Ehrenpreis had proposed to create a Hebrew university in Palestine, he had also been careful to add that the time was not yet ripe. Barely thirty years later, on the afternoon of 1 April 1925, he was seated on a specially erected honorary stand on Mount Scopus in Jerusalem, together with guests from all over the world to witness the fulfillment of the proposal.

Upon his return to Sweden he wrote an article in which he described the ceremony in Jerusalem as an event of universal significance:

> This essentially Jewish event grew into something universal, into a universal promise, and into a refreshing ray of light in our dark times. All that we heard and saw in those wonderful days was meant to strengthen our faith in humankind and in a brighter future. [...] And I thought to myself: perhaps this which is happening here on Mount Scopus on this glorious April day is a turning point, the beginning of a changed relationship between the peoples of the world and Israel. There was an atmosphere of reconciliation—as if centuries of injustice were about to be erased, as if Christianity was about to say to us: from now on we will begin to understand each other. I was taken by the grandeur of the moment, with my own eyes I here could see how East and West reached out to each other.[64]

In conjunction with the visit to Jerusalem, Ehrenpreis made a journey through the emerging Jewish society in Palestine, and everywhere he saw something grander than a plot of land for Jews in a corner of the Orient. To the "incomparable and unforgettable experience" of the ceremony on Mount Scopus was added the experience of a society that seemed free of criminals, alcoholics, prostitutes, beggars, and prisons, as well as the "remarkable discovery" that in Tel Aviv, "the first Jewish city since the destruction of Jerusalem, [...] the Ten Commandments are strictly observed." The names of Jewish prophets, thinkers, and poets greeting him from every street sign stirred his imagination. To Esther in Stockholm he wrote incessantly and excitedly about his impressions. As in a letter from Tel Aviv on 29 March 1925:

> I am with people who mean a lot to me—among our best—many acquaintances from the first congress. I walk through the glorious streets of this Jewish city, which is the opposite of a ghetto, and everywhere I am greeted with warm cheers. Everyone seems to know me, and everyone finds me looking impossibly young. [...] From my very first moment here I don't feel alienated in the way that I usually feel during the first moments in a foreign city. I feel like I've lived here for years.[65]

After having seen Tel Aviv, Marcus Ehrenpreis believed he had gained "a heartening insight into the moral potentials of the Palestine project. [...] We are fortunate to see these beginnings of a moral revival at a time when our old centers of civilization are showing disturbing symptoms of a deepening moral crisis."[66]

These last lines were published a little over a year after Marcus Ehrenpreis's return to Sweden, in a book that would mark his debut as a Swedish author, and in which he would characterize his journey to Palestine as a journey "on the road to myself." That road, however, did not lead to the new settlements of Jewish Palestine, no matter how inspiring, but to a highly idealized spiritual landscape that he time and again would refer to as Österlandet, the Land of the East:

> I wander through Eastern cities, bazaars, mosques, along country roads and across deserts, imperceptibly but irresistibly being absorbed by a new, unfamiliar,

The inauguration of Hebrew University of Jerusalem, on Mount Scopus on 1 April 1925. Marcus Ehrenpreis has marked out himself, Fredrik Böök, and Ahad Ha'am, among others.

atmosphere. [...] The sky is higher, the air is clearer, and the vistas are wider. [...] At times it feels as if you are walking past a large mirror and with astonishment notice that the inside of your coat is turned outward, and the outside is turned inward. We pay attention to that which belongs to the external forms of life, but completely neglect ourselves, our inner human being. [...] Being here, I strongly sense how we Westerners often approach life from the wrong side, from the outside instead of from the inside. "They are always busy with their nets but never have time for fishing," Tagore says of the Westerners. We turn means into ends, and rights into duties. We are slaves to our freedoms.

> On my way through the Land of the East, all this seems clearer to me than at home. In this backward Orient, one feels closer to truth and further from pretense. In this simple, nature-bound world one learns to think *essentially* (not merely *formally*), and the distinction between the core and the shell of existence appears more sharply.[67]

The book, titled *Österlandets själ* (The soul of the East), was received as a literary sensation. In *Svenska Dagbladet*, Fredrik Böök wrote: "It is astonishing that a writer having lived in Sweden for only a decade can write such a masterful Swedish prose; his vocabulary is so rich, his nuances are so soft and accurate that many with Swedish as their mother tongue could envy him. [...] The pathos and poetry that often radiate from his words reflect the beauty of the biblical scriptures. For Swedish readers, he is at once an exotic stranger from the East and a close friend from childhood."[68]

And the reviewer in *Dagens Nyheter*: "It has been noted how astonishing it is that Chief Rabbi Ehrenpreis, after only a few years in Sweden and without any previous knowledge of our language, is able to write such perfect Swedish as in this book, pure, precise, and melodious. This is undoubtedly a most remarkable feat, which we may also consider a great cultural and literary achievement. But perhaps even more remarkable, at least in our latitudes, is the ardor and intensity with which the author, after his pilgrimages, has set about depicting the soul of the East. [...] A deeply religious Jewish book that should be enjoyed by anyone, regardless of nation or religion."[69]

Österlandets själ was printed in several editions and did not only establish Marcus Ehrenpreis as a Swedish writer and cultural personality, but also consolidated his Jewish positions and visions.[70] Everything he saw in Palestine rather confirmed and reinforced him in his belief that there could be no Jewish future without the Jewish Diaspora. He saw it most clearly in the light of "the bright-blue sky of Jerusalem and the generous sun of Palestine" over the "incomparable and unforgettable" inauguration on Mount Scopus, where emissaries from universities and academies all over the world contended to extend "a hand of brotherhood to the ancient Jewish culture" and "the scorn of one side and the bitterness of the other were gone" and "a wind of messianic unity" was touching everybody, and "the figure of Shylock was obliterated," and a "new and better future could be glimpsed at the horizon!"[71]

In *Österlandets själ*, Marcus Ehrenpreis traveled toward a horizon promising nothing less than a new encounter between Jerusalem and Rome, Zion and Diaspora, God and Man. In the light of history, his horizon was a mirage only, but so were many other Jewish horizons at a time when the Jewish existence as a whole was thrown into turmoil, and the floodgates of Jew-hatred were opened anew, and even the most illusory of Jewish horizons could appear to have something real about them.

Against this backdrop, Ehrenpreis's vision of a Jewish renaissance in a small Jewish community in Sweden was perhaps not more of a mirage than so much else, and the fact remains that he went about realizing it with the conviction and vigor of a latter-day prophet. In impeccable and inspiring Swedish he would henceforth take the words of the Prophets in his own mouth, and have the Prophets take his words in theirs.

Marcus Ehrenpreis on a journey for his book on Judeo-Hispanic civilization, Landet mellan öster och väster *(The land between East and West). Bayonne, France, May 1927.*

5.

PHILO OF STOCKHOLM

How weak must be the spiritual life, how shallow the Christian faith, that can have anything to fear for us and our religion, which indeed should have much to hope for, from the people of the Mosaic faith coming into closer contact with our society, our social life, our houses, and homes. May they come, may they come ever nearer to us, may they come so near that one day they will be fully ours!

—Fredrika Bremer, 1854[1]

In about 40 CE, a Jewish writer and philosopher named Philo traveled from Alexandria to Rome to testify before the emperor Gaius, better known as Caligula, about the vicious slander of the Jews in his hometown and the brutal pogroms in its wake.

In 1934, at the end of October to be precise, Marcus Ehrenpreis traveled to Bern to testify in a Swiss court about the malicious libeling of the Jews in the sinister fabrication known as *The Protocols of the Elders of Zion*, which with the full propaganda-backing of the Nazi state, was poisoning the atmosphere for Jews in every corner of the world.

Both men were in their sixties at the time of their travels, and both could look back on a life's work shaped by the conviction that Jews and Judaism had something to communicate to the world. Philo had devoted his life to explaining and interpreting the Jewish scriptures in Greek to the Hellenistic world.[2] Marcus Ehrenpreis had devoted his life to making the world see "the true face" of Judaism in every language he mastered, last but not least the language of Sweden.

But now they were both facing failure. None of their work had managed to stem the wave of anti-Jewish vilification and persecution. In Rome, Philo was to testify in defense of the Jews before a malevolent, if not mad, emperor, and in Bern, Ehrenpreis was to testify in defense of himself and the Jews before a Swiss court, against a Nazi editor. No charge against the Jews seemed too preposterous not to be taken seriously. In Rome, the young Caligula mocked the elder Philo and humiliated him before his court. In Bern, Marcus Ehrenpreis had to testify to the court that the all-mighty Jewish world conspiracy in which he had been inscribed by the Nazi editor did not exist.

The trial in Bern, in due time.

Time, however, to say something about Philo of Alexandria, or Philo Judaeus, since there was more that united him with Marcus Ehrenpreis in Stockholm than the task of defending Jews against libel and slander and persecution. In the eyes of Ehrenpreis, Philo was a role model and source of inspiration, someone who should rank among "the most remarkable figures in postbiblical Judaism."[3]

In this, Ehrenpreis differed from most rabbis in postbiblical Judaism, most of whom had regarded Philo as a heretic of sorts. Philo's crime was to have made the sacred texts of the Hebrew Bible accessible to the Hellenic world, and in so doing taking liberties with them. For example, the liberty to read them allegorically rather than literally, and at times putting his own words in Moses's mouth and Moses's words in his own. When Philo has Moses say that Man was created in the image of God, he also has him explain that this should not be understood to mean that Man is like God or that God is like Man. What makes Man godlike is his Mind, Philo has Moses saying. As God works in the world, so the Mind works in Man; "it has an essence which is undiscernible, though it can discern the essence of everything."[4]

With allegorical interpretations and philosophical explanations, Philo wanted to explain the God of the Jews to a world steeped in the ideas and ideals of Greek philosophy, which was a world in which a large and growing Jewish Diaspora needed to have its God explained, and if necessary defended, in the language that it spoke and understood best, that is, Greek.

Diaspora is a Greek word that in Philo's time, when Judea was still a Jewish province under Rome and the Temple still stood in Jerusalem, denoted the state of territorial dispersion in which a majority of the world's Jews had lived since Babylon. In Philo's time, Alexandria was the largest Jewish city in the world, larger than Jerusalem, which Philo had visited only once in his life. For Diaspora Jews, Jerusalem was a spiritual capital, not a political or national one. This implied that in the time of Philo the majority of the world's Jews had already acquired a more symbolic, or allegorical if you like, relationship to the national and territorial aspects of Jewish doctrine and tradition, and a corresponding inclination to embrace its universal human aspects.

In his work Philo had sought to resolve the conflict between revealed text and philosophical explanation, between Moses and Plato, between a pious adherence to the Jewish Torah and a frank engagement with the non-Jewish world of thought.

Philo could not foresee that his work would also open the door to readings of the Jewish Torah that would be turned against the Jews. The Hellenized Jew Saul of Tarsus may well have read Philo before he became Paul, and with allegorical interpretations of the sacred writings of the Jews, laid the foundations of a movement within the Jewish world that would become Christianity. Such as when Paul in his letter to the Romans takes the liberty of invoking Moses, Joel, Hosea, and Isaiah to proclaim "Christ is the end of the law."[5]

Against this background, it is hardly surprising that Philo was saved for posterity by the Christian Church and not by rabbinical Judaism. In the rabbinical tradition, based on a literal reading of the Hebrew Torah (the Greek translation, the Septuagint, God forbid), Philo Judaeus was seen as a Hellenistic freethinker with little relevance to Judaism.

In part, this was a result of the weakening of Alexandria's position in the Hellenistic world and the demise of the Jewish Diaspora that had flourished in its domain. The subjugation of the Judean state and the destruction of the Temple just a few decades after Philo's death, as well as mounting anti-Jewish rhetoric from the increasingly powerful Christian Church, dramatically changed the conditions of Jewish existence and thwarted for the foreseeable future that encounter between the Jews and the world to which Philo's work had aspired.

Nevertheless, for some centuries Philo's life and work seemed to testify to another path to Jewish development than the national and territorial, and a more universal way of understanding and explaining the teachings of the Hebrew Bible. For a while, the two paths ran side by side in a dynamic relationship—Alexandria and Jerusalem, Diaspora and Zion—only to be resolutely demolished, one at a time, by the steamroller of history.

When, two millennia later, Marcus Ehrenpreis brought Philo of Alexandria back into the Jewish fold, it was his own Jewish path that he hoped to bolster:

> Philo stands before us as the embodiment of noble assimilation. He is not a Jew of the *galut*, of the dispersion, ridden by feelings of inferiority, detached from his roots, a spiritual beggar gathering crumbs from the richly laid tables around him. He is erect and proud, aware of his spiritual nobility, harmonious and whole despite his inner dualism. He feels free and equal in a setting that has enriched him with spiritual values, but that has been spiritually enriched by his own people as well. What he seems to say is: We have appropriated your philosophy and your poetry; in return we bring you our faith in God and our Torah. He sees Alexandria as his home, but to Jerusalem he goes as a pilgrim, to celebrate the great feasts. He senses no contradiction between his love for his homeland and his love for Palestine. [...] The rich work of his life was essentially a philosophical elucidation of Israel's song to God as he had learned it. [...] He did not refute his own particularity to be a Hellene among Hellenes, he did not obscure the profound differences between Judaism and Hellenism to reconcile the irreconcilable. [...]
>
> As far as we understand, Hellenic-Jewish cultural dualism was an honest attempt on the part of the rooted Jewish minority to live and work for the common good in peaceful coexistence with the majority. [...]
>
> [Philo] lived as he learned. It was his tragedy, and not his fault, that the honest attempt ended in disaster,

> that in the end his extended brotherly hand ran into
> the blood-stained arm of Titus.[6]

Ehrenpreis's vindication of Philo as a Jewish thinker was published in 1934 in a book entitled *Israels möten med folken* (Israel's encounters with the peoples), at a time when it was hard to see how yet another "honest attempt" would meet a happier ending. Yet it was to just such an attempt, a Philo-inspired bridge-building between the Jews and the world, that Ehrenpreis would devote most of his Swedish writings. After all, a few times in history it had happened that Israel's encounter with the peoples had resulted in a love affair, more or less short-lived, that sooner or later turned unhappy, but while it lasted the relationship had blossomed and the partners had enjoyed and inspired each other. To be sure, periods of mutual blossoming had been followed by periods of Jewish disasters, but did it have to be that way forever? Could not the ongoing encounter between Israel and the West, between the emancipated children of the ghetto and the peoples of civic liberation, still have a happy ending? After all, there was not only the blossoming encounter between Israel and Hellas to be inspired by and learn from, but also the blossoming encounter on the Iberian Peninsula between Judaism and Islam, lasting nearly five hundred years.

In May 1927, Theodor Ehrenpreis took his final lycée exams in Stockholm, and a few weeks later he joined his father on a journey to explore the remnants of Israel's meeting with the peoples of Spain and Portugal. By now, the leadership of the Stockholm congregation had become well aware, and a bit wary, of Ehrenpreis's penchant for traveling, and when in

March 1927 he applied for yet another leave of absence for yet another journey, it was granted with little enthusiasm: "The trustees feel [...] obliged to point out that in view of your prolonged travels in recent years and the important task incumbent on you to complete the new prayer books for the major holidays, no further leave of absence can be granted in 1927."

On 14 May, Ehrenpreis delivered his last Saturday sermon for the spring season. The already-scheduled sermon for Shavuot on 6 June, the feast marking Moses being given the Torah, had been delegated to the newly hired second rabbi, Emil Kronheim, who after only a year in Sweden had promised to deliver it in Swedish. Ehrenpreis's relief at leaving his daily chores behind was unmistakable:

> The slow journey from Stockholm to Madrid is as liberating as a sea voyage. You are suffused by a delightful sense of freedom, rendering the journey a value of its own regardless of destination. You spend some hundred hours in a railway carriage, alone and unknown, cut off from everything and everyone. You have left the bondage of life behind; no one and nothing can reach you. You have removed the label stuck to your forehead; now you are a human being plain and simple.

Thus opened Marcus Ehrenpreis's book *Landet mellan öster och väster* (The land between East and West), published six months after his return, written amid the pressing daily chores of sermons, funerals, confirmation readings, prayer book revisions, and speaking tours. And it was not hard to see why the congregation only reluctantly had granted him a leave of absence. Making journeys and writing books inevitably competed with the congregational duties. Nevertheless, he was anxious to frame his journey to Spain and Portugal, and the book resulting from it, as a duty as well—to Jews and Judaism at large:

> To me, this is not a tourist trip to a foreign country: Spain is one of my spiritual homelands; a land where in spirit I have spent part of my youth. To me, Jewish Spain has been light and darkness, exaltation and humiliation. This is where I experienced the golden age of the Jewish spirit. This is where, along the Tajo and the Guadalquivir, I mingled with a new generation of God-inspired psalmists and preachers—the bearers of light through the dark Middle Ages. But I also suffered with the victims of religious persecution and the Inquisition; I accompanied the banished from their homeland on their tragic journey into exile. I am spiritually linked to this land, which at once attracts me and repels me. A journey to Spain is a study in cultural challenges from which we all have something to learn.

To Ehrenpreis, the cultural challenges once again facing the Jews of the world were evident. During the two Balkan wars, sometimes with the frontiers in sight, he had personally witnessed how majorities could turn into minorities, and peaceful coexistence turn into fratricidal warfare, and cultural flourishing turn into cultural destruction, sometimes overnight. In a Europe beset by growing ethnic nationalism and strife, the question more than ever begging for an answer was how different peoples could live side by side without the strong devouring the weak.

On their journey to Spain and Portugal, father and son could observe and ponder the remnants of a civilization where for half a millennium Jews, Christians, and Muslims lived side by side, interacted with each other, and at times flourished together. "Here, in blessed times, was achieved something of that fusion of East with West that our own age so eagerly longs for," Ehrenpreis noted.

Among the still-living remnants of this blessed time of flourishing were the poems and songs of Yehuda Halevi, in the eyes of Ehrenpreis "the greatest Hebrew poet of the postbiblical period." Halevi's poems were to live on in the Jewish liturgy and belong to "those rare poems in which the fluttering soul of an entire people is captured in words whose living power has not been weakened by the centuries." In addition, Yehuda Halevi, like no Jewish poet since the Psalmist, had given voice to and embodied the inner contradiction of Jewish life, that "duality of the Jewish soul that [. . .] throughout the Diaspora constituted both the inner richness and the inner distress of noble Jews."

The richness, too, was born from the duality, Ehrenpreis wanted to stress. Yehuda Halevi was born in the duality, agonized in it and flourished in it, as did the philosopher and poet Solomon ibn Gabirol, who wrote one of the masterpieces of the Jewish liturgy, *Keter Malkut*, "the crown of the Kingdom," a meditation named for a concept in the Kabbalah, on the essence and grandeur of God. It is not hard to understand why Ehrenpreis chose to translate part of *Keter Malkhut* for publication in the first volume of *Judisk Tidskrift*, the cornerstone of his Jewish-Swedish bridge-building project.

"See what the Jewish spirit has to offer the world if and when the world allows it to flourish!" he seemed to exclaim to his Swedish contemporaries.

Here, you may get a glimpse of our true face!

My God,
if my sin is too great to be borne,
what will You do for Your great name's sake?

> If I cannot trust in Your mercy,
> Who but You will have mercy on me?
> Therefore, though Thou destroy me, I will hope in Thee.
>
> If Thou seekest after my sin, I will flee from Thee to Thee, and from Thy wrath I will seek refuge in Thy shadow.
>
> And to the skirts of Thy mercy, I will lay hold, until Thou hast had mercy on me …
>
> When Thou places my sins in the balance, lay my sorrows on the other.

Among the surviving remnants of the Jewish flourishing in Spain was the language that Ehrenpreis had encountered among the Sephardic Jews in Bulgaria and Greece, which was a Hebraized form of the Spanish (Castilian) spoken at the time of the Jewish expulsion in 1492. Similarly, Ehrenpreis's childhood language, Yiddish, was a Hebraized form of the High German dialects spoken in the towns and villages along the Rhine valley during the Jewish flourishing there in the eighth and ninth centuries, and which had followed the German (Ashkenazi) Jews on their flight eastward from pogroms and expulsions during the Crusades. The linguistic legacy of Israel's encounters with various peoples also included Hebraized forms of Aramaic, Arabic, and Greek, which to Ehrenpreis was a testimony to the desire of the diasporic Jews to connect to and associate with the peoples among whom they lived:

> They combined their innate Jewish cultural heritage with the language and spirit of their new homelands, into a healthy, viable, constructive synthesis. Jewish literature in the language of the land was a more or less conscious expression of the cultural dualism initiated by the Alexandrian Philo and which to this day is the solid ground on which Jewish life in the Diaspora is resting.[7]

The solid ground under the Jewish Diaspora had certainly been shaken time and again, but the question to which cultural dualism wanted to be an answer remained; "the constant question to which a hundred generations of Jews have sought an answer, the question that weighs on our own generation: how to unite our Jewishness with our Swedishness, Germanness, or Frenchness, how to become part of the life and culture of the land [in which we live] without giving up our own spiritual heritage."[8]

What further confused "our own" Jewish generation was the belief that the question could be answered with a simple choice; either this or that. Either Swedish or Jewish. Either the step out of Judaism or the step into a new Jewish nation. In either case, there would be an end to dualism and contradiction, but also an end to the meaning of the Jewish existence.

> Ever since the Babylonian captivity, the people of Israel has been prepared to live in a dual cultural context: to live fully with their own inherited culture in the richest sense of the word, and at the same time to be a part of the civic and cultural life of the people among whom they lived. [...] We have been in every country, we have adapted culturally, we have learned every

> language, we have become self-sacrificing citizens, but we have never severed our bonds with Israel's spiritual heritage—and therein lies our hope for the future.

For Ehrenpreis, there was also a compelling all-human reason to safeguard the right of the Jewish Diaspora to live as a minority among majorities.

"The fate of Judaism in the world is the fate of the minority par excellence," he told the members of the Jewish Cultural Club in Malmö in the fall of 1932.

By now, Marcus and Esther Ehrenpreis had lived in Sweden for almost twenty years, and their children were rooted in their new country. Theodor studied to be a physician and was to marry Birgit, the daughter of the actor Axel Hultman, who was said not to be entirely happy with having a Jewish son-in-law, just as one may assume that Marcus and Esther were not entirely happy for the opposite reason, but neither family would openly oppose the marriage. Theodor and Birgit were married in a civil ceremony on 7 April 1938, having agreed that "our children, who may be born in the marriage, shall be brought up in the Mosaic faith." Miriam had taken her lycée exams in 1929, and already in the spring of 1931, at the age of barely twenty, had married Gustaf Erik Nathanson, who belonged to one of the most established and wealthy Jewish families in Sweden. It was said that the marriage had been instigated and hastened by Marcus and Esther, as they discovered that Miriam was in love with a non-Jewish man whom she wanted to marry. Whatever Jewish renaissance Marcus Ehrenpreis had hoped to bring about with his Swedish-Jewish bridge-building, he needed only to go to his own children to realize the enormity of the challenge. The "detachment" from Judaism among Swedish Jews was in no small part the consequence of Sweden's ability to detach them from it, with his own children serving as a case in point.

There were no indications, however, that Ehrenpreis was losing faith in his Jewish-Swedish mission, let alone that he was considering leaving Sweden.

Yet there was a brief moment when he seemed tempted to do just that.

A final journey with a taste of adventure.

On 17 December 1925, Marcus Ehrenpreis left Stockholm for Salonika in Greece. He had to be back in his pulpit within three weeks, so he was a bit worried about train connections. Would he risk getting stuck in Prague, from which trains to Salonika only left three days a week, and if so, were there any alternatives? He also worried that his arrival in Salonika would attract too much attention, since he didn't want to create the impression that he had accepted the offer to become Salonika's new chief rabbi. The visit was to be seen as exploratory, he stressed in a letter to the leadership of the Salonika congregation. At the same time, however, he assured them that he considered it an honor to be asked to lead "one of the most-respected Jewish congregations in the world."[9] Furthermore, in a city that before the war had had a Jewish population of 85,000 in a city of 135,000. On Saturdays and Jewish holidays, the shops had been closed and the Salonika port, where most of the workers were Jewish, had been at a standstill.

Ehrenpreis had received the offer a few months earlier, and regardless of whether he was seriously considering it, the name of Salonika must have stirred his imagination. Salonika (or Thessaloniki) was a legendary city in Jewish history, with a documented Jewish presence since antiquity (the apostle Paul had spoken in one of its synagogues), and after the expulsion of the Jews from Spain and Portugal in 1492 it had become a center of Sephardic Jewish culture. The Norwegian poet Alexander Kielland visited Salonika in 1890 and wrote that he had never seen more beautiful men than those Jews who on Sabbath mornings walked in the streets or outside the city walls, with their faces "fearlessly radiating benevolence and dignity." Had he been a Jew residing in northern Europe, Kielland wrote, he would have traveled to Salonika "as to a resort."

Ehrenpreis did not have to read Kielland to know what a unique Jewish milieu awaited him in Salonika.

In addition, there was a forestalled visit to make up for.

It was to have happened in the summer of 1913, during the First Balkan War, as Bulgaria nearly had succeeded in capturing Salonika—which had been part of the Ottoman Empire since 1430—but had been beaten to it by Greece by a day or two. However, Bulgaria still claimed the city, and Bulgarian troops had camped on its outskirts pending a political settlement between the two allies. Bulgaria argued that Salonika, and in particular its Jewish population, had more to gain from being a part of Bulgaria. The victorious Greece seemed to take no notice.

So it was decided that the Grand Rabbi of Bulgaria should go to Salonika to win the Jewish population for the Bulgarian cause by offering formal guarantees for the status of the Jews in a Bulgarian Salonika; the mayor would be Jewish, Jews would be allowed to work on Sundays instead of Saturdays, Jewish schools would be supported by the state.

Some months earlier, however, in what Ehrenpreis perceived to be a private conversation with a French journalist on the train between Adrianople and Sofia, he had generously shared his views on the "more or less unfriendly attitude of the Greeks toward Jews since antiquity" and the "low religious and cultural level" of the Greek Jews.[10]

Just as Ehrenpreis was about to set off on his Salonika mission, his statements were published in a French newspaper, and going to Salonika suddenly became inadvisable, if not life-threatening. The papers in Athens "poured boiling tar over my poor head," he reminisced, and a friend at the French embassy in Sofia informed him of plans afoot to have him killed.[11]

Ehrenpreis never made it to Salonika in the summer of 1913, and Salonika never became a Bulgarian city. Nor did it become an internationalized city, or a multicultural Jerusalem guaranteed by major powers, as some fantasists had dreamed.[12] Salonika or Thessaloniki became part of a nationally aroused Greece, which would be far less protective of its minorities than the Ottoman Empire, which for five hundred years had allowed the Jewish culture of Salonika to flourish.

When Ehrenpreis arrived in Salonika at the end of December 1925, the signs of Jewish decline were in plain sight. A great fire in 1917 had destroyed large parts of the Jewish quarter and the influx of Greek Orthodox Christians displaced from Turkey had reduced the Jewish share of the population to fifteen percent.[13] In order to make the "the new Greece" more Greek, the government in Athens had introduced a mandatory Sunday closure clearly directed at the Jews of Salonika.

In short, the Jews of Salonika were looking for a savior, and Ehrenpreis was largely received as such. The Judeo-Spanish newspapers enthusiastically reported his praise for Salonika as a European-Jewish center worthy of a "European" rabbi, as well as his compliments to the cleanliness and orderliness of the Jewish institutions he visited, a soup kitchen for the poor and a home for orphans. In the newly built Beth Shaul synagogue, he spoke in Judeo-Spanish about the need to strengthen the Jewish congregations in the Diaspora and build a Jewish center in Palestine, which appealed to both the Zionists and the anti-Zionists. While Ehrenpreis was still in Salonika, the formal decision was made to offer him the post of chief rabbi. It came with the promise that the government in Athens would also appoint him chief rabbi of Greece, with offices in both Athens and Salonika, which Ehrenpreis, in a letter to the leaders in Salonika after his return to Stockholm, seems to have made a condition.[14]

The existence of such a letter and such a condition seems to indicate that, at least for a moment, Ehrenpreis was seriously contemplating the offer. In interviews in the Swedish newspapers he did nothing to dispel the uncertainty: "I have been in Sweden for twelve years now, I am a Swedish citizen, my children have been brought up here, I have some important tasks which have not yet been completed, I have learned to love Sweden during my time here, and all this of course means that every little pro and con must be weighed very carefully."[15]

To the arguments against Salonika would be added another, perhaps decisive, factor: a local campaign directed against his person and candidacy. *Le Dr Ehrenpreis, allié á la ploutocratie, ennemi de la démocratie sioniste* [Dr. Ehrenpreis, ally of the plutocracy, enemy of Zionist democracy] was the title of a front-page article in the French-language organ of the religious Zionists in Salonika, *Pro Israel*, on 5 March 1926. The charges were familiar from the campaign of the Bulgarian Zionists against Ehrenpreis twelve years earlier and were mainly taken from there. Or, more precisely, from a book on the Jews in Bulgaria that had appeared a year earlier, and in which it was stated that not only had Ehrenpreis been a bad Zionist in cahoots with the powerful notables, but also a bad Jew, a freethinker and heretic who had been seen eating forbidden food and desecrating the Sabbath, and for those reasons had been forced to resign.[16] The campaign against Ehrenpreis was also joined, somewhat surprisingly, by the Jewish Communists, who in their organ *Avanti* called him an "instrument of the bourgeoisie Zionists."[17] In addition, the dictatorial regime in Athens under Theodoros Pangalos proved reluctant, to say the least, to appoint as the chief rabbi of Greece someone who had acted as a Bulgarian agent in the battle for Salonika in the summer of 1913. To make the government's plans fail-proof, the Greek Ministry of Foreign Affairs ruled that the chief rabbi of Greece must be a Greek citizen.[18]

And suddenly, the decision was not difficult—if it ever had been. A few weeks after the article in *Pro Israel*, Ehrenpreis turned down the offer from Salonika. He announced his decision in a letter to the assembly of the congregation in Stockholm, but made no mention of the opposition to his candidacy. On the contrary, he emphasized that all his demands had been met, but that his decision to stay had been determined by "the signs of confidence and sympathy that have been given to me in such abundance in recent months, both from the leadership of the congregation and from private circles." In an addendum, he quoted a just-arrived telegram from the assembly in Salonika strongly urging him to reconsider his rejection, which undoubtedly served to demonstrate to the leadership in Stockholm how difficult his decision had been.[19]

To the extent that the Salonika adventure had been intended to test and strengthen the support for Ehrenpreis in Stockholm, it had clearly been a success. The relief at his decision to stay was unmistakable. Particularly touching was a handwritten card from Gunnar Josephson, a trustee of the congregation and the brother of Ehrenpreis's co-translator Ragnar Josephson:

> Dear Marcus!
>
> As I have just heard on the radio that Marcus is definitely renouncing Greece, I would like to express my great pleasure. I had some trepidation as long as the matter was pending, and I now congratulate both the congregation and myself that we will be able to keep Marcus here. I sincerely hope that the decision taken will also prove to be a happy one for Marcus himself.[20]

For yet some time, telegrams would pour in from Salonika, and if nothing else they would make clear that the campaign against him had been the work of a minority. In the appeals for Ehrenpreis to reconsider his decision, rather an undertone of anxiety and a tacit question: What will happen to us now?

Salonika would not have a new chief rabbi until 1933, and that one would be the last. In 1943, Salonika's Jews were deported to Auschwitz-Birkenau, where they were annihilated—and Jewish Salonika with them.

By then, Marcus Ehrenpreis had had ample reason to reflect on what he had escaped by turning down Salonika. In the summer of 1931, the first anti-Jewish pogroms in Salonika in living memory broke out, propagated and orchestrated by the Greek National Socialists. On the night of 30 June, parts of the Jewish quarter were set on fire and two hundred houses were destroyed, including the main synagogue and the Jewish hospital.

About this you could read in *Judisk Tidskrift* in October 1931.

And a few years later, in February 1934, appeared an article titled "Salonika—a dying congregation."

Not so the congregation in Stockholm.

The first issue of *Judisk Tidskrift*, "a journal for Jewish thought and culture," was published in January 1928 and opened with an extended Jewish hand to the world. In a Europe where the clouds of war refused to disperse, Marcus Ehrenpreis had become convinced that the spiritual renewal of Judaism had a contribution to make to the increasingly urgent quest for a lasting peace. The very first article of the journal, written by Ehrenpreis himself, was devoted to "the idea of peace in Judaism," and the very first sentence read: "The idea of eternal peace constitutes [...] an essential part of the renewal of Judaism."[21]

In 1928, the horrors of World War I were only ten years away, and a lasting peace was by no means a foregone conclusion. Nationalist conflicts were fermenting, economic divides were widening, political positions were polarizing, and Communism, Fascism, and soon National Socialism were preparing to exploit fear, frustration, and shattered hopes. The Swedish parliamentary elections that year would go down in history as "the Cossack election" for their vitriolic tone and crude intimidations, and one morning there were posters on the streets of Stockholm proclaiming that the Jews were using Christian blood for their religious rituals.

Ehrenpreis recounted the episode with the posters in an article for the tenth anniversary of *Judisk Tidskrift* as an example of the challenge he had to face: "From the very beginning of my work as a rabbi in Stockholm, an observation increasingly intruded upon me, which surprised and disheartened me, [...] the puzzling alienation from all things Jewish, both within and outside the walls [of our community]." In addition, he found an "astonishing ignorance of Judaism in the educated and intellectual non-Jewish circles in this country."

In the first issue, however, everything still seemed possible. After the essay on the idea of peace in Judaism, an essay on the importance of fairy tales and legends in the Jewish tradition. Thereafter, in issue after issue, fearless manifestations of the Jewish spirit that Ehrenpreis wanted to bring to life: poems, short stories, ideas, sermons.

Also, in issue after issue, one or more contributions by Ehrenpreis himself. In the first issue, a tribute to Martin Buber on his fiftieth birthday. And a year later, a tribute from Buber to Ehrenpreis on his sixtieth birthday. In a private letter to Ehrenpreis, Buber stressed how close they were: "Without holding hands, we have walked the same way together, and not just a stretch, but a real way, with aims, stopovers, and retrospections."[22]

In celebration of Buber's fiftieth birthday, also the republication of Ellen Key's article on Buber from 1918, this time with her assertions about the power of the Heine-like Jews over the press and the responsibility of the Rothschild-like Jews for the World War mercifully edited out. Buber, on the other hand, it was assumed, belonged to the "spiritual category" of Jesus-like Jews.

If nothing else, Key's article was a premonition of the fact that Martin Buber, like Philo of Alexandria, would be more appreciated by the non-Jewish world than by the Jewish, and thereby a premonition of the risk that Marcus Ehrenpreis was running with his Swedish-Jewish bridge-building. The balancing act between speaking inwardly to your own and outwardly to the world was historically perilous. On one side the Jews, who had good reason to fear the non-Jewish world and distrust those who wished to speak to it, on the other side the non-Jewish world, with its deep-rooted tradition of vilifying and degrading everything Jewish. At a time when the vilification of everything Jewish was rapidly increasing, and Jewish distrust of the world was rapidly deepening, this would seem to be an ever-harder balancing act to perform.

Over time, the understanding of the Jewish cause would more often take the form of an understanding of the Zionist project in Palestine than of the contribution of Jews and Judaism to the non-Jewish world. With time, some of them would combine their support for a Jewish Palestine with their support for Hitler's Germany. One of them was the aforementioned writer, literary critic, and member of the Swedish Academy Fredrik Böök, who had traveled with Ehrenpreis to Palestine in the spring of 1925, and who had taken a deep, but increasingly problematic, interest in the "Jewish question."

Perhaps time to say something about Fredrik Böök, since Marcus Ehrenpreis had considered him a friend.

In February 1925 Böök published an article that concluded: "In the interaction between Swedish and Jewish patriotism, based on mutual respect and sympathy, lies the solution to the Jewish question, if one day it should come to haunt us too."[23]

The article displayed a mainly welcoming attitude toward the Swedish Jews, highlighting the contributions of a number of Jewish cultural personalities to Swedish society: the poet Oscar Levertin, the literary scholar Karl Warburg, the painter Ernst Josephson, "and other examples of a heartfelt and sympathetic interaction between the Jewish and the Swedish soul." However, the same article also worried about "the incongruity of the Jewish soul with any historically given state and nation," and the risk that this Jewish soul could "pervert into an amorphous and devious internationalism," and as such might get a foothold among "the crowds and contingents of Eastern Jews, who are increasingly seeking to come here, and who are neither able nor willing to assimilate."[24]

Böök's fear of the consequences of a continued immigration of Eastern Jews to Sweden had been nurtured and strengthened by his journey to Poland and Warsaw in the summer of 1916. In a series of articles in *Svenska Dagbladet* he painted in grisly detail the conditions in which thousands of brutally expelled Jews were living; "a teeming anthill full of restlessness, the houses packed with people from attic to cellar."[25] However, these descriptions were less an expression of understanding and compassion than of fear and horror, and even disgust. The predominantly Orthodox Jews in their characteristic garb were portrayed as dirty, derisory, weird, peddling, lazy. "One cannot defend oneself against the horrible impression that this is a people of idlers and drifters, people who do not recognize hard work—they appear like vermin, senselessly crawling vermin. In a flash one understands the abominations of the pogroms [...] understands them with a shudder of horror, pity, and remorse."

A kind of shudder, too, at seeing the Jewish "spiritual frenzy" in the midst of Jewish misery and degradation:

> Spiritual life is more intense in the ghetto than anywhere else. These Jews, who are not firmly rooted in the soil, sprout air roots in all directions, revel in concepts, dialectics, dreams and plans, studies and learning; their muscles are withering, their brains are feverish, nervous, frantic. There can be no talk of a spiritual blossoming, for what pale, feeble, strangely twisted shoots they are, twining around each other in the dark cellars

> of the ghetto; intellectual hypertrophy among Jews is a sign of spiritual malaise, of lost equilibrium.[26]

Böök expanded on his fears of "these Jews" in an article in 1925. He warned that the "destructive form of Jewish internationalism" that had developed in Russia and eastern Europe—"the latent hostility to historically existing societies"—risked leading to an increase in antisemitism and to the disruption of "the relationship between Swedes and Jews based on mutual trust and cooperation."[27]

The deterrent against Jewish internationalism was Jewish nationalism. With a healthy dose of national feelings, the Jews would be like normal people, their pale bodies would recover, their overheated brains would cool, their peddling would be replaced by manual labor, their rootlessness would find solid ground. Buried beneath Böök's growing enthusiasm for Zionism and Jewish nation-building in Palestine was an ill-concealed fear of the Jews themselves. Böök was convinced that the Russian Revolution "was largely the work of Jews," and that "the absolute demand for righteousness" in Jewish messianic thought, "this radical denial of reality, this inability to live securely in interaction with things and nature," could "transform into a destructive force of terrible strength."[28] Against this background, a Jewish national home in Palestine would not only be the salvation of the Jews—but of the non-Jews as well.

During his journey to Palestine and Jerusalem in the spring of 1925 in the company of Ehrenpreis, Böök had met with Chaim Weizmann, the leader of the Zionist movement and Ehrenpreis's friend from their student years in Berlin and the first Zionist congresses. Weizmann had made a strong impression on Böök by admitting, "in a spirit of self-criticism and self-reflection," the fatal role that "Jewish intelligence and fanatical Jewish ideology" played in fermenting discontent in Europe. "The Jews have laid Russia in ruins, they have stormed Hungary, they have even sought to breach the walls of Western European societies. This cannot be allowed to continue. First Europe turns the Jews into vagrants and Bolsheviks, then it punishes them with death and extermination," Böök alleged that Weizmann had said to him.[29]

Whatever Weizmann had said to Böök, it appears that Böök had heard what he was already convinced of:

> The mills that pulverize the lives of Jews around the world, the pogroms and *numerus clausus*, the laws of exception and abuse, the creeping disgrace, the open mockery, all the Jewish sins and weaknesses that give rise to antipathies, all the Christian sins and prejudices that increase the tension, all this forms an army of allies that rush to the rescue of Dr. Weizmann and Zionism. His cause rests on evil and necessity, which in the long run is a viable foundation that will not fail.[30]

When, the following year, Böök wrote his glowing review of Ehrenpreis's Swedish book debut, it became clear that what he had in common with Ehrenpreis was the admiration of the Jewish nation-building in Palestine. In contrast, there was nothing to suggest a corresponding admiration for the transnational universalism that was a central element of Ehrenpreis's Judaism. On the contrary, Böök had no forbearance with Jews who "wanted to cling to the Mosaic creed in anxious denial of all national Jewish values. The suppression of natural feelings, the denial of the calling of blood, can never be the basis of a legal claim or a moral position."[31]

Whatever Ehrenpreis may have thought of Böök's denigration of the very Judaism he himself propagated and believed in, he did not want to engage in a polemic. During their joint journey to Palestine, they had become friends of sorts, sharing boat decks, train compartments, car transports, and dinner tables. After their shared journey from Cairo to Tel Aviv, Ehrenpreis wrote to Esther that he had found Böök to be "a brilliant conversationalist and charmer also in the French language."[32]

A Jewish response to Böök came instead from Ernst Klein, son of the former chief rabbi Gottlieb Klein. Ernst Klein shared his father's criticism of Zionism and Jewish nationalism and was thus probably one of the Jews whom Böök had categorized as "anxious," but his objections to Böök's "nationalist standard solution to the complexity of the Jewish problem" was most likely endorsed by Ehrenpreis.[33]

In his defense, Böök could have said that he had only written what leading Jewish Zionists had already said. Chaim Weizmann's words may not have been verbatim, but they were not taken out of thin air either. Ernst Klein noted the consistency between Böök's view of the Jewish problem and that of nationalist Zionism, but he also noted Böök's "somewhat stronger emphasis on the harmfulness of the Jews to Europe," and perhaps already sensed where this would take Böök.[34]

Where this would take Böök. In due course.

It was not only the non-Jewish friends of Zionism that Ehrenpreis had to convince of the continued significance of a nonnational, diasporic Judaism. In 1932, his close associate, the historian Hugo Valentin, left *Judisk Tidskrift* for *Judisk Krönika* (The Jewish chronicle), a newly founded competitor with an explicitly Zionist agenda. In its first issue, Valentin wrote about his yearning for a Judaism that could appeal "to the fantastic and magnificent in human nature," and it was not hard to see what he was hoping for: "There is something great and gripping in belonging to an oppressed and suffering people seeking freedom and justice. Look how the world engaged itself in the struggle of the Greeks, and then of the Poles! Would it not be possible then to arouse the commitment of ourselves, and especially of our youth, to the cause of Jewish liberation?"[35]

The Jews, a nation like the Greeks and the Poles?

Ehrenpreis could not disagree more.

A year after the launch of *Judisk Tidskrift*, Ehrenpreis added yet another foundation to his Jewish-Swedish bridge-building, in his view the most important one. Just in time for the Christmas sales of 1929, the first in a planned series of three volumes hit Swedish bookstores. It was dedicated to his children, Theodor and Miriam, and consisted of more or less fictitious tales about "The prophets and sages who had built Israel."

"With these pages I want to tell you about my spiritual fathers, who have accompanied me throughout my life," Ehrenpreis wrote in his dedication. "Often their shadows floated in the room, but you did not see them. Often their calls rang through space, but you did not hear them. Often they supported me in difficult moments, but you did not know it."[36]

The language was different, loftier and more archaic, not only because of the many quotations and references from the Hebrew Bible, but also because Ehrenpreis was assuming a new role as a writer. Here he was no longer the traveler and flaneur, poetically describing and reflecting on what he was seeing, but the preacher, or even the prophet, aspiring to give weight and authority to what he had to say. "According to my limited ability, I have tried to bring to life, for you and for our age, these hidden-away figures who should belong to all times. The message they brought to their people and to their kind is a message to all of us," Marcus Ehrenpreis wrote to his children.[37]

The characters of the book, from Moses to Ezra, mostly speak in the voice of Ehrenpreis, and it is to Ehrenpreis's vision of Judaism that they mostly contribute. Moses contributes the idea of human love, Amos the idea of justice, Isaiah the vision of a better world, the second Isaiah "a religion for the world." Sometimes they speak their own words, but mostly they speak the words of Ehrenpreis.

As when Moses on Mount Nebo tells Joshua of his desire to found a new religion of love "that would bind together the children of the earth, and tame their passions, and drive the beast out of them and make them human," and it is unmistakably the voice of Ehrenpreis that we hear.[38]

Or as when he makes Isaiah's message of universal peace resonate against a backdrop of biblical wars and disasters that just as unmistakably bear the characteristics of the European wars and disasters unfolding before the eyes of Ehrenpreis. "Everything is falling apart. Even the faith in God. The generation of Isaiah is living on a rumbling volcano," an elderly Jewish teacher tells his young disciple in a dialogue by which Ehrenpreis attempts to instill the prophecy of Isaiah with a contemporary urgency and relevance.

THE YOUNG MAN: Do you thus, Master, regard Isaiah as the progenitor of our time's endeavors to pave the way for universal peace by disarmament and international tribunals?

> THE OLD MAN: Isaiah's idea of peace rises above our time as the heavens rise above the earth. For Isaiah, war and peace are not political matters, to be resolved by treaties between people. The universal peace that he speaks of will not be achieved by the disarmament of armies, but by the disarmament of souls. Man must improve. Hate must go![39]

The first volume in the series, on Prophets and Sages, was received respectfully by Swedish critics, even if the element of surprise—the foreign debutant with the impressive Swedish language—was gone. "Certainly there are pages in Ehrenpreis's book that suffer from some artificiality, and at times the elevated pitch sounds strained—[but] on the whole the stylistic form is brilliant," the theologian Henning Wijkmark wrote in *Svenska Dagbladet*. He also seemed to confirm Ehrenpreis in his bridge-building ambitions. Although Ehrenpreis is emulating the ancient style of the biblical tradition, Wijkmark wrote, he has nevertheless succeeded in writing a book that "is closer to our own religious and aesthetic perspectives, providing us with a deep insight into the immense power and beauty of the Holy Scriptures."[40]

The second volume, on Saints and Heroes, was published two years later and had an equally respectful reception. "The book was my Christmas reading. You couldn't wish for a better one," wrote the reviewer in *Svenska Dagbladet*.[41] The highlight, he thought, was a story in which Ehrenpreis has Rabban Gamaliel, the grandson of the postbiblical Jewish sage Hillel, discuss with his Jewish contemporary, Saul/Paul, what the Jewish Jesus from Nazareth had really said and meant. In the New Testament (Acts of the Apostles) Gamaliel is mentioned as a highly respected Pharisaic teacher who had defended the apostles in Jerusalem before the Sadducean high priests ("leave these men alone and let them go"), and at whose feet Saul/Paul had received his instruction "in our ancestral law."

In the book, Ehrenpreis has Gamaliel encounter his former disciple as he is being led in chains to the Roman commander in Jerusalem on suspicion of sedition. The imprisonment of Paul in Jerusalem is mentioned in the biblical text, but his encounter with Gamaliel is not. When Ehrenpreis has Paul ask to see his former teacher, it is in the hope that Gamaliel will understand him.

But Gamaliel does not understand him. Instead, he exposes the theological conflict between Paul and Jesus, and thereby the conflict between postbiblical Judaism and the messianic Jewish movement that will become Christianity:

> GAMALIEL: Yeshua [Jesus] was one of us. He lived and died as a Jew. One may say: as a Pharisaic Jew. His teaching was the teaching of Hillel, his voice was the voice of Jeremiah. It had a new and different sound, a sound alien to us, but one thing is beyond doubt: he did not want to tear the bond between Israel and the Torah, he wanted to awaken Israel, and Israel alone, to repentance. He did not want to found a new congregation outside Israel; he did not want to be a prophet to the Gentiles. And most important, he did not want to be what we call the messiah. He said, "You shall not call anyone on earth your father, for one is your father and he is in heaven." He opposed being called the good master: "no one is good but God alone," he said. He spoke the language of Israel, our unshakable faith in the one God, our unyielding: *Adonai Echad!* This language you do no longer speak, Shaul [Saul]. Therefore, I do not understand you.

PAUL: That is so, Master. I do not speak the language of the living Yeshua. I speak the new language that the resurrected Yeshua has taught me. For you, Rabban Gamaliel, Yeshua is a man, a Pharisaic rabbi, like you and your father, but for me he is the Messiah, the Son of God, who took on human form to redeem us all. Gone is the world of sin and the world of the law. A new world has been opened to me, the world of faith and grace.

GAMALIEL: This is your great mistake, Shaul. The world of sin and the world of law are not gone. God has created them both. You, poor man, who is trapped between these two worlds and dares to build a new world on top of them both! Shaul the law-keeper is building a world without the law! This is the abyss that is opening up between you and me, between you and Israel, between you and Yeshua of Nazareth.[42]

With the dialogue between Gamaliel and Paul, Ehrenpreis wished to demonstrate that the conflict between Judaism and Christianity had no basis in what Jesus of Nazareth himself had taught, but rather in the distortions of the Jewish teachings that Paul and his followers had concocted. The true face of Judaism was a face that even good Christians would recognize if only they were allowed to see it.

The reviewer was touched but not convinced. "Dr. Ehrenpreis is possibly somewhat high-handed with the facts. His arguments and counterarguments are not always plausible or even probable. However, the voice of the critic stays silent in face of the gripping atmosphere that rests over the conversation."[43]

The reviewer in *Dagens Nyheter* wrote that the story of Gamaliel and Paul alone would "assure 'Saints and Heroes' a lasting place in our literature."[44]

However, to the extent that Ehrenpreis had hoped that his stories about "those who built Israel" would awaken a broader Swedish interest in "the true face of Judaism," there were no obvious signs of success. Despite the accolades in the reviews, the new books sold far fewer copies than the previous ones.

Instead, ever-new reasons for disappointment.

The third and last volume, on Poets and Visionaries, did not appear until 1943, and its last voice would belong to Chaim Nachman Bialik, who in the poem quoted below may have reflected some of the despair that Ehrenpreis must have felt at the time:

Vainly, my young strength was squandered.
The blame you must take upon yourselves.
In rotten wood I struck my axe;
No anvil for my sledgehammer.

All the same, Swedish-Jewish cultural life seethed with new associations and initiatives. The formation of the Jewish Academic Club had been preceded by stimulating gatherings in the "friendly home of Dr. and Mrs. Ehrenpreis," and neither the Jewish Literary Society nor the Hebrew Club would have come into being without Ehrenpreis's active participation.

With each new issue of *Judisk Tidskrift*, reasons for hope.

With each new issue of *Judisk Tidskrift*, also reasons for fear and anxiety, most so in the monthly review of Jewish events that until 1932 was written by Hugo Valentin and which was colored by his strong Zionist convictions. Wherever Valentin

Marcus Ehrenpreis among the Jewish confirmands of 1930, gathered in the session hall of the Jewish community in Stockholm. Ehrenpreis attached great importance to the confirmation classes and the yearly confirmation ceremony in the synagogue.

looked, he saw growing signs of antisemitism, growing dangers to Jews, and the growing necessity of Zionism.[45] In his last review, in November 1932, before switching allegiances, Valentin summed up his view of the situation: "The Jewish world as a whole presents an extraordinarily dark picture: division, decline, and in many places hopelessness. Only *one* bright spot remains, Eretz Israel [Palestine]."[46]

The difference between Valentin and Ehrenpreis in their views on Judaism and Zionism had become apparent in an article that Valentin had published two years earlier. Against the spiritually and religiously defined Judaism that Valentin had come to associate with Ehrenpreis, he wanted to contrast "a historically and nationally defined Judaism," by which he meant the identification of the Jews with a Jewish nation in Palestine and a corresponding "restraint" in their identification with a "host nation."[47] For Ehrenpreis's faith in the diasporic mission of Judaism, and the Jews as "a nation among the nations," he had almost contempt. Only a *national* goal could galvanize the Jews of the world and save them, Valentin argued, and his call for a Zionist awakening concluded with a passionate cri de coeur:

> Give me a language, give me a land,
> Give beloved bonds to love,
> Give me a circle to which I belong,
> Give me a goal for which to die.[48]

The response to Valentin didn't come from Ehrenpreis but from Simon Aberstén, first librarian in Gothenburg and a regular contributor to *Judisk Tidskrift*, but the concluding sentence could have been written by him: "The rampage of the Nazis must not scare us into creating voluntary ghettos; the most glorious epochs in our exile have been the result of our honorable and successful participation in the cultural work of other peoples."[49]

Replying to Aberstén, Valentin further expressed his distrust in the future of diasporic Judaism. Jews who "recklessly" engaged in the politics of their host country ran the risk of harming the Jewish cause, he argued. By birth and mentality, Jews were not capable of understanding other nations' ways of thinking and being. The communist revolutionary leader Kurt Eisner of Bavaria (murdered in 1919) could no more understand "the soul of a Bavarian peasant than a blind man understands colors, or Georg Brandes understands a Christian Danish nation imbued with Grundtvigianism."[50]

As the gap between the Jews and the world widened, so did the gap between Jews and Jews. Between the choice to be a nation "to die for" and the choice to remain a nation among the nations with a spiritual heritage to carry and a spiritual task to fulfill, an intra-Jewish conflict arose that for a few years seemed to be all-decisive.

So was there someone on the other side of Ehrenpreis's Swedish-Jewish bridge? The sympathetic reception of Ehrenpreis's books might have given cause for hope, as well as the esteem in which he seemed to be held by Swedish society. In September 1935 the Swedish government made him an honorary professor, at the suggestion of the minister of ecclesiastics, Arthur Engberg.

Some ten years earlier, the same Engberg, at the time editor in chief of the social democratic daily newspaper *Arbetet*, had been the author of rabidly antisemitic articles, but had since then had a change of mind. When, in the autumn of 1933, Ehrenpreis published a book to introduce and explain the Talmud to a Swedish readership, Engberg thanked him in an open letter: "Your book is doubly welcome at a time when racial superstition is spreading, and our people's view of your people's greatness and historical achievements is obscured."[51]

Not everyone was equally grateful and appreciative. Reacting to his appointment, a large regional newspaper wrote: "One should not unnecessarily provoke bitter feelings among our unpromoted Swedish scientists and cultural personalities of rank, and create the suspicion that the appointments of honorary professors are made for other reasons than purely objective ones."[52]

This was written a week after the introduction of the anti-Jewish Nuremberg Laws in Germany, at a time when the

Swedish-Jewish bridge of Ehrenpreis was increasingly turning into a Jewish fortress of defense.

In late 1933 Marcus Ehrenpreis published a book on the Talmud. It was a compilation of five public lectures that Ehrenpreis had delivered in the autumn of 1932 and spring of 1933 with the aim of countering the increasingly poisonous attacks on Jews and Judaism, and to demonstrate the common roots and ideals of Judaism and Christianity. The Talmud was the core of Judaism's tradition of interpretations and discussions: an idiosyncratic collection of labyrinthine commentaries, legends, and disputes, written in both Hebrew and Aramaic, prone to be misunderstood, distorted, and quoted out of context. In antisemitic propaganda, Ehrenpreis wrote, the Talmud was presented as "a diabolic work" in which the Jews were taught "to hate the world and to commit every conceivable crime against it."[53]

The impulse to write a book in Swedish on the Talmud, Ehrenpreis recalled, came after a meeting with the Swedish-Danish princess Ingeborg over a cup of tea in her home in the royal domain of Djurgården in Stockholm. The princess had requested to see Ehrenpreis after she had spent time in Copenhagen with some Russian duchesses who had spoken "all evil" about the Jews, using quotations from the Talmud. The liberal-minded Ingeborg sensed that something was wrong, but knew nothing about the Talmud and now wanted his advice on what to read if the matter should come up again.[54]

A few months later, Ehrenpreis gave a well-attended and well-received public lecture on the Talmud in Gothenburg, and the next day the editor of the liberal newspaper *Göteborgs Handels- och Sjöfartstidning*, Torgny Segerstedt, commissioned a series of articles on the topic. "Written in dire times," the reviewer in *Svenska Dagbladet* wrote of the book when it was published six months later, giving Princess Ingeborg something to read if the subject were to come up again.[55]

Seemingly, then, Swedish interest in Jewish matters had grown, but perhaps not in the way and for the reasons that Ehrenpreis had hoped for. The review in *Dagens Nyheter* opened: "What is called by a general and indefinite term the Jewish question has through the events in Germany acquired a new and ominous topicality."[56]

Among those who came to understand and appreciate Ehrenpreis's Swedish-Jewish bridge-building was the historian and writer Lydia Wahlström. In an essay published in the autumn of 1936, with the subtitle "A Man of Cultural Synthesis," she wrote that Ehrenpreis "like no other" had "instilled in the Swedes an interest in the spirit of the Old Testament and late Judaism. [...] Even Christians are flocking to his pulpit in various synagogues around the country. From the Swedish chief rabbi's working study emanates the same ecumenical spirit as once came from the working study of [Archbishop] Nathan Söderblom in Uppsala."[57]

Wahlström also praised Ehrenpreis's efforts to elucidate the common roots and ideals of Judaism and Christianity, and thus to lay bare the unjust foundations of Christian anti-Judaism. "Whatever we do," Wahlström concluded,

> we cannot with impunity cut off the branch we sit on, and therefore the hatred of Christians toward Jews—if authentic and not fabricated—is more unnatural and more unsound than most hatreds in this world. If

> Sweden, with its ancient democracy and its freedom from antisemitism, could serve as a mediating link, no man could be more suited to such a conciliatory mission than Marcus Ehrenpreis, whom we are lucky to have in our midst.[58]

But the time for reconciliation was over, and the need for other missions became increasingly pressing. In mid-July 1933, during a spa sojourn in Karlsbad, Ehrenpreis received a telegram from the Central Organization of Jewish Congregations in Switzerland, informing him that a Swiss Nazi journal, *Der eiserne Besen* (The iron broom), had published an article claiming that Ehrenpreis, in a speech in Stockholm, had testified to the authenticity of the antisemitic forgery *The Protocols of the Elders of Zion*. The source for the article in the Swiss Nazi journal were two articles in the Swedish Nazi journal *Nationen* (The Nation). The first article, dated 1 May 1932, was headlined "Dr. Ehrenpreis and Israel's World Plans," the second, dated 1 October, "Dr. Ehrenpreis Testifies to the Accuracy of the Zionist Protocols."

Ehrenpreis immediately ended his stay in Karlsbad and went to Basel, the site of the First Zionist Congress in the glorious summer of 1897, which was now claimed to be the site of a Jewish world conspiracy allegedly revealed by Ehrenpreis in a speech in Stockholm.

Coming from Ehrenpreis, it had been an unusually "Zionist" speech, delivered on 27 July 1929 before the Jewish Academic Club and dedicated to Theodor Herzl on the twenty-fifth anniversary of his death. It was also an unusually optimistic speech: "Happy our generation, which will witness this momentous event […] the unification of Judaism beyond religious and political differences."[59]

It was this speech that the editor of *Nationen* had twisted into "an unequivocal appeal [by Dr. Ehrenpreis] to all Jews to take an active part, without consideration, in the criminal plan devised by the Elders of Zion to subvert all peoples and states."[60]

Having arrived in Basel, Ehrenpreis made the decision to sue Alfred Zander, the Swiss publisher of *Der eiserne Besen*. He could have sued the Swedish publisher of *Nationen* on the same grounds, but in Basel there was Oscar Meyer, a Jewish lawyer, who convinced him to take the matter to court. "I am suing the author, the publisher, and the distributor," Ehrenpreis announced in a statement to the Swiss telegraphic agency. "The so-called Zionist Protocols, or The Protocols of the Elders of Zion, are, from beginning to end, a forgery, the contents of which are incompatible both with Zionism and with the tenets of Judaism."[61]

Ehrenpreis and Meyer had barely begun the libel proceedings against the publisher of *Der eiserne Besen* in Basel when proceedings were opened in Bern against the Swiss publishers of the protocols themselves, or *Die Zionistischen Protokolle*, "the Zionist Protocols," as they were now called.[62] The lawsuit had been filed by the Bernese-Jewish Community and the Central Organization of Jewish Communities in Switzerland and concerned the distribution of junk literature, *Schundliteratur*, which in the Canton of Bern was an offense. This included writings intended "to incite hatred against a population group and to provoke unrest in the country," and it was from the preface to "the Zionist Protocols" that *Der eiserne Besen* had taken the claim that the chief rabbi of Stockholm in a speech in Stockholm had confirmed the authenticity of the protocols.

On Monday, 27 October 1934, Marcus Ehrenpreis arrived in Bern to testify in what the newspaper vendors on the streets called "The Jew Trial," which Ehrenpreis thought was an apt term for what was at stake. "This was the trial of Judaism, and before the judge in Bern was the cause of Israel," he wrote in an article in *Dagens Nyheter.* "What was prosecuted here was not only a falsification of the minutes of the First Zionist Congress, but a falsification of Judaism as such, of its character and doctrine, of its entire three-thousand-year history."[63] The large courtroom was "crowded with spectators and journalists from every camp and country," where the representatives of the Jewish community and the organized Nazis had been seated side by side, and between them "a yawning chasm of alienation, centuries-old prejudices, hatred and malice, nourished from poisonous springs." Late in life he could not rid himself of the depressing thought that in Bern, like Philo once in Rome, he had been entangled in a millennia-long trial with no end in sight:

> Here Apion once sat, accusing the Jews of annual ritual murders; here had sat Pfefferkorn and Eisenmenger, defaming Judaism by falsifying the Talmud; here sat the inventors of German antisemitism heaping every conceivable filth on their Jewish citizens. [...] And around me in the hall I saw defamed Israel itself, the unknown, misunderstood, disfigured people, defamed for a hundred generations. Would the truth finally emanate from this jury room in Bern and spread across a misguided and troubled world?[64]

For a moment perhaps, he believed so himself. "Like a thunderstorm, the testimonies came crashing down on the heads of the prosecuted. They did not lift a finger to defend themselves. They made not even the slightest attempt to prove what they had had their gullible listeners believe to incite them against the Jews."[65] The verdict of May 1935 seemed unequivocal; the "Zionist Protocols" were "forgeries and plagiarism [with the aim] of sowing hatred against a group of the population and provoking unrest in the country," and the publishers were convicted of having disseminated junk literature. The penalty, however, was lenient (a fine), and the symbolically important demand that the hate-sowing book be confiscated was rejected on the grounds that a confiscation would be of no practical significance.[66]

Nor did the verdict in itself have any real-world significance. The time when a verified truth could defeat a shameless lie was over. Still, when Ehrenpreis was asked by the court to explain the Talmud, he brightened up, as if the minute of truth was only a testimony away.

"I don't know whether the court will allow me to give a lecture on the Talmud," he replied, turning to the presiding judge.

"It depends on the length," replied the judge.

Whereupon Ehrenpreis conveyed the essence of his Talmud book, with the expressed hope that the book would be translated into many languages, and with the unspoken hope that if the world would know, it would understand. His hour-long testimony was apparently an impressive display of scholarship and performance. When another witness at the trial, Chaim Weizmann, was elected the first president of the State of Israel in June 1948, the newspaper *Berner Tagwacht* marked the occasion by recalling the days of the trial fourteen years earlier:

> No one who was there will forget the Chief Rabbi Dr. Ehrenpreis from Stockholm, an old man in whom Lessing's Nathan der Weise suddenly came alive before

> you. One would have given much to be able to say to him that there was no Hitler, no [Theodor] Fritsch, and no [Alfred] Rosenberg, when he placed the genuine Zionist minutes [the stenographic minutes of the Basel Congress of 1897] on the judges' tables, with the words: "In here, you will not find a word, not a sentence, of that which is alleged in the forged 'Protocols of the Elders of Zion'; it is a monstrous forgery of Judaism as a whole, of its worldview, its character and life."[67]

The book on the Talmud was perhaps the last manifestation of Ehrenpreis's conviction that if only the world could be made to see "our true face," another world would be possible. "Ignorance, misunderstanding, and malice have combined to form a hostile force, directed at once against the Talmud and the Jewish people," he wrote.

And against his own person, he might have added. The journal that had propagated the lie about Ehrenpreis and *The Protocols of the Elders of Zion* had also propagated the lie that the chief rabbi of Stockholm was an agent of a foreign power, "the Jewish world government," with the aim "to enslave all peoples on earth to the power of Judaism."[68]

The 1933 book on the Talmud and the 1934 book on Israel's encounter with the nations were darkened by the events of the time. The book that had been intended to demonstrate the blessings of Israel's encounters with the nations concluded with an appeal to the nations to come to their senses:

> The equality of the Jews in Germany is now abolished. The Jewish citizen is banned from the community of people and declared inferior and dangerous. A wave

> of hatred wells through the countries, and not only against the Jews. A world order built on the foundations of humanity has been shaken. Terrible forces are set in motion to break the unity of the human race. Confused and anxious, we stand before the ruins of a world that was our common home. We are all facing a decisive struggle: not only the existence of Judaism is at stake. The Jewish question is an all-human question. It is an all-human interest that conflicts be tempered, and injustices removed, and that even the sorely tested Israel, after millennia of suffering and oppression, should be able to live in dignity and peaceful cooperation with the peoples of the world.[69]

In the final chapter of the book on the Talmud, Ehrenpreis sees himself going back to Salonika, where in a synagogue he meets Paul and discovers that they can "speak to each other without bitterness." Two thousand years of "tragic struggle" had finally demonstrated that what united them was more important than what separated them.

> Today, Paul and Gamaliel need not be irreconcilable adversaries. The enemy of both Paul and Gamaliel, the enemy of both Christianity and Judaism, the enemy of all religion, is coming from the outside, from beyond church and synagogue. Our common enemy is godlessness, the materialistic mind, the spiritual barbarism. Our common enemy is the racial madness that erects walls of separation between human and human, destroying the unity of humankind. In these times of dire tensions, we all have a common cause: to defend

> the eternal values of human existence against the
> life-destructive forces of an erroneous generation.[70]

Eighty years later, I hold in my hand a newly purchased antiquarian copy of *Talmud, fariseism, urkristendom* (Talmud, Phariseeism, early Christianity). I note that it has a hand-written dedication "from the devoted author" to "Professor Torgny Segerstedt, who inspired the writing of this book."

I also note that its pages have remained uncut.

Marcus and Esther Ehrenpreis with their children, Theodor and Miriam, and Marcus's mother, Clara Süss-Ehrenpreis, Vaxholm, summer 1916.

6.

AN UNREQUITED LOVE

When I came, why was there no one?
When I called, why was there no one to answer?
Was my arm too short to deliver you?
Do I lack the strength to rescue you?
By a mere rebuke I dry up the sea,
I turn rivers into a desert;
their fish rot for lack of water
and die of thirst.

—Isaiah 50:2

In the summer of 1916, in the midst of the World War, Marcus Ehrenpreis managed to bring his mother Clara to Sweden from her refuge in Vienna. On a sunny August photo in front of a rented holiday house in the Stockholm archipelago, she can be seen sitting, small, frail, dressed in black, surrounded by her Swedish family, dressed in white; Marcus in a white jacket and waistcoat with a cigar in hand, Esther in a white embroidered dress with a white teapot in hand, Theodor in a white sailor's suit, Miriam in white woolen socks and white bow. In Clara's lowered gaze it is tempting to read alienation and bewilderment at the untroubled summer paradise in which she finds herself. And grief and longing for a home that is irrevocably gone.

For Clara Süss-Ehrenpreis, Sweden never became a home. Physically and mentally weakened, she died in February 1922 at the age of seventy, the first of the Ehrenpreis family to rest in that Swedish soil that her son and his family were now making their own.

Within a few years, the lifestyle of the Ehrenpreis family was indistinguishable from that of the well-established Swedish-Jewish families who dominated the congregation in Stockholm. It was a prosperous world, furnished with arcadian vacation villas and fashionable summer pensions, populated by people with good reason to love a country that so generously had opened its doors to them, and that just as generously was opening them to the Ehrenpreis family.

The chief rabbi of Stockholm did not have an automatic entry ticket to the political and cultural elites of the country, as he had had in his official capacity as Grand Rabbi in Bulgaria, but by virtue of his erudition and personality, Marcus Ehrenpreis soon gained access to both. In bourgeois Sweden, merit and achievement outweighed name and background, and whatever antisemitic noise there was in the background, it rarely stood in the way of public recognition and appreciation. Ehrenpreis's predecessor, the Hungarian-born Gottlieb Klein, had also been awarded the title of professor by the Swedish government (in 1897), and he, too, had come to belong to a well-situated Swedish-Jewish bourgeoisie, with close ties to the cultural elite of Swedish society.

The public standing of Ehrenpreis and the appreciation of his work was most explicitly manifested on his sixtieth birthday, which fell on 27 June 1929 and which the family had chosen to celebrate in the posh seaside resort of Falsterbo. It is in the nature of jubilee tributes to inflate and embellish, but in the telegrams delivered to Falsterbo, and in the letters and articles sent to the editorial office of *Judisk Tidskrift*, you could detect genuine admiration and affection.

From Berlin, Bulgaria's "Royal Envoy and Minister Plenipotentiary" wrote of Ehrenpreis's efforts on behalf of Bulgaria "in a difficult time." They had come to know each other in the turmoil of the Balkan wars, and the minister had not forgotten. "During your successful hold of office in Bulgaria, you were met by a love and a respect that is accorded to only a select few."

Nor had Ehrenpreis forgotten Bulgaria, as would become evident in the spring of 1943.

The spring of 1943. In due course.

The celebratory anniversary in the summer of 1929 was undoubtedly another height in Ehrenpreis's life, but unlike the height in Djakovar in 1897, and perhaps the height in Sofia in 1909, this was a height from which the view backward was considerably clearer than the view forward. Looking backward, there were by now many life achievements to ponder and admire. Looking forward, there was a noticeable uncertainty about where all this would lead. The Swedish-Jewish bridge that Ehrenpreis had set out to build would soon be fortified on the Jewish side with the first part of *De som byggt Israel* (Those who built Israel), but whether there was to be a bridgehead on the Swedish side was still hard to know.

It would soon become clear that 1929 was the high point of Ehrenpreis's bridge-building venture. And the end point.

The high point was there for everyone to see, or rather, everyone could still see what they were looking for.

Hugo Valentin saw "a reverent caretaker of the past and a champion of the reborn Israel."[1] About what kind of Israel to be reborn, they were not yet in public disagreement.

Ragnar Josephson saw a Swedish writer who, with an ingenious mastery of language, imagery, and thought, had been able to capture "a sense of the tangible, magnificent reality of the Old Testament" and to unify "the divine whispers of the biblical forest with the crisp calls of the Nordic pinewoods."[2] About what the crisp calls of the Nordic pinewoods should demand of the Jews of Sweden, they had not yet expressed diverging opinions.

Unsurprisingly, there were more retrospectives than projections, more about Ehrenpreis's path from Lemberg to Stockholm than about the path he had embarked on since then.

From London, Paul Goodman, a leading British Zionist, wrote that Ehrenpreis in Sweden had assumed the role of a pioneer "in a hitherto unsown field," but he left it to "more competent pens" to pronounce on the future of Ehrenpreis's Swedish undertaking. The cause of cultural dualism was not necessarily the cause of Zionism.[3]

For much the same reason, Hugo Valentin chose to stay away from Ehrenpreis's cultural-dualistic enterprise: "It is not up to us but to the impartial observers of posterity to appreciate the new Jewish direction he has introduced and to some extent shaped by his personality."

Still, Valentin could not refrain from reminding Ehrenpreis that in Sweden he would never be able to witness the fulfillment of "the bold hopes of his youth," as he had seen them fulfilled in Tel Aviv, with streets and squares named after his old friends and comrades-in-arms.[4]

What united all those who wanted to celebrate Marcus Ehrenpreis in the summer of 1929 was the respect, bordering on adulation, for his personality. Even those who doubted his cultural Zionism testified to the power of his capacity to instill self-esteem and confidence among the Jewish communities in which he had worked.

Shalom Riwkin testified to the self-esteem and confidence. He belonged to "the small band of Jewish businessmen with intellectual interests" who had sought out Ehrenpreis's lectures at the Hebrew Club. Riwkin had fled Russia in 1915 and had written his tribute in Yiddish and was probably one of the few in Sweden who could fully enjoy a lecture in Hebrew. He could thus testify that Ehrenpreis spoke "in a language so beautiful, so rich in images and so formally perfect, that the listener is completely captivated," and that the small group who had had the privilege of listening to him week after week had been granted the "most beautiful moments in [their] intellectual lives."[5]

A story by Emil Kronheim, the recently hired assistant rabbi of the congregation, contributed to the image of Ehrenpreis's personality. "Let me give you a little guidance for your work among us," Ehrenpreis had said in preparation for Kronheim's installation.

> Coming from Germany, from abroad, you may not yet have a correct understanding of the situation of the Jews in Sweden, the specific circumstances in which our Jewish religious community lives. If you do not take these conditions into account, you could be making serious mistakes in your work. Let me tell you a word about my own experience. It is with love that our children must be brought to our religion, to our services, and to the sources of Judaism; it is with love and patience that we must try to win the adults in our

> congregation for a Jewish religious life. Nothing could be less conducive to the blessings of our activity than harshness and fanaticism.[6]

It was a celebratory text, of course, but Kronheim had nonetheless captured an important aspect of Marcus Ehrenpreis's personality: his ability to immerse himself in new linguistic worlds and cultures. Where others saw something alien and intractable, Ehrenpreis saw a cultural-dualistic opportunity. Where others saw a peripheral country with a peripheral Jewish population, Ehrenpreis saw an uncultivated field. Kronheim had expressed it in terms of patience and love, but it could also have been expressed in terms of empathy and understanding. Empathy with the Swedish Jews detached from their Jewish heritage. Understanding what it might take to bring that Jewish heritage back to them again.

"A priestly human and a human priest," Emil Kronheim concluded his tribute to Marcus Ehrenpreis on his sixtieth birthday, and it was a beautiful and somewhat apt image of the chief rabbi of Stockholm at the high point that was the summer of 1929.

Nevertheless, the end point was on the horizon. The only non-Jewish tribute to Ehrenpreis was written by Emanuel Linderholm, a Christian professor of theology at Uppsala University, and it distinguished itself for not relating in the least to Ehrenpreis and his Judaism, let alone to his ecumenically extended Jewish hand. Instead, it was a narrow, academic account of differing interpretations and translations of an ambiguous passage in Deuteronomy (33:27). The only tribute of sorts that could be discerned was the assertion that the Swedish translation of the passage in question had obscured its original Hebrew meaning by blotting out associations to ancient Egyptian images and representations. Perhaps Emanuel Linderholm's intention was to demonstrate his prowess in Hebrew and his interest in the textual origins of Judaism, but what he managed to demonstrate above all was a conspicuous lack of interest in what a living Jewish theologian could possibly have to say to a Christian theologian of today.

Could something more ominous already be sensed here?

In May that same year, Emanuel Linderholm had become chairman of the Religious Reform League of Sweden, a liberal-theological movement within the national Church of Sweden that would eventually sympathize with the movement within the German Evangelical Church that had aligned itself with Hitler—the Deutsche Christen. Linderholm's Christian theology sought to reform and modernize Christianity by modernizing the Bible, which in Linderholm's case meant purging from it parts of the Hebrew Bible, the Old Testament, especially parts of the Pentateuch, the Torah.[7] From there, the theological step was not too far to Deutsche Christen's desire to purge the Bible of all Jewish influence, and eventually the church of German Christians from all its members of the "Jewish race."[8] Emanuel Linderholm's theology of radical Bible "reform" was ostensibly motivated by something other than the racial antisemitism of the German Nazi Church, yet he would soon become a member of two explicitly pro-Nazi and antisemitic Swedish organizations, Samfundet Manhem and Nysvenska Rörelsen, and by all accounts remain a Nazi sympathizer until his death in 1937.

Linderholm's presence among the contributors to the 1929 anniversary supplement to *Judisk Tidskrift* may be explained by a dinner he had arranged for Ehrenpreis in Uppsala in October

1925. The main purpose of the dinner was to gain the support of Ehrenpreis and the Mosaic Congregation for a new Swedish translation of the Bible, to replace a translation that had been published as recently as 1917. In his dinner speech, Linderholm told of his lifelong love for the Old Testament, "the most wonderful religious document in the world," and of the many times that he "in heavy times of loneliness and distress [had] sought and found comfort, not only in Jesus, but also in the holy words of the prophets and psalmists." It was also perfectly clear to him "that the words of Jesus in their true form were only completing the former, in having the God of the ancestors be the one and only to be worshipped and honored."[9]

This could perhaps be interpreted as a theological rapprochement with Ehrenpreis from a radical Christian theologian who strived to reestablish the affinity of Jesus with the Jewish prophets, and to that end wanted to "bring the Holy Scriptures into our Swedish language in a garb that is fully worthy of them, and which will allow their beauty and poetry, with all their splendid oriental imagery, to come into their own." Linderholm stressed that a new translation should also be in the interest of Swedish Jews. Indeed, that it was their duty to help bring it about: "Your people have been with us for a long time now, and I think that we without arrogance may say that you have done well here, and that your leaders have manifested a good Swedish character." Which brought Linderholm to what the dinner for Ehrenpreis was ultimately all about, getting the Swedish Jews to finance the new Bible translation, since the Church of Sweden apparently had refused to do so.

"I believe that you have the power to bring about this costly enterprise," Linderholm concluded his dinner speech.

Whatever Ehrenpreis may have thought of Linderholm's notions of Jewish duty and Jewish economic power, he seemed, at least for a moment, to have glimpsed the contours of a Swedish-Christian bridgehead on the other side. In any case, according to Linderholm, Ehrenpreis had replied with "an unforgettable speech," saying "that it was perhaps the first time that Jewish and Christian scholarship had personally met to collaborate on a matter of this kind."

Nothing came of the collaboration, nor of the matter at hand; the Bible translation of 1917 would survive until 2000, and Linderholm's passion for a new translation would prove to be based on anything but respect for Judaism. In the eyes of Linderholm and many other Christian theologians, Judaism was a fundamentally obsolete and outdated precursor to Christianity, a narrow and primitive tribal religion that no longer had any validity. The Hebrew prophets and psalmists whom Linderholm had said he valued so highly turned out to have a value only as harbingers of Jesus and Christianity, not as an inseparable part of a living Jewish tradition worth knowing and respecting.

Of course, Emanuel Linderholm was not the only Christian theologian with difficulties having an unprejudiced view of Judaism. For centuries, strongly negative perceptions of "the Jews" had been deeply ingrained in the liturgy and theology of the Christian Church, and the Church of Sweden was no exception. The degrading *Judensau*, Jew-pig, in the Cathedral of Uppsala dates from the fourteeenth century, and Martin Luther himself had written one of the most virulent anti-Jewish tracts ever, *On the Jews and Their Lies* (1543). Thus, in Sweden there existed firm views about Jews and Judaism long before any Jews had set foot there. That country in the periphery of

Europe untainted by anti-Jewish prejudice, which Ehrenpreis might have fantasized about, did not exist.

What did exist was a specifically Swedish or German Protestant variant of anti-Jewishness that at first could be mistaken for interest and benevolence. It spoke the language of the modern Enlightenment, it draped itself in the notions of reason and progress, it claimed to advocate religious tolerance and universal brotherhood, but it nevertheless regarded Judaism as spiritually and morally inferior to Christianity. What was morally sublime and universally valid in the biblical heritage was being preserved by Christianity, and Jews who wished to claim that part of their heritage should draw the proper conclusions.

Such notions of Judaism, of course, had nothing to do with the Judaism whose "true face" Ehrenpreis wanted the world to know. In fact, they were drawn almost directly from the anti-Jewish stereotypes formulated in the early phases of the Christian Church, and which were ultimately rooted in a theological need to invalidate a Judaism that continued to lay claims on the covenant with God and the legacy of the Hebrew Bible. Since the story of Jesus as the Christ was ultimately legitimized by the prophecies of the Hebrew Bible, and since the Christian Church claimed to be the embodiment of a renewed covenant, "the new Israel," the continued existence of Judaism was perceived as an affront, and for a time as a contender for the souls of the "pagans" in a Hellenic-Roman world where the synagogue still maintained some power of attraction.

The Jews must therefore be portrayed as recalcitrant, obstinate, stubborn, and downright evil, since they had had the Truth before their eyes but had refused to receive it. This theological need found expression in a particular genre of writings, *adversus Judaeos*, "against the Jews." Some pamphlets were explicitly titled as such, others were titled somewhat less bluntly, but they all drew the same irreconcilable dividing line between the old Israel and the new, between the Jews and the Church, between Flesh and Spirit, between Law and Grace, and thus laid the foundations for the anti-Jewish tropes that were to take deep root in the Christian world. At the end of the third century, John Chrysostom compared the Jews to untamable and obstinate animals who served no purpose but to be slaughtered,[10] and only a few years later the first "Christian" pogroms against Jews broke out, blessed by the bishop of Milan, the Church Father Ambrose. In the fight against Judaism, the Spirit was proclaimed to be literally above the Law.[11] The lawlessness against the Jews went so far that another Church Father, Augustine, felt the need to provide a theological justification for why the Jews should not be killed. The divine task of the Jews, according to Augustine, was to continue to live in disgrace and humiliation and thereby be a living testimony to the truth of Christianity.[12]

This vindictive image of the Jews, formed in the theological tension between Ambrose and Augustine, between killing and forbearance, was to reemerge not only in the anti-Jewish fantasies of the Middle Ages and the Renaissance, but also in the anti-Jewish stereotypes of the European Enlightenment. In a Christianity reformed along the lines of Emanuel Linderholm, there was as little room for Judaism as in Immanuel Kant's universal order of morality and reason. Kant had imagined that such an order presupposed a universal religion of reason, which he could not conceive of as anything other than Christianity in its enlightened Protestant form. Judaism was not only intellectually inferior to Christianity, but it was also an expression of *heteronomy*, a pre-enlightened state of moral dependency that man must leave behind in order to attain *autonomy*, the higher state of moral independence postulated by Kant's philosophy. Only when Christianity had freed itself from its "Jewish" residues could it become a universal religion for all humanity.[13] Kant predicted, or even hoped, that Judaism would thereby perish of its own accord, or as he put it in an ominous but difficult-to-interpret phrase: "The euthanasia of Judaism is the pure moral religion, with the abandonment of all precepts [*Satzungslehren*], some of which, however, must be retained also in Christianity (as a messianic faith)."[14] Kant imagined that even enlightened Jews would embrace the religion of reason, or at least weed out the superseded features of Judaism and make it more "Christian."

But soon Kant's philosophical problem with Judaism as a doctrine and a way of life had turned into a problem with the Jews as human beings. Kant's disciple, Johann Gottlieb Fichte, regarded the Jews as an alien element in the nation, a state within the state, no matter how much they reformed themselves.

"In order to protect ourselves from them [the Jews]," wrote Fichte, "I see no other way than to conquer their promised land for them and send them all there."[15] The Christian Church, as Fichte saw it, must "eradicate the last spark of Jewish faith [*letzte Funke des jüdischen Glauben ausgerottet*]" and separate the figure of Jesus from the Messiah of the Jewish prophets.[16] Fichte's Christ was not the Messiah, and his Christian Church did not need its Jewish roots. Instead, it had fallen to a new chosen nation, the German people, the German soul, to transform Christianity into a religion of reason. "Jewish" Christianity had been an alien "Asian" import of mute submission and blind faith. The Christianity of the free German spirit, on the other hand, in symbiosis with a free German state, heralded the political and moral emancipation of humankind.[17]

It was not hard to see the line from Fichte to Deutsche Christen. Nor, indeed, from the liberal-minded priest and theologian Friedrich Schleiermacher. Schleiermacher, unlike Fichte, believed that Jews must be allowed to become full citizens, and his theology seemed to admit that there could be multiple paths to God. Nevertheless, Schleiermacher considered Judaism "a long-dead religion [...] a withered fruit [...] a husk without content."[18] On the one hand, he feared that the Jewish faith in the messianic redemption of the world would make Jews less loyal to the state and therefore proposed that in order to become citizens, Jews must "formally and publicly renounce the hope of the Messiah" (*daß sie der Hoffnung auf einen Messias förmlich und offentlich entsagen*). On the other hand, he feared that Jews who wanted to convert would bring Jewish ideas and beliefs into the Christian "religion of religions" he wanted to lay the foundations for, and therefore opposed conversions for the sake of convenience or conformity. Or, as he put it sarcastically, "a Judaizing Christianity—that would be the right disease to inoculate ourselves with!"[19]

That Schleiermacher's notions about Judaism also reflected notions held by many reform-striving German Jews did not preclude them from being notions molded in centuries of Christian-colored anti-Jewish rhetoric. Whatever arguments Schleiermacher may have had for his reservations about Judaism, whether political or theological, the result was that these notions and reservations lived on in the liberal circles of the German Lutheran Church, and thus in the liberal circles of the Swedish Lutheran Church, and thus in those circles where Ehrenpreis might have expected to gain most sympathy and understanding for his bridge-building project.

Did not the liberal theologians' quest for a renewed Christianity go hand in hand with his own quest for a renewed Judaism?

And were they not a prospective partner in that World League of Religions he had proposed in 1923, and for which he had thought to have found an ally in no other than Archbishop Nathan Söderblom when they had run into each other at the railway station in Munich in the spring of 1925?

And had not Nathan Söderblom himself told him that the ecumenical world movement which he was about to create should have a place for Judaism as well?

And in this time of all-devastating wars, didn't it seem as if a new cross-confessional understanding was emerging about the spiritual battle that lay ahead; a battle not between one way to God and another, but between a world with God and a world without?

And that in this battle, Judaism had a contribution to make?

At least that's how Ehrenpreis viewed it.

However, that's not how even reform-minded Swedish theologians viewed it, no matter how much interest they seemed to take in Ehrenpreis and his work. The fact that there were groups and individuals within the Church who were openly anti-Jewish, and who in some cases would become openly Nazi-friendly, was perhaps not surprising, but that a liberal theologian like Emanuel Linderholm would be one of them was hardly what Ehrenpreis had anticipated—not after his contribution to the anniversary in 1929, and the dinner at his home in Uppsala in 1925, and the promising encounter between Christian and Jewish scholarship in fine-tuning the Swedish translation of the Hebrew Bible.

But even the open-minded Nathan Söderblom probably did not literally mean what Ehrenpreis remembered him saying at the Munich railway station, that at the world ecumenical table there would be a place for Judaism too. The young Nathan Söderblom had certainly had a long and friendly relationship with Ehrenpreis's predecessor Gottlieb Klein, and in one of his letters to him had spoken of "the unity of spirit that, despite differences in confession, prevails between you and some young colleagues of yours within our church." In the same letter he had also, not for the first time, emphasized and affirmed the Jewish roots of Christianity: "Every time the Church has gained new supplies of faith and strength, she has retrieved them from their Israelite origin."[20]

It soon became clear, however, that in the eyes of Söderblom too, the primary raison d'être of Judaism was to serve as a source of power for Christianity, and not as spiritual tradition with a significance and relevance of its own. Like many liberal theologians, Söderblom had embraced an evolutionary view of the development of religions, from the spiritually lower to the spiritually higher, with Christianity at the pinnacle of the spiritual evolution. Only Christianity had evolved to become that religion of religions that could accommodate the spiritual experiences and needs of modern enlightened men.

From this perspective, it was not difficult to understand the friendship, and even the affinity, between Nathan Söderblom and Gottlieb Klein, since Klein, in his work as both rabbi and scholar, had not only emphasized the Jewish roots of Christianity but had also argued that what was worth preserving in Judaism, the prophet religion or prophet doctrine, could also be found in the radically reformed Christianity that Söderblom and his young liberal theologians were fighting for. At a conference on religious studies convened in Stockholm in 1897, both Söderblom and Klein spoke. Söderblom spoke of Christianity's position as the religion of modern society. Klein spoke on the subject of religion and morality from a Jewish-Biblical perspective, but at the same time, somewhat surprisingly, seemed to confirm Söderblom's contention: "No other system has been shown to possess the power to morally elevate barbaric peoples and fill their lives with new meaning, as the Christianity that has grown out of Judaism."[21]

Marcus Ehrenpreis would not have said such a thing. Christianity may have sprung from Judaism, and Christianity may have embraced parts of the prophetic heritage, but the Judaism to which Ehrenpreis wanted to give voice had far greater claims to relevance and importance than in the role of being the origin of Christianity. While Gottlieb Klein was steeped in German Reform Judaism, which in many respects sought to make Judaism more like Christianity, Ehrenpreis was the child of a different generation and a different environment. Both had certainly studied at the same Reform rabbinical school in Berlin, but the idea of a Jewish cultural renaissance that would so profoundly influence Ehrenpreis found no resonance in Klein. Even less so the idea of a Jewish return to Palestine.

There may have been several reasons why Ehrenpreis did not manage to establish as close a relationship with Nathan Söderblom as his predecessor had. Söderblom had become the Archbishop of Sweden only a few months before the arrival of Ehrenpreis in Sweden, and perhaps the duties and considerations of the office simply got in the way. But probably the difference between Klein's more subdued Judaism and Ehrenpreis's more ambitious kind also played a role in the end. When Nathan Söderblom was invited to contribute a text to the 1929 anniversary supplement of *Judisk Tidskrift*, he declined on the grounds that he was inundated with proposals of a similar kind "from a number of persons very close to me," and one might perhaps conclude that Marcus Ehrenpreis was not one of them.[22]

Two years later Nathan Söderblom died, and he was thereby spared the harsh trials that the Church would be put to in its relationship to Jews and Judaism. To the very end, he seemed to question whether in Sweden there would be any trials at all. When a member of the Mosaic Congregation in Gothenburg wrote to Söderblom in April 1925 asking what the Church had to say about the antisemitic propaganda spreading in the country, he replied: "In this country we are fortunate enough not to have a Jewish question. [...] I ask you to mention a single such case in our country, and if so, I shall immediately react to it."[23]

As late as 4 April 1931, when there could hardly be any doubt about the existence of a "Jewish question" in Sweden as well, Hugo Valentin wrote a letter to the archbishop in which he pointed out that in Germany the Catholic bishops had "reacted against the National Socialist hate orgies, [...] but no Protestant churches." He therefore appealed to Söderblom "as a Nobel Peace Prize laureate, a renowned friend of Germany, a leading cultural personality, and the most authoritative of our generation of evangelical bishops, to do something about this." Söderblom replied that what was going on in Germany was "a disgrace to Christianity and to humanity" and promised to contact his colleagues in Germany: "I am extremely anxious that something be done on the part of the Evangelical Church."[24]

Three months later Nathan Söderblom was dead, and the question of how the Church of Sweden would act in the approaching anti-Jewish storm fell to his successor.

By this time it must have been clear to Ehrenpreis that friendliness toward his person and interest in his work, and even glowing reviews of his books, were not necessarily the same as sensitivity and receptivity to what he had to say about Judaism. What Ehrenpreis had hoped for was a new understanding of Judaism as a living spiritual force in its own right. What he encountered instead, even in the seemingly most broad-minded Christian circles, was a striking lack of understanding of just that. No matter how hard Ehrenpreis tried to bring forth the "true face" of Judaism as he saw it, he was met by a deeply entrenched Jewish stereotype that grinned stubbornly at him from the Lutheran Swedish "folk soul."

To the very last, Ehrenpreis seemed to have found it difficult to reconcile himself to the fact that people who had recently lauded the role and significance of Christianity's Jewish origins could begin to hate not only Judaism but also the Jews. When, as late as 1933, in his book on the Talmud, Ehrenpreis had pinned his hopes on "the progressive improvement in the relationship between Christian and Jewish theology," he had done so with reference to what he perceived as a steady development of Christian Talmudic research "toward a fairer appraisal of postbiblical Judaism." Among the Christian scholars he pointed to in this regard was "the eminent German historian of religion" and Protestant theologian Gerhard Kittel, who in his "exemplary work" of 1926 on Palestinian late Judaism and Christianity had shown that in the view of God there was no essential difference between Jesus and Judaism, and that "all Christian culture and Christian ethics were rooted in the ethical consciousness of Old Testament piety." In a parenthesis, Ehrenpreis noted that Kittel, in a later pamphlet (1933), had been "less fair to Judaism."[25]

That was an understatement. Kittel's later pamphlet on the "Jewish question" was an antisemitic tract that not only argued for the expulsion of the Jews from German society but also touched on the idea of physically exterminating them,

The inauguration of the national bishop of Germany, Ludwig Müller, in Berlin, September 1934. The denomination he represented, the German Evangelical Church, and the movement within it, Deutsche Christen, were anti-Jewish and friendly to the Nazis, and had adherents within the Swedish church, including Ehrenpreis's former friend Emanuel Linderholm.

although Kittel considered such a solution to the "Jewish question" to be practically difficult.[26]

It was as if Ehrenpreis had not been able to imagine that the seemingly welcoming climate in which he had gone about his Jewish-Swedish endeavor could shift so rapidly and so radically: that a Linderholm or a Kittel who had just seemed to affirm the importance of Judaism for Christianity had suddenly joined a movement that wanted to wipe it out.

For yet some time Ehrenpreis wrote and spoke as if the battle for the position of Judaism could be fought and won, and for the same reason that he had gone to Bern to testify against the lies of *The Protocols of the Elders of Zion*, he began to devote ever more of his work in Sweden to the defense of Israel's honor, as he called it:

> I considered it my inevitable task to shed as much light as possible on the seemingly impenetrable darkness. In lectures to both Jewish and non-Jewish audiences in various parts of Scandinavia, in interviews in the press, in my essays and writings, I sought to do the only thing necessary: to explain what was actually happening, to let the quiet voice of truth drown out the boisterous and mendacious propaganda of incitement. I avoided both polemics and apologetics: it is futile to polemicize against a malice that seeks no truth, and there is no reason to apologize, to defend oneself against, accusations that are utterly groundless: I merely wanted to open the eyes of the ignorant to these "secrets" that were no secrets at all. I wanted to say to those around me: Here is a Jew telling you what Judaism is and what it is not. He speaks because of his intimate familiarity with the teaching and living of Israel; he does not want to show off, he does not want to persuade, he certainly does not want

> to proselytize. He wants to give you an opportunity to develop your relationship with Jews and Judaism *en pleine connaissance de choses* [in full knowledge of the facts], and not under the influence of vicious, hateful propaganda.[27]

Ehrenpreis would soon have to defend his Judaism not only against external vilifications but also against internal criticism. When *Profeter och gudsmän* (Prophets and Sages) appeared in German translation, it was reviewed in the Hebrew press by none other than Josef Klausner, professor of history and Hebrew literature at the Hebrew University of Jerusalem. Already in 1919, Klausner had made good on his Zionist convictions and emigrated from Odessa to Jerusalem. In many respects, Klausner and Ehrenpreis were close. They had both been at the First Zionist Congress in Basel in 1897, they had both belonged to the cultural-Zionist circle of Ahad Ha'am, and they had both endeavored to bring forth the Jewish origin and character of Christianity, Klausner through his internationally acclaimed study *Jesus of Nazareth* (1929), Ehrenpreis through his fictional dialogue between Rabban Gamaliel and the apostle Paul in Saints and Heroes, the second volume of his series on "those who built Israel" (1931).

Yet something had come between them, and that something was the assessment of the Jewish Diaspora. In his review, Klausner praised the book for its grand poetic language ("in its entirety a masterpiece"), but criticized the author in surprisingly harsh terms for downplaying the Jewish-national agenda of the Prophets and exaggerating their universal ambitions. The prophets whom Ehrenpreis had cited in support of his view of Israel as a nonnational people had in fact said something else. Even the most "universal" of the biblical prophets spoke in national and territorial terms, Klausner argued. To overlook the Jewish-national aspect of the prophetic message was to express a "Christianizing" view that had little to do with Judaism, neither religiously nor nationally.[28]

Klausner ended as he began, by praising the book "for a language as prophetic as its content," but this did not appease Ehrenpreis. His response to Klausner's review, published in Swedish translation in *Judisk Tidskrift*, showed that he had taken offense. It was one thing to be misunderstood and maligned by Christian theologians, quite another to find yourself misrepresented by someone who had been at the same cultural-Zionist barricades you had.

The dividing point was the nature of the Jewish nation. Klausner in Jerusalem had come to take an increasingly Hebrew-territorial view of the matter, and a correspondingly critical view of the continuing role and significance of the Jewish diaspora. When in 1927 it was proposed that a professorship in Yiddish be established at the Hebrew University, Klausner was one of its most ardent opponents. He even planned to join a group of students in protesting the lectures of the prospective professor. Diaspora Yiddish had no place at a Hebrew university, Klausner believed, and subsequently the proposal for a Jerusalem chair in Yiddish came to nothing.[29]

In his response, Ehrenpreis recalled what they had once fought for together, and above all what they had not fought for—to make the Jews a people like all other peoples.[30] And herein lay the crux of the conflict between them. Ehrenpreis continued to regard the Diaspora as the main form of Jewish life, through which "Israel" would be able to uphold its peculiar spiritual task in the world. Jewish nation-building in Palestine, however much Ehrenpreis supported and admired it, and however much importance he attached to its potential significance for the spiritual and cultural renewal of Judaism, could never be a substitute for the Diaspora. To Ehrenpreis, the Jewish diaspora embodied a moral-political ideal, a world in which minorities and majorities, like the lamb and the wolf in Isaiah's prophecy, would live side by side. The ethos of Judaism had been shaped by the memory of slavery and alienation, and the Jews of the Diaspora had made the cause of the minority and the alien their own, and he never tired of quoting Leviticus 19:33 to stress his point: "When a stranger dwells with you in your land, you shall not oppress him. The stranger that sojourneth among you shall be counted as a native among you, and thou shalt love him as thyself: for ye were strangers in the land of Egypt. I am the LORD your God."

Only a few years later, as the Jews of Germany were deprived of their humanity, and desperately were seeking refuge, and country after country closed their borders, Ehrenpreis again pointed to the universal significance of the Jewish minority existence.[31] Had not humanity just been reminded of how majorities could be transformed into minorities overnight? From this perspective, the Jewish existence was not an anomaly to be rectified, but a vivid and at times inspiring reminder of the human condition: the minority and the stranger could one day be us. "World history shows that every people and every group must be prepared for such possibilities and devise its actions accordingly," Ehrenpreis wrote in June 1939, when it was humanly too late to anticipate anything but another major war, and another wave of expulsions and persecutions of minorities, and this time with "the annihilation of the Jewish race in Europe" as an explicitly pronounced goal.[32]

Also far too late, of course, to make the world see the true face of Judaism.

Between the Jews and the world, a widening chasm that words could no longer bridge.

The true face of Judaism. An aged Talmudic folio kept by the Jewish community in Stockholm.

7.

THE TRUE FACE OF JUDAISM

In general, the Jew has a peculiar lack of ability to see himself in a proper light. Having lived in a country for a long time and fully assimilated its language, customs, and culture, he feels himself to be a son of that country and believes himself to be a full-fledged German, Englishman, Frenchman, or Swede. He does not understand that the others do not regard him in the same way, but strongly sense his uniqueness and feel him as something essentially alien from themselves.

—Efraim Briem,[1] 1940

Marcus Ehrenpreis never authored a systematic presentation of Judaism. That which can be pieced together from his writings is disjointed and at times contradictory. The Ehrenpreis who stood on the barricades of the Young Hebrews did not see Judaism in the same way as the Ehrenpreis who only a few years later looked back on his "youthful hubris," and the account of Judaism that emerges from his Swedish writings is colored not only by a new language but also by a new task late in life: to build a bridge between Judaism and the world in the periphery of Europe.

In Sweden, if not before, it became clear that Marcus Ehrenpreis was a rabbi who was also a writer, with a writer's eye for the literary power of the Hebrew Bible and the sources of Judaism, and with a writer's ability to breathe life into its characters and stories. In the sources and matters of Judaism, Ehrenpreis was more erudite than most and he would certainly have been able to compile a systematic presentation of Judaism, but already in his grandfather's house in Lemberg his mind was set on literature, and his hope was increasingly set on the capacity of literature to build that Jewish bridge to the world that the early Jewish Enlightenment, the Haskalah, had failed to do. Where Immanuel Kant's friend Moses Mendelssohn had hoped to speak to the mind of the Christian world, it remained for Ehrenpreis and his generation to try to speak to its heart.

From this followed that what Ehrenpreis had to convey about the true face of Judaism not only had the purpose to enlighten and inform, but as much to create understanding and sympathy, and perhaps even to inspire a certain love for the spiritual power and poetic beauty of the Hebrew heritage.

The greatest challenge would be to create understanding and sympathy for those parts of Judaism that had been distorted, slandered, and misunderstood for centuries, and to which Ehrenpreis would have to devote an increasingly large part of his work to explain and defend as the wave of anti-Jewish propaganda swept over Europe:

The Jewish God.
The Jewish Law.
The Jewish Chosenness.
The Jewish Messianism.

The Jewish God, according to Ehrenpreis, was first and foremost no other God than the God that had inspired Jesus of Nazareth. When Jesus taught that Man should love his neighbor, he taught what he himself had been taught. In three of the Gospels (Mark, Matthew, Luke), Jesus is asked about the most important commandment of the Law, and in all three he answers with the Jewish confession of faith, taken from Deuteronomy.

"Hear, Israel, you shall love the Lord your God with all your heart, with all your soul, with all your mind, and with all your strength."

To this Jesus adds another commandment, taken from Leviticus:

"You shall love your neighbor as yourself."

"There is no greater commandment than these," Jesus says, according to Mark.[2]

"On these two commandments rests the Law and the Prophets," Jesus says, according to Matthew.[3]

The Jewish God was also the God of Christian love, Ehrenpreis wanted to show.

He was aware that the God of the Hebrew Bible could be understood in other ways. Anti-Jewish propaganda was replete with such ways. There was the zealous God and the avenging God and the exclusive God of the chosen people. In his Sunday sermon in the synagogue of Norrköping on 22 January 1939, with many non-Jews in attendance as usual, Ehrenpreis explained that the Hebrew Bible must not be read like any other book. It contained parts that were local and temporal and parts that were universal and eternal. To allow the temporal to obscure the eternal was to miss "a call from God to Man, from eternity to this day, from infinity to this place [...] an imperative, a demand, a claim on Man." At a time when the Jews of Germany were having the letter *J* stamped across their passports, so that they could more easily be sorted out at the Swedish border, the God of the Bible called upon Man: "Be holy! Love your neighbor! Love the stranger among you, for you yourselves have been strangers!"

"To us, these are not laws or legal norms," Ehrenpreis preached to the gathering in the synagogue of Norrköping. "These are divine imperatives with which we must wrestle and from which we cannot free ourselves."[4]

Not everyone understood the Jewish God and the Jewish Law that way.

The Jews as "legalists" was a deeply rooted trope in the anti-Jewish tradition. Jewish Law versus Christian Grace. The stereotype of Judaism as a "legalistic" religion was carried forth by the early European Enlightenment and was also to be found in the early German-Jewish Reform movement, whose demands for the adaptation and modernization of the commands and rituals of Judaism could at times be framed as an escape from "legalism."

It was thus not only to the non-Jewish world that Ehrenpreis had to explain that the Law, the commandments of the Torah, meant freedom, not slavery. Or more poetically, "the free submission of the soul to the yoke of the kingdom of heaven." He was happy to highlight a rabbinic comment that the Hebrew word for "engraved," *charut*, could also be read "freedom," *cherut* (spelled the same way in vowel-free Hebrew), and that this was ultimately how the Law was to be understood, not as dogma engraved in stone but as an ongoing conversation between God and Man about the conditions of freedom.[5]

Legalism was hardening the Law into dogma and silencing the conversation with God in empty rituals. Legalism was an evil in all religions, not least in Judaism. What was the Hebrew

The true face of Judaism. Rabbi Abraham Heschel and the Reverend Martin Luther King Jr. at a joint demonstration in February 1968. In 1937 Ehrenpreis introduced the German-born Heschel to readers in the pages of Judisk Tidskrift*; like Ehrenpreis, he was a strong advocate of the prophetic heritage of Judaism.*

Bible but a perpetual reckoning with rigid dogma and empty rituals?

Law was the opposite of legalism, Ehrenpreis argued.

The Law was "God's eternal demand on Man; be righteous, be pure in heart, be a seeker of the good."[6]

The tension between "external legalism and internal religiosity" was inevitable in all religious life, Ehrenpreis stressed. "Every religious belief, every longing for God and eternity, will in the course of time be encapsulated in visible and tangible forms, by liturgical and ritualistic ceremonies, by time-honored texts, by symbols [...]. Sometimes the forms can become dominant and obscure what is essential, the elevation of the mind."

The notion of the Jews as a chosen people was hard to explain, easy to misunderstand, and easy to turn against the Jews themselves. And the more it was turned against the Jews in the Europe of the 1930s, the more Ehrenpreis was forced to move from explaining "chosenness" to defending it. One of those who had turned "chosenness" against the Jews was the priest and professor of religious history in Lund, Efraim Briem, who in 1940, when so much had already been turned against the Jews, published a book on the causes of antisemitism. The all-explanatory cause that Briem had found was chosenness, or particularism, as he called it, the tendency of the Jews to separate themselves from other peoples, their "inner isolation," the "coldhearted coldness" toward the Gentiles nurtured in them by their rabbis.

"Here we must search for the innermost core of antisemitism," Briem wrote.[7]

The charge that the Jews only had themselves to blame for being persecuted was a key element in Nazi propaganda that was poisoning public opinion in Sweden as well, and Ehrenpreis felt compelled to respond. "Without noticing it, [Briem] provides legitimacy to antisemitism as a justifiable and understandable reaction against the Jews' intolerable claim to some kind of chosenness," he wrote. With his explanation, Ehrenpreis argued, Briem had joined a long tradition of anti-Jewish rhetoric, from Haman in Xerxes's Persia ("there is a people in your kingdom whose laws are different"), through the pogroms in Philo's Alexandria, "to the present-day extermination campaign against the Jews in large parts of Europe." What made the charge of "particularism" against the Jews specifically treacherous was that unlike purely trumped-up accusations of ritual murder, well-poisoning, and world conspiracies, it contained a grain of truth.

"If by particularism we mean religious and historical self-assertion, fidelity to your ancestral heritage and kin, then no one can deny that such a Jewish particularism exists, just as there is a Swedish or Protestant particularism," Ehrenpreis wrote. The problem with Briem's explanation was that it measured Jewish particularism by other standards: "What is considered a virtue, as something worthy of respect among other peoples, is made into a national culpability when it comes to the Jews, explaining and justifying the atrocities being committed against them."[8]

In fact, there was nothing in Jewish particularism that made it incompatible with Swedish or Protestant particularism. Had not the prophet Jeremiah instructed the Jews in the Babylonian exile to be loyal to the land in which they lived and to pray for its welfare? And did not rabbinic tradition decree that the law of the land should be the law of the Jews? "Contemporary Jews who wish to reconcile Jewishness with Swedishness do openly and honestly subscribe to this noble form of particularism," Ehrenpreis wrote. "This composite form of life, which at the same time is our historical destiny and our historical mission, we call the dual loyalty or the dual identity."[9]

Briem, however, had turned the dual loyalty into an accusation. However much the Jews felt at home in the land in which they lived, however much they made its culture and history their own, and however wholeheartedly they shared in its sorrows and joys, they would eventually, "if they are genuine Jews, feel an even greater solidarity with their own people and put its interests, needs, and goals first."[10]

In addition, Briem explained, Jewish particularism was especially provocative and conflict-generating because it was based on the Jews seeing themselves as "the nobility of the earth, who will not only bring the light of true divine knowledge to other peoples but who will also, as God's chosen priests, rule over other peoples."[11] With out-of-context quotations from obscure sources, Briem wanted to prove that the Jews looked down on other peoples and despised them, using them for their own purposes when necessary. Against the narrow-minded particularism of Judaism, he contrasted the "openness and universalism" of the Christian creed.

By the time Ephraim Briem had finished explaining the "innermost core" of antisemitism, he had condemned the Jews of the Diaspora to eternal persecution.

"No other solution seems possible," he concluded.[12]

Ehrenpreis's explanation of the Jewish "chosenness," the particular heritage and mission of the Jewish people, was of course different from Briem's. Chosenness was a burden, not a privilege, as was made abundantly clear at Sinai: "You shall keep all my commandments and my statutes and perform them. Otherwise you will be expelled from the land, the land to which I will bring you and in which I will let you live."[13]

Or in the words of the prophet Amos, "I have chosen you alone out of all the families of the earth; therefore will I also punish you for all your iniquities."[14]

Or in the words of the prophet Amos through the mouth of Marcus Ehrenpreis: "In what way have you earned the right to be chosen? All nations are God's people, each in the place He has assigned to it. Do not delude yourselves that the sun of God will continue to shine on you when it sets on others."[15]

The fact that the children of Israel had been specifically chosen to receive the Law meant only that they had specifically committed themselves to obey it and to be specifically accountable to God for their (mostly imperfect) observance of it. The covenant at Sinai had given the Jewish people a peculiar task, a task that could easily be misunderstood, but it was nonetheless a task for which Jews throughout history had chosen to live and die.

Ehrenpreis was straightforward about the demands of the task. Being Jewish was not an organizational formality, let alone an ethnicity with no substance. To be a Jew was to be the guardian of a spiritual heritage. He was at times critical, even irritated, by what he saw as the lack of substance in Jewish activities in Sweden. In a lecture at the Jewish Club in Stockholm in December 1939, he did not mince words: "For years, your lecture evenings have dealt with subjects that must be considered peripheral: Am I a Jew? Why am I a Jew? What is Judaism? and much else of the same kind." Rather than getting bogged down in peripheral Jewish matters, the people in the audience should "finally open the door to the spiritual home of Judaism, enter its vast halls, one after the other, and partake of its treasures":

> There you will see the prophets of Israel walking, now as then, on the heights of the human spirit, showing us the ways of human progress, of incessant development toward the final goal, which we Jews call the messianic age. And there, now as then, God-inspired poets are giving voice to our Creator and Father and to the indestructible values of life. Jewish self-awareness and humanitarian universalism are here united in an indestructible force of life. [...] The Bible is a book of all humanity, but in a certain sense, historically and religiously, it is a Jewish book.[16]

When the rabbis of the Talmud debated which was the most important saying of the Bible, they settled on Man being created in the image of God. "The awareness of our divine origin," Ehrenpreis clarified, "is the source of both our religion and our morality; from this flows our sense of human dignity and human responsibility, the sense of human obligations that no individual and no people can violate with impunity."[17]

Such was the combination of Jewish self-assertion and humanitarian universalism, according to Ehrenpreis. Judaism's particular world of laws and rules drew its power from a universal vision of God, Man, and the World, and the particular task of the Jewish people was to keep that vision alive. The diaspora, the dispersion, the exile, or whatever one preferred to call the state in which most Jews had lived for over two thousand years, was not a parenthesis in Jewish life but the existential condition of Judaism. In this Ehrenpreisian narrative, the founder of Judaism was not only Moses but also Ezra "the scribe," who on his return from the Babylonian exile to Jerusalem wanted to build "an Israel without a king, without a state, without a temple even, held together only by its Holy Scripture: not a people like any people, but something that has never existed before—'a priestly realm and a holy nation.' Was not Moses *before* David? Was not Sinai *before* Jerusalem?"[18]

That is at least how Ehrenpreis imagined Judaism as he wanted to see it, or rather as he dreamed and hoped it would become.

"Can a people live without a king and without a country?" he has someone in the crowd ask Ezra.

"Israel can and Israel must!" he has Ezra reply.

"Perhaps it will dawn on future generations that the Diaspora is Israel's destiny, Israel's way of life, part of its mission, part of its strength," he has Ezra continue. "Is this unnatural?

Perhaps to others, but not to us. Not everyone is clinging to the earth. Ask the fish if they find it unnatural to live in the water, ask the birds if they find it unnatural to fly in the air?"

Whereupon he has Ezra deliver a clear-cut argument for the cultural Zionism of Marcus Ehrenpreis:

> I want to save the people, not the land. The land is a means, not an end in itself. A dispersed Judaism needs a center for its religion, for its spirit, for its kind. The more we disperse, the more we will need a life-giving point that can bring us together. I want to restore Jerusalem, not as the royal capital, but as the heart of Israel. I will dare what has never been dared before: from the shambles of the Jewish people I will create a spiritual power that will defy the changes of the times. I will build a people without an army, without a state, without a kingdom: *Judaism*.[19]

This was much more Ehrenpreis than Ezra. Actually, this was not Ezra at all. Nowhere in the books of Ezra and Nehemiah, the two books in which Ezra appears and which are both set at the time of the return from Babylonia and the rebuilding of the Temple in Jerusalem, does he say anything even resembling this. The book of Nehemiah tells how Ezra is gathering the people in the square before the Water Gate in Jerusalem to read the Law to them, explaining and interpreting it so that "the people understood what was read," but nowhere is he saying anything about a people without a country or state or temple. On the contrary, both books are filled with the tribulations of temporal and earthly state and temple building. And not least, as Josef Klausner had reminded him, of far-from-universal questions about tribal purity and temple ritual.

When the biblical Ezra rips his clothes and tears his hair, it is not in grief over the cruel edict to dissolve all "intermarriages" and send away all "foreign" women and children, but in grief over the faithlessness of those who have mixed "the holy race" with "the peoples of the land."[20]

In short, it was a literary and theological challenge for Ehrenpreis to extract the timeless and eternal from the temporal and at times terrifying story of Ezra the scribe. In order to make the one compatible with the other, he had to provide Ezra with remorse for the pains that the dissolution of mixed marriages would inflict on people and make him "refuse to pronounce a death sentence on these families, on these women who will become widows, on these innocent children who will become fatherless."

But the book of Ezra is what it is, and Ezra does pronounce what amounts to a death sentence, and Ehrenpreis must somehow fit this into his story of how Ezra wanted to lay the foundation for a Judaism without nation, state, and temple.

"It seems odd," Klausner had noted, that Ehrenpreis would make Ezra the founder of a Judaism without state or temple, and at the same time have him praise Nehemiah for restoring the walls of Jerusalem and "once again providing the Temple with its protective shelter."[21]

What Klausner had put his finger on was the seemingly most contradictory aspect of the Judaism of Marcus Ehrenpreis. On one hand the Diaspora as the existential condition of Judaism, on the other hand the Jewish return to Zion/Palestine as the precondition for the survival of Judaism. The contradiction might not have been obvious from the start, since few had initially imagined that Zion/Palestine would replace the Diaspora, but as the winds of hatred and malice battered the Jews of Europe, the one came to be set against the other.

For a long time, Ehrenpreis had seen no contradiction at all, since his cultural Zionism had not been aimed at saving the Jews (from the Diaspora), but at saving Judaism (in the Diaspora). This was the Zionism he had been advocating at the First Zionist Congress, and this was the Zionism he still believed in. "We must embrace both Palestine and a Diaspora Judaism struggling for its survival," he proclaimed in December 1931, speaking at a Scandinavian Jewish Youth Congress in Stockholm, "We must build with both our hands: with one the new Palestine, with the other the renewed Diaspora!"[22]

Yet the contradiction was being pressed upon him. Ephraim Briem was not alone in thinking that "as long as the Jews continue to live among other peoples without giving up their national distinctiveness," they must put up with "the suffering that goes under the dismal name of antisemitism. No other solution seems possible."[23]

Nor did any other solution seem possible for the Zionist movement that wanted to liberate the Jews from the Diaspora and make them a people like all the others. The controversy with Klausner about Ezra was ultimately about the nature of Judaism. For Klausner in Jerusalem, Judaism was historically inscribed in a national and territorial narrative from which it could not extricate itself. For Ehrenpreis in Stockholm, postbiblical Judaism had inscribed itself in a new narrative in which the national and territorial element (Jerusalem, Zion) had taken on an allegorical meaning. "Next year in Jerusalem" did not mean next year on a temple mount in Judea. It meant next year in a messianically redeemed world.

Hence, a heroic figure in the Judaism of Marcus Ehrenpreis was Yohanan ben Sakkai, a learned Pharisee who at the Roman destruction of Jerusalem had smuggled himself out of the city together with a Torah scroll, for the purpose of founding a Judaism without Jerusalem. In *Helige och hjältar som byggt Israel* (Saints and Heroes), from 1931, Ehrenpreis puts his vision of a nonnational and nonterritorial Judaism in the mouth of ben Sakkai:

> Farewell Yerushalayim [Jerusalem]! I leave you forever. Your day has come to an end. I leave you to build a new Yerushalayim. In place of an earthly city that cannot be saved, I will establish a spiritual Yerushalayim, which will reach across the earth to resist the forces of destruction. Not a city that can be destroyed, not a temple that can be burned to the ground—but a faith, a doctrine, a spiritual power that no one and nothing can destroy.[24]

It was not hard to see how the vision of a nonnational and nonterritorial Judaism would come to be at odds with a Zionist movement feverishly bent on territorial Jewish nation-building, and perhaps even more so with the rapidly hardening conditions of Jewish life in the Diaspora.

In early August 1937, Marcus and Esther Ehrenpreis were invited to the twentieth World Zionist Congress in Zurich to celebrate the fortieth anniversary of the First Congress in Basel. In a train decorated with Hebrew plates the delegates were taken from Zurich to a special jubilee gathering in Basel, where Marcus Ehrenpreis in his presentation was pressed to explain, defend, and temporarily withdraw from the nonnational and nonterritorial Judaism he still deep down believed in:

> To you, the generation of 1937, I dare not bring the prophetic call, Not with hosts, not with might, but

> with the spirit. I myself, like a large part of my generation, still believe that this will happen one day, that this is our future, our destiny, the meaning of our existence, that we live and suffer and struggle to fulfill this prophecy. Yet I know that at this moment this prophetic call is entirely untimely. I know as well as you do the catastrophic conditions under which we all live and work in this demoralized age of cruelty, reckless power, and barbarism. And I fully know that in times like these a new life cannot be built without the support of material and physical power. But when we, the generation of 1897, to our great sorrow hear that some of you are turning the prophetic call on its head, saying, Not by the spirit, but by hosts and might only—then we must raise our voices. Such a way of thinking is as unhistorical as it is un-Jewish. What is Zion to us without the Teaching of Zion?[25]

Ehrenpreis's speech did not make any waves in the debate. The Zionist movement was intensely preoccupied with acute national and territorial issues, this summer with a British proposal (put forth by the Peel Commission) to divide Palestine into a Jewish and an Arab state and thus put limits on the territory for Jewish colonization, to which the Zurich congress had expressed opposition. Upon his return, the Swedish delegate, Hugo Valentin, explained that what the Congress had demanded was a territory large enough to accommodate at least "one-third of the Jews who otherwise, humanly speaking, were doomed to destruction."[26]

Inexorably then, the Jewish path of Marcus Ehrenpreis was being blocked by nation and territory, might and host, defamation and persecution.

Marcus and Esther Ehrenpreis as guests of honor at the twentieth World Zionist Congress in Zurich, August 1937, on the fortieth anniversary of the first congress in Basel (front row, fourth and fifth from the right).

Who could still believe in the spiritual destiny and mission of the Jewish people?

Or in the cultural and spiritual blessings of Israel's encounters with the nations?

Or in a world where minorities and majorities would live in peace side by side, like the wolf and the lamb in Isaiah?

Against the rapidly darkening horizons of Europe, the messianic element in the Judaism of Marcus Ehrenpreis becomes increasingly visible.

Messianism is a central element in Judaism, as it is in Christianity. Without messianism there is no Messiah ("the anointed one" in Hebrew), and without the Messiah there is no Christ ("the anointed one" in Greek). In Christianity, the

Messiah has already come in the form of Jesus of Nazareth, with all its implications for Christian life and thought. In Judaism, the Messiah has yet to come, and Jewish life and thought cannot be imagined without the anticipation, at times acute, of the coming of the Messiah and the redemption of the world. When Ehrenpreis in a 1948 radio address was asked to declare in what he believed, he quoted the twelfth principle of Moses Maimonides: "I believe in the coming of the Messiah, and even if he tarries, I will be waiting daily that he shall come."[27]

What did Ehrenpreis mean by the coming of the Messiah? And what did Judaism mean?

What Judaism meant the rabbis in the Talmudic tradition had a hard time sorting out, and at times a hard time reining in, since Jesus of Nazareth was not the first and not the last Messiah in Jewish history. Some of the latter, Sabbatai Zvi in the seventeenth century and Jacob Frank in the eighteenth century, had sparked ecstatic revivals and created chaos and division in large parts of Jewish Europe. Messianism was an inexhaustible source of hope and joy in Jewish life, a shining horizon that gave meaning to the most agonizing Jewish trials and sufferings, but the promise of a coming Messiah was also a source of self-destructive eruptions of acute expectations of its imminent fulfillment.

Maimonides devoted much effort to taming the messianic impulse within Judaism: the temptation, at times hard to resist, to move from timeless expectation to historical fulfillment. Maimonides sought to downplay the expectations of fulfillment: "Let no one think that in the days of the Messiah anything will change in the natural course of the world, or that anything new will be introduced into Creation. No, the world order will remain as it has been. [...] The Messiah comes solely to make peace in the world. [...] How all this will happen no one knows until it happens."[28]

To Maimonides, faith in the Messiah was about approaching God in the world "as it is." To live a righteous, Jewish, everyday life was to prepare for the coming of the Messiah every day. As in the Talmudic story of Rabbi Joshua ben Levi, who meets the Messiah in the guise of an ailing beggar at the gates of Rome and asks him when he will come. "Today," the Messiah replies to the bewilderment of Rabbi Joshua.

"Today, if you all will hear his voice," the Messiah adds.

The Messiah will come when the reign of the Messiah is a fact.

Who needs to wait for the Messiah when the lambs are lying down with the wolves?

The messianism of Ehrenpreis was squarely in the spirit of Maimonides. The messianic prophets were "no dim-eyed fantasists, no dreamers out of touch with reality. [...] They firmly believed in the possibility of a more rational and better world order. [...] What they sought was both reasonable and possible."[29]

Thus Marcus Ehrenpreis spoke in his Passover sermon in the Great Synagogue of Stockholm in April 1940. Hitler's armies had just occupied Norway and Denmark and were standing at the borders of Sweden, and it seemed almost reasonable to express the belief in a more rational and better world in messianic terms:

> God has created wolves and lambs, strong and weak, great powers and small. Who gives the strong the right to destroy the weak? Why should the weak not be able to live their lives, to contribute to the progress of mankind according to their means and powers? [...] The

lamb cannot in the long run withstand the supremacy of the wolf. But the faith of the prophet is unshakable: *The time will come when the wolf shall live with the lamb.*[30]

During the early years in Lemberg and Berlin, the messianic idea in the Judaism of Marcus Ehrenpreis had been closely interwoven with intense Jewish hopes for a renewal of the world "as it is." The rebirth of Hebrew literature, the awakening of the Jewish soul, the renaissance of Judaism, the Jewish return to Zion, these were all dreams and expectations that could all too easily be merged into a messianically charged narrative of the fulfillment of Jewish destiny in a dawning age of universal peace and brotherhood. For a brief moment, there also seemed to be a messianic figure in Ehrenpreis's life, Theodor Herzl, "a man of royal stature, both in the grandeur of his appearance and the nobility of his soul."[31]

However, apart from the fact that Ehrenpreis would soon clash with Herzl on the ends and means of Zionism, he remained fundamentally averse to personal and extra-historical interpretations of the messianic prophecies. The reign of the Messiah was a reign of this world, not of a world beyond time and space, and the Messiah was an allegorical figure, not a physical person. When he invoked the messianic prophecies, it was in support of indeed utopian but nevertheless earthly proposals for the betterment of the world "as it is"; a league of world religions, international treaties to protect minorities against majorities, universal disarmament and peace. At times it was difficult to see what distinguished Ehrenpreis's Jewish messianism from the secular progressivism of his time and its plethora of visions for a new and better world.

But the difference did not rest in the vision. The difference rested in God.

In the visions of secular progressivism there was no place for God.

Much less so for God in the course of human history.

In the messianic vision of Ehrenpreis there was both a God and a divine course of history.

Increasingly so, the more godless and aimless the course of history appeared to be.

In November 1939, God entered firmly into Marcus Ehrenpreis's rendering of the course of history, or more precisely into his attempt to explain a course of events that was making it increasingly difficult to imagine any presence of God whatsoever.

Where was God in Auschwitz? was the question that would ultimately emerge, and Ehrenpreis's answer would steadfastly remain the same: there is a higher meaning also in the seemingly most destructive and meaningless of historical events.

For Ehrenpreis, to answer otherwise would have been to abandon what he regarded as Judaism's most important contribution to human thought, the idea of the moral development of humankind and the fulfillment of God's creation. The faith in a direction and a purpose to human existence was to him a cornerstone in the Jewish tradition, and the origin of the concept of history as such. "What we mean by history is fundamentally a religious concept, and its emergence in biblical Israel is intimately connected with the biblical concept of God," Ehrenpreis preached in the dark fall of 1939 to assure his congregation that God was present even when this was hard to see:

> What we mean by history is, in fact, that there is coherence, consistency, a law-bound plan, and, above all,

> justice in the apparently confused, capricious, incomprehensible course of events. [...] The prophets' teachings about the course of history are borne by their firm belief in the evolution of human existence—that the path of history is the path from the primitive to the perfect, from cruelty to refinement, from war to peace, which is what we call messianism. Israel's historical belief is that the perfection of humanity is not behind us but before us—at the end of time [...]. This upward path is rich in obstacles and inhibitions, it is beset with stumbling blocks of various kinds, human weakness, cowardice, and evil. From time to time there are interruptions, sometimes we deviate from the path we have marked out, sometimes we are pushed back by destructive forces—but the path goes forward; we have come a long way and we are moving on toward the goal. This is Israel's messianism, the culmination of the biblical idea of the meaning of history.[32]

In this perspective, even all-destroying catastrophes, historical cataclysms, as Ehrenpreis called them, could be given a higher meaning. When "the Lord and the world come into conflict with each other [...] the higher power intervenes to restore order from chaos. A rotten world must make way for a new world, sounder and better."[33] The sufferings and devastations brought about by every such cataclysm could be likened to birth pangs. The Hebrew term *Chevlei Mashiach*, the birth pangs of Messiah, denoted the particularly severe trials and torments that were to precede the coming of the Messiah.

Jewish history had no lack of trials and torments that could be interpreted as the birth pangs of Messiah. The messianic eruption of Sabbatai Zvi followed upon another devastating disaster in the history of eastern European Jewry, the Chmielnicki Massacre of 1648, when tens of thousands of Jews in today's Ukraine, Lithuania, and Poland were murdered, and hundreds of Jewish villages were ransacked.

Ehrenpreis did not say that the present Jewish disaster might be the birth pangs of a new messianic age, but he did his utmost to save the Jewish faith in the divine purpose and meaning of history from the impact of its most severe test ever. This looming historic cataclysm, too, however unfathomable, was part of an endless chain of events, "stretching from eternity to eternity," in which destruction would always be followed by renewal. "A deluge is once again laying waste to large parts of our earth, and once again there will be those who, like Noah and his family, will survive the devastation in order to rebuild what has been destroyed."[34]

Perhaps Ehrenpreis was still hoping that the Jews in the far north would find a place in the ark when the sea rose above the earth, and perhaps that is why he allowed himself to speak in such abstract, messianic terms about a catastrophe that he very well knew would destroy the greater part of European Jewry. Gone was a messianism that had been able to glimpse, at least for a brief moment, a higher meaning in some promising events of history. In its place came a messianism that had to find a higher meaning of history in yet another cataclysm, a messianism for the chosen few who would walk out of the ark "to build a better and happier world in a purer air under a clearer sky."[35]

It was a messianism of despair, of course, one of unspeakable suffering and death to make for a better world, and a horrible price to pay for saving God in history.

So why save God in history? Especially since a number of Jewish thinkers of Ehrenpreis's generation had been hard at work trying to save God *from* history, not least after the cataclysm that Europe had just gone through, the First World War. That God could have had an ever-so-unfathomable finger in such a devastating and meaningless historical event was increasingly hard to believe. If Jewish messianism were to have any meaning, God must be rescued from the course of events.

The Jewish thinker who most interestingly tried to do so was the young Franz Rosenzweig, who from an antiaircraft post in Macedonia during the First World War began to write his philosophical magnum opus *Der Stern der Erlösung* (*The Star of Redemption*), in which he attempted to save the messianic hope in the world "as it is" by freeing it from all expectations of history; the messianic time was not a historical time, and the messianic era was not a historical era. In historical time, each day was a stepping stone to tomorrow; in messianic time, each day was a stepping stone to eternity.[36] The reign of the Messiah was a reign in messianic time, a reign that could establish itself at any moment as a spark in historical time and shed on it a light of eternity. Or as Rosenzweig beautifully put it:

> [The reign of God] is always as much here as it is in the future. It is forever not yet here. It is forever to come. Eternity is not a very long time, but a tomorrow that might also be today. Eternity is a future that—without ceasing to be future—is nevertheless also a present. Eternity is a today [*ein Heute*] that knows that it is more than a today.[37]

Whatever historical time might hold, and after the war Rosenzweig knew it could hold anything, it had nothing to do with the messianic time—and therefore nothing to do with God. The task of the Jewish people (the covenant, the chosenness) was to bear witness to the eternal presence of a messianic time measured by what *ought to be*, in contrast to a historical time measured by *what is*. Rosenzweig's messianism was a messianism in defiance of history; the ever-existing possibility at every moment in history to assert right against might, and thus at every moment an existing possibility to prepare the world for the coming of the Messiah. Rosenzweig's messianism was a call for eternal preparation, not a promise of historical fulfillment.

The ambition of Rosenzweig to liberate messianism from the expectations of history also made him a critic of Zionism, since in Zionism there was a promise of historical fulfillment that all too easily could be rendered a messianic interpretation. In the Jewish return to Palestine, even self-declared secular Zionists could be tempted to see if not the hand of God, then still the higher meaning of history, and if not the portending of the messianic age, then still the portending of a new and better world.

But to Rosenzweig, as to Ehrenpreis, Jews were not a people like any other, nor could they become one without giving up their spiritual destiny and undermining the very meaning of Judaism. To both Rosenzweig and Ehrenpreis, the Diaspora was the existential condition of the Jewish destiny, and both were critical of a Zionism that wanted to make the Jewish return to Palestine the fulfillment of that destiny.

Rosenzweig died all too young, in 1929, at a time when it still seemed possible to imagine a future for Jews and Judaism in Europe. In 1920 Rosenzweig had founded a Jewish teaching house, Lehrhaus, in Frankfurt, with the purpose of bringing Germany's assimilated Jews into renewed contact with the spiritual roots of Judaism, and with the founding of *Judisk Tidskrift* in 1928 Ehrenpreis had hoped to achieve something similar with his "detached" Swedish Jews. Both projects were conceived at a time when the Jews of the Diaspora were still physically present enough to be envisioned as a "people of eternity," *das ewige Volk*, whose destiny it was to perpetuate a messianic light of divine law and justice over the godless course of history.

Only a few years after Rosenzweig's death, the godless course of history was set on stamping out the very bearers of the messianic light, and consigning any idea for the renewal of diasporic Judaism to the dustbin of history. All while the question of God in history returned with a vengeance.

Why did Marcus Ehrenpreis want to preserve God in history? After all, in the Jewish tradition there was also a God who had withdrawn from the world, diminished his presence in it, having left Man to take responsibility for God's creation. In the Kabbalah there was the concept of *tzimtzum*, shrinking or diminishing, to denote God's withdrawal. Ehrenpreis, who had written his doctoral thesis on the Kabbalah, must have been well aware of all the Jewish venues that existed for keeping God out of history.

God, who had hidden his face from Man.

God, who had placed his destiny in the hands of Man.

God who had left Man a shattered world to mend (*tikkun olam*).

So why did Ehrenpreis insist on God's presence, even in the most unfathomable and unbearable of historical events?

Perhaps because he, in this dire moment for Judaism, had to be more rabbi than philosopher, more prophet than politician. There was, as Ehrenpreis saw it, no rescue for the German Jewry, nor for the Polish Jewry, and therefore no rescue for that European-Jewish world into which he had been born and for which he had had such great hopes and plans. At this point, to give up on God in history would have been to give up on too much. It would have been to give up on everything he had believed and said and written throughout his life. It would have been to give up on Isaiah and Amos and Job's wrestling with God, it would have been to give up on the power of the spirit over the sword, it would have been to give up on the messianic promise of a new and better world. How could there be a promise of a new and better world if the course of history was set by godless and meaningless chance? If the philosophers and theologians had long since been forced to confront the problem of theodicy—how to reconcile God's omnipotence and justice with the evils of the world—Ehrenpreis chose to make God's hand visible even in the most evil of historical circumstances.

In May 1940, as Hitler's armies were standing at the borders of Sweden (and soon would be allowed to transit troops across them), he felt compelled to prepare his young confirmands for the worst—and to make them see a meaning in that too:

> Out of the ravaging fire that is spreading over a whole world, that crushes countries and peoples, that throws kings from their thrones and turns flourishing youngsters into heaps of corpses, out of a fire that threatens to destroy a whole generation, we sense the voice of God, the call of God to us all. [...] The Lord is testing us as he tested Abraham, testing our strength, our courage, testing whether we are prepared for the sacrifices that are necessary. [...] Perhaps, Israel has not yet fulfilled its task in world history. Perhaps the task will be there for us when the storm has subsided, and a happier tomorrow is dawning, and a rejuvenated humanity is preparing to build a new, peaceful, and happy home for mankind on

> the ruins of a shattered world [...]. Your path, my dearest, will be a path between worlds, between a decrepit world that is perishing and a new world that is being born to life in distress and agony.[38]

Perhaps Marcus Ehrenpreis had to hold on to his belief in God in history for his own sake as well, to provide meaning to the personal pain and despair he must have felt at the devastation of the world in which most of his family still lived, and the friends of his childhood and youth, and the people and organizations and congregations with whom he had come into close personal contact over the years, and whose increasingly desperate pleas for help were now piling up on his desk in Stockholm.

Already in 1937, on the tenth anniversary of *Judisk Tidskrift*, Ehrenpreis had voiced his sense of inadequacy and powerlessness in the face of what was happening. He was nearly seventy, physically weakened and with declining eyesight, which may have affected his mood, but his memory and intellect were as sharp as ever, and he could not suppress his frustration with not having been able to make himself better heard and understood in his new *Kinderland*.

> More than once, I was overcome by the dark mood expressed by the unknown prophet in Babylon in the words: "Why was no one there when I came? Why was there no one to answer when I called?" It is the most agonizing of disappointments. You call out loud and clear, and you call again and again, but there is no answer, your voice does not resonate.[39]

A love unrequited. A Judaism besmirched.
Wherever God might be, History was running its course.

Visiting Marcus's family in Lemberg in the summer of 1933. None of the people surrounding Marcus and Esther in the photo—Marcus's sisters, brothers-in-law, and nieces—would survive the Holocaust. At the far right is the poet and writer Debora Vogel, daughter of Marcus's sister Lea (next to Debora).

8.

MALACHI'S CALL TO THE WORLD

I am a Jew. Hath not a Jew eyes? Hath not a Jew hands, organs, dimensions, senses, affections, passions? Fed with the same food, hurt with the same weapons, subject to the same diseases, healed by the same means, warmed and cooled by the same winter and summer, as a Christian is? If you prick us, do we not bleed?

—WILLIAM SHAKESPEARE, *The Merchant of Venice*

Passover of 1933 fell on 11 April. It was a Tuesday, and on its front page *Svenska Dagbladet* could report a "brightening" in the situation of Jewish lawyers in Germany. The brightening consisted in the exemption of Jewish lawyers who had served as front soldiers in the First World War from the ban on Jewish lawyers from state employment. Only a few days earlier, the new Nazi regime had banned from employment not only Jewish lawyers but all Jews employed by state-controlled institutions. Only a few days before that, the Nazi Party had organized a boycott of Jewish-owned shops and announced public burnings of "Jewish" books, making no secret of its intention to turn the Jews of Germany into outlaws in their own country. The same front page would also report that Fredrik Böök would be traveling to Germany to assess the situation there "without preconceived notions" and without shying away from "the burning question of the relationship between the new German state and the Jewish race."

That same morning, Marcus Ehrenpreis delivered his Passover sermon in the Great Synagogue of Stockholm with no brightening whatsoever in sight. Nor did he have to wait for Fredrik Böök's assessment of the situation in Germany to know what the expulsion of the Jews from German society meant, not only for the Jews but for the entire "Christian" civilization to which Germany had seemed to belong.

"The whole world trembles at the prospect of the human race sinking back into the barbarism of the Middle Ages," Ehrenpreis called out to his congregation.

"Have we not all *one* Father? Have we not all been created by *one* God?" he had the prophet Malachi call out to the world. "No one can be indifferent to this call. No one can avoid answering it. He who does not answer consents, promotes evil, becomes an accessory to the tragedy now unfolding."[1]

It was a long and emotional sermon, in which Ehrenpreis wove together the persecution of the Jews in Hitler's Germany with the persecution of the Jews in Pharaoh's Egypt, and the air in the synagogue was saturated with anxiety.

> In this hour of bewilderment, I sensed that these worried men and women were waiting for a word of guidance, a word that could alleviate the unbearable pressure on them. I myself was gripped as rarely before, I felt the need to cry out my resentment and despair. Passionately, the words tumbled out of my mind, without any consideration for the rules of preaching. The emotion in the people assembled was unmistakable. They left the synagogue somber and serious.[2]

Outside the synagogue, waiting in the courtyard, was Gustaf Stridsberg, the editor of *Svenska Dagbladet*, who, "almost tearful," pressed Ehrenpreis's hand, "as if to apologize that Christian people could behave so shamefully toward the Jews."[3]

In an initial moment of shock, the world appeared to have heard the call of Malachi. In country after country declarations were made stating that the attack on the Jews in Germany was not only a matter for the Jews, nor only a matter for Germany. On 1 April 1933, *Dagens Nyheter* characterized the events in Germany as "a crime against civilization," and the following day, in the same newspaper, a member of the Swedish Supreme Court, Nils Alexanderson, characterized the dismissal of Jewish judges "as a stab in the heart of the [Western] constitutional state."

"One almost fears that our species is sliding back into barbarism," the local daily *Eskilstuna-Kuriren* wrote on 3 April.

"A purer form of barbarism cannot be imagined," the local daily *Oscarshamns Nyheter* chimed in.

"This is a barbarism which hardly had any equivalent, even in the Middle Ages," the local daily *Östersunds Länstidning* added.

On 26 April, a Christian manifesto against antisemitism was published in several Swedish newspapers. Among the signatories were bishops, pastors, priests, professors, editors, and writers. "He Who Does Not Denounce Antisemitism Denies His Master," read the headline over three columns on the front page of *Dagens Nyheter*:

> The undersigned see it as their inescapable duty to express their concern and anguish in the face of the antisemitic movement, and to appeal to Swedish Christians of all denominations to assert the human

> dignity and brotherly love of Christ against racial hatred [...]. There is no time to lose. The coercive power of mass delusion is not yet upon us. Free speech is not yet restricted. The gospel of truth and love can still ring out.[4]

The time was quickly lost. Soon enough, the unthinkable was normalized. The gospel of truth and love was drowned in antisemitic propaganda, and the claim that the Jews were to blame for their own persecution rapidly gained traction.

When the text of the sermon was published as a booklet under the title *Malachis rop till tiden* (Malachi's call to the times), it was reviewed by the professor of classical languages in Gothenburg, Vilhelm Lundström, who began by stating that this Jewish sermon was among the most moving texts he had ever read. He thereafter did his utmost to cast doubts on what it had to say. Was the blame for the persecution of the Jews on the Germans only? Lundström asked. Didn't he personally know of several "men of high moral and cultural standing" in both Germany and Austria who had unanimously testified before him that the persecution of the Jews in Germany was aimed at curbing "an undue and pernicious, nationally and morally corrupting Jewish influence"? He even went on to reproach Ehrenpreis for not having used his Passover sermon to scold the Jews as well: "One may listen with admiration and approval to the words of the Jewish preacher and yet ask oneself: Is there not something missing? Is there not missing what the prophets of the Old Testament never lacked: a word of warning and reprimand, a word of punishment and judgment against their own people?"[5]

If Ehrenpreis had not yet completely given up on the power of the word, he must have felt a pang of despair at such a review. In a written response to Lundström published in *Judisk*

Tidskrift together with the review itself, Ehrenpreis pointed out that a time of anti-Jewish book burnings, boycotts, and purges was perhaps not the right moment for a Jewish rabbi to pass judgment on his own people: "When a boy is half-beaten to death by his brutalized mates and hovers between life and death, it is hardly the time for a father to admonish him."[6]

The response of Ehrenpreis was tinged with a tone of bewilderment, or of suppressed desolation perhaps. How was it possible that a highly educated man like Lundström could embrace the Nazi propaganda accusing the Jews of being guilty of their own persecution? He still wanted to believe that with people like Lundström it was possible to argue with facts, although he now had to argue in a climate where even the most obvious facts had to be stated and the most basic human rights defended: "We Jews certainly do not believe that we are faultless, and we do certainly have words of admonition for those among us who are prepared to listen. But what we most reasonably are asking of the world is that we, like all other peoples, shall have the right to live."[7]

The futility of facts was soon to manifest itself anew, in the form of Fredrik Böök's reports from Hitler's Germany in May and June 1933. They made perfectly clear that Ehrenpreis's traveling companion to Jerusalem, the concerned observer of the Jewish plight in eastern Europe, the enthusiastic supporter of the Zionist project in Palestine, and the self-proclaimed friend of the well-adjusted Swedish Jewry had turned into a propagandist for the Nazi regime. In any case, he was now parroting the Nazi claim that Germany's "war on the Jews" was a response to the war of the Jews on Germany, and that German antisemitism was a response to Jewish "anti-Germanism," and that "the breaking of the overpowering Jewish influence in the public cultural life of Germany [...] *was a necessary and inevitable act of self-defense*" (emphasis mine). This was said to happen in a country where self-identified Jews constituted one percent of the population, of which an increasing number identified more as Germans than as Jews, and it thus would take a heavy dose of alternative facts to paint the Jews as a threat to Germany. The undisputed assumption underpinning Böök's "unprejudiced" reports on the "relationship between the new German state and the Jewish race" was the "fact," propagated by the Hitler regime, that the Jews were an alien and harmful element that had to be expelled from German society.

Consequently, Böök knew how to inform his readers about the degrading influence of German Jews on German culture: "Neither German literature and learning nor German public opinion, can in the long run be left in the hands of Jewish power." To the "conscious threat of Jewish anti-Germanism," Böök also knew to add "the unconscious corruption of true German culture by cultural Semitism." The international reaction of shock and horror to the anti-Jewish measures in Germany, Böök explained away as the result of "talented" Jewish propaganda.[8]

Böök's captivation by the anti-Jewish rage in Nazi Germany became, if possible, even more pronounced on the night of 10–11 May 1933, when he witnessed the burning of "Jewish" and other "anti-German" books outside the University of Berlin. From his vantage point, on a balcony on the second floor of the Dresdner Bank building, he could feel the hot gusts from the bonfire on his face and hear the cheers and applause from the crowd, as one author after another was thrown onto the flames, and observe "the omnipresent Dr. Goebbels, smiling and optimistic in the midst of his restless work." When an American banker on the balcony reacted by saying that he was witnessing "something unprecedented since the Middle Ages," Böök could assure him "that no irreplaceable treasures were lost here [...] and that the solemn burning of displeasing writings was a venerable tradition in the world of German students." From his balcony, Fredrik Böök had no problem joining in the cheers and applause: "Fire is a purifying element, and the midnight bonfire in front of the university will undoubtedly have many effects that only the desiccated specialist, the rigid aesthetic expert, should be inclined to deplore."[9]

When Böök's newspaper reports from Hitler's Germany were published as a book,[10] his assertions about "the Jews" were patiently scrutinized by Simon Aberstén, first librarian in Gothenburg and a frequent contributor to *Judisk Tidskrift.* No, it was not true that "nine-tenths of all the filth in German literature and art" came from the Jews. No, it was not true that "almost every German village" had had an "intimate experience of the Jewish usurer." No, it was not possible for Böök to know in which voice "the Jews in unguarded moments spoke about peasants, craftsmen, and workers." As Aberstén remarked, this would have required the author to have "a hearing comparable to that of Heimdall, the Nordic god who could hear the grass grow."[11]

Yet in Aberstén's refutation of Böök's allegations, there was a tone of resignation as well. How to argue with a member of the distinguished Swedish Academy who could see a bright future in the burning of books? The seemingly cultivated and educated Böök had suddenly become an *advocatus diaboli* ready to defend "his criminal client" by whatever lies and half-truths.

A tsunami of lies and half-truths that no factual arguments could stem was now sweeping over the Jews of Europe.

Ehrenpreis would have to get used to this.
Get used to arguing with a tsunami.
Get used to the futility of words.

Ehrenpreis would never get used to it. The power of the word was the foundation of everything he had believed in and fought for. The power of the word was the power of the Prophets. The power of the word was the power of the spirit. The power of the word was the power of the *ought to* of the Law against the *what is* of Nature. When, in the summer of 1934, he traveled to Bern to testify in the trial against the publishers of *The Protocols of the Elders of Zion*, it was the power of the word that he put his trust in. For a brief moment, he fantasized that the ruling of the court had opened the eyes of the world: "In Bern, this phantasmagoric work of fiction evaporated like smoke. The sinister network, so scrupulously fabricated by the protocols, was torn asunder like a spider's web. The two days in court undid for all the world what thirty years of lies and propaganda had created."[12]

The world took no notice, however. *The Protocols of the Elders of Zion*, with Nazi Germany as its all-powerful purveyor, continued to whip up anti-Jewish sentiment all over Europe, and soon the very word *Jew* became poisoned with malice. In October 1933, only a few months after the boycotts and book burnings and the purge of Jews from the German state apparatus, an appeal for assistance to "intellectuals exiled from Germany" appeared in several Swedish newspapers. At the top of the list of signatories were Princes Eugen and Wilhelm of the royal family, followed by prominent representatives of the Swedish elite: bishops, professors, governors, doctors, lawyers, writers, editors, artists, military officers, academics. The brief appeal described how "the political upheavals in Europe" had forced thousands of people to flee Germany, people who "in many cases had been among the most eminent in society" and had made important contributions to "our shared European culture," and argued that an international effort should therefore be made "to enable them to reside abroad for the time being to pursue their life's work."[13]

At the same time, the people behind the appeal were careful to point out that this wasn't necessarily "about trying to make a place for these exiles in our own country, where unemployment is such a big problem."

In what country they would find that place was not made clear.

Nor was it made clear that the vast majority of the "intellectuals exiled from Germany" were Jews.

The word *Jew* did not appear in the appeal.

In its efforts to commit Sweden to nothing and to antagonize nobody, including Hitler, the appeal was a foreboding of the Evian Conference in the summer of 1938 and the collapse of an internationally coordinated effort to provide asylum to the persecuted and ostracized Jews of Hitler's Germany and Austria.

Evian in the summer of 1938. Soon enough.

A more outspoken protest against the persecution of the Jews in Germany, though not public, was a letter written on 4 April 1933 by the president of the Swedish Red Cross, Prince Carl, brother of King Gustaf V, to the still president of Germany, Marshal General Paul von Hindenburg. When the letter was made public after the war, Prince Carl revealed that it had been prompted by an appeal from "the Swedish Chief Rabbi, Professor Marcus Ehrenpreis [...] urging me to do whatever I could do to make the German government treat the Jews more fairly and put an end to the pogroms."[14] It was Prince Carl's wife, Princess Ingeborg, who had invited Ehrenpreis to her home a year earlier to learn about the Talmud. In his letter to Hindenburg, Prince Carl reminded the former commander-in-chief of Germany what the Swedish Red Cross had done for millions of German prisoners of war during the First World War to ensure their humane treatment, and that the same should now apply to the Jewish population in Germany:

> I urge Your Excellency to do whatever is in your power to save the world from the depressing spectacle of racial persecution among a German people admired for its high level of culture. Believe me, Your Excellency, this will do more harm than you may imagine to the German Empire and to the German people, for whom I have had the deepest sympathies since my youth.[15]

The answer came from Hitler's office, not from Hindenburg, and was a piece of propaganda.

The futility of words, once again.

Ehrenpreis never lost his penchant for traveling, and the leadership of the congregation in Stockholm had gotten used to the chief rabbi packing his suitcases every now and then. "Next to books, travel was my most passionate hobby," he confessed toward the end of his life. "The art of travel is to widen your field of vision, to learn how to compare and discern, to sharpen your eye for the essential. As you in sixty years travel through three continents—without a Baedeker, without a guide, without museum catalogues, and above all without the persistent ambition to see *everything* in the province or city you are visiting—then *something* of the meaning of the world slowly reveals itself to you."[16]

Even as the meaning of the world became increasingly difficult to discern, Ehrenpreis continued to travel. In the summer of 1933 he traveled with Esther to the city of his childhood and youth, Lemberg, which was now called Lwów and was part of Poland. A photo from the visit shows the two of them surrounded by Marcus's three sisters, Lea (Lonja), Maryam (Marinja), and Gittel (Gusta). The photo also shows the lawyer David Maltz, the husband of Maryam, together with their son Edin and his wife Edit. On the far right, next to Lea, is Lea's daughter, the poet and writer Debora (Dvojra) Vogel.

None of the family members surrounding Marcus and Esther in the photo would survive the cataclysm.

When, much later, Marcus Ehrenpreis reminisced about the journey in the summer of 1933, it was not the family reunion in Lemberg he remembered. The event that "in an illuminating glow" had stayed in his memory was an excursion to "the interior of the Eastern Carpathians," to the wild mountainous regions south of Lemberg, to follow in the footsteps of Baal Shem Tov, the founder of the Hasidic movement. "In a landscape of untouched wilderness, the enigma of Baal Shem dawned on me," Ehrenpreis wrote. "Here, where there are no words, where no human voice is heard in the eloquence of cosmos, here is where visions are born."[17]

The romantic gaze was the inseparable travel companion of Marcus Ehrenpreis. Wherever he traveled, he saw more than met the eye; a flow of biblical associations and historical references colored the places he visited. He could be quick, perhaps too quick, to discern qualities and characteristics in people. "What you discover when you travel is not the common but the peculiar, that which constitutes the richness and diversity

Marcus and Esther Ehrenpreis walking in their beloved Karlsbad, summer 1935.

of life, [...] the more landscapes you experience, the more cultures you encounter, the more people with their different ways of life you get to know, the more lives you live."[18]

Maybe this was a way for Ehrenpreis to provide his lust for travel with a philosophy of sorts, but more likely, his lust for travel served to reinforce a philosophy that was already there: a deep faith in the messianic potential of encounters between peoples and cultures:

> After a long life, I have found that universalism and nationalism are two forces necessary to build our lives. One without the other is evil. It will tear down instead of building up. In the course of traveling through the world, preserving your own historical distinctiveness,

> you will become something of a citizen of the world. If you have been brought up to follow the basic religious precepts of the relationship between human and human, if you have learned that a stranger is not inferior because he is different, if you have become accustomed to taking a clear view of the world, then you are cured of ingrained prejudices, of religious and racial hatred, of conceit and mistrust, then you are a human among humans.[19]

When Ehrenpreis wrote this in 1946, the European world that he had crisscrossed back and forth was in ruins—and his messianic philosophy of travel had become a defiant declaration of faith.

Ehrenpreis was not a hardship-seeking traveler, at least not as soon as his position allowed for some comfort. He liked to travel in style, staying at good hotels and exploring the world in hat, vest, and spats. His international network was extensive, and wherever he went, doors opened and excursions and dinners were arranged. In a combination of weakened health and undiminished wanderlust, his travels in the 1930s were increasingly to be combined with sojourns in venerable Habsburg health resorts. In the few years left for travel in Europe, the spa stays in Karlovy Vary together with Esther would become a tradition, just as it would become a tradition of sorts that the spa stays in Karlovy Vary would be interrupted by urgent calls for participation in the fight for "the honor of Israel."

In the summer of 1935, it had to be interrupted for a meeting in the nearby spa town of Marienbad to discuss a Jewish effort to awaken world opinion. Among the Jewish personalities arriving at the magnificently situated Café Egerländer was the writer Stefan Zweig. When previously, Zweig had been asked by *Judisk Tidskrift* to provide a comment on the "state of world Jewry," he had kindly declined, arguing that it would be to no avail for Jews to act on their own behalf. Zweig thought of himself more as a European than a Jew, and for yet some time he wanted to believe that Europe was teeming with good Europeans like himself. When Ehrenpreis had met Zweig in London the year before, the only rigidity that he could detect in him was "his belief in a European man."[20]

By the time of the Marienbad meeting, Zweig had learned that the good Europeans were few and far between, and he was now ready to join an initiative in which Jews indeed would act on their own behalf. Or, as Ehrenpreis put it, "his sense of solidarity with the suffering Israel had awakened."[21]

In August that same year, Ehrenpreis traveled to a Zionist Congress for the first time in twenty-eight years. He had been invited as a guest of honor and had agreed to attend, since he sensed that the gravity of the moment had dampened "the fruitless" battles over the aims and means of Zionism, and mellowed the antagonism between Zionists and anti-Zionists. "A cruel reality is settling these differences more quickly and thoroughly than might be expected," Ehrenpreis reported from Lucerne, Switzerland. "Today, Palestine is one of the few bright spots in the darkness of our time, perhaps the only real plank of salvation for tens of thousands of our haunted coreligionists."[22]

A few months earlier, in April 1935, Marcus Ehrenpreis had traveled to Palestine for the second time in his life, this time having been invited to give a lecture on the occasion of the tenth anniversary of the Hebrew University, and once again he had been impressed by the economic and political vitality of the Zionist project. He still believed that the goal of Zionism must be to establish in Palestine a spiritual-cultural center for the Jews of the world, but he realized only too well that Palestine must now also become a territorial refuge for the increasing numbers of Jews to whom the world was closing its borders.

This time Esther traveled with him, and in her travel diary she revealed a lifelong and deep affection for Zionism—perhaps deeper than her husband's.

"I have been preparing for this journey since my earliest youth," Esther Ehrenpreis wrote. "I travel not as a tourist and not out of curiosity, but out of longing to experience in Palestine the realization of the great dream of my life."[23]

Nor was it as an accompanying wife only that the twenty-year-old Esther Haskler/Ehrenpreis had attended the First Zionist Congress in Basel in 1897. Her very personal recollection of Theodor Herzl, "that wonderful, God-inspired man," was matched by an equally personal relationship to the Zionist project she was now seeing realized before her eyes. After visiting the headquarters of the Jewish Administration in Jerusalem, she wrote: "Your self-esteem as a Jew is strengthened by being on your own soil, within this first government building in which Jews are allowed to work out their own destiny. From this undeniable fact, so eloquently and tangibly materialized, you may gather strength."

The steamship on which they traveled back and forth across the Mediterranean was the *Polonia*, and twice a month it was filled with Jewish refugees from Germany. On the way to the port of departure in Constanța, Romania, Esther had taken the opportunity to visit her family in what was now Poland, and she had been horrified by the anti-Jewish atmosphere in the country. Not like it was in Germany, but ominous enough.

Marcus and Esther among friends and fellow rabbis during a meeting in Marienbad in the summer of 1935 to discuss a common Jewish defense against the poison of Nazi propaganda. Also pictured: Jakob Klatzkin, a Jewish thinker and writer who had fled from Germany to Switzerland; Moritz Rosenmann, a rabbi in Vienna; Samuel Arie, a rabbi in Prague; and Moses Schorr, a rabbi in Warsaw.

"Seeing with your own eyes the great distress of the Jewish masses in Poland, and following with trepidation the ongoing collapse of German Jewry, the experience of the great miracle in Palestine will make you believe in the inner coherence of things, in the logic of historical events," Esther Ehrenpreis wrote, and it seemed that neither could she imagine History without God.[24]

In a way, Stefan Zweig had been right about the good Europeans, they still existed, but those who still existed were increasingly also Jews. When, at the meeting in Marienbad, Zweig proposed the founding of a multilingual, pan-European journal to assert the ideals of Europe against the ideals of Nazi Germany, he was in effect addressing himself to a shrinking circle of Jewish intellectuals. The Jews were the last Europeans, and a pan-European journal to assert the values of Europe never came about.

What would emerge from the meeting in Marienbad, and a subsequent meeting in Lucerne, was a joint prayer to be read in the synagogues of the world on the eve of Yom Kippur, the Day of Atonement, on 6 October 1935. The task of drafting and distributing the text of the prayer had been entrusted to Marcus Ehrenpreis and the chief rabbi of Paris, Maurice Liber, and when, in a Stockholm synagogue filled to capacity, Ehrenpreis prayed "for the Jews of Germany and their persecutors," he prayed to the world:

> On this holy day, we, the children of Israel, flee from a hostile life to the peace of our synagogues to seek strength in the reconciliation between God and Man. This year, our wounded hearts turn in compassion and sorrow to our sorely tried brethren, who are robbed of the foundation for their existence as human beings and Jews. A defenseless people is being deprived of its human rights and dignity. The unifying bond between all humans, that we have all been created in the image of God, is torn asunder by a fallacious idea that wants to make [biological] race the foundation of social life. The religious and moral foundations of mankind are shaken.
>
> O God, Father of all men and leader of all nations, who hast founded the universe on love and justice,

open the eyes of the blinded, enlighten the hearts of
the lost, give knowledge to all, fill all with mercy.[25]

The last Europeans continued to travel in Europe as long as they could. In the summer of 1935, the members of the Stockholm congregation were offered a bus tour of Germany, Czechoslovakia, Austria, and Hungary.

"Promoting tourism in Austria may help to protect Austria's Jews from a tragic future," the organizers explained. They emphasized that the travel agency had promised to donate five percent of the proceeds to the congregation's emergency relief fund for Germany's Jews.

The trip included two overnight stays and a day tour of Berlin.

Yes, even to Hitler's Germany the last Europeans could travel for yet some time.

In January 1937, Marcus Ehrenpreis was also about to do so. Invited by two embattled but still permitted Jewish institutions, the Franz Rosenzweig Memorial Foundation in Hamburg and the Vereinigung Jüdisches Lehrhaus in Cologne, he was to speak about the medieval poet Yehuda Halevi and his journey to Palestine. He was to speak in Cologne on 7 January and in Hamburg on 9 January. The organizers in Cologne had respectfully asked if he would agree to have the chief cantor of the congregation perform one or two of Halevi's poems set to music in conjunction with his lecture. Everything seemed set to go, the prepaid German train tickets were to be picked up at the ferry terminal in Sassnitz, the hotels and venues were booked, the events were announced.

Nevertheless, there was an unmistakable undertone of uncertainty and anxiety in the letters from the organizers.

Although all seemed set to go, it could all still fall apart. Jewish lecture evenings required permits from the secret state police, the Gestapo, and permits could be handed out and taken back with humiliating capriciousness. The organizers in Cologne believed they had a permit and assumed that Hamburg would be given one too, and if not Hamburg then perhaps Karlsruhe or Mannheim or Gelsenkirchen.

"I welcome you on German soil," wrote Mr. Grünebaum in Cologne in a letter Ehrenpreis received before his departure from Stockholm.

On 3 January, Mr. Grünebaum wrote again to Ehrenpreis, who by then had made a stop in Vienna, informing him that everything had fallen apart. There would be no permit for Cologne or Hamburg or for any other place in Germany. The letter was restrained in tone, since the Gestapo would read what Mr. Grünebaum had written. "Everyone here regrets that the lecture has had to be canceled. Several hundred people had already signed up for it."[26]

In July 1938, Marcus Ehrenpreis made his last journey as a good European, with one last hope that the conscience of world would awaken, and its nations open their doors to the Jews of Germany and Austria. "Traveling from Stockholm to Evian, there is a sense of optimism growing within me that is really quite out of place," he noted. "Bad news is pouring in every hour, every paper brings new warning signs—but my awakened faith remains unshaken. Evian shines from afar like a promise, giving warmth to your heart. [...] At last humanity will raise its voice; at last, after months and years of hopeless suffering, the hunted, tormented Jewry will have a sense of vindication."[27]

The conference in the French resort of Evian had been convened by President Roosevelt of the United States to negotiate an intergovernmental agreement to "facilitate the involuntary emigration from Germany, including Austria." On the way to Evian, Ehrenpreis had stopped in Lausanne, on the Swiss side of Lake Geneva, to be reminded of another intergovernmental agreement that had been concluded fifteen years earlier, concerning the forced removal of one and a half million people of the "wrong" religion from Greece to Turkey and vice versa, in apparent contradiction to everything Ehrenpreis had believed in and fought for. But as he gazed at the bronze plaque commemorating the Lausanne Peace Conference of 1923 in the entrance to Château d'Ouchy, he saw it as a sign of hope that a similar intergovernmental will and capacity would manifest itself in Evian.

But the only thing manifesting itself in Evian was the lack of intergovernmental will and capacity: no European country committed itself to anything. The Swedish representatives declared that the "Jewish question" must be solved by the settlement of Jews outside Europe, and a few months later Sweden (together with Switzerland) prompted Hitler's Germany to stamp a prominent *J* in the passports of German Jews so that no Jew would accidentally be allowed to cross the border.

On 23 November 1938, a newspaper report confirmed that the policy worked as intended. German Jews arriving daily at the port of Trelleborg were turned away. "Foreigners who are not allowed to return to their homeland are not allowed to enter here," the city's chief of police assured readers.

Ehrenpreis was not unaware of the risks of failure in Evian, he was just unduly optimistic about the possibility of a miracle. For two weeks in his observer's seat, he had tried with "all his senses to catch a glimpse of warm humanity." But no,

Marcus Ehrenpreis (bottom right) serving as an observer at the Evian conference in the summer of 1938: "A painful disappointment."

no glimpse, no miracle, just the "cold and barren words" of high-positioned gentlemen—and a "painful disappointment."[28]

A year later, in the summer of 1939, he imagined what would have happened if he had stood up from his seat and read to the assembled delegates the injunction from the Hebrew Bible, Love the stranger as thyself!

> And then at once, their finely crafted prevarications would have burst like soap bubbles, and of this whole grandly touted world conference would have remained an empty and dejected nothingness. [...]
>
> When I stepped out of the conference hall in Evian, onto a magnificent height on which a lavish sun was

> pouring so much warmth, so much light and goodness on poor lost human children, it was hard to fathom that I had just been nearly freezing to death from all the stinginess, coldness, and hardness of heart inside the hall.[29]

Already before the Nazi takeover, the letters had begun pouring into the chief rabbi's office in the house of the Stockholm congregation on Wahrendorff Street. The day after the German presidential elections on 10 April 1932 (in which Hitler won 36.8 percent of the vote), Erik Italiener in Berlin appealed to Ehrenpreis for help to make it possible for him and his family to return to Sweden, where he had spent some "happy years" during the war. He addressed himself in perfect Swedish to "the Reverend Chief Rabbi," explaining that although he had an "excellent position" as a program director at the German radio, the recent election had shown "with frightful clarity" that the antisemitic movement was growing stronger by the day, that life in Germany had become unbearable, and that he could not be responsible for his children's misfortune. No material help was necessary, he stressed, "I have the best recommendations, I am fluent in six languages and have good knowledge of six more, I have a solid liberal arts education and a solid musical education, and I do not anticipate any difficulties in finding a job."[30]

After Hitler's ascent to power on 30 January 1933, the dams broke, every day new bundles of letters, and in each letter an appeal for help, usually addressed to Marcus Ehrenpreis personally.

Sehr Geehrter herr Doktor.

Euer Hochvolgeboren, sehr geehrter herr Professor.

Euer Ehrwürden, hochverehrter herr Oberrabbiner.

The writers of the letters often seemed embarrassed, almost ashamed, for having to appeal for help. In the wave of letters that came from Vienna after the German annexation of Austria in March 1938, with the immediate and brutal humiliation of its Jews, some had to convince themselves that they were human beings. Still in disbelief, they told of their learning, skills, and qualities and what they might be able to contribute to Sweden.

"Dear Rabbi, we do not want to be a burden to anyone, we are young people who take pride in making a living for ourselves, but here there are no longer any possibilities for us to do that," wrote Jane Ladenheim on Obermüllerstrasse in Vienna on 29 September 1938. She wrote on behalf of herself, her mother, and two siblings, making sure to emphasize everybody's capacity and willingness to work. She was somewhat concerned that her younger brother, who was "an academically schooled painter," might be perceived as being economically less valuable, and therefore added that he was an "unusual man," *ein ungewöhnlicher Mensch*, who with his art "could accomplish more than just to make money."

"I appeal to you in the firm belief that able people should not be allowed to perish," Jane Ladenheim concluded her letter to Marcus Ehrenpreis.[31]

Many letters had a similar ending. Help us. Don't let us perish. We want to support ourselves and not be a burden to anyone.

Sometimes the answer would give hope, but mostly it would not.

Usually the answer would inform them of the severe restrictions that applied to Jews wishing to come to Sweden, and that in their case the possibilities were small.

As in the answer to the rabbis Prof. Dr. M. Papo and Prof. Dr. K. Kupfer, who in a joint letter from Vienna on 10 July 1938 (written in Swedish) had appealed for help to receive a temporary permit of stay in Sweden for the student Hans Ledermann, "this extremely serious, talented, and capable young man, who with Your Eminence's kind assistance could be enabled to continue his university studies. He is of course prepared to take on any practical job that corresponds to his abilities."[32]

Ehrenpreis's answer, in German, was a catalogue of obstacles and difficulties. Foreigners who wished to study at a Swedish university must commit themselves to leaving Sweden after completing their studies. Permits of stay could only be issued to students who could present guarantees in advance for the financing of their studies and living. Grants were not available to foreign students. The congregation's own resources were "stretched to the limits of exhaustion in providing the bare necessities of life for destitute refugees."

"Therefore, unfortunately, as much as we would like to, we cannot meet your request. It pains me not being able to give you any other answer," Ehrenpreis concluded his letter to the two rabbis in Vienna.[33]

Several answers were written "on behalf of Dr. Ehrenpreis," informing the sender that he was unable to respond in person due to illness or travel or overload. As in the answer to the twenty-eight-year-old medical doctor Perla Kraszewska in Vienna, who in a letter on 18 April 1938 had appealed on behalf of herself, her mother, and her younger sister, a medical doctor too. But again, for foreign medical doctors no chances for work, and with no work and subsistence no permit, and without a permit no entry.

"Professor Ehrenpreis deeply regrets that he cannot give you a more positive answer. He wishes to emphasize that it is not in his power to change the objective facts, *die objektiven Tatbestände*. Should you and your sister seek other employment opportunities, where a word from Professor E. might make a difference, you should feel free to contact him again."

The "objective facts" also applied to non-Jewish Swedes trying to appeal for permits of stay for Jews. On 14 February 1939, the pastor in the small village of Färila, Anker Korn, appealed on behalf of his German sister-in-law's "very skilled" dentist in Berlin, Dr. Carl Fuchs. The pastor admitted that Dr. Fuchs would probably not find any work in the surroundings of the parish in the "remote forests" of Hälsingland, where he would "be dependent on the mercy of others," but were he only allowed to come to Stockholm, he would surely be able to sustain himself. "I therefore thought that Dr. Ehrenpreis might possibly—I understand very well that Dr. Ehrenpreis is already overloaded with cases of a similar kind—find some way out. The man is prepared to do any honest work."[34]

Three weeks later, Ehrenpreis replied, apologizing for the delay, explaining that the letter had "got lost in the piles of papers currently covering my desk," but still having to inform the pastor in Färila that the Fuchs case was just one of hundreds of similar cases. "The pastor knows the mood in the country and knows the difficulties we have in being able to help. We shall of course see what we can do in the matter, which is why we have today put ourselves in direct contact with Dr. Fuchs."

On 13 March, an emotional letter of thanks arrived from Dr. Fuchs. Ehrenpreis had indeed contacted him, as had the

Mosaic Congregation in Stockholm, and in his letter Dr. Fuchs made promises and assurances that if only he and his wife could be given a refuge in Sweden, he would not compete with anyone or take the bread out of anyone's mouth. "From the bottom of our hearts, we appeal for a positive answer as soon as possible."[35]

In some cases hopes were fulfilled. In most cases not.

In some cases Ehrenpreis undertook to try to do something about it. In most cases not.

In most cases, a sting of powerlessness.

> Every morning I am visited by the postman, and as he arrives I know that he is not only bringing ordinary letters; he is bringing tragedies. I know that almost every letter carries a tale of heart-wrenching suffering, that every such letter is filled with desolation and despair, with laments for a happiness lost, for families blown apart, for elderly people having their lives disintegrate, with no venue left. So every morning I sit sadly in front of these mute visitors, sensing the living life beneath the sheets of paper. [...] Why are you silent, they ask, why don't we hear a word of sympathy and comfort? Why do you not help us in our great distress? When we were well-off, we helped Jews all over the world, wherever there was need and disaster. Now we ourselves are waiting for help. Let us not wait in vain.[36]

The "objective facts" spoke their own cold language. People who had been defined as Jews in Germany and Austria, and thereby deprived of their human dignity and their means of existence, were in Sweden not defined as refugees in need of protection, but as "involuntary emigrants" in need of a livelihood. The material support had to be guaranteed in advance, either by private individuals or by the congregation in Stockholm. What also had to be guaranteed in advance was that the stay in Sweden would be limited in time, which in turn required that a visa to a third country must be secured. The number of involuntary emigrants to be admitted to Sweden under these conditions was decided by the Aliens Bureau at the Swedish National Board of Health and Welfare. Permits of stay were granted for six months, with the condition that involuntary emigrants must not compete for jobs with ordinary Swedes. Another condition was that there should not be too many of them. Or as it was formulated in the 1927 Aliens Act still in force: "A more substantial settlement in this country of immigrants who are very different from us in race will be detrimental to us."[37]

It was not hard to trace the spirit of the Aliens Act behind Sweden's refusal to consider racial persecution as grounds for asylum. Or, as it was more bluntly put in a letter from the Aliens Bureau in November 1938; if "all persons of Jewish descent" were to be regarded and treated as political refugees, Sweden would "become the door through which the so-called non-Aryans of Germany would seek their escape."[38]

The objective facts determining how many of Germany's and Austria's Jews would be allowed a temporary refuge in Sweden during the 1930s have been succinctly summarized by the Swedish historian Karin Kvist Geverts:

> The overall aim of the [Swedish] refugee policy was first not to accept Jewish refugees at all, and second to select those who would be able to travel on. Underneath this policy was a fear of not being able to get rid of this group, and the notion that an increase in the

> number of Jewish refugees would lead to a flare-up of antisemitism. This policy of selection was made on the basis of "race," using the Aliens Bureau's special form for "German citizens of Jewish descent" and the Foreign Office's question number nine about "ethnic race" in the application form for a passport visa.[39]

From the outset, it was clear that the financial and social responsibility for the "involuntary emigrants" that Sweden might accept would rest squarely on their Swedish "coreligionists." Just as the attempts to organize the rescue of Germany's Jews would rest mainly on the Jews of the world.

After the initial shock to the world came the silence and the adaptation.

And the Jewish loneliness.

The Jewish loneliness befell Ehrenpreis early on. In an interview during his stay in Karlsbad in the summer of 1933, he warned that the "antisemitic poison" from Germany would create an atmosphere, "a mood of souls," the effects of which would be more serious and lasting than the ever-so-brutal Jewish policies of one government.

"The stab now being directed at the Jews of the world is an exhortation to joint [Jewish] action," Ehrenpreis declared.[40]

Yet, what joint Jewish action could there possibly be? Whatever fantasies about Jewish world power that Nazi propaganda was disseminating, there existed no Jewish world organization, let alone a Jewish world conspiracy. What characterized the Jews of the world was rather the absence of a common organization and a unifying authority. Jewish life differed from country to country, and from congregation to congregation. Jews spoke different languages (including different Jewish languages), were influenced by different cultures and traditions, and had widely differing understandings of what it meant to be Jewish. There were Sephardic Jews and Ashkenazi Jews, Orthodox Jews and Reform Jews, Zionist Jews and anti-Zionist Jews, Western Jews and Eastern Jews, and wherever different Jews tried to come together for common action, there was often more that separated them than united them, which was one of the reasons why Ehrenpreis had stopped going to Zionist congresses: too much disagreement and bickering.

It was also one of the reasons why Ehrenpreis, in the Karlsbad interview, rejected the American-Jewish proposal to establish a World Jewish Congress to organize joint actions: "Congresses degenerate all too easily into talking exercises, and we have truly no time for talk. At this fateful moment, we should instead make use of our historical form of organization, having stood the test of two and a half millennia: the Jewish congregation. Together they constitute the authorized representative of world Jewry—albeit not a fully democratic one."[41]

Another reason for Ehrenpreis to reject the proposal was the concern he shared with other Jewish leaders in Europe, not least in Germany, that the convening of a World Jewish Congress would be exploited by Nazi propaganda and presented as evidence of a Jewish world conspiracy. It was from the congregations and the synagogues that the defense of Jews and Judaism must emanate and be organized, Ehrenpreis concluded.[42]

The congregation in Stockholm had quickly moved from words to action. In April 1933, Ehrenpreis delivered his much-noted Passover sermon, and a week later, a newly formed

Committee for Emergency Aid to the Jews of Germany issued an appeal to the Jews of Sweden. The committee was formally independent of the congregation, but it had been set up on the congregation's initiative; the director of the congregation and its two rabbis, Marcus Ehrenpreis and Emil Kronheim, were signatories and patrons. The declared purpose of the funds raised was to "bring first aid to distressed refugees who may arrive in our country."[43]

In a first account of funds and activities six months later, it was emphasized that the initiatives of the committee had been planned in close cooperation with the German Jews themselves, through their own aid organization, Zentralausschuss der deutschen Juden für Hilfe und Aufbau, and what the German Jews primarily had asked of the Swedish Jews was to receive and prepare Jewish youth for further emigration to Palestine. This also became one of the committee's first undertakings: to negotiate with the Swedish authorities a quota for agricultural training of a few hundred *chalutzim*, pioneers, "for a maximum of eighteen months."[44] Similarly, and again at the request of the German Jews, to negotiate a quota for the education of a few hundred German-Jewish children at a privately run boarding school in southern Sweden, again on the condition that the stay would be limited in time and result in continued emigration. After the German annexation of Austria in March 1938, two further quotas were to be added, a child quota and a transmigrant quota, both limited to a few hundred individuals, both permitting a time-limited stay pending further emigration, both requiring that people within the quotas "not be a burden on society."

This was to be the main form of the Jewish aid effort in Sweden up to the outbreak of the war: to negotiate, finance, and organize the reception of "involuntary emigrants" within the framework of officially predetermined and strictly limited quotas, with the provision that their "coreligionists" assume responsibility for their subsistence and further emigration.[45] Repeated attempts by the aid committee to widen the quotas, sometimes with only a few people, or to add new quotas, were mostly disregarded by the Swedish authorities, who referred to the labor market situation, or the mood of public opinion, or simply to the official immigration policy, which stated that Sweden would only receive Jews who could document their intention to leave the country "within a short space of time."[46]

Only in 1939, when it became clear that involuntary Jewish emigrants would have little chance of leaving Sweden in a preset span of time, and that the costs of their subsistence and education were becoming too much for their Swedish "coreligionists" to bear, did the government decide to subsidize the aid effort. Most of the funds raised by the congregation had been used, "as a natural obligation," to assist the increasing number of Jews who had managed to get to Sweden without the congregation's help. In its application for a state grant in November 1940, the congregation pointed out that many of these people were too old and too sick to be retrained and put to work. "In addition, there are the difficulties for foreigners as such to obtain jobs and work permits."[47]

Until the outbreak of war in September 1939, when Jewish emigration from Germany and German-occupied territories was effectively halted, Sweden had given temporary residence to perhaps a total of four thousand persons of Jewish descent, largely with the assistance, directly or indirectly, of the Mosaic Congregation in Stockholm. We don't know for sure, since the counting was done in several places and in different ways. It was also difficult to keep track of how many had traveled on and when. What we do know is that in light of how many might have been saved had they been given an ever-so-temporary refuge in another country, it was a vanishing trickle.

There would come a time when the question would be asked whether the "coreligionists" in Sweden, the emergency aid committee and the congregation in Stockholm, not least Marcus Ehrenpreis personally, could not have acted in a more forceful way to make Sweden open its doors to more Jews trying to escape Nazi terror. There were even suspicions that the congregation, and explicitly Ehrenpreis, had actively acted against accepting more Jews, fearing that it would increase Swedish antisemitism.

Contributing to the suspicions was the fact that the Stockholm congregation had not only taken it upon itself to negotiate the quotas with the authorities but had also agreed to suggest which people should be proposed for the quotas, based on an assessment of their chances to pass through the eye of the needle at the Aliens Bureau. The eye of the needle was a reality: not everyone who was put on the list was allowed to enter, and trying to select the most eligible to fill the list might thus have seemed a rational and reasonable thing to do, but the impression remained that the congregation had allowed itself to become an accomplice in the execution of an essentially anti-Jewish refugee policy.

This impression would not be significantly affected by the fact that the congregation also had pushed for increases in the quotas, and for Sweden to receive people outside the quotas, and by the apparent fact that it was not possible for Jews to act more aggressively in pushing Sweden to accept more Jewish refugees, in a country that would rather not have any Jewish refugees at all. For Jews to press for more Jews might rather have the opposite effect. Not even Jews with relatives or close friends in Sweden could hope for more than, at best, a temporary permit of stay.

Nor could there be any doubt that Jewish fears of increased antisemitism were justified. Swedish political opinion, reflected in the Swedish Aliens Act, was hostile to foreigners in general, and to a feared "Jewish invasion" from Germany in particular. Antisemitic propaganda in Germany fueled antisemitic sentiments and opinions in Sweden as well, and even seemingly well-established and well-assimilated Swedish Jews were given reason to consider their positions. A demand was soon presented for the "aryanization" of Swedish companies wishing to do business with Germany, as was a demand that German citizens wishing to marry in Sweden had to certify that both groom and bride were "Aryan." The German demand for the aryanization of companies never gained legal force in Sweden, but the requirement of an Aryan certificate for German citizens wishing to marry in a Swedish church was accepted by the Swedish state. "German Racial Law a Barrier to Marriage Even in Our Country. Sweden Bound to Respect German Marriage Bans," read the headline in *Dagens Nyheter* on 4 December 1935.

"I hereby declare on my honor and conscience that, to the best of my knowledge, none of my grandparents have belonged to the Jewish race or religion," read the "Aryan Declaration" that the Swedish Foreign Ministry's legal department had drawn up in September 1937 and that at least 430 couples in which one of the parties was a German citizen had to sign in order to be legally married in Sweden.[48]

In short, there was good reason to fear that Jewish pressures for more Jews being allowed to seek refuge in Sweden might have the opposite effect, and thus good reason to argue that the accommodating stance of the congregation was based not only on a justified fear of antisemitism, but perhaps even more on a realistic assessment of the political conditions for receiving any Jews at all.

As if any reminder of the political conditions was needed, at a meeting on 17 February 1939 (three months after Kristallnacht and two weeks after Hitler's open threat to exterminate the "Jewish race" in Europe), the students in Uppsala voted against giving ten (!) Jewish physicians a safe haven in Sweden. The students in Lund did the same at a meeting on 6 March 1939.

When, in early April 1933, Ehrenpreis wrote to his rabbinical colleague in London, Joseph Hertz, asking for advice on how Swedish Jews should act, he was answered by a spokesman for the British Jews, Neville Laski, telling him that the main task was to muster non-Jewish opinion for the demand that Germany restore the civil and human rights of the German Jews. Specific Jewish actions against Germany, such as Jewish boycotts of German goods, were not advisable, and "exaggeration should be avoided."[49] Ehrenpreis had received similar advice in his contacts with his German colleague and friend from his student years in Berlin, Rabbi Leo Baeck, and now the president of the organization for German Jews (Reichsvertretung der Deutschen Juden).[50]

"Chief Rabbi Marcus Ehrenpreis, an extraordinarily wise and experienced person, did not believe that Hitler's reign would last long," his 1929 confirmand and later secretary Inga Gottfarb would reminisce after the war. "Without the contribution of the Jews the German economy would soon collapse, I remember him saying."[51]

In any case, Ehrenpreis made the same assessment as his German and British colleagues: what the situation called for was caution. The caution of Ehrenpreis was manifested in a statement in March 1933 against a Swedish-Jewish boycott of Germany.[52] And subsequently, in a reluctance to publicly criticize the immigration and refugee policies of Sweden. In retrospect, this would come to be perceived as an expression of complacency and conformity, or even coldness and unwillingness, but in light of "the objective facts," and not least in light of what Ehrenpreis simultaneously wrote and said, it would be more justified to perceive it as the result of a hopeless balancing act between one Jewish impotence and another, between the impotence in facing Hitler's Germany and its barrage of anti-Jewish propaganda, and the impotence in facing a Swedish alien policy with an unmistakably anti-Jewish bias.

For a short time it might have seemed possible to wield the power of words to make the cause of the Jews the cause of the world, and thereby to make the world put pressure on Hitler's Germany. Even as it became increasingly clear that the world would not, the power of words was still what remained for the Jews of Europe.

At the end of October 1933, Ehrenpreis traveled to London to attend a worldwide Jewish conference for aid to the Jews of Germany. Not a permanent Jewish World Congress, nota bene, but an ad hoc convened council of representatives of Jewish organizations and congregations from all over the world. The meeting in London was an event that "carved itself unforgettably" into the mind of Ehrenpreis, "the image of a *united Judaism*!" Never before had all branches and parties of Judaism been brought together in this way, "taking part in brotherly discussions, side by side," all closing ranks behind the need for the German Jews to leave and the emerging importance of Palestine as a place of refuge.

"The building of Palestine has ceased to be a partisan matter and is becoming an all-Jewish concern," Ehrenpreis reported on his return.[53]

The most apparent cause for Jewish unity was the fact that country after country was closing its doors to Jews, but perhaps just as significant, a Nazi-inspired "racial madness" that threatened "to undermine the position of Jews, not only in Germany."

"The realization of this rested heavily on the conference," he stressed in his report, as if to show that it was not only Swedish Jews who were facing a morally corrosive balancing act between solidarity and self-preservation. And that not only the fate of the German Jews was at stake. And that the crucial challenge to the Jews of the world, in addition to saving Germany's Jews, was to save Israel's honor:

> Our adversaries have set up megaphones in which they scream to the world that Jews are inferior, despicable, harmful. They castigate us, mock us, slander us. Against the incitements resounding all around us, we must defend ourselves. [...] Surely we cannot convince antisemites who do not want to be convinced. But there are millions of just and unprejudiced men and women who seek the truth, who ask and who deserve answers.[54]

Still, preparing for the worst.

Well, not the worst. The worst Ehrenpreis could not imagine. What he could imagine was a looming defeat in the battle for Israel's honor. As the skies darkened, he therefore made it his task to strengthen Jewish self-esteem and resilience. Talking to the confirmands of May 1933, he prepared them for a time of suffering and trials:

> My beloved, moved to tears I read in your confessions the anxiety that fills you. I perceived in your young and pure hearts a genuine and simple cry of pain. At the same time, your stories were filled with hope. You seemed to be saying: It is night over the world, it is night over Israel, but a new morning is approaching after all. Your words were words of faith, faith in justice, faith in Israel—reminding of the exultant faith of the Psalmist: "The Lord is my shepherd, I shall not want. […] Though I walk through the valley of the shadow of death, I will fear no evil, for you are with me."[55]

It would take twelve years to the day to reach that "morning," and at the age of sixty-four Marcus Ehrenpreis was faced with the task of carrying his Jews through the night. Fate had brought him to a country on the periphery of European Jewry, and fate would make it one of its few surviving habitats, and Marcus Ehrenpreis one of its few rabbis with a congregation left to lead.

He would thus be forced to play a role for which he had not prepared himself and which was not really his to play: politician, diplomat, rescue organizer, savior of last resort.

Anyone seeking advice on whom in Sweden to write for help would probably get the name Ehrenpreis. It was thus inevitable that Marcus Ehrenpreis would come to be associated with the efforts—or lack of efforts—of the Swedish Jews to help their German "coreligionists."

Ehrenpreis himself was hoping that aid and rescue operations would become an international undertaking, since the limitations of the national level were becoming all too clear. Thus, when the League of Nations in October 1933 appointed a High Commissioner for Refugees, James McDonald, to bring about an internationally coordinated rescue of the German Jews, he glimpsed a "ray of hope in all the darkness."

Two years later, James McDonald resigned in protest at the world's inability to stem Germany's racial policy and offer protection to its victims:

> When domestic policies threaten the demoralization and exile of hundreds of thousands of human beings, considerations of diplomatic correctness must yield to those of common humanity. I should be recreant if I did not call attention to the actual situation, and plead that world opinion, acting through the League and its Member-States and other countries, move to avert the existing and impending tragedies.[56]

Ehrenpreis's translation and publication of McDonald's letter can be seen as his way of indirectly criticizing the Swedish government for its callous policies toward the German Jews seeking protection. A more directly expressed Jewish critique was probably not conceivable in a climate poisoned by anti-Jewish propaganda.

Instead, in September 1935, with McDonald still in office, the Jewish congregations in Stockholm, Gothenburg, and Malmö tried to voice their concerns by sending a telegram to Edvard Beneš, the foreign minister of Czechoslovakia, in his capacity as president of the League of Nations. The telegram was signed by the chairmen of the congregations but most likely initiated by Ehrenpreis. During his stay in Karlsbad a few months earlier, Ehrenpreis had been informed that Beneš, with the blessing of the Czechoslovak president Tomáš Masaryk, considered bringing the racial laws of Germany before the League of Nations, which had sparked the unmistakably Ehrenpreisian idea of an appeal to Beneš directly (as he himself had appealed directly to Clemenceau, the prime minister of France, in 1917):

> The Jewish congregations in Sweden, together with right-minded people all over the world, are deeply shaken by the new Jew-laws in Germany [...]. By introducing for the first time the principle of race as a legal category, civilized humanity is thrown back centuries; the attack on the Jews of Germany is a threat to the legal foundations of the entire world. The League of Nations, whose purpose is to safeguard the peaceful coexistence of peoples, must raise its voice of warning at this moment of uppermost emergency.[57]

A few months later, McDonald would be gone, as would Masaryk, and soon Beneš and Czechoslovakia. The League of Nations would never concern itself with racial laws, and in the summer of 1938 at Evian the world would finally turn its back on the Jews.

Whatever conflicts about Zionism and Palestine that had existed among the Jews of Sweden, they were to take second stage as it became increasingly clear that Palestine might be the only place on earth in which the persecuted Jews of Germany would be received and even welcomed. It would also become a source of Jewish confidence and self-esteem in facing the onslaught of anti-Jewish propaganda.

The recurrent propaganda attack against the Jews for not being fully loyal to the nation in which they lived, for having "dual loyalties," was deeply hurtful to many Swedish Jews. One of them was Ragnar Josephson, Ehrenpreis's friend and co-translator of Hebrew poetry. In the spring of 1936 he gave a talk to Jewish associations in Stockholm and Gothenburg in which he spelled out what the plight of the German Jews demanded of the Swedish Jews. "We feel the heavy pressure of the dual loyalty," Josephson candidly confessed. He began with a heart-wrenching rendering of the isolation and vulnerability of "all those thousand Germans with Jewish blood [...] scattered on the roads of Europe," hoping for a refuge somewhere. He then went on to plead an almost unconditional support for a Swedish policy that had closed its doors to them, making it perfectly clear that in the choice between loyalty to the scattered Jews hoping to find a refuge in Sweden and loyalty to a Swedish policy that did not allow for more than a few of them, he did not hesitate:

> It may be to a country's advantage to accommodate within it a few honest men who, by their nature-given gifts and talents, are able to contribute to the creation of cultural and material values; and when we plead that

> a few such exiled men should be given a right of residence in Sweden, we are acting for the benefit of our fatherland. However, it would be to a country's disadvantage to receive large groups of foreigners who have no bonds with it, and in which a larger group of aliens may create distrust, fear, and disorder.[58]

Josephson admitted that his position could be perceived as narrowly self-serving. And so it seemed, undoubtedly. Out of concern for their historically attained position in Sweden, Josephson argued, the Swedish Jews must uphold confidence in their "unconditional national trustworthiness." His fear for a weakening of that position was apparent: "The epidemic that is now raging has not failed to infect a good many weak Swedish men."[59]

Ragnar Josephson's declaration of loyalty was a moving manifestation of his deep affinity with Sweden, and a proud account of the contributions of Swedish Jews to Swedish society, and an agonizing expression of that morally grueling balancing act between one loyalty and another that every Jewish leader in Europe would be facing, including Ehrenpreis.

Nevertheless, Ehrenpreis felt a need to distance himself from his friend. "[A] one hundred percent Swedish loyalty and a twenty-five percent Jewish one, that I find difficult to accept," he wrote to Josephson on 7 May 1936.

What exactly Ehrenpreis was referring to was unclear, there were no quantifications of loyalties in Josephson's manifesto, and to the very notion of dual loyalties Ehrenpreis had no objections; on the contrary, "it is the twin brother of that 'cultural dualism' which is an inseparable part of my Jewish creed." Yet something had prompted his reaction, perhaps a sense of unease at what seemed like an unabashed commitment to one loyalty against another, and the potentially callous consequences of a conflict of loyalties that Ehrenpreis refused to acknowledge.[60]

Josephson thanked Ehrenpreis for his frankness, but then ventured to explain the difference in their views with the difference in their ties to Sweden, Ehrenpreis being a newcomer compared to Josephson. "Perhaps your son will already feel closer to what I am saying," he added. The reason for putting more emphasis on loyalty of the Swedish Jews to the Swedish "fatherland" than on their loyalty to Jews, Josephson argued, was because that was the only loyalty questioned. "That Swedish Jews are Swedes is denied by many, that they are Jews by none."

The difference between them should not be exaggerated. Josephson argued that his undivided Jewish loyalty had been expressed clearly enough for not having to be measured by percentage points.[61] And, essentially, Ehrenpreis did not have any other response to the current attacks on Jewish loyalty than, time and again, having to state and confirm it.

What seems to have disturbed Ehrenpreis, nevertheless, was a statement of Jewish loyalty that entailed the endorsement of a fundamentally anti-Jewish immigration and refugee policy.

To Ehrenpreis, the humiliation of Jews and Judaism was the worst of all, and defending "the honor of Israel" his overriding task, and in Josephson's version of "dual loyalty" he saw too much honor being sacrificed on the altar of subservience.

"A people can overcome everything, but it cannot live without honor," Ehrenpreis proclaimed in his New Year sermon of 1935, a few weeks after Nazi Germany had made the Jews legal outcasts in their own society, this "most severe insult that has befallen Israel for centuries."

> They have deprived our brethren of all human rights, of every possibility to make a living, but one thing no

> one can take away from them and from us, and that is our honor and our good name, which we have borne for thousands of years, and which we will bear as long as it is God's will to let us live among the peoples of the earth.[62]

"For the Honor of Israel" was the title of the sermon when it appeared in print, and it made perfectly clear how central the issue of Jewish honor and self-respect had been in the life of Marcus Ehrenpreis. The world's understanding and recognition of the true values of Judaism were what his Jewish Renaissance had been all about, and his Hebrew Revolution, and his cultural dualism, and his Jewish-Swedish bridge-building, and his dream of Zion as a spiritual and cultural center for the Jews of the world. The true face of Judaism must also be the face of Jewish honor, manifesting itself to a world that for so long had mocked and defiled it.

Never before, however, had "the honor of Israel" been more trampled on as now, since never before had the vilification and defamation of everything Jewish been so all-embracing and so unconditional, and never before had so many Jews lacked the self-respect and inner strength to resist and endure. Ehrenpreis recounted the legend of King Solomon, wandering in the world dressed as a ragged beggar, everywhere being met by scorn and contempt, saying to himself: "I am Solomon. I know who I am. I carry my royal stature within me, and no mockery can take it away from me."

Like King Solomon, we must know ourselves and stand up for ourselves, Ehrenpreis urged. "This will give us the moral strength to withstand the onslaught that we are subjected to, and which may at any time cross the border from one country to another."[63]

Contributing to Jewish honor and self-respect was now also Palestine. From the young men and women "who, under the most difficult hardships, are building flourishing communities [...] emanates a living force whereby the disgraced Jew regains something of his good name, something of the honor that has been taken away from him."[64]

For Ehrenpreis, Jewish Palestine was no longer merely a path to the Jewish spiritual and cultural renaissance of which he had dreamed all his life, but increasingly a defense against that degradation and humiliation of Jews and Judaism he feared more than anything else, and which the German Jews had shown themselves to be defenseless against, and which was now creeping under the skin of Swedish Jews as well. Not even a person with Ehrenpreis's inner conviction could remain unaffected by propaganda systematically aimed at degrading everything Jewish, and against which there proved to be no defense.

Nor was there any defense against the making of a world in which Jewish leaders were forced to make moral choices that were bound to demoralize them. Marcus Ehrenpreis wanted to save Germany's Jews, but he also wanted to defend Sweden's Jews, and when the one was deviously pitted against the other, he had to maneuver between one dispiriting compromise and another.

The "Gray Zone" was what Primo Levi would later call the sinister world of demoralizing compromises that the Nazis had constructed around the Jewish leaders in the ghettos of the extermination machine. Sweden was not Nazi Germany, and the Jewish catastrophe to which the leaders of the ghettos had been co-opted to contribute, was, to say the least, of another dimension than the anti-Jewish immigration policy of Sweden in which the Mosaic Congregation in Stockholm had agreed to play a limited advisory role.

However, the question of how and why would arise in Sweden too.

Could the Swedish Jews have done more for the fleeing German and Austrian Jews?

Could Marcus Ehrenpreis personally?

In the summer of 1939 Ehrenpreis turned seventy. No commemorative booklet as ten years earlier, just a few "autobiographical aphorisms" in the June issue of *Judisk Tidskrift*. "My path," he titled them, and where he now found himself, the "hour was dark" and the day of tomorrow "shrouded in impenetrable darkness."

> The world that welcomed me in the spring of my youth is wiped out, humanism has ceased to be a force of life, civil emancipation is in ruins. Large parts of Israel are stricken to the ground—a nation of castaways that no one is saving.

Marcus Ehrenpreis on his last trip to Europe before the war, a Zionist congress in Geneva in August 1939, with the aim of forming a joint Scandinavian-Jewish action to have Britain reopen the gates to Palestine.

9.

THE END OF THE WORD

And the Lord put forth his hand, and touched my mouth, and said:
I put my words in your mouth. Today I give you power over peoples and kingdoms. You will uproot and overthrow, destroy and break down, build up and plant.

—Jeremiah 1:9–10

In the pile of letters on Ehrenpreis's desk in November 1939, a letter from a thirty-four-year-old rabbi in Vienna: "Dear Mr. Chief Rabbi, I don't know whether you have heard of me, and I therefore take the liberty of attaching to my request a brief biographical sketch. I was born in Lemberg on 9 June 1905, and hold both a doctorate in philosophy and a rabbinical degree from the Jewish-Theological Seminary in Vienna, both with excellent distinction. Since 1931 I have been a lecturer at the Seminary and a rabbi in the congregation in Vienna, first in the 20th district, which has a sizable Jewish population, and more recently in the large synagogue in Leopoldstadt."

The similarities with Ehrenpreis were striking: the upbringing in Lemberg, the dual education, philosophy and theology, the early rabbinical career, the broad erudition, the writing skills and ambitions. The latter could be deduced from the attached summary of published texts in German and Hebrew. The most recent had been published only a few months earlier and was an attempt to view the ongoing forced emigration of Jews from Vienna and Austria in a historical, and perhaps messianic, light. Between the lines it was made clear that the young rabbi had had a role to play in this as well. "Since May 1938 I have held a leading administrative position in the Jewish community in Vienna," the letter continued, without detailing the nature of his administrative tasks, only that they had prevented the rabbi and his family from emigrating earlier. "I therefore take the liberty, Most Reverend Chief Rabbi, of humbly asking you whether within the framework of your activities you might find a suitable position for me."

The letter was dated 16 November 1939.[1]

Four days earlier, Swedish newspapers had reported on the forced transfer of Jews from Austria to a newly established "Jewish reservation" in eastern Poland. "Every week a transport of 2,000 Jews is to depart from Vienna," *Svenska Dagbladet* wrote, adding that the transport at the end of October had numbered no more than 1,400, "as a large number of Jews had sought to escape deportation by committing suicide or hiding. During the last week there were 82 suicides in Vienna, 36 of which were committed by women."[2]

What the writer of the letter had failed to detail about his administrative task in the Jewish community was that it had been about organizing the forced emigration of Jews from Vienna, and that in doing so he had been forced to cooperate with an SS officer named Adolf Eichmann, who was in charge of the terrorization and plundering of Vienna's Jews.

Neither did the writer mention that on 15 October 1939 he had been ordered to accompany the first transport of forcibly deported Jews to Eichmann's planned Jewish reservation in eastern Poland, and that he had witnessed with his own eyes how thousands of Jews were left there to perish, and how the reservation plan collapsed in a matter of weeks. By the time he was ordered back to Vienna in early November to resume his previous administrative tasks, he had come to understand that mass deportation of Jews to "the East" was the next step of the Nazi regime, and he began to look for an emigration route of his own.

A few days later he wrote to Ehrenpreis in Stockholm.

The response of Ehrenpreis and the congregation can be deduced from a second letter from the same rabbi written six years later, again asking whether there might be any use for him in the congregation in Stockholm. In the response from the congregation in November 1939 he had been informed that a rabbinical position was later to be advertised, was the position possibly still vacant?

The letter was dated Theresienstadt, 26 May 1945, and the writer was the last and only surviving leader of its Jewish Council of Elders, the *Judenältesten*. Theresienstadt was a garrison town in Czech Bohemia that Nazi Germany had converted into a deceptive combination of propaganda device, Jewish ghetto, and concentration camp. One hundred and fifty thousand Jews from Nazi-occupied Europe were deported to Theresienstadt, tens of thousands died of starvation and hardship, tens of thousands were deported to Auschwitz, but in May 1945, when Theresienstadt was liberated, some tens of thousands were still alive, which Dr. Benjamin Murmelstein, the writer of the letter, in part wished to see as a result of his efforts. He did not say so outright, nor at what cost, only that he was pleased to have been able to deliver the "Jewish community" that had been entrusted to him "unharmed" into the hands of the liberating forces, *unversehrt den befreienden Kräften übergeben konnte.*[3]

Benjamin Murmelstein had apparently received a discouraging but not definitive answer to his request in November 1939. In the summer of 1941, the congregation had contacted him again, asking whether he would be able to travel to Stockholm to give a test sermon for the as-yet-unfilled position of "first rabbi." The proposal must have seemed wholly unrealistic at the time—an Austrian rabbi on a business trip through Nazi-dominated Europe—but as Murmelstein nevertheless began to explore the possibility of obtaining a travel permit through his connections in Vienna, the Stockholm congregation unsurprisingly announced that the recruitment of a new rabbi had been indefinitely postponed.

In early 1943 Murmelstein was deported from Vienna to Theresienstadt, in December 1944 he became leader of the Jewish Council in Theresienstadt, and in May 1945 he wrote his letter to the congregation in Stockholm. In a separate letter addressed to Ehrenpreis personally, Murmelstein emphasized that in addition to his formal qualifications, he had also come to learn a few things about "the tough obligations that work in the service of the community may entail."[4]

Among the liberated in Theresienstadt along with Murmelstein was Ehrenpreis's longtime friend and colleague Leo Baeck, the prewar leader of Germany's Jews, who in a handwritten attachment vouched for Murmelstein's "excellent" qualities and stressed that he was still young enough to have a life's work ahead of him. "After these years of interruption, I would deeply appreciate if he could be given a chance to resume his rabbinical and Jewish scientific activities," Leo Baeck wrote to Marcus Ehrenpreis.[5]

What neither Murmelstein nor Baeck anticipated was that only a few weeks later Murmelstein would be arrested on suspicion of collaborating with the Nazis and held in custody for eighteen months, after which he was cleared of all charges. Nor that he would spend the rest of his life explaining to posterity that his "collaboration" with the Nazis in both Vienna and Theresienstadt had been "in the service of the community"; that through his collaboration with Eichmann in Vienna he had succeeded in getting the majority of Austria's Jews to emigrate before it was too late;[6] that in Theresienstadt he had "collaborated" with the Nazis because it was the Nazis who ruled over life and death. Those who had subsequently accused him of being a collaborator had simply failed to understand the "objective facts" (to use Ehrenpreis's expression) that the Nazis had created for the Jews of Europe, which meant that Jewish leaders were forced into situations and faced with decisions from which no human being, Jew or not, could emerge morally unscathed. "No other group of people or victims could have acted differently under the same circumstances," the Austrian-Jewish author Doron Rabinovici writes in his book on "Eichmann's Jews," referring to the Jewish leaders in Nazi Vienna, among them Benjamin Murmelstein.[7]

Many would testify in retrospect that Murmelstein had indeed sought to serve the community. Many would also testify that in doing so he had taken part in morally appalling decisions, such as choosing which names to put on the lists for deportation to "the East" that the German camp command regularly ordered the Council of Elders to compile. Not the number of names, that question was beyond the council's power, nor essentially which names (members of the Council of Elders were also deported and murdered), but in the choice between a person deemed important to the survival of the camp and a person deemed less so, the Nazi regime had handed Murmelstein a power that was cunningly designed to demoralize and humiliate both the Jewish leaders and their subjects. This would in time make Murmelstein a prominent symbol of what Hannah Arendt would term "the darkest chapter of the whole dark history"—by which she meant the complicity of Jewish leaders "in the extermination of their own people." Without the Jewish councils, Arendt argued, the Nazis would not have been able to murder as many Jews as they did.[8]

This Hannah Arendt could not know, of course. On the Nazi killing fields in Ukraine and Russia, up to one and a half million Jews were killed in a short time without the slightest participation of any Jewish councils. The Councils of Jewish Elders was a Nazi invention, not a Jewish one. In the new state of Israel, the councils would nevertheless come to be seen as symbols of the inability or unwillingness of the "ghetto Jews" to defend themselves. What was worth remembering and honoring were the Jewish uprisings, however few and doomed; what had to be repressed was the shameful memory of millions of Jews having been led like lambs to the slaughter.

Consequently, when Adolf Eichmann was put on trial in Jerusalem in 1961, Benjamin Murmelstein was not called on to give testimony. The prosecutor in Jerusalem had no interest in reminding the world of the Jewish Councils of Elders. Benjamin Murmelstein was not only the sole surviving "Jewish Elder" in Europe, but also the only one who could have testified to the devious moral maze the Nazi perpetrators had created for their Jewish victims in order to weaken and dehumanize them, and which the Jewish leaders in Europe had all been condemned to confront. In Łódź there had been Chaim Rumkowski, in Warsaw Adam Czerniaków, in Vilnius Jakob

Gens, and in Theresienstadt, before Murmelstein, Jakob Edelstein and Paul Eppstein. They had all collaborated with their tormentors, they had all told themselves that their collaboration was in the service of the community, and they would all be murdered (Czerniaków by his own hand). Their common mistake was to believe that their Nazi masters would choose to exploit the Jews to death rather than murder them straightaway. A moral universe in which the murdering of Jews was more important than their exploitation, none of them could fathom.

Neither could Zvi Koretz.

In 1933, a thirty-year-old rabbi from Galicia accepted the position in Salonika that Ehrenpreis had turned down in 1926 and that had remained vacant ever since. Like Ehrenpreis, Zvi Koretz had a doctorate in philosophy and a rabbinical degree from the Institute for Jewish studies in Berlin, and like Ehrenpreis he was an Ashkenazi rabbi who had become the leader of a Sephardic community. Had Marcus Ehrenpreis accepted the offer to become the chief rabbi of Salonika, he would have been in the clothes of Koretz when Nazi Germany occupied Greece in April 1941.

In December 1942, after having been imprisoned for more than a year, Zvi Koretz was installed by the German commander in Salonika as the leader of the Jews and offered to negotiate their fate. The negotiations went on for a few months and consisted in getting Salonika's Jews to pay large ransoms to avoid deportation. In March 1943 the charade was over and the deportation of Salonika's Jews to "labor camps" in Poland began. Koretz continued to negotiate as if there were something to negotiate, but in the Nazi moral universe there wasn't. Within four months, virtually the entire Jewish population of Salonika had been transported to the gas chambers of Auschwitz-Birkenau. Zvi Koretz was deported to Bergen-Belsen, and in April 1945 was moved to Theresienstadt, and a month after liberation he died of illness and hardship, thus escaping the verdict of posterity: that by his "cooperation" with the German occupiers he had facilitated the deportation and extermination of Salonika's Jews.

Few would in retrospect understand that he, too, clinging to a moral universe that did not exist, believed that he was serving the community. In hindsight, it was all too convenient, and suited all too many purposes, to make the "cooperating" Jewish leaders co-responsible for the Nazi extermination of the Jews.

Marcus Ehrenpreis did not end up in the clothes of Zvi Koretz, nor in the clothes of Benjamin Murmelstein, but with a different turn at one or another junction of his life, he might very well have. Whatever twists of fate that made Ehrenpreis end up as a Jewish leader in non-occupied Stockholm, he, too, would find himself in a moral maze from which he could not come out unscathed. How did you serve a Jewish community squeezed between an all-powerful Germany bent on destroying its Jews and an accommodating Sweden imbued with antisemitic propaganda that would rather not open its gates to any of them?

Ehrenpreis and the congregation in Stockholm never had to face the choice to cooperate or bargain with Nazi commanders over life and death, but they were nevertheless faced with the choice to cooperate or bargain with the Swedish authorities over the number of Jews to be allowed a temporary stay in Sweden. The "objective facts" were as they were: Sweden didn't allow for more than a few of them, and the conditions for receiving them were harsh, and the political opinion for not receiving more was persistent. For Ehrenpreis and the congregation to press for more, as they sometimes did, was to risk precisely the kind of accusations of "dual loyalties" and lack of patriotism that had prompted Ragnar Josephson to state his undivided Swedish loyalty to the point of self-abasement.

"Typical of the actions of the Mosaic Congregation in Stockholm was the acceptance of the existing framework," the Swedish historian Klas Åmark would later write, with an undertone of reproach. Why didn't the Jews do as "the ladies in the Committee for Exiled Intellectuals, who went to the officials at the Board of Social Welfare to plead individual cases, and who refused to leave until they had got what they wanted. The actions of the Mosaic congregation were much more cautious."[9]

Why didn't Ehrenpreis and the leaders of the Jewish community act in the same manner as the non-Jewish ladies in the Committee for Exiled Intellectuals?

Well, because there was a difference between a Jewish plea and a non-Jewish one. A Jewish plea could easily have the opposite effect and lead to rejection.[10] There was an anti-Jewish bias in Sweden's alien and immigration policy, reflecting existing anti-Jewish stereotypes in Swedish society, that would most likely color the official responses to "Jewish" pleas. Jewish caution in pressing for more Jewish "immigrants" was not a choice but a necessity.

Nevertheless, the Swedish Jews would be accused not only of having collaborated with the Swedish state in its de facto anti-Jewish policy, but of having supported it as well. Again, according to Klas Åmark, the demand that Jewish permits of stay be temporary only, and be made contingent on guarantees for further emigration, was "an important feature of both the Mosaic Congregation's and the Swedish state's view on refugees."[11]

Both the Mosaic Congregation and the Swedish state—in that order.

This conjured up the image of the Swedish Jews as being at least as responsible for Sweden's anti-Jewish refugee policy as the Swedish state itself. Toward the end of the war, as the extent of the Jewish catastrophe was becoming clear to all, this image would be disseminated by the Swedish government as well. On 18 January 1945, the minister of social affairs, Gustav Möller, was asked in the Swedish parliament whether he thought that the Swedish policy toward the Jews had been "humane."

This is how he answered:

> What characterized Swedish policy toward certain kinds of refugees before the world war—I must say not only before the war but also at least during the first two years of the war—was that it entailed a restrictive visa rule. For a number of reasons, this meant that the very large numbers of people who wanted to come to Sweden were not readily received. There is no denying that these people were mainly persecuted Jews who wanted to find a safe haven in this country and who therefore sought to come here in masses. At that time, it is true, there was a great reluctance to accept any larger number of people who were persecuted in their countries because they were Jews. But while there may have been, and of course will continue to be, much disagreement as to whether this restrictive policy was justified or not, we should not forget that we have Mosaic Congregations in this country, and *I venture to*

assure the members of this chamber that the Swedish Government, when it came to admitting Jews to the country, was at least as generous as the Mosaic Congregation in Stockholm. I wish to have that taken to the protocol as well.[12]

As for the role of the congregation, Möller's answer was not only misleading, but could easily be perceived as an attempt to shift the blame for an essentially anti-Jewish Swedish refugee policy onto the Jews themselves. Or, as interpreted by another Swedish historian, Mikael Byström: "If only the Swedish Jews had been more willing to help 'their own' [...], the situation would have been different."[13]

Möller's attempt to make the Jewish leaders in Stockholm complicit in a policy which they had very little possibility of influencing, but which the Swedish government at the end of the war felt the need to defend and explain to the outside world, showed, if nothing else, that Marcus Ehrenpreis in Stockholm had more in common with Benjamin Murmelstein in Theresienstadt than met the eye.

The rabbinical post that Murmelstein had hoped for was not to be filled until 1948, and then by Kurt Wilhelm, a rabbi who had left Germany for Palestine in 1933 and thus had escaped the kind of choices and decisions that would put into question not only the role of Benjamin Murmelstein but also the role of Marcus Ehrenpreis. Gustav Möller's statement that the congregation in Stockholm had been as unwilling as the Swedish government to give refuge to German Jews proved to be a mild insinuation compared to the vehement accusations and reproaches that would soon be directed at Ehrenpreis personally and cast a shadow over his final years.

In an ironic twist of fate, the accusers would be joined by Benjamin Murmelstein's son, Wolf Murmelstein, bitter at what he had come to see as a failure by Ehrenpreis to take in his father in the spring of 1939, making little Wolf, three years old at the time, spend part of his childhood in Theresienstadt.

"While the congregation in Stockholm lost time on idiotic correspondence, we were forced to live in the darkness of hell until the war was over," Wolf Murmelstein wrote to me in December 2020. He would spend much of his life defending his father against the accusations and reproaches of posterity, trying to make the world understand the conditions under which Benjamin Murmelstein in Theresienstadt had been forced to act.

For Marcus Ehrenpreis in Stockholm, however, he had no understanding.

The accusations against Ehrenpreis, in due time.

Time, however, to state the obvious: the Jews of Europe were becoming an increasingly isolated minority, with little power to influence the political events that were to seal their fate. The hindsight suggestion that Jewish leaders should have been more forceful in their actions toward their governments and less cooperative seems all the more absurd in view of how even powerful states and governments "cooperated" with Hitler, bowed to his language of power, kept silent about his crimes, and, when provoked to act more forcefully, were overrun by his armies.

The "objective facts" determining the options and actions of Ehrenpreis and the Stockholm congregation in the rescuing of Jews before the war became, if possible, even more intractable when the war broke out and Germany locked its doors on the Jews and started deporting and killing them, and the question of how many Jewish "emigrants" Sweden could accept lost its relevance. In that situation, it would not have taken the Swedish government much to give temporary refuge to the very few Jews who still had a chance to escape.

Instead, the Swedish immigration authorities showed an iron fist. Increasingly desperate appeals for entry were rejected repeatedly—often in defiance of recommendations and pleas from the congregation in Stockholm. The harsh restrictions on Jewish "emigrants" continued to apply as before; the applicant had to have close relatives in Sweden, not have close relatives in Germany, be below eighteen or above forty-five years of age, and have material support guaranteed for three years. As late as February 1942, when the deportations of Jews to "the East" were already known to the Swedish Foreign Ministry,[14] Jewish "involuntary emigrants" (they were still not considered refugees) were refused entry permits to Sweden. For the few who were, it was usually too late.[15] From the congregation in Stockholm, a stream of similarly worded telegrams in English went out to anxious relatives, mostly in the United States:

- Entrance for Schorr Kon family unfortunately refused. (25.2.1942)
- Very sorry Swedish visa and departure from Germany impossible. (2.4.1942)
- Very sorry Swedish visa and departure from Germany and Holland impossible. (23.4.1942)
- Nearest relatives in Sweden and sufficient economic guarantees necessary but departure from Germany impossible. (29.5.1942)[16]

A parliamentary commission set up after the war detailed some of the cases. Each case was followed by a commentary, and each commentary was critical of the handling of the case:

- Should have been approved immediately.
- The Commission finds it remarkable that Mr. F was not granted an entry permit.
- The refusal by the Ministry of Foreign Affairs to refuse Mr. E an entry permit, the Commission finds remarkable.
- The Commission finds that the application submitted in April 1941 [in the case of D] should have been granted by the Ministry of Foreign Affairs immediately after its approval by the National Board of Health and Welfare. The Commission finds it remarkable that this was not done.[17]

The last commentary concerned a twelve-year-old girl who had been admitted in November 1939 under the agreed-upon quota for children, but who was unable to leave Germany at that time. If and when conditions changed the congregation would bring forth her name again. On 3 April 1941, the congregation asked that the now fourteen-year-old girl be granted a permit of stay on the grounds that she had relatives in Sweden—Swedish citizens at that—who had offered to provide for her. On 2 July 1941, the application was put on hold by the Ministry of Foreign Affairs. In a letter of 31 July 1941, the Refugee Section of the congregation asked what had happened. On 6 August 1941, the application was rejected.

"According to the Refugee Section, which brought the case to the attention of the commission, D has been deported," the commission concluded its account of the case.[18]

In the final report by the commission, there was not the slightest suggestion that the congregation in Stockholm in any way had supported Sweden's policies forbidding entry to refugees, and even less, of course, that it had had any shared responsibility in it. Instead, a self-critical account of "the objective facts" that the Swedish Jews had to face:

> The Commission of Inquiry is fully aware of the insurmountable difficulties that could have arisen from an unlimited flow of refugees into our country. However, in view of the considerable number of refugees received in this country at a later stage of the war [seven thousand Danish Jews in October 1943], the commission has come to the conclusion that the difficulties which, before and at the beginning of the war, were thought to arise from a more liberal entry policy regarding refugees from Germany, especially Jews, would not have been impossible to overcome. It was only in the autumn of 1941 that Sweden changed its entry policy toward Jewish refugees from Germany. At about the same time, however, Germany had transitioned from a policy of eliminating the Jews through forced emigration mainly, to their elimination by mass deportation and subsequent liquidation, with a ban on Jews leaving Germany being put into effect. Unfortunately it must be said that the turnabout in Sweden's refugee policy came too late.[19]

Nevertheless, it was Gustav Möller's insinuation that the Mosaic Congregation in Stockholm had supported the restrictive Swedish policy toward Jewish refugees, rather than the commission's account of how the Swedish authorities in case after case had run roughshod over the congregation, that would live on in posterity and tarnish the reputation of both Ehrenpreis and the congregation. It was of little help that the chairman of the congregation, Gunnar Josephson, in a statement published in several Swedish newspapers, declared that the congregation "obviously" had not wished for more restrictive policies, but on the contrary, had wished for many more Jews to be rescued in Sweden. However, Josephson explained, "the Mosaic Congregation has been bound in its efforts by the rules and regulations mandated by the Swedish authorities. There are many cases in which applications for entry permits were submitted and advocated by the congregation, but where the authorities still refused to grant them."[20]

Historical research has confirmed Josephson's version of events. "The Swedish Jews tried as best they could, and in many different ways, to help their brethren in Europe," the historian Pontus Rudberg concludes in his study of the role and actions of the Swedish Jews in the era of the Holocaust: "Considering the restrictive refugee policies of Sweden and other countries during this time, and the vulnerability of the small and dependent Jewish minority in Sweden, its reactions were determined more by the restricted room for maneuver and a sense of powerlessness than lack of will or imagination."[21]

To the challenge of maneuvering restrictive policies and hostile opinions must be added the challenge of standing up to an unprecedented vilification of Jews and Judaism. All his life Marcus Ehrenpreis had been prepared for the task of defending Judaism as a faith and tradition, and he had taken it upon himself with enthusiasm and conviction, but in facing the task of defending Jews as equal human beings he seemed to be at a loss.

As when a distinguished law professor at Uppsala University, Carl-Axel Reuterskiöld, warned against accepting refugees of "Jewish descent," since they would always remain strangers in their host country, and always regard their hosts as enemies, and therefore always make themselves undesirable, which was why they were now undesirable in Germany. "The very fact that a person has become a refugee shows that—for one reason or another—he has not so adapted himself in his homeland that he could or should remain there," Reuterskiöld wrote.[22]

Ehrenpreis rarely engaged in public controversy, but at the request of people close to him he did so now. "I must admit," he wrote in a response to Reuterskiöld, "that in view of the acknowledged scientific authority of the author, I was both saddened and surprised."[23]

Saddened and surprised, since Reuterskiöld's brutal attack on people of "Jewish descent" seemed to confirm that words and arguments no longer sufficed to defend them. Having to argue with a professor of law that Jews were human beings like all others, and that refugees were "innocently persecuted men, women, and children," whether they were Jews or not, must have been a disheartening experience. The entire life and work of Marcus Ehrenpreis had been formed in the belief in the power of the word; the power of truth against lie, the power of spirit against sword, the power of reasoning against propaganda.

Particularly painful it must have been to witness how people affiliated with the Swedish church began expressing affinity with the Nazi-affiliated Protestant denomination in Germany, Deutsche Christen, which had banned members of the Jewish "race," no matter how Christian in faith.[24] To Ehrenpreis, this was a betrayal of the core tenet of both Judaism and Christianity, the equality of all humans before God, and it so deeply disturbed him that he felt compelled to defend Martin Luther against a Church that was using his name to justify the racial persecution and denigration of Jews.

Luther had indeed written one of the most blatantly anti-Jewish pamphlets in history, *The Jews and Their Lies* (1543), but for most of his life he had looked upon the Jews with benevolence, since what he hoped for was their conversion, not their destruction. After all, Luther had also written that if he were a Jew he would rather have been tortured than be subjected to the pope, and had emphatically stated that Jesus Christ was born a Jew, which was in glaring opposition to the attempts by the Deutsche Christen to make Jesus an Aryan. "A policy of persecuting people with a drop of Jewish blood regardless of their creed has no right to seek support from Luther," Ehrenpreis wrote.[25]

And most importantly, perhaps, Luther had believed in the power of words, not least the words of the Hebrew Bible. It was with these words that Luther had hoped to win the Jews for Christianity, and it was with the same words that Ehrenpreis had hoped to win the Christian world for a new understanding of Jews and Judaism. Against the power of blood and race, however, the power of words proved futile.

As Ehrenpreis realized how little his words seemed to inform the view of Jews and Judaism in Sweden, he increasingly turned to the Swedish Jews themselves, hoping to instill in them the self-esteem needed to endure the anti-Jewish gale sweeping over Europe. In the spring of 1933, Ehrenpreis had summoned the prophet Malachi to alert the time and the world. But the time had passed, and the world had turned its back on the Jews, and in the spring of 1936 he directed his call to the young Jewish confirmands standing before him in the synagogue of Stockholm:

> Fear not! Do not be afraid of the dangers that surround us and that will surround you. [...] Remember your Jewishness in all that you do, in all that you undertake, because as a Jew you are more exposed to the criticism

> of the world, to the malice of the world, than any other youth. [...] May the events of the times never lead you to self-abandonment.[26]

Thus Ehrenpreis turned from building a bridge to building a fortress. The dream of a new encounter between Israel and the nations was shattered, and the struggle for the renaissance of Judaism had become a struggle for its very survival. To Ehrenpreis, it was still mainly a matter of spiritual survival, of saving not only the house of Jacob, but more importantly "the inestimable treasures that this house harbors." But faced with the prospect of the treasures having no house at all, the cause of political Zionism, a Jewish national home in Palestine, became Ehrenpreis's cause as well. Whatever Jewish home Palestine should become, and whatever people the Jews were or should be, Jewish Palestine had become a refuge of last resort, and a growing source of self-esteem, even for Swedish Jews who did not consider themselves Zionists.

Toward the end of August 1939, two weeks before the outbreak of the war, Marcus Ehrenpreis once again traveled to a Zionist congress, this time in Geneva, and this time with the specific aim of bringing about a joint Scandinavian-Jewish action to keep Palestine open for Jewish refugees from Hitler's realm of terror.

> Here we were sitting on this bright August morning in a cold schoolroom temporarily transformed into a conference hall, listening with sadness to the grave appeals of the Palestinian representatives. [...] And I heard the trembling voice from Ramah, of which the prophet Jeremiah speaks: "Rachel weeps for her children and she cannot comfort herself because her children are

> no more." And here again, Rachel was weeping in a schoolroom in Geneva: My children are gone, they cannot return to me: homeless and helpless they crowd outside their parents' home, knocking desperately at the gate, unable to enter. And there is no Jeremiah to comfort her: stop weeping, your children shall return to their land.
>
> Never before has this return been such a burning necessity, never has the knocking on the gates of Eretz Israel sounded so despairing, so heart-wrenching, as in this time of distress.[27]

Ehrenpreis still remained faithful to his cultural-Zionist ideals and thus remained critical of a Zionism that wanted to make of the Jews a people like all the others, with a state like all the others, a Jewish Serbia or Montenegro, as his cultural-Zionist mentor Ahad Ha'am had put it sarcastically. Nor did he see a Jewish state in Palestine as the solution to what was increasingly being termed "the Jewish problem" or "the Jewish question." To political Zionism, the "Jewish problem" was a consequence of Jewish "alienation" and would be solved when the Jews had been normalized into a people like all the others, in their own land like all the others. For Ehrenpreis, on the other hand, Diaspora was a fundamental condition of Jewish existence; it was in the Diaspora that Judaism had formed, developed, and at times flourished; it was in the Diaspora that "Israel" had become a people founded on the spirit and not the sword. "We are not a people because we have a common enemy. We have enemies because we are not a people like other people," he would insist to the very end.[28]

If Ehrenpreis had for a few years thought that in his new *Kinderland* he would be able to devote himself to the spiritual and cultural renewal of Judaism and the building of a bridge between Judaism and the world, he by now knew very well that those years were past. Marcus Ehrenpreis was Sweden's most well-known Jewish personality, and his formally limited role as chief rabbi of a small congregation on Europe's Jewish periphery soon merged with the larger political and diplomatic role that the "objective facts" were forcing him to play. There was simply no one else among the Jews of Sweden who could have filled it with the same authority and experience.

As a consequence, the name of Ehrenpreis, perhaps more than anything else, would be associated with a heated postwar controversy about what the Jews of Sweden did or did not do to save their "coreligionists."

Time then, perhaps, to say something about what Marcus Ehrenpreis did or did not do, since lies and slander would soon come to distort it.

Marcus Ehrenpreis at home in Stockholm, 1933.

10.

SERVING THE COMMUNITY

The man at the writer's desk, or in the pulpit, is free but not sovereign.
Above him is a cause, a time, a destiny.
What he writes or speaks comes from within,
but when and how are determined by forces from without.

—Marcus Ehrenpreis, 1944[1]

There is no denying that Marcus Ehrenpreis played a central role in the efforts of the Mosaic Congregation in Stockholm to bring help to the Jews of Germany, and to "bring first aid to the distressed Jewish refugees who may arrive in our country."[2] After Hitler's annexation of Austria and the November pogrom in Germany in 1938 (Kristallnacht), he pleaded with the Swedish government to allow for more "involuntary emigrants" than the minimal transit quotas and the tacitly anti-Jewish visa restrictions allowed for, leading to the creation of two additional quotas, one for unaccompanied minors (500) and one for the elderly (150), and an increase in the existing quota for young pioneers destined for Palestine (300).[3] In the spring and summer of 1939, the refugee section of the congregation also proposed the creation of a transit camp in Sweden for some thousand people, largely funded by the American-Jewish aid organization JDC, the Joint Distribution Committee, with which Ehrenpreis had close ties. That same summer, Ehrenpreis asked the JDC to be the financial guarantor of an application to the Swedish government for the creation of an additional transit quota for Jews in Germany who were considered stateless, or who as "Polish subjects" were in a particular danger of being assaulted by the Nazi state.[4]

Then came the war. On 2 October 1939, the aid committee met at Ehrenpreis's home to discuss the new situation. To the contributions of Ehrenpreis, it should be added, was an open and hospitable home where meetings and gatherings were interspersed with dinners and informal discussions. At the meeting on 2 October, Ehrenpreis proposed a special transit quota for Jews whose transit visas to countries now at war had been revoked.[5]

In fact, the minutes and documents from these meetings are replete with proposals and initiatives that eventually would bring some result, just as they were filled with proposals and initiatives that would not.

No transit camp for some thousand Jews.
No transit quotas for particularly endangered Jews.
No transit quotas for Jews with revoked transit visas.

In October 1941, Ehrenpreis formed the Association for Aid to the Jews of Poland: "Speechless, we stand before the shed blood of our brothers, wondering and pondering what will become of them. We must now make every effort to help them, firmly believing [...] that this part of the Jewish world will once again be able to fulfill great and important tasks in the history of our people."[6] In its appeal for contributions, the association stated: "We Swedish Jews are among the few remaining Jewish groups on our continent who are still able to help. This grace of God, which has been bestowed upon us, creates an obligation for each and every one of us. We must extend a helping hand to our despairing brothers in faith. We must save those who can be saved."[7]

It seems that the association had not yet fully grasped the challenge in delivering aid packages to people locked up behind ghetto walls and isolated from the outside world. "We have received definite assurances from the proper authorities on location that our aid will reach its addressees in full," the appeal said.[8]

A later report on the association's activities noted that the emergency food and clothing parcels sent via Portugal to recipients in Poland were a "drop in the ocean," that it had taken three to six months for them to reach their addressees, and that in many cases it had not been possible to confirm their reception. It was also noted that the funds collected up to the summer of 1942 had been embarrassingly small.

"It appears that the Swedish Jewry had not grasped what the hour of need demanded," the report concluded.[9]

In October 1942 Ehrenpreis proposed that the scope of the association be extended to "the Jews of Europe," and shortly thereafter the Jews of Sweden would find out what was meant by "the Jews of Europe." With the mass roundup and deportation of one-third of Norway's Jewish population on 26 November 1942, it became only all too clear that Nazi Germany was bent on exterminating the Jews on the periphery of Europe as well.

"It is horrible to see with what inexorable consistency the Nazi war of extermination against the Jews is being carried out:

the innocent victims stretching from the internment camps in the Pyrenees to the wilderness of northern Norway," Ehrenpreis wrote a week after the Norwegian roundup. The Jews of Stockholm had just lit their Hanukkah candles in celebration of the "Maccabean miracle," but with no new miracle in sight. The eight candles that were to bear witness to the power of the spirit over matter had now to witness the opposite, "a brutal material force, trampling spirit, law, and humanity under its boots."[10]

Nevertheless, the deportation of the Norwegian Jews would be a turning point in Sweden's attitudes and policies. "The tragedy that has befallen the Jews of Norway has triggered a spontaneous, powerful reaction in Sweden, unbendingly spreading from town to town, from group to group," Ehrenpreis wrote in December 1942. "Shame and disgust reverberate through the protests, and an unshakable determination that such barbarism must not be allowed to penetrate the borders of Sweden."

On 17 January 1943, Ehrenpreis spoke to 1,400 people at a fundraising event "for the Jews of Europe" in the City Hall of Stockholm, a record number in the annals of the Jewish community in Stockholm, and in one evening was raised more than half of the amount that the Association for Aid to the Jews of Poland had managed to raise in ten months.[11]

On 15 March 1943, another appeal, this time for the Jewish children of Europe, and another public event, a packed opera house in Stockholm, and another keynote speech by Marcus Ehrenpreis:

> The darkened ghettos of Europe are hidden behind a veil of smoke. We do not know what is going on. We can only guess, and there is a danger that our worst fears will be surpassed by reality. When the day comes for the

> veil to fall, when the destruction will be revealed in all its cruel nakedness, the world will be struck with horror and terror, and the angels in heaven will blush at the sight of the unspeakable crimes committed by humans against humans on this earth. The tragedy of children is the most shocking aspect of the tragedy that has befallen Jewry, the darkest point in a dark picture. Hundreds of thousands of Jewish children and young people, crammed into overcrowded ghettos.[12]

The aim of the event was to raise money for the rescue of Jewish children in Europe by organizing their evacuation to Palestine. No other rescue seemed possible. Although the "industrial" details of the "final solution to the Jewish question" were not widely known yet, everyone understood by this time that "the solution" was the physical annihilation of the Jews.

No other explanation seemed possible anymore.

The response to the appeal for the rescue of Jewish children was overwhelming. The organization Save the Children sent a check for more than the total amount raised so far for the Jews of Poland and Europe. It was conditioned upon the money being used for children's and young people's evacuation to Palestine. When, in September 1943, Save the Children impatiently wondered why the full amount had not yet been used for this purpose, Ehrenpreis patiently explained that the conditions for the rescue of children had "deteriorated considerably." The Soviet government had halted all emigration of Polish Jews, and the Bulgarian government had reneged on its promise to release 4,000 Jewish children. "The fact that we have used a small amount of the provided funds for helping suffering and abandoned Jewish children in France and elsewhere—and that we intend to do so to the extent possible [awaiting new openings for evacuation]—needs no further explanation. It was our common understanding from the beginning that although the action was mainly intended to promote child *aliyah* to Palestine, temporary aid to starving and freezing Jewish children, wherever they may be, would not be excluded."[13]

Apparently, Save the Children could not fully imagine what it would take to evacuate Jewish children from Europe, and that most of the children intended for rescue were already beyond rescue.

Where to, for example, had 260,000 Jews in the Warsaw ghetto, children and all, been transported during the summer of 1942? As late as October 1942, a Swedish-Jewish magazine (*Judisk krönika*) could only imagine that they had been taken farther east, "and since they are more or less incapable of work due to starvation and disease, one can only imagine what fate awaits them."[14]

In November 1942, following a telegram from the Jewish Agency in Tel Aviv, Marcus Ehrenpreis contacted the Swedish Foreign Ministry for information about the Jews in Warsaw, but whatever information the Foreign Ministry had to share, it was not willing to share it with Ehrenpreis. The Swedish minister in Berlin, Arvid Richert, suggested in a telegram to Ragnar Kumlin at the Ministry of Foreign Affairs that Ehrenpreis be told that rumors of "a larger or smaller" evacuation of the Warsaw ghetto had not been verified. Richert was also careful to emphasize that whatever information Ehrenpreis was to be given "about the treatment of Jews, etc." must not be shared with the outside world.[15]

By this time Richert already knew what his colleague at the Berlin Legation, Göran von Otter, had learned on 20 August 1942, at a meeting with the SS officer Kurt Gerstein on the night train between Warsaw and Berlin, about the mass gassing of Jews at a makeshift killing facility in Bełżec, outside Lublin. Presumably Richert also knew more about the deportations from the Warsaw ghetto than he wanted Kumlin to tell Ehrenpreis. What Kumlin told Ehrenpreis, in a telephone conversation on 22 November 1942, seems to have led Ehrenpreis to believe that the Jews "rumored" to have been evacuated from the Warsaw ghetto were to be exploited for road construction. In any case, this was what Ehrenpreis reported to the Jewish Agency in New York two days later: "According to uncontrollable rumors the main of Warcovie [*sic*] ghetto has been evacuated, partly for building roads."[16]

It is hard to believe, writes the historian Pontus Rudberg, that Ehrenpreis would have reported this if Kumlin had not taken pains to make him believe it.[17] It is also hard to believe that the Swedish legation in Berlin did not know (or understand) more than that. By this time, Richert, and therefore Kumlin, had received reports that the population of the Warsaw ghetto had decreased from 400,000 to 30,000 in a matter of months, and whatever German excuses the report had forwarded (road construction, starvation, disease, et cetera), Richert already had firsthand information of what Germany had in mind for the Jews who were transported "farther east."

One possible explanation for Richert's concerns about what Ehrenpreis should be allowed to know, and even more what he would be allowed to spread, was that he did not want the German government to be able to trace information and testimony about the extermination of the Jews to Swedish sources. This could also explain why von Otter's report about the gas chambers in Bełżec did not immediately come to the attention of the outside world. Indeed, the question was no longer whether

Nazi Germany was killing the Jews, but how. Ehrenpreis and most of the world could not yet imagine how, and what the Swedish legation in Berlin learned in August 1942 about how it was being done in Bełżec was not allowed to be forwarded to Ehrenpreis and the world.[18]

What the world did not have to imagine any longer, since it was taking place before its eyes, was how the Jews in every corner of Europe were hounded and herded into concentration camps and ghettos for further deportation. In August 1942, Ehrenpreis wrote about the deportation of the Dutch Jews, the descendants of the Sephardic Jews in Amsterdam among whom Rembrandt had lived, and whose faces had inspired many of his portraits and paintings:

> Now the children of the Rembrandt figures are marched in black herds to the internment camps. After four hundred years of life and work in a country to whose culture and economic prosperity they have made invaluable contributions, they are headed off into the darkness to meet their martyrdom as laborers in a distant land.[19]

Even in countries not occupied by Nazi Germany but still part of the Nazi axis, Jews were treated as outlaws, herded into newly erected ghettos and subjected to "every conceivable degradation," Ehrenpreis noted.

He also noted that one such country was Bulgaria.

Fourteen years in Bulgaria had left a lasting mark on Marcus Ehrenpreis, not least in shaping his view of the possibilities and future of the Jewish Diaspora. He remembered Bulgaria's relationship with its Jewish minority as a model for the Balkan countries, and although his memories had become shrouded in nostalgia, the rumors in the spring of 1943 of the imminent deportation of the Bulgarian Jews must have come as a shock. With his former friend and protector King Ferdinand, who abdicated in 1918, Ehrenpreis had continued to exchange birthday greetings, and now Ferdinand's son, Boris III, was in the process of sacrificing the very Jews that his father had protected and safeguarded. To Ehrenpreis, the Jews of Bulgaria were still very much "his" Jews, and in the Jewish world his role and position in Bulgaria were well remembered.

Consequently, at the end of March 1943, Marcus Ehrenpreis received two telegrams in rapid succession appealing to him to use his contacts and influence to stop the deportations. One was from Vitalis Nachmias of the Committee for the Rescue of Bulgarian Jews in New York: "Please use all available means to help brethren." The other was from Rabbi Stephen Wise, President of the World Jewish Congress: "Do everything to prevent this ghastly crime which would constitute unbridgeable barrier between the Bulgarian people and humanity of today and tomorrow."[20]

Ehrenpreis acted immediately, and in a telegram to Stephen Wise on 12 April he could report that the deportations from Bulgaria had been suspended.

However, for the Jews in the territories of Greece and Yugoslavia that Bulgaria had invaded in 1941 with German support, it was too late. At the end of March 1943, the Jews of Macedonia, Thrace, and parts of Serbia, 11,350 in all, were deported in sealed boxcars to a place along the railway line between Warsaw and Białystok where over a quarter of a million Warsaw Jews had already been murdered, and which would be known to the world as Treblinka.[21]

Left for deportation in April 1943 were 28,000 Jews in "old" Bulgaria.

What happened next has been described as one of the few bright spots in the dark history of the deportation and destruction of Europe's Jews. Under the pretext that Bulgaria needed "its" Jews for the building of roads (always these roadbuilding projects), the Bulgarian government in May 1943 had them evacuated to labor camps in the countryside. At the same time, leading political and church representatives demanded that Bulgaria refuse to hand over its Jews. One of the most outspoken was the leader of the Bulgarian Orthodox Church in Sofia, the metropolitan Stefan, and when rumors began to spread that the deportations would resume in the summer, it was to him that Marcus Ehrenpreis sent a telegram on 21 June 1943:

> Despairing cries from my former Jewish congregations, coming to me through Palestine and America, prompt me to plead with Your Eminence for your moral assistance. You know the absolute loyalty of the Bulgarian Jewry. You know of my successful efforts, during a long period as the religious head of the Bulgarian congregations, to promote the integration of my fellow believers into the life of the liberated Bulgarian nation. I know that Your Reverence has repeatedly spoken on behalf of my defenseless fellow believers, and there are expectations that in this hour of supreme danger you will continue your efforts. The friends of Bulgaria in the world, among whom I have the right to count myself, have full confidence in the wisdom of King Boris, being convinced that he will spare the loyal innocent Bulgarian Jewry that utmost fate and thus do an invaluable service to the Bulgarian name in the eyes of the world.[22]

On 2 July 1943, the Swedish Legation in Sofia confirmed that the telegram from Ehrenpreis had been delivered to Metropolitan Stefan, and that he had expressed "his appreciation of the confidence shown in him by Chief Rabbi Ehrenpreis. He himself was very concerned about the fate of the Jews, and he foresaw that they might find themselves in a critical situation during the coming autumn and winter. The metropolitan would do his utmost to assist them, and he hoped that his efforts would not be fruitless."[23]

That the telegram to the metropolitan was the initiative of Ehrenpreis and not of the Swedish government is evident from the handwritten note on the copy of the reply telegram from Sofia forwarded to Ehrenpreis, specifying the costs for which the Ministry of Foreign Affairs asked to be reimbursed.[24]

On 14 August 1943, Metropolitan Stefan sent a telegram informing the Swedish Ministry that he had received a personal assurance from King Boris that "no further action would be taken against the Jews and that they would not be deported."[25]

Two weeks later, King Boris died under unclear circumstances at the age of forty-nine, but his promise held. The deportations from Bulgaria were halted, not to be resumed again. In Plovdiv, where in early March 1943 the Jews had been assembled in a school awaiting deportation, Metropolitan Kirill declared himself prepared to be deported with them. And from Kyustendil, where the Jews had been herded into a tobacco warehouse, a civic delegation left for Sofia to demand that the deportation be stopped.

And so it happened.

"In Bulgaria, the significance of the Jewish question is simply not understood," the German ambassador in Sofia, Adolf-Heinz Beckerle, complained to his superiors in Berlin. "To the simple Bulgarian, brought up among Greeks, Turks, and

Gypsies, the struggle against the Jews, indeed the very nature of the racial question, seems completely incomprehensible."[26]

At this fateful moment, Bulgaria, which had been so close to Ehrenpreis, and for whose Jews he had had such great prospects, confirmed his brightest memories and hopes. Of all the countries in Europe exposed to Nazi Germany's anti-Jewish propaganda and policies, Bulgaria proved to be one of the most resilient. At least, that is how Ehrenpreis wanted to see it. In a lengthy interview in *Dagens Nyheter* on 31 August 1944 (on the occasion of Bulgaria's abolition of its anti-Jewish racial laws), he spoke at length about his Bulgarian experiences, resolutely stating that antisemitism had always been alien to the Bulgarian people.[27]

Ehrenpreis's intervention on behalf of Bulgaria's Jews would later be characterized by the World Jewish Congress as one of the organization's greatest rescue efforts,[28] but whatever contributed to the rescue (there were other actors and pressures at play), the appeal to the metropolitan of Sofia was characteristic of Ehrenpreis's mode of operation: using personal contacts with religious leaders to evoke and appeal to a common spiritual responsibility.

"It seems to me that it in this dark hour it would be both desirable and useful if the church in our country were to raise its voice and speak a word of comfort and guidance," he wrote to the Swedish archbishop, Erling Eidem, the day after the deportation of the Norwegian Jews.

And again to Archbishop Eidem after the deportations of Hungarian Jews in April 1944: "As the situation is now, when political authorities seem powerless to intervene, the ecclesiastical authorities are the ones who can and must raise the voice of humanity, to what benefit it might have. Here, if anywhere, the saying applies: *in magnis et voluisse sat est* [in big things it's enough to have wanted it]."[29]

After the deportation of the Norwegian Jews, the ecclesiastical authority in Sweden had at last begun to raise its voice. On 3 December 1942, the first Sunday of Advent, a statement from the bishops of Sweden was read in the churches: "Whatever we can do to assist the poor victims of this hatred, it is our simple duty both as Christians and as human beings to do. But even if we cannot do much to help the unfortunate, we can and should carry them and their plight in our hearts."[30]

The ecclesiastical authority in Sweden did not raise its voice any more than that. Throughout the war, the Church of Sweden cautiously refrained from "interfering in politics" and never publicly criticized the German government for its persecution of the Jews or the Swedish government for its forbidding immigration and refugee policies.

Theologically, the restraint of the Swedish church was justified by the Lutheran doctrine of two kingdoms: strict separation between earthly power (the sword and the law) and divine power (the grace and the gospel). In a Swedish context, this led to the Swedish church subjugating its moral and spiritual voice to the *raison d'état* of the Swedish government—even when the policies of that *raison d'état* stood in sharp contrast to fundamental Christian values and beliefs.

When, in early October 1943, the turn came for Denmark's Jews to be deported by the German occupiers, the Church of Sweden did not have to put the two-kingdom doctrine to the test. This time the earthly power did what was reasonably the Christian thing to do. In any case, there was no longer any discussion about how many persecuted Jews Sweden could take in; the Swedish government declared itself willing to receive them all. Subsequently, in the course of a few nights, the Jews of Denmark were carried in small fishing boats across Øresund, the strait between Denmark and Sweden. The rescue of more than seven thousand Jews from deportation and extermination was the second bright spot after Bulgaria—and this time much of the light fell on Sweden.

About the new light on Sweden, the Swedish Ministry of Foreign Affairs reported willingly and repeatedly to Ehrenpreis. On 24 November 1943, he received a letter from the head of the political department enumerating the Jewish organizations around the world that had sent tributes and thanks to Sweden. Three days later, another letter with another list of grateful organizations. Ehrenpreis was now entrusted with copies of confidential letters from the Swedish ambassador in Washington to the foreign minister in Stockholm concerning "the reaction in Jewish circles to Sweden's action on the Danish-Jewish question."

It was not hard to understand the willingness of the Ministry of Foreign Affairs to share its diplomatic reports from the United States. "In this darkness of Teutonic rage and cruelty, the name of Sweden will forever shine like the brightest of stars," the Swedish ambassador quoted from *Der Tog*, a Yiddish newspaper in New York.[31]

Undeniably, a new Swedish policy on Jewish refugees was now emerging, and Ehrenpreis's central position in the Jewish world made him a valuable contact for the Swedish government in its ambition to communicate its newly awakened willingness to help and save.

With the arrival of the Danish Jews, Jewish congregations in Sweden were faced with a new task. Although the Swedish government this time contributed financially to their reception and accommodation, large sums were donated by Jewish individuals, and many private Jewish homes were opened to the new arrivals, and the Mosaic Congregation in Stockholm made another fundraising appeal to the Jews of Sweden:

> Why do we need to help?
> Out of compassion.
> Out of a sense of dignity.
> Out of concern for the verdict of the future, which will be considering what sacrifices we made to alleviate the plight of our fellow believers in this time of disaster.[32]

The verdict of the future. Not yet.

In April 1944 began the deportation of Hungary's 800,000 Jews, the largest remaining Jewish population in German-occupied Europe, and within two months 435,000 men, women, and children were murdered in the gas chambers of Auschwitz. The purpose of the deportations was no longer in any doubt, and it was no longer difficult to make the Swedish government accept even far-reaching plans for saving those who could still be saved.

In the last week of June 1944, Marcus Ehrenpreis received two telegrams, each suggesting that the Swedish Jews should appeal to Sweden's head of state, King Gustaf V, to intervene with Hungary's head of state, Miklós Horthy, to stop the deportations. One was from the chief rabbi of Zurich, Zvi Taubes, the other from Itzchak Grünbaum of the Jewish Agency in Jerusalem. Ehrenpreis immediately forwarded the two telegrams with the handwritten addition *periculum in mora!* [danger in delay!] to the Swedish foreign minister Christian Günther, who in turn forwarded the information from Ehrenpreis to

Prime Minister Per Albin Hansson, who in turn raised the matter at the cabinet meeting of 28 June 1944, where it was decided that the king would make a personal appeal to the Hungarian regent.[33]

Around the same time, a group of Hungarian Jews had written to the Swedish minister in Budapest, Ivan Danielsson, pleading for the same thing. The letter was forwarded to the Foreign Ministry on 24 June, together with a detailed report on the ongoing mass deportations, and an eyewitness account from the death camp at Auschwitz-Birkenau.[34] A few days later, Danielsson reported "that the campaign of persecution against the Jews has taken such forms that one can fear for the almost complete destruction of the Jewish population in Hungary."[35]

On 30 June 1944, King Gustaf V sent an appeal to Admiral Horthy:[36]

> Having learned of the extraordinary harshness of your government's treatment of the Jewish population of Hungary, I take the liberty of addressing Your Excellency personally, in the name of humanity, to ask you to take steps to save those of this unfortunate people who remain to be saved. This appeal is prompted by my long-standing feelings of friendship for your country and by my sincere concern for the good name and reputation of Hungary in the community of nations.[37]

Horthy replied that he would do everything "in [his] power under present circumstances to ensure that the principles of humanity and justice are respected."

A few days later, the Swedish government was informed that deportations of Jews would be suspended, and that Jews who were Swedish citizens or had close relatives in Sweden would be allowed to emigrate to Sweden, and that Jewish children under the age of ten would be allowed to emigrate to Palestine.[38]

However, the matter was no longer entirely in Horthy's hands. Three months earlier, on 19 March 1944, Germany had invaded Hungary, and a man named Adolf Eichmann had taken control over the fate of its Jews and organized their deportation with frightening efficiency: train after train of cattle cars filled to bursting with humans, most of whom were already dead by the time of the king's appeal. When the deportations were halted on 7 July, large parts of Hungary had already been emptied of their Jewish population.

Remaining to be deported were Budapest's two hundred thousand Jews.

Thereby remaining was yet another Swedish rescue operation.

In mid-April 1944, Marcus Ehrenpreis received a letter from Norbert Masur, the Swedish representative of the World Jewish Congress in New York, who had been in contact with Iver Olsen, the representative of the War Refugee Board, an American organization newly established by President Roosevelt to "rescue Jews and other vulnerable groups in German-occupied countries." Olsen was stationed at the American Legation in Stockholm and worked for the Office of Strategic Services (OSS), the United States' intelligence service, and had been involved in covert rescue operations in the Baltic States, some of which had been carried out with the assistance of Swedish military and intelligence services. Olsen wanted to explore if something similar could be done in Hungary.

In his letter to Ehrenpreis, Masur wrote: "Recalling our conversation on Saturday, I would like to specify my proposal:

we should look for a personality, skilled, with a good reputation, non-Jewish, who is willing to travel to Romania/ Hungary to lead a rescue operation for the Jews. This person must be trusted by the Foreign Ministry, be equipped with a diplomatic passport, and be given assurances of assistance from the [Swedish] legations in Bucharest and Budapest. We must place a large sum of money at his disposal. [...] If we find the right man, get the support of the Foreign Ministry, and have the money, I believe this plan will save hundreds of people."[39]

Ehrenpreis was easily convinced by Masur, whom he knew well and trusted, and immediately began to search for the right man. His first thought was to search among people within the non-Jewish aid organizations in Sweden. On 4 May, in his capacity as chairman of the Committee for Aid to the Jews of Europe, he wrote a letter to Hugo Cedergren, secretary-general of the Christian organization Aid to Victims of War, referring to the "unspeakable" emergency of the Jews of Hungary and Romania, and reminding him of the "well-known obstacles that we as a Jewish organization have to face." He therefore wished to raise with Cedergren the question of "committing to the regions in question, beginning with Budapest, a [non-Jewish] confidant equipped with the necessary credentials who would come into contact with the authorities and organize the work in consultation with Jewish leadership. [...] I will be happy to provide you any further information and I am looking forward to your kind reply."[40]

The kind reply came in a phone call on 12 May, by the secretary of Aid to Victims of War, who informed him that such an initiative would imply an extension of the organization's stated mission, and that a decision on the matter would have to be referred to the meeting of the General Assembly at the end of May, and that it therefore might be worthwhile to make contact within business circles, Save the Children, and the Swedish Central Bank."[41]

A few days later Ehrenpreis contacted a Hungarian-Jewish businessman in Stockholm, Kálman Lauer, to ask him whether he knew a suitable person who could be sent to Budapest to investigate "the Jewish question." Lauer had been running a small food-export-and-import firm, Mellaneuropeiska Handels AB, since 1941, and at the recommendation of his Swedish partner, the shipowner Sven Salén, he had employed a talented young man with a gift for languages who had already made several trips to Hungary, most recently in September–October 1943, and who Lauer without hesitation recommended for the assignment.[42]

To the extent that Ehrenpreis had doubts about Raoul Wallenberg's suitability for the assignment—after their first meeting at Ehrenpreis's home in mid-May he found him a bit too young and inexperienced, and perhaps too ambitious[43]—those doubts were soon to be dispelled. Just a day later, Lauer wrote to Ehrenpreis, informing him that he had discussed with Raoul Wallenberg the forming of a Swedish "aid association" in Budapest, perhaps as a chapter of Save the Children, to be put under the auspices of the Swedish Legation. "Within such an arrangement, Mr. Wallenberg will have many opportunities to help, although it is of course not yet possible to know how far the arrangement may extend."[44]

Marcus Ehrenpreis responded by contacting a friend in the leadership of Save the Children, the countess Ebba Bonde, to put her in touch with Raoul Wallenberg. Ebba Bonde was the sister of Raoul's godfather, the industrialist and banker Jacob Wallenberg, and a cousin of Raoul's father. A year before, Ebba Bonde had initiated the Committee for Racially Persecuted

Children, which had been contributing to Ehrenpreis's Committee for the Relief of Europe's Jewish Children.

The immediate relief effort that Ehrenpreis seems to have had in mind was the transportation and distribution of lifesaving supplies to the Jews in Hungary with the help of the Swedish Legation in Budapest. At least this was what Ebba Bonde had discussed with Wallenberg when they met, and it was the result of this discussion that Wallenberg, in a letter to "Herr Professor M. Ehrenpreis" on 3 June 1944, wished to inform him about. Countess Bonde had by then already spoken to the Swedish foreign minister, "His Excellency Günther," who was "fully prepared to help" and who had promised to contact the Swedish minister in Budapest immediately, about "possible ways of getting shipments to the ghettos."[45]

Thus, by early June 1944 Ehrenpreis had not only reassessed Raoul Wallenberg but had begun working with him. According to a letter from Kálman Lauer to Jacob Wallenberg a year later, Ehrenpreis had told Raoul that he would "be eternally grateful to him if he would undertake the mission."[46]

With the gratitude of Ehrenpreis at hand, Lauer arranged a meeting between Raoul Wallenberg and Iver Olsen on 12 June, and that same afternoon the head of the U.S. Legation in Stockholm, Herschel Johnson, telegraphed to the U.S. secretary of state, Cordell Hull, informing him that he had found "a Swede who will shortly be going on a business trip to Hungary and who seems willing to assist in every possible way in the Hungarian problem."[47] The following day, 13 June, Wallenberg was summoned to a meeting with the top civil servant at the Foreign Ministry, Cabinet Secretary Erik Boheman, where he was asked to join the Foreign Service and "travel to Budapest in the capacity of legation secretary."[48] On 21 June, Herschel Johnson in Stockholm recommended that the U.S. government, through the War Refugee Board, give its full support to the mission that Wallenberg had been given by the Swedish government.[49]

On one of the first days of July 1944, Ehrenpreis received Raoul Wallenberg in the synagogue. According to a later account, he embraced the young Wallenberg with tears in his eyes and read God's blessing over him.[50]

On 5 July 1944, on the eve of his departure for Budapest, Wallenberg visited the chief rabbi in his summer home in Saltsjöbaden. It remains unclear why. Perhaps Ehrenpreis had information he wanted to pass on in person: contacts, lists of names, addresses.

Whatever the reason, Ehrenpreis seems to have been one of the last people in Sweden to have seen Wallenberg alive.[51]

The rest, as they say, is history, and in that history Ehrenpreis played an early but important role; not by virtue of his formal capacity as chief rabbi, but again by virtue of his personal authority and position. So it came that the Swedish government in July 1944 dispatched a non-Jewish representative by the name of Raoul Wallenberg to the Swedish Legation in Budapest with the task of rescuing those who could still be rescued.

Ehrenpreis, together with other Jews in Sweden, would henceforth be personally involved in the decisions about who would or would not be eligible for rescue. Hungarian Jews who sought the protection of the Swedish Legation still had to declare a personal connection to Sweden. In mid-August 1944, Ehrenpreis received a letter from the head of the legal department at the Foreign Ministry, Louis De Geer, stating that "Dr. Tanne, a lung specialist from Lemberg, with his sister, daughter, and brother-in-law," had provided the name of Ehrenpreis as his Swedish connection, but that the legation in Budapest, "due to lack of documentation, had not been able to provide any assistance." "In view of this," the letter continued, "I have the honor to request that you provide the Foreign Ministry in writing with information concerning the nature of your relationship with the person in question."[52]

Ehrenpreis's secretary, Inga Gottfarb, replied truthfully that the chief rabbi had been away from Lemberg for fifty years and could not possibly remember "all the Lemberg refugees who refer to him," but that he would gladly endorse Dr. Tanne's application, "and if he comes here, Professor Ehrenpreis will do everything in his power to assist him and his family."[53]

A trace of irritation could be detected in the answer: How could the Swedish Foreign Ministry be indulging in time-consuming demands for written documentation when everybody knew that this was a race against time about life or death?

Not so for Raoul Wallenberg. The thousands of protective Swedish passports issued by Wallenberg and the legation in Budapest in the autumn of 1944 required no written documentation, and eventually not even a fictitious Swedish connection.

No one knows exactly how many lives Raoul Wallenberg helped to save in this way, but the dimensions of his rescue action would grow with the buildup of testimonies from those who had witnessed it, just as the manifestations to celebrate and remember it would increase with the questions surrounding Wallenberg's arrest in January 1945 and his subsequent disappearance without a trace in Stalin's Soviet Union.

On 11 January 1948, some thousand people gathered in the Stockholm Concert Hall to demand that "Generalissimo Stalin" tell his fate.[54] For health reasons Ehrenpreis had to refrain from appearing in person, but his written tribute to Raoul Wallenberg was read from the stage:

> From my personal encounters with Raoul Wallenberg, I have retained an unforgettable impression of a straightforward, selfless humanitarian, a shining figure in an age darkened by hatred and division.[55]

The health reasons had long made themselves present: cancellations of lectures and conferences, written greetings instead of personal appearances, recurring leaves of absence. His eyesight was failing, his heart was troubled, and his physical strength was waning. In the dark summer of 1944, Marcus Ehrenpreis turned seventy-five, and in other circumstances it would have been an appropriate time to retire. The tributes published in *Judisk Tidskrift* were largely attempts to summarize his life. At the same time, it was hard to summarize a life that was still devoted to tasks and duties from which it was hard to retire.

The bishop of Visby, Torsten Ysander, wrote with empathy and insight about being a Jewish leader in a Europe beset by Jew-hatred:

> During the war years and the years immediately preceding it, the Chief Rabbi of Stockholm has been in a protected place, and at the same time in a terrible position. Few have had greater insight than he into the bottomless atrocities visited upon the Jewish people. Hardly anyone can have been more passionate than he about reaching out with help to the suffering. At the same time, he must also assume responsibility for the Swedish Jews, who are facing the creeping contagion of our northern climate with Jew-hatred.[56]

The last, not the least. Bishop Ysander had seen enough of the creeping contagion of "our northern climate," including the Church of Sweden, to know the tightrope that Ehrenpreis and the Swedish Jews had to walk between solidarity and self-preservation. "Dad often came home in a depressed mood," his daughter Miriam recalled. "He kept trying to increase the Jewish immigration quotas, but he had a very hard time getting a hearing. 'I have to fight on two fronts,' he used to complain."[57]

The chairman of the congregation, Gunnar Josephson, had also seen enough, and devoted his entire contribution to Ehrenpreis's still-ongoing rescue activities. Together with Ehrenpreis, Josephson personified Swedish Jewry during these years, and better than most he had come to see the "terrible" nature of Ehrenpreis's position.

> Certainly he has been able to share with the rest of us the unimaginable happiness of living in this sheltered and richly endowed land, to which only a faint breeze of the raging storm has reached. But to witness the devastation, the extermination of our brothers in faith, the destruction of all Jewish life, it is for a man like Marcus Ehrenpreis, considering his life and work, heavier than for most of us, however intensely we may feel the horror and distress.[58]

It was a celebratory text, no doubt, but it captured quite well the central role that Marcus Ehrenpreis had played in Swedish-Jewish relief work since the spring of 1933: the committees, the fundraising, the appeals, the courtships, the interaction with the outside Jewish world.

> Appeals and requests are directed to Marcus Ehrenpreis from all over the world; his person and his position have become central to the whole of the remaining European Jewry. To the extent of the limited possibilities offered by our country, Professor Ehrenpreis seeks to help Jews in need beyond our borders.[59]

And pretty much that's how things were, but as Ragnar Josephson, Gunnar Josephson's brother and Ehrenpreis's co-translator of new Hebrew poetry, remarked, this was not what Marcus Ehrenpreis had imagined when, thirty years before, he had moved "far out into the Jewish periphery [...] where the congregations were small and Jewish life was dwindling." Neither could he have imagined that thirty years later he would be one of few remaining rabbis in Europe with a Jewish congregation to lead and a synagogue to preach in, and that this might ultimately prove to be "the deepest meaning" of Ehrenpreis's choice of Sweden as his home.

> In the rest of Europe, Jewish life is fundamentally destroyed; nowhere is there a safe place for a Jewish preacher. Marcus Ehrenpreis, however, has enjoyed the Swedish peace and the Swedish freedom, and he has known how to use it. Tirelessly, he has been speaking, writing, and preaching, as if he sensed that he was one of the very few remaining who could still speak for the Jewish people.[60]

Nevertheless, in the midst of an unfolding Jewish catastrophe of which Ehrenpreis was more aware than most, with a congregation to lead, with sermons to prepare, with services to conduct, with a journal to edit, with meetings and conferences to chair, he found time to withdraw to his private library to fulfill the task he had set to himself fifteen years earlier; to present in his new language, in his new *Kinderland* on the periphery of the Jewish world, the true face of Judaism.

In the fall of 1943, he completed the third and final volume of stories about the people "who built Israel," in a last literary attempt to bring to life some of the central figures in the Jewish heritage. However, when the book landed in the bookstores in time for Christmas sales, it was hard not to read it as an elegiac tribute to a heritage about to be annihilated.

The last of Israel's builders to be presented in the book, "perhaps one of the greatest seers and preachers that the genius of Israel has ever produced," Ehrenpreis had brought forth from his own dear circle of new Hebrew poets and writers. Chaim Nachman Bialik had died on 4 July 1934, aged sixty-one, having put down his pen long before, but was already considered the undisputed master of the new Hebrew poetry. It was probably also a poem by Bialik that best captured Ehrenpreis's state of mind as he, time and again, had to put down his pen in order to save what could still be saved.

> Son of man, what are you doing here?
> Get up and flee to the desert! Carry with you the
>   chalice of suffering.
> Tear your soul into ten pieces, tear into a rag,
> and dedicate your heart to impotent rage,
> and shed your tears on the crest of the rock,
> and send your cry—to vanish in the storm![61]

It is hardly possible to understand Ehrenpreis's positions and actions in the role that "the objective facts" had cast him without understanding the Jewish world that looked down on him every morning from the bookshelves in his study, and that spoke to him from all corners of the Jewish world in all its languages. It was this world that Marcus Ehrenpreis had come to see as his task to save, if only a remnant of it. Not long ago it had seemed possible to renew it and make it touch the world. What now remained was to save the "treasures from the house of Jacob" from total destruction.

Some of these treasures had been collected by Ehrenpreis during his lifetime and were now housed in his ever-growing library. Their significance to the life and work of Ehrenpreis had not escaped Ragna Aberstén-Schiratzki, the editorial secretary *of Judisk Tidskrift* since its founding in 1928. In her contribution to the jubilee of 1944, she provided an endearing image of the world in which Ehrenpreis largely lived, thought, and wrote.

> Books of all varieties, from venerable folios with graciously chiseled characters on yellowed paper to unassuming pamphlets with a modern, straightforward appearance, cover the walls from floor to ceiling and rise in towering piles on tables and chairs in the master's workshop. [...] These tall and densely packed bookshelves are the very soil from which Marcus Ehrenpreis's literary work has sprung: out of the dust and darkness of this book world, the long line of prophets and men of God, of holy men and heroes, of poets and seers, has emerged over the years, yearning to be reimagined, to be brought to life anew.

It was to Ragna Aberstén-Schiratzki that Ehrenpreis had dictated many of his books and articles, and as his eyesight weakened he proved to her that he didn't have to see his library to know it from within and without.

> If he asks me to fetch a thin book in brown leather slightly torn at one corner, which should be found on the bottom shelf to the right, or a blue linen folio, about two inches thick, to be found in the middle of the third shelf from the top, I can be sure of finding them right there. And if he asks me to look for a name or a year at the top of a left-hand page about twenty pages from the end, it's usually there too—and these are often books that he hasn't held in his hand for years.

As the Jewish world of Marcus Ehrenpreis was disappearing, ever-new book chapters, essays, speeches, and sermons kept springing from his library. He rarely put down his sermons in writing, and if they were to be printed and published, it had to be from shorthand notes.

As was the sermon Ehrenpreis delivered on 18 September 1944, entering the Jewish Year of 5705, which when published was entitled "Vägen uppåt" (The way up):

> If there is any meaning to our earthly life—and there must be—*it can only be one: to go up*, to rise from the animal to the human, from the material to the spiritual, to the enduring, eternal values of life.[62]

Preaching was central to Marcus Ehrenpreis. His sermons were much talked about, and people came to the synagogue only to hear him speak. In a sermon a few years earlier, he had talked about the centrality of preaching in the Jewish tradition, and the unbroken chain of prophets and preachers, from Moses to Jeremiah—and to Marcus Ehrenpreis. Indeed, it was as a link in this chain that he saw himself, and it was to his beloved prophets that he compared himself when he defined his mission as a rabbi: "to educate and to edify your congregation through your preaching, your action, your life. [...] You do not become a spiritual leader by a degree or a diploma. You are selected."

> Faced with this great and demanding task, the preacher and the rabbi of today must speak the word of Israel to the congregation, as he must carry the word of Israel to the world at a time when our existence and character, our teaching, our history, our place in the world, are all being distorted and falsified. It is upon him to tell us and the peoples of the earth what Israel is, what Israel teaches, what meaning the Lord has assigned to us and our historical existence of struggle and suffering.[63]

His sermons also left traces in contemporary Swedish literature. In a 1942 novel, an aged rabbi stands before the young (non-Jewish) protagonist, "at the velvet-clad pulpit in front of the altar" in the synagogue. "In his voice not a trace of unction, it was natural, yet with a passionate power. He seemed alive with spirit and thought, and his words appeared to be striving to come as close as possible to the truth, not to sedate us with rhetoric or soak us with emotionalism." The words left no doubt as to who the rabbi was: "The awareness of our divine origin is the source of our religion and our morality... We humans carry the divine on our shoulders, says one Talmud teacher... The way we respond to the call from God, as individuals or as God's people, is central to our lives, and it may be central to the course of history."[64]

No doubt, this was Marcus Ehrenpreis preaching.

In addition to the sermons and essays and the book about the poets and visionaries "who built Israel," there were now also the memoirs. It his seventy-fifth year, 1944, he finally began to look back on his life, initially through a series of articles in *Judisk Tidskrift*. In the January issue, memories of growing up in Lemberg; in the February issue, memories of his student years in Berlin; in the March issue, memories of his activist years "between the ghetto and the world"; in the April, May, and September issues, memories of his years in Bulgaria. In the Christmas issue, a walk through his library, which he by now had donated to the congregation in Stockholm "to be preserved under my name to serve future scholars, without distinction, for their benefit."[65] The handover was to take place after Ehrenpreis's death, but Ehrenpreis was still very much alive, and so was his relationship to his books:

> We have become friends over time, my books and I. We have walked together through ages and countries, we have grown and developed alongside each other. [...] My book collection is as multilingual as I am; the confusion of languages increased with every turn in my life. Here they stand side by side, section by section: Hebrew and Yiddish, next to Polish and Bulgarian, Spanish next to Nordic. [...]
>
> This is the purpose of the volumes before which I now stand. They are intended to be the voice of Israel in the world. They have sought to bring to life

> the great and enduring creation of the Spirit of Israel among the Jews and non-Jews of the North. They have sought to open a window on a Jewish world that is still unknown and misunderstood, but which hides no secrets and has nothing of which to be ashamed.[66]

It might have been seen as a form of escapism, writing your memoirs in the midst of the dark Holocaust year of 1944, with an apparent fondness for remembering the bright moments, not least the meetings with kings, ministers, metropolitans, and great names of a still-vibrant Jewish world. Maybe Ehrenpreis foresaw and feared that the memory of the Holocaust itself would suppress the memory of the Jewish world that had preceded it, and with it the memory of its spiritual vitality and meaning. In any case, time was running out—for the Jewish world and for Ehrenpreis.

Published in March 1946 under the title *Mitt liv mellan öster och väster* (My life between East and West), the memoirs of Marcus Ehrenpreis were largely memories of a world that no longer existed.

"An important book that provides a rich perspective on an era that is doubly past," wrote the reviewer in *Dagens Nyheter.*[67]

It was also a memoir that stood out for what it did not tell.

Or for what it did not want to remember.

The memoirs end in Evian in the summer of 1938.

Saving those who could be saved. Survivors of Ravensbrück and Bergen-Belsen on their way to Sweden, May 1945. After the deportation of the Norwegian Jews in November 1942, Sweden began to open its doors to Jewish refugees and survivors. How many more could have been saved if those doors had been opened earlier?

11.

THE VERDICT OF THE FUTURE

Only that historian will have the gift of fanning the spark of hope in the past who is firmly convinced that even the dead will not be safe from the enemy if he wins. And this enemy has not ceased to be victorious.

—WALTER BENJAMIN, 1940[1]

It is probably not saying too much to say that the food parcels distributed in the Ravensbrück concentration camp on 15 April 1945 saved the life of the young Jewish man who would become my father. The parcels came from Sweden and contained twenty Camel cigarettes, a package of vitamin tablets, a bar of soap, half a kilo of dry milk, chocolate, sugar, biscuits, half a kilo of margarine, a can of corned beef (marked kosher), a can of cheese, a can of tuna fish.

About the young man and his fate I have written elsewhere, but it may be worth reiterating that it was the package that saved his life.[2]

The shipments of food parcels that reached thousands of Jews in Nazi concentration camps such as Bergen-Belsen, Ravensbrück, and Theresienstadt in the last months of the war were a remarkable rescue operation in every respect, not least because it was carried out while the killing of Jews was still going on. The Jews reached by the food parcels were not meant to survive. They were all destined to be killed, and by April 1945 they were on their way to being killed one way or another.

Without the food parcels, they would not have survived.

The rescue of prisoners in concentration camps with food parcels coincided with the rescue of prisoners from concentration camps in white buses, and both rescue operations coincided with a dramatic change in the "objective facts." In April 1945 Germany's defeat and surrender was a matter of weeks, and in the top German leadership someone was prepared to negotiate the rescue of Jewish lives in the hope of saving his own.

The story of how the SS chief Heinrich Himmler, the man in charge of the extermination program, played a duplicitous game of life and death with Swedish Red Cross vice president Folke Bernadotte and the representative of the World Jewish Congress in Sweden, Norbert Masur, is well known. Also known is the central role that a Jewish businessman in Stockholm, Gilel (Hillel) Storch, played in both contexts.

Less well known is the role played by Marcus Ehrenpreis.

Or rather, the role played by Marcus Ehrenpreis has been misrepresented.

Partly it has to do with the food parcels and Gilel Storch.

Gilel Storch had been granted a visa to enter Sweden from Soviet-occupied Latvia in the autumn of 1940. It was not easy to obtain such a visa, but Storch was a successful and wealthy businessman, and soon enough he had built a position in Sweden of his own. Soon he also began promoting his own ideas on how to help and save the Jews of Europe. In doing so, he came into conflict with the leadership of the Mosaic Congregation, which he blamed for not having done enough. Most importantly, it had not done enough to help a group of Latvian and Lithuanian Jews get transit visas for onward travel to Palestine, and had thus, Storch believed, contributed to their deaths. Soon Storch also promulgated the view that it was the Mosaic Congregation in Stockholm, not the Swedish government, that was behind the harsh requirements for persecuted Jews to enter Sweden. "This is nothing but the work of the Mosaic Congregation," Storch wrote in a 1942 letter to the head of the American-Jewish relief organization the JDC in New York.[3]

In both cases, Storch had at best misunderstood and misjudged the power of the congregation in such matters. As late as 1940, it was still hard for the congregation to make the Swedish authorities give refuge to Jews fleeing Hitler's Germany. Trying to make them give refuge to Jews from still "only" Soviet-occupied Latvia and Lithuania would have been even harder. That Germany would invade the Baltic states in the summer of 1941 and kill its Jews, including most of Gilel Storch's family, was not yet known to anyone, including Storch. Storch was also wrong about who was behind the restrictions on giving refuge to Jews, but the impression that the congregation in Stockholm had had a part in it would in time be reinforced by the Swedish government and be spread throughout the Jewish world. Contributing to Storch's negative views of the congregation was most certainly the fact that he was not allowed to become a member of it. The congregation admitted only Swedish citizens, and whatever Jewish rescue activities Storch intended to initiate, he could not do so from a position within the congregation.

As if this were not grounds enough for potential conflicts over how the Swedish-Jewish rescue work should be conducted and who should take responsibility for it, Gilel Storch was also a strong-willed personality with an energetic, entrepreneurial spirit and a fiery temperament. This meant that he saw opportunities that no one else saw, and got things done that few others would have succeeded in doing, but it also meant that he was not easy to work with and easily could fall out even with people who valued his ideas and initiatives and whose support he needed to implement them.

For example, Marcus Ehrenpreis.

He also had a tendency to downplay rescue efforts other than his own.

For example, those initiated and organized by Ehrenpreis and the Refugee Committee of the congregation.[4]

When, in the autumn of 1944, Gilel Storch organized the recently unthinkable, the delivery of forty thousand food parcels straight into the Nazi concentration camps, he not only sidelined the Refugee Committee and Ehrenpreis but also communicated to organizations in the outside Jewish world a stark image of their inefficiency and lack of commitment.[5] When, in early November 1944, the food parcel initiative was discussed at a meeting of the newly formed Swedish section of the World Jewish Congress, of which Ehrenpreis was to become chairman, it turned out that Ehrenpreis had not even been informed about it. His annoyance at what he saw as Storch's selfish and "inappropriate" behavior was evident from the minutes of the meeting.[6]

Less than two weeks later, Storch resigned from the Swedish section of the WJC and persuaded the central leadership of the WJC in New York to have him organize his own rescue operation under their auspices, citing "the problems" with

Ehrenpreis and the congregation. Many tried to persuade Storch to stay on, not least Ehrenpreis himself: "Irrespective of our differences in details, we have all appreciated your untiring efforts, not least your successful work with the parcel shipments," he wrote to Storch on 5 December 1944.[7]

But Storch stuck to his resignation, and the remarkable package operation was mainly carried out under his direction. Storch was also to play a central role in the equally remarkable operation to save people directly from Nazi concentration camps. Originally, Storch had planned to fly to Berlin himself and negotiate the matter directly with Himmler. The fact that it was another person, Norbert Masur, a soft-spoken Jewish businessman protected by Swedish citizenship, who finally did so, was probably in the best interests of the cause, but it does not detract from Storch's role as mastermind.

It must be stated, however, that Storch's rescue operations were carried out with the full support of Ehrenpreis and the leadership of the Stockholm congregation. After all, the new parcel shipments were only a continuation of the parcel shipments organized since the outbreak of the war by the committees for aid to the Jews of Poland and Europe, albeit on a spectacular scale. The formal sender of the new parcels was still the non-Jewish organization Help the Victims of War, which had also been the sender of the parcels from the aid committees. Only in the spring of 1945 would the International Red Cross be listed as the sender, and then only after yet another change in the constellations of "objective facts."

Until the summer of 1944, the International Red Cross had refrained from speaking out against the Nazi persecution of the Jews, and furthermore from actively trying to help them. The Jews, no matter how persecuted and mistreated, were deemed not to be regular prisoners of war and therefore deemed to be of no concern to the Red Cross. As the winds of war shifted and the pressure for a change increased, the "objective" conditions for the Red Cross to send parcels with cans marked kosher to Jews in German concentration camps dramatically improved.[8]

In the meantime, the shipments of aid packages organized by the Jewish aid committees in Stockholm since 1940 were still going on, albeit on the limited scale that the conditions so far had allowed for. Each package must have an individual addressee and be granted a Swedish export license. On 20 September 1944, Marcus Ehrenpreis was informed that his application for an export license regarding a package with "various foodstuffs to Bohemia and Moravia" had not been approved. The unapproved parcel was addressed to Mr. Benjamin Igre in Theresienstadt.[9]

That licenses were still granted, and food packages from Sweden still reached Theresienstadt, is shown by the handwritten card that Ehrenpreis's friend and rabbinic colleague in pre-Hitler Berlin, Leo Baeck, managed to get through the camp censors on 12 December 1943: "A small package with the finest butter and flour arrived today from Stockholm and I allow myself to assume that it is you who are behind it. For this you are to be thanked. *Haben Sie vielen Dank.*"[10]

Still, each package required an individual recipient, and no matter how many individual recipients the aid committees in Stockholm managed to scrape together, they remained a drop in the sea. There was also no guarantee that the recipients were still at their addresses, or at all.

Among the new facts changing the conditions for rescue operations were the lists of thousands of individual names and addresses provided by Jewish relief organizations in the United States, as well as the fact that the American Red Cross had started to use the port of Gothenburg for food shipments to U.S. prisoners of war in Germany, as well as the fact that the U.S. government had formally decided to contribute to the rescue of "Jews and other vulnerable groups" in countries occupied by Germany.

In short, the long-running rescue work in Sweden was now being supplemented by new and powerful players, and Gilel Storch saw earlier than most the new rescue venues that were opening up.

However, in his efforts to realize them Storch chose to sidestep Ehrenpreis and the aid committee, and in the process he could offend and even hurt people. One of his closest friends and associates, the exiled German-Jewish businessman Fritz Hollander, testified that Storch could be "extremely aggressive." Once, he had gotten very angry with Hollander as well, saying that he didn't want to have anything to do with him anymore, only to apologize a few days later: "But Fritz, you can't be taking me seriously! You know how I am."[11]

Temperamental clashes of this kind may very well have played a part when Ehrenpreis, at a couple of meetings in November 1944, expressed his distrust of Storch and his way of organizing the parcel shipments. It was probably not so much the matter itself that divided them; on the contrary, sending aid parcels was entirely in line with what Ehrenpreis and his committee had been doing for four years, but when Storch, without Ehrenpreis's knowledge, managed to get the support of the World Jewish Congress in New York to take the parcel operation into his own hands, Ehrenpreis could not avoid expressing his irritation. The conflict lurching beneath Storch's appeal to the WJC in New York—which of two American-based Jewish organizations JDC or the WJC, should sponsor Swedish rescue efforts—proved to be of no practical consequence whatsoever.

It was soon to become evident that the ongoing Jewish disaster demanded rescue actions on a scale that transcended organizational boundaries.

In this context, nothing more should have had to be said about the conflict between Storch and Ehrenpreis. In practice, Ehrenpreis came to support Storch in full and lend his authority to strengthen Storch's position, and could not but rejoice as thousands of food parcels from Sweden were distributed to half-dead Jewish men and women in the concentration camps of Bergen-Belsen, Ravensbrück, and Theresienstadt.

Somehow the two men also respected each other, or just realized that they needed each other. On Ehrenpreis's seventy-fifth birthday in June 1944, Storch cabled his warmest congratulations to "the old Zionist veteran, the champion of Jewish rights," and a year later likened him to "a diamond in the center of a brooch of fake stones."[12] And although Ehrenpreis's irritation with Storch shone through at some meetings in October and November 1944, he was fully aware of Storch's capacity to get things done, and at other occasions expressed his appreciation. "'Now my favorite antipathy is calling,' Dad used to say every time Storch called," his daughter Miriam recalled.[13]

Perhaps they complemented each other after all, the diplomatic rabbi and the blunt entrepreneur, and despite their age difference (Storch was only in his early forties) recognized themselves in each other: two eastern European Jews who had been forced to see their world being annihilated, and their families with it, and who both in their different ways, with their different temperaments and personalities, struggled to save from it what could be saved.

Nevertheless, the damage was already done. With his stubborn and at times high-handed modus operandi, Gilel Storch contributed successfully to spreading the rumor that the leaders of the Swedish Jews didn't do what they could have done, or even worse, that they had prevented the Swedish government from doing more. Storch would thereby provide a "Jewish" legitimacy of sorts to the insinuation from the Swedish minister of social affairs, Gustav Möller, that if it had not been for the Swedish Jews, the Swedish government might have been more generous in its policy toward Jews in need.

It was an insinuation that was to be reinforced and further corrupted, and eventually give rise to a smear campaign against Ehrenpreis and the congregation in Stockholm that would tarnish their name in the verdict of the future.

The verdict of the future, soon enough.

The first Jewish remnants arrived in Sweden in the spring and summer of 1945, some tens of thousands in all. They were meant to stay no longer than necessary to recover and then find a new home elsewhere. Most of them eventually did so and continued their journey—to the Jewish Diaspora in the United States and to the emerging Jewish state in Palestine—but a few thousand would try to make a home for themselves in Sweden, among them the young man who had been saved by the Swedish food parcels in Ravensbrück and who had come on a Red Cross transport to Malmö on 18 July 1945 and who was to become my father.

With the arrival of the remnants, conditions for Jewish life in Sweden changed rapidly. Those who were to be incorporated into the Swedish-Jewish community brought with them not only unspeakable traumas and memories, but also experiences of being a Jew in an increasingly antisemitic Diaspora that were difficult to reconcile with Ehrenpreis's vision of a new and fruitful encounter between Israel and the peoples. They were afraid and suspicious even of people who claimed to wish them well, and so did not always announce that they were Jewish. It also meant that in his final years as chief rabbi, Ehrenpreis had to step into yet another role: that of a spiritual counselor and comforter.

On 17 July 1945, the first issue of *Exodus*, a monthly newsletter in Yiddish, Polish, and German for the Jewish remnants in the Swedish archipelago of transit camps, carried on its front page a greeting in Yiddish from Marcus Ehrenpreis to the "rescued of 1945" that was perhaps more condescending than comforting:

> What we wish for you at this time is *the power to forget.* [...] That you may tear yourselves away from the bloody images that are burned into your minds, tear yourselves away from the hatred and the revenge and all the bitterness and ugliness that years of calamity have created in your hearts. Forget the old disputes and misunderstandings: a new age demands a new mind. You must force yourselves to return to the normal life that lies before you, force yourselves to regain faith in life, faith in man, faith in a merciful Father in heaven.[14]

Exodus was published by the Mosaic Congregation in Stockholm for a total of four issues in the summer and autumn of 1945, and was filled, among other things, with page-long lists of names under the heading *Kennen Sie jemanden von diesen Personen*, "Do you know any of these people?" It was also filled with articles on how to search for missing relatives and on the possibilities of emigrating to Palestine. No articles, however, on the possibilities of staying in Sweden. This prompted someone to interpret the name of the newsletter, Exodus, as an exhortation to further emigration, which in turn prompted the editors to clarify their position:

"The name is of course not intended to express any wish to have the rescued leave Sweden as soon as possible. [...] On the contrary, by this name we wanted to recall the happiest event in Jewish history, the exodus and liberation from Egypt, with which we wanted to compare the fate of the rescued."[15]

Whoever had "misunderstood" the name and disseminated "false interpretations" of its intentions had nevertheless shone light on a wall of mistrust and suspicion, behind which false interpretations of many things could easily gain a foothold, not least of the intentions and actions of the Swedish government and the Swedish Jews. "You must have faith in those who are doing their best to pave your way to a secure future," Ehrenpreis said to "our rescued" in his greeting address, and he had reasons to say so.

In September 1945, *Exodus* was succeeded by *Via Suecia*, published by a Swedish organization, the Committee for Democratic Reconstruction, that seemed to have as its main task to propagate the social visions and ambitions of Social Democratic Sweden to the people in the transit camps. On the front page of the first issue, Prime Minister Per Albin Hansson expressing his hope that as the people of the camps returned to their home countries, they would have learned that Sweden was a friendly country that strived to "preserve, defend, and improve the democratic order, increase social progress, and create work for all."[16]

Still, *Via Suecia* was a fascinating mix of both Swedish and Jewish topics. On the same page you could read about the fight against the housing shortage in Sweden and what the Talmud had to say about the equal value of all human beings. There were also articles that could be assumed to have an appealing effect on camp residents who were considering the possibility of staying on. Sweden was a country in which you had "modern schools for a new era," an "ongoing democratization of society," and new autumn fashions. It was also a country in which the exiled German-Jewish poet Nelly Sachs had written a poem to "you who are building the new house," *An Euch, die das neue Haus bauen*, which was also published in *Via Suecia*:

> When you rebuild your walls—
> Your hearth, your bed, your table, and your chair—
> Don't hang your tears on them, the departed,
> Who will no longer live with you
> On the stone
> Not on the wood—
> Or weeping will intrude on your sleep,
> The short one that you must have.[17]

"Via Suecia," like "Exodus," could be interpreted literally: as the way via Sweden to somewhere else, but also as the way of Sweden, the peculiar Swedish way to a new society, or even a new world, in which the horrors of the past would be succeeded by the promise of a new life.

Perhaps also a new Jewish life.

The efforts of the Swedish government to disseminate a positive image of Sweden's actions during the war seemed to have an impact on the Jewish world as well. In August 1946, the American magazine *Jewish Frontier* described Sweden as a country that "on more than one occasion had put its humanitarian duties before the interests of the state."[18]

Nothing about Sweden's immigration and refugee policies before 1942.

Nor any reference to the brutal Jewish attack on the Mosaic Congregation in Stockholm—and on Marcus Ehrenpreis personally—that had been unleashed only a few months earlier.

On 29 January 1946, the American Yiddish daily *Der Tog* (The Day) published an article with the blistering headline THE SECRET REVEALED. OUR JEWISH QUISLINGS. A TRUE SWEDISH PATRIOT SPEAKS OUT. The article recounted a meeting that the editor of *Der Tog*, Samuel Margoshes, accompanied by Gilel Storch and others, had had with Per Nyström, the right-hand man of Gustav Möller, the minister of social affairs. The purpose of the meeting was to find out whether Sweden would be willing to accept more Jews from the camps for "displaced persons" in Europe. Per Nyström gave no firm response, but when asked about Swedish opinion on the matter, his answer was unequivocal: "The Swedish opinion has always been very friendly to Jewish immigration, but the problem is the Swedish Jews, they don't want any immigration, and therein lies the crux of the problem."[19] Nyström was also alleged to have said that the Stockholm congregation had admonished the Swedish government not to encourage Jewish immigration, since they feared that this would increase antisemitism. Upon hearing this, another participant at the meeting, an Orthodox Zionist leader named Rabbi Mordechai Nurock, had proclaimed that he had more respect for Sweden than for the Jewish community in Stockholm. Whereupon Per Nyström had "laughed heartily and slapped his hands on his thighs."[20]

After the meeting, Gilel Storch had informed Margoshes of what Nyström's boss, Gustav Möller, had said in parliament about the Swedish Jews and Sweden's refugee policy, and the story was confirmed: the Jewish leaders in Stockholm were quislings who had prevented true Swedish patriots like Per Nyström and Gustav Möller from saving the Jews of Europe.

Margoshes's article resonated throughout the Jewish world. New York's influential *Jewish Daily Forward* sent a telegram to Ehrenpreis asking for comment.[21] Ehrenpreis in turn contacted Per Nyström to get his version of what had happened, and a few days later Nyström responded with a denial of sorts: "I hereby wish to state the Mosaic Congregation has exerted no pressure whatsoever on the Swedish authorities to prevent or discourage the immigration of Jewish refugees to Sweden."[22]

Nyström could have been clearer. He could have admitted what a parliamentary commission would soon conclude; that the Swedish authorities had very often ignored appeals from the congregation on behalf of fleeing Jews applying for permits of stay. He could also have expressed his indignation at the defamation of the Jewish leaders in Sweden that was now being disseminated in the world, and his regret at the role that he and the Swedish minister of social affairs might have played in this, whether they had been misunderstood or not.

Whatever Per Nyström had said or not said, Margoshes's image of Marcus Ehrenpreis changed radically after the meeting. Only a month earlier, on 21 December 1945, the same Margoshes had sent an ingratiating telegram to Ehrenpreis, inviting him to join the circle of "outstanding" Jewish leaders and literary personalities on the editorial board of a new magazine, *Yiddish Welt*, sponsored by the World Jewish Congress. In the telegram, Margoshes stressed that "we would be greatly honored to have your name associated with the council."[23]

But now Ehrenpreis was a quisling, and the Swedish government, in an unholy alliance with Gilel Storch, had laid the foundation for a harsh verdict on the Mosaic Congregation in

Stockholm and Marcus Ehrenpreis personally on their role in the efforts to save what could be saved.

In a letter to several American-Jewish newspapers and organizations, Ehrenpreis and Gunnar Josephson, the chairman of the congregation, made an attempt to counter the accusations:

> The Mosaic Congregation in Stockholm [...] denies in the strongest terms that it has sought to discourage any rescue of European Jews. There were years before and at the beginning of the war when Swedish opinion was strongly hostile to immigration and the Swedish government felt compelled to issue very rigorous immigration regulations. Repeatedly, the congregation made requests to the authorities for permits to immigrate. Unfortunately, in many cases such requests were refused, in other cases the congregation was successful. In its efforts, the congregation was of course bound by the rules laid down by the Swedish authorities, but in loyal cooperation with them it sought to provide as much help as possible. [...] We do not wish to claim that we, the Swedish Jews, who in our fortunate country have been so wondrously spared from the harrowing catastrophe, have done all that we ought to have done. However, the Mosaic Congregation in Stockholm, together with the other Mosaic Congregations in Sweden [...] has sought and is seeking, to the best of its ability, to help its brethren in faith who have suffered such terrible fates. They have every reason to reject with indignation the attack on the Swedish Jews by Dr. Margoshes.[24]

But there would be more accusations—and more serious ones. On 19 January 1947, an Orthodox rabbi in the United

States, Pinchas Wohlgelernter, launched a new attack on the Jewish leaders in Sweden, this time claiming that the congregation in Stockholm had thwarted the Swedish government's plans before the war to rescue a hundred thousand (!) Jews. To this was added the claim that out of five hundred Jewish children who had come to Sweden in 1939, only two (!) had remained Jews, as well as the claim that the Mosaic Congregation had allowed fourteen Jewish girls to be baptized in a transit camp in Dalarna.[25] The allegations were all untrue, if not absurd, but they were nevertheless given a semiofficial legitimacy by being disseminated by the weekly press review of the Jewish Agency in Palestine.[26]

Whence Wohlgelernter had received his "information" is not clear, but there is reason to believe that it had been hatched in the circles of the Jewish Orthodox community in Stockholm that harbored a long-nurtured animosity toward the non-Orthodox Jewish leadership in general and Ehrenpreis in particular. In their eyes, Ehrenpreis not only represented a watered-down and assimilated form of Judaism, but he was also perceived as an outright opponent to their claims and interests.

The Orthodox animosity toward Ehrenpreis was demonstratively expressed in January 1946, when on the cover sheet of a new prayer book, a siddur, dedicated to "the annihilated Jewish congregations" was printed: "supervised by Chief Rabbi Marcus Ehrenpreis." This was enough to make members of the small Orthodox synagogue in Stockholm tear out the cover page, which made their prayer books fall apart.[27] Wohlgelernter had recently visited Stockholm as a representative of the Union of Orthodox Rabbis of the United States and Canada, and had almost certainly met with people who not only tore the cover sheets out of their prayer books but also provided him with stories about the "machinations" against Orthodox Jewish life in Sweden by Ehrenpreis and the congregation.[28]

At the time of Wohlgelernter's visit, the dissemination of malicious rumors about leadership in Stockholm had in fact been going on for some time. As early as October 1945, Ehrenpreis had received a letter from the head of the information department of the National Council for Jewish Palestine, *Ha'vaad Ha'leumi*, asking him to comment on a rumor "creating alarm and confusion among us." The rumor said that in the spring of 1945 Nazi Germany had agreed to release five thousand Jews and transport them on a ship from Danzig to Sweden, and that the Swedish government had agreed to take them in, but that the congregation in Stockholm had protested, citing "the danger of increased antisemitism." The letter from Palestine was written in a reverential tone and the signatory assured him that "we cannot imagine that there is even a shred of truth in this rumor." Nevertheless, he added, "in order for us to credibly refute it in this country, we must ask you to inform us on the matter."[29] The letter did not say where the rumor came from, but again it is not difficult to imagine how Gilel Storch's recriminations against the leaders of the congregation had been passed from mouth to mouth, and along the way had become increasingly distorted and coarsened.

On 12 February 1947, Ehrenpreis and Josephson authored a response to Wohlgelernter as well, and this time their exasperation was apparent. The Jewish Agency was not just any Jewish institution, and Ehrenpreis had personally known several of its leaders, and its contribution to the spreading of baseless defamation must have been a shattering experience for Ehrenpreis. To the most outlandish of the accusations, that the Stockholm congregation had prevented the Swedish government from rescuing hundreds of thousands of Jews, Ehrenpreis and Josephson responded with impressive self-restraint:

> The Swedish government, which in many respects has shown an admirable willingness to help, has never been prepared to rescue 100,000 or more Jews, and the Mosaic congregation in Stockholm has never raised any objections "for fear of antisemitism," or taken any steps whatsoever to prevent possible relief efforts. On the contrary, the congregation has with varying success—before, during, and after the war—appealed to the authorities for the rescue of persecuted Jews in Europe. [...]
>
> The Mosaic Congregation in Stockholm, its rabbis and directors, see themselves as completely untouched by the libelous accusations directed against them from certain Jewish quarters. [...] False and malicious allegations of the kind made by Rabbi Wohlgelernter, however, are likely to seriously damage Jewish interests, both internally and externally, and it is most regrettable that an organ of the Jewish Agency has seen fit to disseminate defamation of this kind.[30]

In a reply to Ehrenpreis on 20 February 1947, the information department of the Jewish Agency in Jerusalem explained that its weekly press review had only relayed what Rabbi Wohlgelernter had said at a press conference, and that it had no means of verifying the veracity of every news item it relayed, but that it was nonetheless prepared to publish the response by Ehrenpreis and Josephson in a coming issue.[31]

The incident, however, did not prompt any change in the practice of not verifying the veracity of relayed news items. In the issue of the *Jewish Agency Digest* published on 4 May 1947, another attack on the Stockholm congregation appeared, this time in a report of what Mordechai Nurock, the Orthodox rabbi present at the meeting with Per Nyström in Stockholm, had said in a press conference in Jerusalem.[32] And this time there could be no doubt whence the information originated: Rabbi Nurock had again been echoing Gilel Storch's old grievances against the congregation for failing to help a group of Jews in Riga to obtain transit visas to Sweden in June 1940. Nurock also alleged that Gunnar Josephson had told Gilel Storch "that we do not want any foreign Jews here."

In yet another letter to the editor of *Jewish Agency Digest*, Gunnar Josephson responded that it was "completely out of the question" that he had said such a thing, and that Storch, against his better judgment, had misled Nurock. As for one of the Jews in Riga whom Storch had accused the congregation of abandoning, the revered Jewish historian Simon Dubnow, Josephson explained that the congregation had applied for a visa for Dubnow on 18 July 1940, that is before Storch had even arrived in Stockholm, and that a visa for Dubnow had in fact been granted, but that it "for reasons unknown to us" had not been used.[33]

No number of refutations, however, could prevent the rumors from spreading. On 16 May 1947, *The Jewish Chronicle* in London gave further publicity to what Nurock had said. "Grave charges of indifference to and even opposition to the rescue of Jews facing Nazi domination were leveled against Swedish Jewry," the paper informed its readers. And once again, the Swedish government was portrayed as more willing to take in fleeing Jews than the Swedish Jews themselves.

Upon Margoshes's attack in *Der Tog*, Hugo Valentin, as the newly appointed chairman of the Swedish section of the

World Jewish Congress, had intended to cosign the response from Ehrenpreis and Josephson, but when members of the section disapproved, he wrote his own response and resigned as chairman. The Swedish section consisted largely of newly arrived refugees who had little knowledge of the congregation's leadership and its activities, and who were therefore more prone to believe the rumors. In his article, Valentin not only countered the accusations but showed how they fit into an antisemitic tradition of blaming the Jews for their own misfortune. "Shouldn't we Jews, humanity's scapegoat *par préférence*, be especially careful not to fall victim to such psychosis ourselves?" asked Valentin.[34]

On 16 July 1947, Hugo Valentin wrote another letter, this time to *The Jewish Chronicle*. He began by explaining that as an active Zionist and longtime chairman of the Zionist Federation in Scandinavia, he had often disagreed with the leaders of the Stockholm congregation. "However, I cannot, for the sake of righteousness, pass over in silence the defamation of these persons which for the past two or three years has been perpetrated by Jewish papers all over Europe and America."[35]

Well into the 1950s, Valentin would explain to the Jewish world that the rumors about the reluctance of Swedish Jews to accept Jewish refugees were unfounded and that the moral judgment that had been passed on them was unjust. In a study published by YIVO, the Yiddisch Scientific Institute in New York, Valentin pointed out that even the Jews in Germany had not understood at the beginning what was in store for them. "Had it been possible in those years to foresee the full range of the Nazi policy, no doubt both the Jews in the Scandinavian countries and the governments would have acted differently. To judge them harshly today is unfair."[36]

But it was too late. The image of a Swedish-Jewish community less willing to accept its fleeing brethren in faith than the Swedish government was to be reinforced by anecdotes and memories, often directed against Marcus Ehrenpreis himself.

In a white paper commissioned by the Jewish congregation in Stockholm more than fifty years later, investigating the wartime rescue activities of the congregation, the negative statements about Ehrenpreis were abundant, and the impression was created that whatever hesitance and reluctance that could be observed in the actions of the congregation often had to do with Ehrenpreis personally. "It was said of him," the white paper quoted from a secondhand source, "that he had personally visited the minister of social affairs, Möller, to point out that a greater influx of Jews might provoke a stronger antisemitic movement in Sweden."[37]

Perhaps even more devastating was the rumor that Ehrenpreis had admonished the Swedish government not to receive the Danish Jews. When two young Danish Jews, canoeing across Øresund, had walked into his office to inform him of the secret escape plans, he allegedly had picked up the phone to the Foreign Ministry to sound the alarm. The author of the white paper, Svante Hansson, had heard the story twenty-five years later from one of the young Danes, Werner David Melchior, and chose to publish it without further verification, emphasizing instead that Ehrenpreis's attitude "was in no way representative of the leadership of the Mosaic Congregation." Upon the slightest critical examination, the story would otherwise have turned out to be just as implausible as Svante Hansson seems to have suspected from the start. "I was doubtful and wondered whether he might not have misunderstood the meaning of Ehrenpreis's words," Hansson wrote.[38]

Indeed, could two young Danish Jews possibly have misunderstood or misinterpreted what Ehrenpreis had said in a phone conversation in Swedish? And how plausible was it that

Ehrenpreis would pick up the phone for such a conversation in front of two persons who had just risked their lives to inform him?

What had prompted Melchior to disseminate such devastating rumors about Ehrenpreis remains unclear. As well as why the white paper consistently chose to give precedence to negative anecdotes and secondhand accounts.

Quoting from a private letter: "It is said of Ehrenpreis that he was known as an enemy of refugees."[39]

Quoting from a book of fiction: "It is rumored that Chief Rabbi Marcus Ehrenpreis had courted [the Swedish prime minister] Per Albin Hansson to have him restrict the immigration of Jews from Germany—so that Sweden would not run the risk of bringing in uncontrollable elements and having the good climate of cooperation deteriorate. To which Per Albin had sniggered."[40] There is no evidence whatsoever that the meeting ever took place, and even less, if possible, that the prime minister had sniggered at Ehrenpreis.

The white paper also quoted long passages from an anonymous letter to the editor of *Judisk Krönika* in 1987, concluding: "To us refugees, the name Ehrenpreis was a nightmare."[41] This, despite Hansson himself acknowledging that the letter was full of errors and exaggerations. In addition, the letter made the claim that Ehrenpreis had been more feared among the Jewish refugees than the head of the Aliens Bureau of the National Board of Health and Welfare, Robert Paulsson. At this point, if not before, Svante Hansson should have recoiled, since Robert Paulsson was an unapologetic antisemite who in 1944 had been convicted of espionage in forwarding the names of Jewish refugees to the Gestapo. Instead, Hansson omitted the comparison between Ehrenpreis and Paulsson and used the remaining quote as further evidence of how insensitively

Ehrenpreis had treated refugees who had turned to him "for help and support."[42]

Hansson could otherwise have quoted a passage or two from a letter to the editor published in the same issue of *Judisk Krönika*, by the lawyer Ragnar Gottfarb, "one of the few survivors of a difficult time," as he introduced himself. Gottfarb had reacted to how the congregation's refugee activities had been characterized in a previous editorial.[43] The editorial, in turn, was based on a book by the American writer Steven Koblik, who had given full credence to Storch's criticism of the congregation and singled out its "assimilated" chairman Gunnar Josephson as a symbol of its fearfulness and passivity.[44]

"Koblik has it completely wrong," Ragnar Gottfarb retorted indignantly.

> Gunnar Josephson was wise, warmhearted, and dedicated. Almost daily he spent his time in the offices of the congregation, neglecting his noble vocation as a bookseller. In his hospitable home we came together for serious deliberations, always hoping to do something for the persecuted. [...] Certainly there was little we could do, but Koblik may not know that we faced a strongly hostile administration, and at least initially an uncomprehending popular will and press [...]. It's convenient to sit in California and write history with the course of the events at hand.[45]

Koblik's claim that there had been an active opposition from "pro-Zionist" groups to the positions and actions of the congregation had little base in facts. Rather, there seemed to have been a common understanding among the Jews in Sweden of what could be done under the circumstances. No explicit criticism of the rescue activities of the congregation can be traced in the documents, since no Jew in Sweden could have been unaware of the hostile public mood prevailing in the country.

With the course of events at hand, it is easy to say that more should have been done, but perhaps not primarily by the small and vulnerable Jewish minority in Sweden, but by the Swedish government, which until the deportation of the Norwegian Jews in late November 1942 had pursued a de facto anti-Jewish immigration and refugee policy.

However, this was a story that Sweden now wished to leave behind and replace with the loftier story of what it had done for the fleeing Danish Jews, and the encircled Jews in Budapest, and the doomed Jews in the Nazi concentration camps. And to the extent that the story of a welcoming and humanitarian postwar Sweden could not fully supplant the story of a xenophobic Sweden closing its borders to Germany's fleeing Jews, the temptation to place some of the responsibility on the Jews themselves arose early on, with the simmering intra-Jewish conflict between Storch and the congregation as a source of inspiration. When, in January 1945, Gustav Möller claimed that Sweden had been "at least as generous as the Mosaic Congregation in Stockholm" in its position toward Jewish refugees, he was not only speaking against the facts of the matter but in his own interest. "Into the new Swedish self-image, the story of the refugee-restrictive Swedish Jews fitted perfectly," writes historian Pontus Rudberg.[46] If there were Jews in Sweden who could claim that the chief rabbi of Stockholm himself had been reluctant to receive Jewish refugees, it was not hard to see how the government could exploit such claims, however false, for its own purposes. "Over the years," Rudberg writes, "the apologetic excuses and allegations of the Swedish state and the claims made by Jewish anti-establishment groups have cross-fertilized each other by 'confirming' each other's biased claims and accusations."

There were certainly Jewish groups and individuals who had reason to be critical of the Swedish-Jewish "establishment" and of Ehrenpreis personally. Orthodox Jews had their reasons, radical Zionists had theirs, frustrated refugees had theirs, and Gilel Storch had his, but what might otherwise have remained an intra-Jewish affair would now feed into the readily exploited story of how the Jews themselves, through the evasion and cooperation of their own leaders, from Murmelstein in Theresienstadt to Ehrenpreis in Stockholm, had contributed to the scale of the Jewish catastrophe.

Given the scale, it was hardly surprising that the surviving remnants would ask their leaders why more had not been done to save them. When the congregation in Stockholm in 1947 published an account of its rescue activities, Gunnar Josephson admitted that it had not perhaps lived up to "the expectations put on us by our hard-hit brethren in faith," but noted again that until 1942 the Swedish government had rather not received any Jews at all: "With sadness we think how a more liberal immigration policy on the part of the Swedish authorities might have saved many of those who later perished."[47]

But the image of an overly cautious and accommodating congregation took hold. For the time being, the need to find someone to hold accountable for lives not saved was greater than the desire to understand why the Jewish leaders in Sweden had not done more to save them. What also took hold was the image of Ehrenpreis as insensitive and dismissive. In the white paper he is said to have given the cold shoulder to refugees seeking his help, asking them curtly why they did not go back to Germany, having his secretary tell them that he had no time for them. In a Swedish novel published in 2009 Ehrenpreis is alleged to have told a family of Jewish refugees asking for his help: "We have no problem with antisemitism. So far. And we don't want to have any now either. So sorry, but thank you for your visit."[48]

The fact that this starkly negative image of Ehrenpreis, based mainly on rumors and secondary sources, was hard to reconcile with what Ehrenpreis had actually said and done during "the difficult years" did not prevent it from being reinforced and sanctioned by the white paper and thereby further etched into his legacy.

This is not to say that the image didn't also reflect genuine memories and experiences. With the intensified pressures on Ehrenpreis during those years, with the mounting pile of letters of pleas and hopes attached to his name, it is hardly surprising that people who had sought his personal attention and help could be disappointed and even bitter. In such situations, Ehrenpreis may also have been perceived as brusque and dismissive. The frustration of having to explain time and again the current rules and regulations for "involuntary emigrants," of having to explain time and again that there was nothing more that he or the congregation could do for them, may very well have affected his mood and behavior. The congregation had set up a special office to receive refugees and process their applications, and people who had hoped to speak to Ehrenpreis personally were mostly asked to take their case to the refugee office, which might have been interpreted as a token of uninterest and indifference.

Add to this that Ehrenpreis could be hard to read and understand, and that pastoral care in a more individual and psychological sense was not his forte. In his sermons and texts there was often a demanding and even moralizing element, which when addressed to the congregation in the synagogue or to a group of Jewish confirmands could be perceived as uplifting and inspiring, but when manifested in personal contacts with people seeking his help could be perceived as harsh and insensitive. In dealing with individual refugee cases, Ehrenpreis could also be more inclined to go by his inner intuitions than by formal procedures. "Theoretical reasoning or presuppositions were valid for him only as long as they corresponded to his subjective feeling," noted Wilhelm Michaeli, the legal adviser to the congregation on refugee matters.[49]

However, for better or worse, that is how Marcus Ehrenpreis had always been. Throughout his life he had believed in the power of the spirit, as he preferred to put it. On one hand, it gave him the strength to see possibilities in the seemingly impossible, and meaning in the seemingly meaningless, on the other hand it fostered a tendency to act on his own. From his very first years as a Jewish public figure he resisted committing himself fully to any of the established interests and categories of the Jewish world. The Jewish path of Marcus Ehrenpreis was very much his own, and those who believed that he was fully on their side would sometimes be disappointed. The Zionists never quite got the hang of his Zionism, the Orthodox never quite got the hang of his Judaism, and newly arrived refugees, who did not know who he was and where he came from, and did not always understand what he said and meant, could easily be given the impression that he belonged to a Swedish-Jewish establishment that was more on the side of the authorities than on theirs.

It is certainly true that Marcus Ehrenpreis was a part of the Swedish-Jewish establishment, but in many respects he was also an outsider. On the whole, he lived up to being the unifying and inspiring leadership figure that the Stockholm congregation had hoped for when it recruited him, but with his idiosyncratic visions and plans for the renewal of Jewish life in Sweden, he remained a solitary figure. Partly this lay in his role as chief rabbi, having to stay above the fray of internal struggles and conflicts, but partly it lay in his self-chosen role as a spiritual renewer and prophet of sorts. As a consequence, when postwar accounts were to be settled, and responsibilities were to be assigned, and history was to be written, Ehrenpreis was again vulnerable to intra-Jewish attacks and accusations, not unlike the intra-Jewish crossfire he managed to draw upon himself after fourteen years of service in Bulgaria.

Nor did he seem too eager to defend himself. After his two responses in the international Jewish press, he never raised the matter again.

As if what he had said and done over the years should speak for itself.

Or maybe he was just too tired.

In the summer of 1948, Ehrenpreis gave a radio talk on what he believed in as a Jew, and in which he confessed that he had wrestled with doubts about the "multimillennial" religion into which he had been born. "The religious life of my early years was marked by vacillations: Is that true what I believe and have been taught to believe, or is that true what I see with my eyes and feel with my senses?" Putting an end to his vacillations were the "honest and courageous words" of a natural scientist telling him, when he was still a student in Berlin, that the ultimate secrets of existence would always remain a secret, "which in due course," Ehrenpreis explained, "weakened my illusions about the omnipotence of knowledge, and brought me to the saving harbor of faith."

He then declared in what he believed:

The Jewish-Swedish painter Isaac Grünewald working on a portrait of Marcus Ehrenpreis, Stockholm 1939. On the desk is a picture of Marcus's father, Jacob Ehrenpreis.

The Jewish faith has taught me to believe in the majesty of the human being, the human being whom God has created in his image, the human being as the bearer of the divine and the eternal in our existence. The Bible places all human beings on the same level of equality and fraternity and proclaims respect for the majesty of human life, and for human dignity as the highest tenet of religion and morality. [...] We are all meant to make the divine a reality on earth, assigned to us as a common home. My religion teaches me to develop a sense of equality with my fellow human beings, regardless of race, religion, status or origin, as

Marcus Ehrenpreis delivers his farewell sermon at the Stockholm Synagogue on 11 December 1948.

> expressed by the imperative in Leviticus: "Love your neighbor as thyself!"[50]

This was the last time Marcus Ehrenpreis's voice was heard in public—and from this occasion the voice is preserved: the careful intonation, the crisp articulation, the hard-to-pin accent, tinted by so many languages. The voice in front of a mute microphone is certainly not the same as the voice in front of a packed synagogue, or in a teeming congress hall, or in front of a group of expectant confirmands, but the faith is the same—and it is unmistakably his.

On 11 December 1948 he delivered his farewell sermon in the Stockholm synagogue. He was now practically blind, and in a photograph from the occasion he is wearing glasses that serve to hide the weakness of his eyesight rather than to strengthen it.

And maybe this was for the best. Whatever remained to be seen was now mostly beyond the horizon of his life. The Jewish world into which he had been born was irrevocably gone, and even for the most sharp-eyed it was hard to see what would come in its place.

Marcus Ehrenpreis spent his last years at Saltsjöbaden Sanatorium outside Stockholm, where he died on 27 February 1951. The funeral ceremony took place in the synagogue on 2 March, and was officiated by his successor Kurt Wilhelm, who in his words of remembrance quoted freely from a poem by Ehrenpreis's dearest poet, Chaim Nachman Bialik, translated into Swedish thirty years earlier by Ehrenpreis himself:

> At my death, O, lament for me:
> Behold, this was a man. He is no more.

> Great is the pain, very, very great.
> Alas, one song, a single song, still lived,
> in his breast, passing forever,
> dying forever.

Ehrenpreis's last book was a collection of essays, written between 1923 and 1948, entitled *Frågetecknet Israel* (The question of Israel). The title essay was from 1943 and dealt with the solution to the "Jewish problem." Perhaps, he wrote, this was a problem so "wide and complicated" that it could never be fully solved. In any case, the establishment of a Jewish Palestine would only be a partial solution to it, and a partial solution with unforeseeable consequences.[51]

To Marcus Ehrenpreis, the solution to the "Jewish problem" remained inseparably linked to the solution of that fundamental human problem that had followed him throughout his life and which he one last time formulated in his characteristic way:

> Peace must be made, not only between the world and the Jews, but more widely, between the weak and the strong, between minorities and majorities, between the oppressed and the oppressors. [...] The strengthening and cementing of minority rights is a sine qua non for a lasting peace, and an imperative requirement for both Jews and other minorities.[52]

Where others saw a new Jewish answer appearing, Marcus Ehrenpreis saw an old question remaining.

Isaac Grünewald's portrait of Marcus Ehrenpreis. From the Jewish congregation in Stockholm.

Saving the treasures of Jacob. Volumes of Bikorei Ha'etim *(The first fruits), the Hebrew-language journal published by the Jewish Enlightenment movement in Galicia between 1820 and 1831. From the private library of Marcus Ehrenpreis, donated to the Jewish congregation in Stockholm.*

12.

THE QUESTION OF ISRAEL. AN EPILOGUE

What do I have in common with the Jews? I hardly have anything in common with myself and should just stand quietly in a corner, content to breathe.

—Franz Kafka

It is said that history is written by the victors, which is probably true, but sometimes a pity. I believe that the history of the losers can be just as interesting, especially when the losers have right and justice on their side.

Yes, I know, right and justice are big words, and one man's right can easily become another man's wrong, and the victors usually make sure that the right is written on their side. But for Marcus Ehrenpreis, the big words were more than just words. They were the foundation of his Judaism. The big words of the Prophets were also his words, and he took them in his mouth in the firm belief that they reflected the true face of Judaism and provided Jewish heritage and tradition with their meaning and significance. For him, Judaism was the historic bearer of faith in the power of the spirit over the sword, and the right of the weak against the strong.

And for most of his life, there was little to disprove it. Jews and Judaism were certainly the bearers of much else, and not everything was perhaps worth passing on, but in the two-thousand-year history of postbiblical Judaism, there were no instances of Jews and Judaism executing the right of the strong over the weak, or wielding the sword against the spirit, or being a majority oppressing a minority, or being a nation like all the others.

There were those who had made this into a problem, indeed, into the very essence of what throughout the life of Marcus Ehrenpreis had been designated the Jewish problem. The Jews as an anomaly among the peoples of the world. The Jews as a people outside the political orders of the world. The Jews as a people united by something other than kings, armies, and borders. The Jews as an eternal minority in the midst of majorities.

The antisemites, of course, made it a problem, but so did the political Zionists. Hannah Arendt did it when, as a still-active Zionist in 1944, she described the Jews as a pariah people, by which she meant a people who had placed themselves outside "a world of political realities" in order to preserve "the illusion of liberty and unchallenged humanity."[1]

This we now know is no longer possible, she wrote.

And undeniably, that's how it appeared to be.

But Marcus Ehrenpreis didn't see it that way. Not even in 1944. He couldn't or wouldn't imagine a Jewish existence that had forfeited its spiritual destiny, as he saw it. And even less, of course, a Judaism that could be invoked for territorial conquest, military occupation, minority oppression, and ethnic cleansing.

However, if he had looked back on the time before the Roman conquest of Judea and the destruction of the Temple in Jerusalem, he would have seen such a Judaism as well. For a century or so Judea was a kingdom ruled by a Jewish priestly dynasty, the Hasmoneans, who hardly distinguished themselves by leniency and tolerance toward minorities and dissenters, and who did not hesitate to use the power of the sword to subjugate them.

This less-tolerant side of Judaism Ehrenpreis had tasted himself; the recurring attacks on his Jewish "liberalism" and his "assimilationism," and the whispering rumors about his "un-Jewish" way of life, and the cover sheets with his name torn out from Jewish prayer books were all rooted in a different interpretation of Judaism than his.

The Judaism of Marcus Ehrenpreis was founded when, symbolically, one of his heroes, Yochanan ben Sakkai, smuggled a Torah scroll out of the Roman-besieged Jerusalem "to establish a spiritual Yerushalayim, which shall extend over the earth and resist the powers of destruction." This was a Judaism grounded in the legacy of the biblical prophets, which was a legacy founded on a small people's experiences with slavery and captivity, with political weakness and powerlessness, and from these experiences it had bequeathed to the world a faith in the right of the weak and the justice of the powerless. A Judaism betraying this faith he could or would not imagine, and when he imagined a Jewish state in Palestine, he convinced himself that it would not be a state like all the others.

He had certainly already noted that the Jewish state emerging in Palestine was still based on the power of the sword, and on a majority oppressing a minority, and thus violating some central tenets of his Judaism. But I believe that he convinced himself that these were temporary deviations due to external circumstances. To the extent that the "deviations" were noted and discussed in the Jewish world, they were largely being silenced by the story of the miraculous return, the miraculous reconstruction, the miraculous resurrection of the Hebrew language and the miraculous flowering of the desert.

For a while there was hope among the remaining proponents of cultural Zionism that the State of Israel would not become a state like all the others. Or as Chaim Weizmann, Ehrenpreis's fellow activist and friend during the student years in Berlin and the first president of Israel, wrote in his memoirs in 1949, expressing what I believe was their common idea of how a state wishing to embody the tenets of Judaism should act:

> There must not be one law for the Jews and another for the Arabs. We must adhere to the ancient principle that has been taught in our Torah [Exodus 12:49]: "The same law shall be for the native and for the stranger who dwells among you." [...] I am sure that the world will judge the Jewish state by its treatment of the Arabs, just as the Jewish people at large will be judged by what we do or fail to do in this state where we have been given such a wonderful opportunity after thousands of years of wandering and suffering.[2]

Similar expectations were voiced by another soulmate and friend of Ehrenpreis, Hugo Bergmann, professor of philosophy at Hebrew University, who in 1947, at the request of Ehrenpreis, had been invited to Stockholm to "enhance the spiritual life" of the Jewish congregation. In October 1949 Bergmann published an article in *Judisk Tidskrift* where he outlined how "this quantitatively minuscule state" must evolve in order to fulfill "the messianic longing of all generations of Israel to begin history anew":

> Day by day, hour by hour, it will be tested whether the State of Israel has chosen this path or the path of mainstream politics. Every single law is a test, be it a law regulating our relations with the outside world or a law regulating the State's relations with its inhabitants and above all with its minorities. [...] If the State of Israel proves worthy of its great name and does not bear it unjustly, a new conception of man and society will emerge from here. A new chapter of Judaism has begun.[3]

In the last sentence Hugo Bergmann was undeniably right, a new chapter of Judaism had begun, but this was a chapter that neither he nor Ehrenpreis could have imagined, since the external conditions for such a chapter, Jewish military power and territorial supremacy, had not existed for two thousand years. What both of them could well imagine, and both of them feared, was a state that would be too little Jewish, that it would be a Jewish nation without roots in the teachings of Judaism, as they understood them. From his position in Jerusalem, Bergmann observed a growing contempt for the "degradation, bondage, and impurity" of the Jewish diaspora, and the emergence of groups calling for the renunciation of two thousand years of Judaism and a reconnection with the ancient Hebrews. He also noted tendencies toward a fetishistic, idolatrous worship of "every turf of Palestinian soil and every biblical Palestinian name."[4]

What both Bergmann and Ehrenpreis believed in and hoped for was a state that would embody in its laws and institutions a Judaism formed by faith in the right of the weak and the justice of the powerless. Exactly how this would materialize, and what kind of laws and institutions it would require, remained unclear, but for a brief moment it seemed possible to imagine that the teachings of Judaism might serve as a spiritual and moral corrective to the temptations and excesses of political and military power.

But temporary deviations became the rule, and minority oppression and expulsion became embedded in the history of the new state, and in its exercise of power it became increasingly difficult to trace the tenets of Judaism according to Marcus Ehrenpreis. For some time yet, this could perhaps be explained by arguing that the state was still too little Jewish and that the true ethos of Judaism had yet to be realized. But with time it would become clear that the new state had created conditions for hitherto unthinkable forms of Judaism—violent, nationalist, colonialist—and that the problem for people with another view of Judaism would turn out to be that the Jewish state could become *too* Jewish, not too little.

If not sooner, the problem became evident in the summer of 1967, when, after another war with its Arab neighbors, the State of Israel took control of the most biblically charged places in Jewish history, and religious and messianic arguments for occupation and colonization began to emerge alongside the entrenched arguments of national security.

Henceforth, the idea of Judaism as a religion proclaiming the right of the weak and the justice of the powerless would be hard to sustain.

I cannot know, of course, how Ehrenpreis would have reacted if he had lived to see such an interpretation of Judaism put into practice, but I've gotten to know him well enough to suspect that he would have been horrified. A Zionism spearheaded by armed settlers invoking Jewish commands for racist terror and ethnic cleansing would have exceeded his worst fears. A Jewish state based on the continuous occupation, oppression, and dispossession of its Palestinian population would have been beyond his imagination.

I suspect that other developments would have frightened him as well. The growth of ultra-Orthodox Judaism, for example, and the reemergence of an inward-looking and sectarian ghetto culture, far from the ideals of his Jewish renaissance. More predictable was a development that Ehrenpreis had long wrestled with in his writings and sermons: the secularization of Jewish identity and the weakening of the spiritual content of Judaism. His criticism of political Zionism was ultimately rooted in the fear that being Jewish would be reduced to a national affiliation, and the Jews become a nation like any other.

In his recurrent exhortations to his Swedish-Jewish congregation and his young confirmands to reconnect with their Jewish heritage, and become aware of its richness, and make themselves self-conscious bearers of the destiny and mission of the Jewish people, there was a tone of concern. Not only for not being heard and understood, that concern was there too, but from a sense that the times were against him: the morally disoriented, materialistic, individualistic times that dissolved the bonds between generations and made it hard to carry forth and sustain a spiritual heritage.

This, however, seemed less a crisis of Judaism than a crisis of humanity. The problems of Jews and Judaism, as Ehrenpreis saw them, were very much the problems of modern man as a whole. Not only Jews and Judaism had difficulties in sustaining inherited beliefs and spiritual traditions, and the criticism of "an unhealthy pursuit of profit and pleasure" was not specifically Jewish. At some point, he might even have been struck by the blasphemous thought that had it not been for historical

Jew-hatred and modern antisemitism and murderous Nazism, Judaism might have ended up withering away, which is what Kant had in mind when in 1798 he coined the ominous phrase "the euthanasia of Judaism."

In this respect, Hugo Valentin was perhaps more right than Ehrenpreis, when in their public discussion in March 1945 he insisted that it was antisemitism that had held the Jewish people together, and that if and when antisemitism subsided—which Valentin expected would happen when the Jews had their own state and became a people like all the others—the process would be unstoppable.

In the light of history, they were both wrong.

Valentin was wrong about the decline of antisemitism and the demise of the Diaspora.

Antisemitism, essentially a conspiracy theory that invents the Jews it needs, has shown no signs of going away. The Jewish Diaspora is certainly not what it once was, and in some parts has taken on the characteristics of an Israeli Diaspora in exile, but it has remained an independent, fractious, and vital Jewish form of existence, with a complex and tense relationship with the Jewish state.

Ehrenpreis was wrong about the true face of Judaism.

The Judaism that he portrayed and preached and wanted the world to see, however unrealistic it may have seemed even in his time, cannot exist even as a messianic fantasy in my time. This has to do not only with the emergence of a Judaism that would concoct a messianic fantasy based on territorial occupation and ethnic cleansing, but also with the rapid secularization and individualization of Jewish life. The idea that the people of "Israel" carry a common spiritual destiny, as Ehrenpreis preached, is not only impossible today, but as I see it, also dangerous, since it has shown itself capable of fomenting movements of messianic extremism, both Jewish and Christian. There has even emerged a Christian strand of Zionism, according to which Israel's collective destiny is to return to Zion, heralding the second coming of Jesus, the conversion of the Jews to Christ, and the end of times.

Ehrenpreis was also wrong about antisemitism.

For the greater part of his life he believed that antisemitism could be fought with truth.

With testimony in a court in Bern.

With a journal to build a bridge between Judaism and the world.

With books that would have the "builders of Israel" touch the hearts and minds of the people in his Swedish *Kinderland*.

To the very last, he wanted to believe that hatred of Jews and Judaism was rooted in two thousand years of Christian misrepresentation and defamation, and as he rejoiced at every manifestation of Christian soul-searching and understanding, he was disappointed, and even outraged, at how rapidly Christian understanding could turn into animosity. But as he would find out, against antisemitism no truth whatsoever about Jews and Judaism would make any difference.

Still, as Ehrenpreis saw it, the history of the Jews should not be written as an endless litany of defamation and persecution, but as the manifestation of a destiny—to live as a people amid the peoples. Even if in so doing, the Jews had once again, and with more devastating consequences than ever, become just as unavoidable targets of defamation and persecution, as Valentin had argued against him.

Thus, as Marcus Ehrenpreis saw it, the solution to the Jewish problem, defined as the Jews being an eternal minority among majorities, was inextricably linked to the solution of that all-too-human problem that had preoccupied Ehrenpreis ever since the Balkan wars: how to make majorities and minorities live side by side, peacefully and fruitfully, in a world where ethnic, cultural, and national boundaries would always overlap.

For Marcus Ehrenpreis, the question of Israel was not a Jewish question only.

So what did he leave behind?

Except for a question.

Let me say in a few words what he left to me.

He left the traces of a deep and heartfelt love for our common Jewish heritage, its poetic and literary beauty not least, and showed that there was something for me to love as well.

He showed me that the Jewish questions he was asking were not questions for Jews only. He asked them from a specifically Jewish experience and a specifically Jewish tradition and gave them a specifically Jewish form, but he never doubted that the Jewish experience and the Jewish tradition had something important to contribute to the non-Jewish world as well.

Not least, he wanted to show that Jewish heritage was primarily about upholding an ethical-moral obligation and not an ethnic-national community. It is true that he saw the obligation as an explicit undertaking of the Jewish people, or for "Israel" as he preferred, and that this was the meaning of the much-misunderstood chosenness, and that a Judaism that did not carry the obligation was not worth preserving.

That's how Marcus Ehrenpreis saw it, and that's how I tend to see it too.

A Jewish community deprived of its ethical and moral foundations may be considered worth preserving for other reasons, ethnic and national, for example, but that is not reason enough for me.

A Jewish community kept together by defamation and persecution appeals to me the least. Antisemitism, however deadly it has shown itself to be, remains for me an uninteresting reason to be Jewish. An unavoidable reason, perhaps, depending on circumstances, but uninteresting.

I will confess that in many Jewish eyes I would probably be considered a bad Jew. Rules and rituals, however beautiful and meaningful, are not my strong suit. Nevertheless, I feel naturally at home in the Jewish tradition, and in the Jewish texts, and in the Jewish prayers, and in the relation between humans and God that I find in the Judaism of Marcus Ehrenpreis.

No, I don't believe there is a God in history, or in a God that humans can have any claims on. But I do believe in a God who can make humans assume responsibility for the world we live in, however we believe that this world has come about, because it is only humans who, for better or for worse, have been endowed with the capacity to create the world they live in, and to destroy it, and to assume responsibility for what they create and destroy. Which for me is the meaning of the basic tenet of Judaism, that humans are created in the image of God.

The Jewish faith that Ehrenpreis gave voice to in his radio talk in 1948, a few months before I was born into Judaism, I therefore have no problem making into mine.

The question of Israel remains, and will always remain, and I hereby add it to my declaration of faith.

BIBLIOGRAPHIC REFERENCES

Ahad, Ha'am. *Essays, Letters, Memoirs*, Oxford: East and West Library, 1946.

Åmark, Klas. *Att bo granne med ondskan. Sveriges förhållande till nazismen, Nazityskland och Förintelsen* [Living next door to evil. Sweden's relationship with Nazism, Nazi Germany, and the Holocaust], Stockholm: Albert Bonniers Förlag, 2011.

———. *Främlingar på tåg* [Strangers on a train], Stockholm: Kaunitz-Olsson, 2021.

Andersson, Lars M. *En Jude är en jude är en jude... Representationer av »juden« i svensk skämtpress 1900–1930* [A Jew is a Jew is a Jew. Representations of "Jews" in the Swedish humor press, 1900–1930], Lund: Nordic Academic Press, 2000.

Andersson, Lars M., and Kvist Geverts Karin (eds.), *En problematisk relation? Flyktingpolitik och judiska flyktingar i Sverige 1920–1950* [A problematic relation? Refugee policy and Jewish refugees in Sweden 1920–1950], Uppsala: Opuscula Historica Upsaliensia, 2008.

Arendt, Hannah. *Eichmann in Jerusalem: A Report on the Banality of Evil*, New York: Viking Press, 1963.

Benjamin, Walter. *Selected Writings, Volume 1: 1913–1926*. Cambridge: Harvard University Press, 2004.

———. *On the Concept of History*, 1940, translated by Dennis Redmond, 2005. https://www.marxists.org/reference/archive/benjamin/1940/history.htm

Berkowitz, Michael. *Zionist Culture and West European Jewry before the First World War*, Chapel Hill: The University of North Carolina Press, 1993.

Böök, Fredrik. *Resa till Jerusalem* [Journey to Jerusalem], Stockholm: P.A. Norstedt & Söner, 1925.

Bredefeldt, Rita. *Judiskt liv i Stockholm och Norden—ekonomi, identitet och assimilering 1850–1930* [Jewish life in Stockholm and Scandinavia: economy, identity, and assimilation, 1850–1930], Stockholm: Stockholmia Förlag, 2008.

Briem, Efraim. *Antisemitismen genom tiderna, orsaker och historia* [Antisemitism through the ages, causes and history], Stockholm: Natur och Kultur, 1940.

Brumlik, Micha. *Deutscher Geist unden Judenhaß*, München: Luchterhand, 2002.

Buber, Martin. *Die Erneuerung des Judentums. Reden über das Judentum*, Frankfurt am Main: Literarische Anstalt Rütten & Loening, 1923.

Dubnow, Simon. *Weltgeschichte des Jüdischen Volkes, Band III*, Berlin: Jüdischer Verlag, 1937.

Ehrenpreis, Marcus. *Die Entwicklung der Emanationslehre in der Kabbala des XIII. Jahrhunderts*. Frankfurt a/M: J. Kaufmann'sche Buchhandlung, 1895.

———. *Nationernas bibliotek. Judarna* [Library of nations: Judarna], Stockholm: Norstedt & Söner, 1920.

———. *Österlandets själ* [The soul of the East], Stockholm: Hugo Gebers förlag, 1926.

———. *Landet mellan öster och väster* [The land between East and West], Stockholm: Hugo Gebers förlag, 1927.

———. *De som byggt Israel I. Profeter och gudsmän* [Prophets and sages who built Israel], Uppsala: Hugo Gebers förlag, 1929.

———. *De som byggt Israel II, Helige och hjältar* [Saints and heroes who built Israel], Uppsala: Hugo Gebers Förlag, 1931.

———. *Malakis rop till tiden* [Malachi's call to the times], Stockholm: Bonniers, Stockholm 1933.

———. *Talmud, fariseism, urkristendom* [Talmud, Phariseeism, early Christianity], Uppsala: Hugo Gebers Förlag, 1933.

———. *Israels möten med folken* [Israel's encounters with the nations], Stockholm: Hugo Gebers förlag, 1934.

———. *De som byggt Israel III, Skalder och siare* [Poets and visionaries who built Israel], Stockholm: Bonniers, 1943.

———. *Mitt liv mellan öster och vaster* [My life between East and West], Stockholm: Bonniers, 1946.

———. *Frågetecknet Israel* [The question of Israel], Stockholm: Bonniers, 1948.

———. *Vad jag tror på* [What I believe in], Radiotjänst 1948.

Ehrenpreis, Marcus, and Josephson Ragnar (trans. and ed.), *Nyhebreisk lyrik (1870–1920)* [New Hebrew poetry], Stockholm: Norstedt & Söner, 1920.

Einhorn, Lena. *Handelsresande i liv* [A traveling salesman in lives], Stockholm: Prisma, 1999.

Ek, Sven B. *Nöden i Lund*, Lund: Liber, 1971.

Filon, Judaeus. *The Works of Philo, Complete and Unabridged* (English translation C. D. Yonge), Massachusetts: Hendrickson Publishers, 1993.

Fredriksen, Paula, *Augustine and the Jews. A Christian Defense of Jews and Judaism*, New York: Doubleday, 2008.

Fruitman, Stephen. *Creating a New Heart, Marcus Ehrenpreis on Jewry and Judaism*, Umeå: Department of Historical Studies, 2001.

Gottfarb Inga. *Den livsfarliga glömskan* [The dangerous oblivion], Stockholm: Langenskiöld, 2006.

Gunnarsson, Lars. *Kyrkan, nazismen och demokratin, åsiktsbildning kring svensk kyrklighet* [The Church, Nazism, and democracy: Opinion formation in the Swedish ecclesiastical movement 1919–1945], Stockholm: Almqvist & Wiksell International, 1995.

Hansson, Svante. *Flykt och överlevnad. Flyktingverksamheten i Mosaiska församlingen i Stockholm 1933–1950* [Flight and survival. Refugee activities in the Mosaic Congregation in Stockholm], Stockholm: Hillelförlaget, 2004.

Hermansson, Magnus. *Hur skall det gå med judarna?* [What will be with the Jews?] Stockholm: Harriers förlag, 1936.

Herzl, Theodor. *Valda skrifter, utgivna och inledda av Marcus Ehrenpreis* [Theodor Herzl, selected writings, edited and introduced by Marcus Ehrenpreis], Stockholm: Förlags A.-B. Herzlia, 1944.

Jangfeldt, Bengt. *Raoul Wallenberg, en biografi* [Raoul Wallenberg, a biography], Stockholm: Wahlström & Widstrand, 2012.

Jarlert, Anders. *Emanuel Linderholm som kyrkohistoriker* [Emanuel Linderholm as Church Historian], Lund University Press, 1987.

———. *Judisk »ras« som äktenskapshinder. Effekten av Nürnberglagarna i Svenska kyrkans statliga funktion som lysningsförrättare 1935–1945* [Jewish race as marriage impediment. The effects of the Nürnberg Laws on the official functions of the Church], Malmö: Sekel Bokförlag, 2006.

Josephson Ragnar, *Den dubbla lojaliteten* [The dual loyalty], Stockholm: Bonniers, 1936.

Katz, Jacob. *Out of the Ghetto, the Social Background of Jewish Emancipation 1770–1870*, New York: Random House, 1988.

Kechales, Haim. *Korot Yehudei Bulgaria* [The history of Bulgarian Jews], Tel Aviv: Davar Publishing, 1972.

Kittel, Gerhard. *Die Judenfrage*, Stuttgart, Berlin: W. Kohlhammer, 1934.

Klein, Ernst (selection and translation). *Den stora tiden och de små människorna. Civila brev från galiziska flyktingar* [The big war and the small people. Letters from Galician refugees], Stockholm: Bonniers 1916.

Klein, Gottlieb. *Religion och moral. Föredrag hållet vid religions–kongressen i Stockholm 1897* [Religion and morality. Lecture given at the Congress of Religion in Stockholm 1897], Stockholm: Gullberg & Hallbergs boktryckeri, 1898.

Koblik, Steven. *The Stones Cry Out, Sweden's Response to the Persecution of the Jews. 1933–1945*, New York: Holocaust Library, 1988. Swedish translation by Erik Frykman: *Om vi teg skulle stenarna ropa. Sverige och judeproblemet 1933–1945*, Stockholm: Norstedts, 1987.

Kohn, Hans (ed.). *Nationalism and the Jewish Ethic. Basic Writings of Ahad Ha'am*, New York: Schocken Books, 1962.

Kvist, Geverts Karin. *Ett främmande element i nationen. Svensk flyktingpolitik och de judiska flyktingarna 1938–1944* [A foreign element in the nation. Swedish refugee policy and the Jewish refugees 1938–1944], Uppsala: Studia Historica Upsaliensis, 2008.

Lauritzen, Monica. *Karl Warburg. Den varsamme vägvisaren* [Karl Warburg. The careful guide], Stockholm: Albert Bonniers Förlag 2018.

Levai, Jenö. *Raoul Wallenberg: His Remarkable Life, Heroic Battles and the Secret of His Mysterious Disappearance*, Melbourne: WhiteAnt Occasional Publications, 1989. Original in Hungarian, 1948.

Levi, Primo. *Tre böcker: Är detta en människa/Fristen/De förlorade och de räddade* [Three books: *If This Is a Man/The Truce/The Drowned and the Saved*], Stockholm: Albert Bonniers Förlag, 2013.

Levine, Paul A. *From Indifference to Activism: Swedish Diplomacy and the Holocaust, 1938–44*, Uppsala Studia Historica Uppsaliensis, 1998.

Mendes-Flohr, Paul, *Martin Buber, a Life of Faith and Dissent*, New Haven and London: Yale University Press, 2019.

Meyerson, Per-Martin. *På jakt efter den judiska anden: en resa i judisk historia* [In search of the Jewish spirit, a journey in Jewish history], Stockholm: Fischer & Co, 2002.

Naar, Devin E. *Jewish Salonica, Between Ottoman Empire and Modern Greece*, Stanford: Stanford University Press, 2016.

Narrowe, Morton. *Zionism in Sweden, Its Beginnings until the End of World War I*, New York: The Jewish Theological Seminary of America, 1990.

Nirenberg, David. *Anti-Judaism. The Western Tradition*, New York: Norton, 2013.

Nordlund, Sven. *Affärer som vanligt: ariseringen i Sverige 1933–1945* [Business as usual. Aryanization in Sweden, 1933–1945], Lund: Sekel Bokförlag, 2009.

Nussenblatt, Tulo (ed.). *Theodor Herzl Jahrbuch* [Yearbook], Vienna: Dr. Heinrich Glanz Verlag, 1937.

Penkower, Monty Noam. *The Jews Were Expendable: Free World Diplomacy and the Holocaust*, Urbana and Chicago: University of Illinois Press, 1983.

Rabinovici, Doron. *Eichmann's Jews. The Jewish Administration of Holocaust Vienna, 1938–1945*, Cambridge: Polity Press, 2011.

Rabinovitch Simon (ed.). *Jews and Diaspora Nationalism, Writings on Jewish Peoplehood in Europe and the United States*, Waltham, MA: Brandeis University Press, 2012.

Ronen, Shoshana. *A Prophet of Consolation on the Threshold of Destruction: Yehoshua Ozjasz Thon, an Intellectual Portrait*, Warsaw: Elipsa, 2017.

Rosenberg, Göran. *Det förlorade landet, en personlig historia* [The lost land, a personal history], Stockholm: Albert Bonniers Förlag, 1996.

———. *Ett kort uppehåll på vägen från Auschwitz* [*A Brief Stop on the Road from Auschwitz*], Stockholm: Albert Bonniers Förlag, 2012. Translated by Sarah Death and published in English in 2015 by Other Press.

Rosenfeld, Harvey. *Raoul Wallenberg*, New York: Holmes & Meier, 1995.

Rosenzweig, Franz. *Der Mensch und sein Werk. Gesammelte Schriften I. Briefe und Tagebücher, I, 1900–1918* [Man and his work. Collected writings I. Letters and diaries, I, 1900–1918], Rachel Rosenzweig and Edith Rosenzweig-Scheinmann (eds.), Haag: Martinus Nijhoff, 1979.

———. *Der Stern der Erlösung*, Frankfurt: Suhrkamp, 1988. Published in English as *The Star of Redemption*, Madison, WI: The University of Wisconsin Press, 2005.

Rovner, Jay (ed.). *The* Ma'sar Kesafim *Ledger of Mordcai Zeev Ehrenpreis of Lvov. With an Examination of the Practice, and its Meaning for the Donor*, New York and Jerusalem: The Jewish Theological Seminary of America, 2003.

Rudberg, Pontus. *The Swedish Jews and the Holocaust*, London and New York: Routledge, 2017.

Shanes, Joshua. *Diaspora Nationalism and Jewish Identity in Habsburg Galizia*, New York: Cambridge University Press 2012.

Suber, Margareta. *Vänd ditt ansikte till mig* [Turn your face to me], Stockholm: Norstedt & Söner, 1942.

Svanberg, Ingvar, and Tyden Mattias, *Sverige och Förintelsen, debatt och dokument om Europas judar 1933–1945* [Sweden and the Holocaust, debates and documents about Europe's Jews], Stockholm: Dialogos, 2005.

Valentin, Hugo. *Judarnas historia i Sverige*. Stockholm: Bonniers, 1924.

———. *Det judiska folkets öde. Forntid—nutid—framtid* [The fate of the Jewish people. Past—present—future], Stockholm: Kooperativa förbundets bokförlag, 1944.

Urban, Martina. *Aesthetics of Renewal, Martin Buber's Early Representation of Hasidism as Kulturkritik*, Chicago: University of Chicago Press, 2012.

INDEX OF NAMES

NOTES

1. BEING JEWISH. A PROLOGUE

1 In 1996, I published *Det förlorade landet* [The lost land], a personal exploration of the history of Zionism. In Swedish, the "The Lost Land" and "The Promised Land" differ by one letter only (*Det förlorade landet* versus *Det förlovade landet*). In German the book was *Das Verlorene Land* (Jüdischer Verlag, Frankfurt 1998), and in French *L'utopie perdue* (Denöel, Paris 2000).
2 *A Brief Stop on the Road from Auschwitz*, New York: Other Press, 2015.
3 Marcus Ehrenpreis, "Tragisk försoningsdag" [A tragic Day of Atonement], *Judisk Tidskrift*, October 1943.
4 Psalms 69:2–6.

2. PREMONITIONS OF SPRING

1 Ehrenpreis, *Mitt liv* [My life], p 106.
2 Ehrenpreis, *Mitt liv*, p 113.
3 Marcus Ehrenpreis, "Die junghebräische Literatur," *Die Welt*, Vol. 1, No. 7 (16 July 1897), pp 14–16. A short passage from the text was later published in Swedish in Ehrenpreis, *Mitt liv*, p 124. The text reproduced here is drawn from both sources.
4 Ehrenpreis, "Die junghebräische Literatur," pp 14–16. Ehrenpreis, *Mitt liv*, p 124.
5 Ehrenpreis, "Die junghebräische Literatur."
6 Hillel Halkin, "The Most Tragic Jewish Writer of Modern Times," *Mosaic Magazine*, February 2017. https://mosaicmagazine.com/observation/2017/02/the-most-tragic-jewish-writer-of-modern-times.
7 Marcus Ehrenpreis, "Zwei Junghebräer," *Die Welt*, Vol. 5, No. 49, (6 December 1901), pp 18–19.

8 Ehrenpreis, "Zwei Junghebräer," p 20.
9 Ehrenpreis, *Mitt liv*, pp 94, 95.
10 Marcus Ehrenpreis, "Conversation with Berdyczewski," *Judisk Tidskrift*, December 1931, p 298.
11 Marcus Ehrenpreis, "Den historiska sommaren 1897" [The historical summer of 1897], *Judisk Tidskrift*, September–October 1932.
12 Theodor Herzl, *Valda skrifter, utgivna och inledda av Marcus Ehrenpreis* [Theodor Herzl, selected writings, edited and introduced by Marcus Ehrenpreis], Stockholm: Herzlia 1944, p 15.
13 Letter from "Verein Jung Israel" to like-minded associations and friends in Austria, Russia, Germany, France, and Romania, dated Lemberg-Berlin, 14 July 1893, and signed by three persons, including Ehrenpreis. Reproduced in *Theodor Herzl Jahrbuch* [Yearbook], ed. Tulo Nussenblatt, Vienna: Dr. Heinrich Glanz Verlag, 1937, p 187.
14 Letter from "Verein Jung Israel." Reproduced in *Theodor Herzl Jahrbuch*, pp 193–194.
15 Letter from "Verein Jung Israel." Reproduced in *Theodor Herzl Jahrbuch* p 194. About the meeting in Vienna, also in Ehrenpreis, *Mitt liv*, p 129: "A Jew of his kind [...] we had never met before. Perhaps he was still learning from us, but he was already our master."
16 Tulo Nussenblatt (ed.), *Theodor Herzl Jahrbuch*, p 195.
17 Ehrenpreis, *Mitt liv*, p 130.
18 Ehrenpreis, *Mitt liv*, p 116.
19 Marcus Ehrenpreis, "The Historical Summer of 1897," *Judisk Tidskrift*, July–August 1932, p 135.
20 Ehrenpreis *Mitt liv*, p 123.
21 Letter from Ahad Ha'am in Odessa to Marcus Ehrenpreis in Djakovar, 8 March 1898. Ahad Ha'am, *Essays, Letters, Memoirs*, Oxford: East and West Library, 1946, p 248.
22 Ehrenpreis, *Mitt liv*, p 131.
23 Marcus Ehrenpreis, introduction in Theodor Herzl, *Valda skrifter*, Stockholm 1944, p 30.
24 *Theodor Herzl Jahrbuch*, p 196.
25 *Theodor Herzl Jahrbuch*, p 196. Willy Bambus was an important figure in the Zionist circles in Berlin, but during the summer of 1897 he had gone from being a supporter of the Congress to an opponent of it.
26 Ehrenpreis, *Mitt liv*, p 21.
27 Ehrenpreis, *Mitt liv*, p 29.

28 Ehrenpreis, *Mitt liv*, p 22.

29 Ehrenpreis, *Mitt liv*, p 35.

30 Debora Vogel (1902–1942) was the daughter of Marcus's sister Lea and emerged in the 1930s as a pioneering Yiddish poet, essayist, and art historian. She was a close friend of the writer and artist Bruno Schulz and also maintained contact with her uncle in Stockholm, whom she visited on at least one occasion. Her description of her grandfather, Jacob Ehrenpreis, appears in an illustrated essay, "The Jewish Quarter in Lemberg," published in Swedish translation in *Judisk Tidskrift*, October 1935. She writes with sensitivity and warmth about the Jewish life that still looked in part as it did in her grandfather's time and still filled the streets of the ghetto.

31 Ehrenpreis, *Mitt liv*, p 23. In July 1941, the temple in Lviv was destroyed by the invading Germans, and the site where it stood is now a park with a memorial stone.

32 In the early 2000s, Mordechai Zeev Ehrenpreis's diary, preserved in Stockholm, was acquired by the Jewish Theological Seminary of America, which published it in 2003 in an annotated edition in English and Hebrew. Jay Rovner, *The* Ma'sar Kesafim *(Income Tithe) Ledger of Mordecai Zeev Ehrenpreis. With an Examination of the Practice, and its Meaning for the Donor.* New York and Jerusalem: The Jewish Theological Seminary of America, 2003 (5763), p 57.

33 Ehrenpreis, *Mitt liv*, p 33.

34 Ehrenpreis, *Mitt liv*, p 34.

35 From "Die Ersten" by Adolf Stand in *Jüdischer Nationalkalender* 1918–1919, quoted by Hugo Valentin in "Marcus Ehrenpreis 60 Years," *Judisk Tidskrift*, September 1929.

36 See also Joshua Shanes, "Mikra Kodesh," in *The YIVO Encyclopedia of Jews in Eastern Europe*. http://www.yivoencyclopedia.org/article.aspx/Mikra_Kodesh

37 Ehrenpreis, *Mitt liv*, p 81.

38 Ehrenpreis, *Mitt liv*, pp 64–65.

39 Ehrenpreis, *Mitt liv*, p 73.

40 Ehrenpreis, *Mitt liv*, p 63.

41 Ehrenpreis, *Mitt liv*, p 78. Marcus Ehrenpreis, "Möte med västjudendomen" [Encounter with Western Judaism], *Judisk Tidskrift*, February 1944, p 58.

42 Ehrenpreis, *Mitt liv*, p 78. Marcus Ehrenpreis, "Möte med västjudendomen," *Judisk Tidskrift*.

43 Marcus Ehrenpreis, *Die Entwickelung der Emanationslehre in der Kabbala des XIII. Jahrhunderts* [The development of the doctrine of emanation in the Kabbalah of the XIIIth century]. Frankfurt a/M: J. Kaufmann'sche Buchhandlung, 1895. The quotations reproduced are from the private Swedish translation that Ehrenpreis's son Theodor commissioned in the 1970s. The original had been given to Theodor by his father on the fiftieth anniversary of his doctorate, 11 March 1945.

44 Ehrenpreis, *Mitt liv*, p 100.

45 Martin Buber, "Jüdische Renaissance" (1900) in *Die Jüdische Bewegung, Gesammelte Aufsätze und Ansprachen 1900-1915*, Berlin: Jüdische Verlag, 1916, p 8.

46 Ehrenpreis, *Mitt liv*, p 101.

47 Congress speech, *Die Welt*, 10 September 1897, p 12. "Dr. Ehrenpreis regrets that this point, which everyone takes so seriously, will not be negotiated until the twelfth hour."

48 Congress speech, *Die Welt*, 10 September 1897, p 12. Michael Berkowitz, *Zionist Culture and West European Jewry Before the First World War*, Chapel Hill: University of North Carolina Press, 1993, pp 48–49.

49 Letter dated Berlin 18 March 1903. National Archives, Stockholm. The reply from Ehrenpreis added by hand. In an essay in the magazine *Ost-West*, April 1903, Ahad Ha'am had severely criticized Herzl's recently published visionary novel *Altneuland*, which he believed showed political Zionism's lack of realism and fundamental lack of understanding of the Jewish cause. Max Nordau reacted violently in an article in *Die Welt* (13 March 1903), in which he accused Ahad Ha'am of abhorring tolerance.

50 Marcus Ehrenpreis, "Meine Kongressrede," in Martin Buber's journal *Der Jude*, 7–8 1923, pp 389–395.

51 Marcus Ehrenpreis, "Den historiska sommaren 1897, del 2" [The historical summer of 1897, part 2], *Judisk Tidskrift*, September–October 1932, p 170. Ehrenpreis, *Mitt liv*, p 132.

3. A TASTE OF ADVENTURE

1 Elias Canetti, *The Tongue Set Free—Remembrance of a European Childhood*, New York: Farrar, Straus and Giroux, 1983, translation Joachim Neugroschel.

2 Ehrenpreis, *Mitt liv*, pp 138–139.

3 Ehrenpreis, *Mitt liv*, p 141.

4 Ehrenpreis, *Mitt liv*, p 146.

5 Ehrenpreis, *Mitt liv*, p 146.

6 Marcus Ehrenpreis, "Bei Georg Brandes," *Die Welt*, 18 October 1901. "Ett möte med Georg Brandes 1899" [A meeting with Georg Brandes], *Israeliten*, March 1927.

7 Ehrenpreis, *Mitt liv*, p 149.

8 *Mitt liv*, pp 189–190. *Priaporets* newspaper, 10 September 1909. Vladimir Paunovski: "Inauguration of the Central Synagogue in Sofia." *La Estreya* 2/2009. For the translation into English of this and other texts in Bulgarian I am indebted to Prof. Dr. Rumyana Marinova-Christidi.

9 Marcus Ehrenpreis, "När kung Ferdinand invigde synagogan i Sofia" [When King Ferdinand inaugurated the synagogue in Sofia], *Judisk Tidskrift*, September 1944.

10 Ehrenpreis, *Mitt liv*, p 157.

11 Ehrenpreis, *Mitt liv*, p 155.

12 *Encyclopedia of the Jewish Diaspora. Bulgarian Jews*, Vol. 10, Jerusalem, 1965, quoted by Yulina Danova, "Rabbi Dr. Marcus Ehrenpreis between East and West," *La Estreya*, Sofia, 2/2009." For the translation from Bulgarian into English I am indebted to Prof. Dr. Rumyana Marinova-Christidi.

13 Ehrenpreis, *Mitt liv*, p 183.

14 Founded in 1860 by the French-Jewish statesman Adolphe Crémieux, the Alliance Israélite Universelle built up a large network of French-language schools in the Sephardic world in the late nineteenth and early twentieth centuries.

15 Ehrenpreis, *Mitt liv*, p 183.

16 Ehrenpreis, *Mitt liv*, p 181.

17 Haim Kechales, *Korot Yehudei Bulgaria* [The history of Bulgarian Jews], Tel Aviv: Davar Publishing, 1972, part II, pp 202–204. The demonstrations were intended to celebrate Yom Hashekel, Shekel Day, which was instituted to commemorate and financially support the Zionist project in Palestine in the Diaspora.

18 Ehrenpreis, *Mitt Liv*, p 180.

19 Ehrenpreis, *Mitt Liv*, p 168.

20 Ehrenpreis, *Mitt Liv*, p 160.

21 Marcus Ehrenpreis, "Die Hebräische Sprache und Literatur. Referat für den V. Zionistencongress in Basel" [The Hebrew language and

literature. Presentation to the Fifth Zionist Congress in Basel]. Jewish Congregation, Ehrenpreis, Swedish National Archives.

22 "Stenographisches Protokoll der Verhandlungen des V. Zionisten-Congresses in Basel," Vienna 1901, p 156.

23 *The American Jewish Year Book*, Vol. 4, (2 October 1902 to 21 September 21 1903 / 5663), p 82. https://www.jstor.org/stable/23600078

24 Ehrenpreis, *Mitt liv*, pp 201–202.

25 Ehrenpreis, *Mitt liv*, pp 205–206. Marcus Ehrenpreis, "When King Ferdinand got a Torah scroll," *Judisk Tidskrift*, January 1933, p 13 ff.

26 Ehrenpreis, *Mitt liv*, p 207.

27 Ehrenpreis, *Mitt liv*, p 213.

28 Ehrenpreis, *Mitt liv*, p 213.

29 Ehrenpreis, *Mitt liv*, p 213.

30 The signatory powers of the Berlin Congress were Germany, England, France, Italy, Austria-Hungary, and Russia. They demanded that as a condition of independence, Romania should delete Article VII of the Romanian Constitution, which stipulated that only Christians could become citizens of Romania.

31 Ehrenpreis, *Mitt liv*, p 220.

32 Ehrenpreis, *Mitt liv*, pp 218–219.

33 Marcus Ehrenpreis, "Clemenceau såsom religionsfrihetens försvarare" [Clemenceau as defender of religious freedom], *Judisk Tidskrift*, December 1929. "Die konfessionelle Minoritäten auf dem neuen Balkan," *Neue Freie Presse*, Wien, 24 October 1913.

34 Ehrenpreis, *Mitt liv*, p 263.

35 Ehrenpreis, *Mitt liv*, p 249.

36 Marcus Ehrenpreis: "Hos Viktor Emanuel i San Rossore" [With Victor Emmanuel in San Rossore], *Judisk Tidskrift*, April 1944.

37 Ehrenpreis, *Mitt liv*, p 267.

38 Ehrenpreis, *Mitt liv*, p 272.

39 Ehrenpreis, *Mitt liv*, p 280.

40 Ehrenpreis, *Mitt liv*, p 278.

41 Ehrenpreis, *Mitt liv*, pp 280–281.

42 Ehrenpreis, *Mitt liv*, pp 281–282. Also Marcus Ehrenpreis, "När Bulgariens heliga synod vittnade för judendomen. Minnen från Beilisprocessen 1913" [When Bulgaria's Holy Synod testified for Judaism. Memories of the Beilis trial of 1913], *Judisk Tidskrift*, May 1944.

43 Kechales, *Korot Yehudei Bulgaria* [The history of Bulgarian Jews], p 204.

44 Ehrenpreis, *Mitt liv*, p 289.
45 Ehrenpreis, *Mitt liv*, p 288.
46 "Dr Ehrenpreis und der Gemeindekongress," *Die Welt*, No. 17, year 18, 8 May 1914, p 470.
47 Ehrenpreis, *Mitt liv*, p 292. Genesis 31:40.
48 *Svenska Dagbladet*, 15 September 1914.
49 *Svenska Dagbladet*, 27 August 1914.
50 Ehrenpreis, *Mitt liv*, p 281.
51 M. J. Cohen, "M. Ehrenpreis' Wirksamkeit in Bulgarien," *Judisk Tidskrift*, June 1929.

4. A NEW CHILDHOOD

1 Oscar Levertin, *Kung Salomon och Morolf*, Stockholm: Albert Bonniers Förlag, 1905. Translation by the author.
2 *Nyhebreisk lyrik (1870–1920)* [New Hebrew poetry], Stockholm: P. A. Norstedt & Söner Publishers, 1920.
3 Marcus Ehrenpreis: "The Hebrew Literature," *Nationernas bibliotek. Judarna* [Library of Nations: Judarna], ed. M. Ehrenpreis and Alfred Jensen, Stockholm: Norstedt & Söners, 1920, p 200.
4 *Svenska Dagbladet*, 8 November 1926.
5 Anders Österling, "Nyhebreisk lyrik," *Svenska Dagbladet*, 13 February 1921.
6 Gottfrid Johansson, "Nyhebreisk lyrik," *Dagens Nyheter*, 17 January 1921.
7 *Nyhebreisk lyrik*, pp vi–vii.
8 "Literature does not do justice to the Jews." *Svenska Dagbladet*, 17 January 1921.
9 Ehrenpreis, *Mitt liv*, pp 357–358.
10 "The Jewish Literary Society," *Svenska Dagbladet*, 4 July 1919.
11 Fredrik Böök, "Jewish History," *Svenska Dagbladet*, 21 December 1922.
12 Böök writes: "If the Russian Revolution is largely the work of Jews, is it then premature to see in it a new proof of the homelessness and rootlessness of the Jewish soul?"
13 Ellen Key, "A Sorrow of a Thousand Families," *Forum*, No. 7, 1921, quoted in "Ellen Key and Judaism," *Israeliten*, December 1924.
14 "Ellen Key and Judaism," *Israeliten*, December 1924.

15 Ehrenpreis, *Mitt liv*, p 302.
16 Ehrenpreis, *Mitt liv*, p 285.
17 Monica Lauritzen, *Karl Warburg. Den varsamme vägvisaren* [Karl Warburg. The careful guide], Stockholm: Albert Bonniers Förlag 2018, p 370.
18 Ehrenpreis, *Mitt liv*, p 299.
19 Ehrenpreis, *Mitt liv*, p 301.
20 Ragnar Josephson, "Den svenske författaren Marcus Ehrenpreis" [The Swedish writer Marcus Ehrenpreis], *Judisk Tidskrift*, June 1929.
21 Ehrenpreis, *Mitt liv*, p 308–309.
22 Ehrenpreis, *Mitt liv*, p 308.
23 *Dagens Nyheter*, 19 April 1915.
24 *Den stora tiden och de små människorna. Civila brev från galiziska flyktingar, samlade och översatta av Ernst Klein* [Civilian letters from Galician refugees, collected and translated by Ernst Klein]. Stockholm: Albert Bonniers Förlag 1916.
25 *Svenska Dagbladet*, 28 April 1916.
26 Marcus Ehrenpreis, "Rysslands judar under världskriget" [The Jews of Russia during the World War], *Svensk Tidskrift*, Vol. 6, 1916.
27 "I, Woodrow Wilson, President of the United States, in compliance with the suggestion of the Senate, do hereby appoint and proclaim January 27, 1916, as a day upon which the people of the United States may make such contributions as they feel disposed for the aid of the stricken Jewish people." "Relief Day for Jews: President Sets Aside Jan. 27 for Collection of Funds," *New York Times*, January 13, 1916.
28 "Jewish emergency conference in Stockholm for emergency aid to the Eastern Jews," *Dagens Nyheter*, 22 Janurary 1916.
29 "Open letter to Clemenceau," *Svenska Dagbladet*, 20 November 1917.
30 Rita Bredefeldt, *Judiskt liv i Stockholm och Norden—ekonomi, identitet och assimilering 1850-1930* [Jewish life in Stockholm and Scandinavia: economy, identity, and assimilation 1850–1930], Stockholm: Stockholmia Förlag, 2008.
31 Anna Besserman, "Mosaiska församlingen i Stockholm inför den östjudiska invandringen till staden 1860–1920" [The Mosaic Congregation in Stockholm in the face of Eastern Jewish immigration, 1860–1920], *Nordisk judaistik*, 5 (2) 1984, p 23.
32 Besserman, "Mosaiska församlingen i Stockholm," p 26.

33 Bredefeldt, *Judiskt liv i Stockholm och Norden*, p 64.

34 *Dagens Nyheter*, 5 April 1917.

35 For a penetrating examination of the antisemitic background noise in the Sweden in which Ehrenpreis worked, see Lars M. Andersson, *En jude är en jude är en jude. Representationer av "juden" i svensk skämtpress 1900–1930* [A Jew is a Jew is a Jew. Representations of "Jews" in the Swedish humor press, 1900–1930]. Lund: Nordic Academic Press, 2000.

36 Bengt Lidforss, "Storsvenska semiter," *Arbetet* 14 October 1905, in Lars M. Andersson, *En jude är en jude är en jude*, p 356.

37 Ehrenpreis, *Mitt liv*, p 354.

38 Gottlieb Klein, "Hvarför äro de svenska judarna icke Zionister?" [Why are the Swedish Jews not Zionists?], *Dagens Nyheter*, 7 January 1913.

39 "The Zionist Congress in Stockholm. A lecture on the Jewish state by Dr Bloede," *Dagens Nyheter*, 7 January 1913.

40 Morton Narrowe, *Zionism in Sweden, Its Beginnings until the End of World War I*, New York: The Jewish Theological Seminary of America, 1990, p 56.

41 Narrowe, *Zionism in Sweden*, pp 115–116.

42 Narrowe, *Zionism in Sweden*, p 109.

43 *Svenska Dagbladet*, 20 March 1916.

44 M. Ehrenpreis: "Yehuda Halevi. The First Religious Zionist." *Judisk Tidskrift*, April 1936.

45 "Dr M. Ehrenpreis anförande vid Oscar Levertins grav den 22 september 1926" [Dr. M. Ehrenpreis's address at Oscar Levertin's grave, 22 September 1926], *Israeliten*, October–November 1926. "Stämningsfull högtidlighet vid Oscar Levertins grav" [Solemn ceremony at Oscar Levertin's grave], *Svenska Dagbladet*, 23 September 1926.

46 Gustaf Stridsberg, "Oscar Levertin och den svenska kulturen" [Oscar Levertin and Swedish culture], *Svenska Dagbladet*, 30 September 1906.

47 Daniel Brick, "Our Youth and the Future of Judaism," *Israeliten* 1–2, October–November 1924.

48 Olof Valentin, "Am I a Jew?" *Israeliten* 8, June–July 1925.

49 Leon Fried, "Am I a Jew? A Reply and a Characteristic," *Israeliten* 9, August–September 1925.

50 Hirsch Nissalowitz, "Abuses in Sweden's Jewish Congregations." Appendix to *Israeliten* 9, August–September 1925.

51 Marcus Ehrenpreis, "Frågetecknet Israel" [The question of Israel], *Israeliten*, October–November 1924.

52 Ehrenpreis, "Frågetecknet Israel."

53 Ehrenpreis, "Frågetecknet Israel."

54 Marcus Ehrenpreis, "Hebreiska klubbens femårsdag" [The fifth anniversary of the Hebrew Club], *Judisk Tidskrift*, January–February 1932.

55 Ehrenpreis, "Hebreiska klubbens femårsdag."

56 Marcus Ehrenpreis, "Är konfessionell fred möjlig? Tankar om ett Religionernas Förbund" [Is confessional peace possible? Thoughts on a league of religions], *Israeliten*, December 1923, pp 1–3.

57 Marcus Ehrenpreis in a letter dated 18 February 1937 to Söderblom's former colleague, the vicar Herman Neander in Gävle. Jewish Congregation Archives, Ehrenpreis, National Archives. Also in Ehrenpreis, *Mitt liv*, p 341.

58 Marcus Ehrenpreis in a letter dated 18 February 1937 to Herman Neander. Also in Ehrenpreis, *Mitt liv*, p 341.

59 "Mixed marriages have changed the original composition of Swedish Jewry, new layers are increasingly emerging, but this natural change need by no means mean dissolution." *Israeliten*, October 1923.

60 Marcus Ehrenpreis, "Judendomens uppgift inom fredsrörelsen" [The task of Judaism in the peace movement], *Judisk Tidskrift*, January–February 1930.

61 Marcus Ehrenpreis, *De som byggt Israel I. Profeter och Gudsmän* [Prophets and sages who built Israel], Uppsala: Hugo Gebers förlag, 1929, p 53.

62 Josef Klausner and Marcus Ehrenpreis, "Har judendomen en 'mission'? Ett tankeutbyte," [Does Judaism have a "mission"? An exchange of ideas], *Judisk Tidskrift*, April–May 1931. The Ahad Ha'am quote is from an article in the Palestinian-Hebrew daily *Ha'aretz*, 1 September 1922. The continuation of the quotation in brackets, omitted by Ehrenpreis, is taken from the translation of the article reproduced in Hans Kohn (ed.), *Nationalism and the Jewish Ethic: Basic Writings of Ahad Ha'am*, New York: Schocken Books, 1962, pp 26–27.

63 The Balfour Declaration of November 2, 1917: "His Majesty's Government view with favor the establishment in Palestine of a national home for the Jewish people, and will use their best endeavors to facilitate the achievement of this object, it being clearly understood

that nothing shall be done which may prejudice the civil and religious rights of existing non-Jewish communities in Palestine or the rights and political status enjoyed by Jews in any other country."

64 Marcus Ehrenpreis, "Festen på Skopusberget skapade framtidstro och försoningsstämning," *Dagens Nyheter*, 19 April 1925.

65 Ehrenpreis, Central Zionist Archives, Jerusalem.

66 Marcus Ehrenpreis, *Österlandets själ* [The soul of the East], Stockholm: Hugo Gebers Verlag, 1926, pp 95, 96.

67 Ehrenpreis, *Österlandets själ*, pp 174–175.

68 *Svenska Dagbladet*, 23 November 1926.

69 *Dagens Nyheter*, 21 October 1926.

70 Ehrenpreis, *Österlandets själ*, p 134.

71 Ehrenpreis, *Österlandets själ*, pp 144, 147–148.

5. PHILO OF STOCKHOLM

1 Fredrika Bremer, "Sursum Corda" [Uplift your hearts], *Svenska Tidningen*, 3 May 1854, quoted in *Judisk Tidskrift*, March 1928.

2 The first Greek translation of the Hebrew Bible (and the first translation of it at all), the Septuagint, was produced in Alexandria around 200 BCE.

3 Marcus Ehrenpreis: *Israels möten med folken* [Israel's encounters with the nations], Stockholm: Hugo Gebers, 1934, p 72.

4 "On the Creation II," *The Works of Philo, Complete and Unabridged* (trans. C. D. Yonge), Massachusetts: Hendrickson Publishers, 1993, p 11. (The original title of Yonge's 1854 translation: "A Treatise on the Account of the Creation of the World, as Given by Moses.")

5 Romans 10:4–13. Note that the Hebrew word *torah*, which means "teachings," was translated as "law."

6 Ehrenpreis, *Israels möten med folken*, pp 74–79. Titus was the Roman general, later emperor, who in 70 CE razed and sacked the Temple in Jerusalem.

7 M. Ehrenpreis, "Hur jag blev svensk författare" [How I became a Swedish writer], *Judisk Tidskrift*, July 1935.

8 M. Ehrenpreis, "Den personliga judefrågan" [The personal Jewish question], *Judisk Tidskrift*, December 1932.

9 Marcus Ehrenpreis in letters to Albert Pipano, 24 September 1925, and to the Jewish community in Salonica, 25 October 1925. Devin

E. Naar, *Jewish Salonica, Between Ottoman Empire and Modern Greece*, Stanford: Stanford University Press, 2016, p 111.

10 Ehrenpreis, *Mitt liv*, pp 227–228.

11 Ehrenpreis, *Mitt liv*, p 230.

12 N. M. Gelber, D. Florentin, Adolf Friedmann, and G. F. Török, "An Attempt to Internationalize Salonika, 1912–1913," *Jewish Social Studies*, Vol. 17, No. 2 (April 1955), pp 105–120.

13 In a protocol signed in Lausanne on 30 January 1923, Greece and Turkey agreed on a "population exchange" of at least 1.6 million people: 1.2 million Greek Orthodox Christians were moved from Turkey to Greece and 350,000 to 400,000 Muslims were moved from the "Turkish" areas conquered by Greece to Turkey. As a result of the population transfer, the population of Thessaloniki multiplied.

14 Naar, *Jewish Salonica*, p 211. Naar cites as a source a letter from Ehrenpreis dated 20 January 1926 to the Jewish *Communal Council of Salonica*, kept in the Ben Zvi Institute in Jerusalem.

15 "Ehrenpreis Chief Rabbi in Greece?" *Dagens Nyheter*, 13 January 1926.

16 Saül Mezan, *Les Juifs Espagnols en Bulgarie* [Spanish Jews in Bulgaria]. Quoted in Naar, *Jewish Salonica, Between Ottoman Empire and Modern Greece*, p 112.

17 Mezan, *Les Juifs espagnols en Bulgarie*. Quoted in Naar, *Jewish Salonica*, p 113.

18 Mezan, *Les Juifs espagnols en Bulgarie*. Quoted in Naar, *Jewish Salonica*, p 114.

19 Marcus Ehrenpreis to the director of the Mosaic congregation, 25 March 1926. Archives of the Jewish Congregation, National Archives.

20 Gunnar Josephson to Marcus Ehrenpreis, 28 March 1926. Archives of the Jewish Congregation, National Archives.

21 Marcus Ehrenpreis, "Fredstanken i Judendomen" [The idea of peace in Judaism], *Judisk Tidskrift*, January–February 1928.

22 "Ich meine, wir sind, ohne einander an die Hand zu halten, doch gemeinsam einer Weg gegangen, nicht bloss eine Strecke, sondern einer wirklicher Weg, mit Zielahnung, Stationen und wechselnden Rückblick." Letter from Martin Buber to Marcus Ehrenpreis, 24 June 1929. In private ownership.

23 Fredrik Böök, "De svenska judarna" [The Swedish Jews], *Svenska Dagbladet*, 7 February 1925.

24 Böök, "De svenska judarna."
25 Fredrik Böök, "Judarna i Warschau I" [The Jews of Warsaw I], *Svenska Dagbladet*, 23 June 1916.
26 Fredrik Böök, "Judarna i Warschau II" [The Jews of Warsaw II], *Svenska Dagbladet*, 2 July 1916.
27 Fredrik Böök, "The Swedish Jews," *Svenska Dagbladet*, 7 Feburary 1925.
28 Fredrik Böök, "Judisk historia," *Svenska Dagbladet*, 11 December 1922.
29 Fredrik Böök, *Resa till Jerusalem* [Journey to Jerusalem], Stockholm: Norstedt & Söners Förlag, 1925, p 160.
30 Fredrik Böök, "Zionismens framtid" [The future of Zionism], *Svenska Dagbladet*, 18 July 1925.
31 Böök, *Resa till Jerusalem*, p 158.
32 Letter from Marcus Ehrenpreis to Esther Ehrenpreis, Tel Aviv 27 March 1925, Central Zionist Archive, Jerusalem.
33 Ernst Klein, "Professor Bööks Palestinaresa" [Professor Böök's Palestine journey], *Israeliten*, January 1926.
34 Klein, "Professor Bööks Palestinaresa."
35 *Judisk Krönika*, May 1932.
36 Marcus Ehrenpreis, *De som byggt Israel. Visioner från tre årtusenden. Första serien: Profeter och Gudsmän* [Prophets and sages who built Israel. Visions from three millennia.]. Stockholm: Hugo Gebers förlag, 1929, p v.
37 Ehrenpreis, *De som byggt Israel*, p vi.
38 Ehrenpreis, *De som byggt Israel*, p 12.
39 Ehrenpreis, *De som byggt Israel*, p 70.
40 *Svenska Dagbladet*, 29 December 1929.
41 *Svenska Dagbladet*, 5 January 1932.
42 Marcus Ehrenpreis, *De som byggt Israel II, Helige och hjältar* [Saints and heroes who built Israel], Uppsala: Hugo Gebers Förlag, 1931, pp 106–109. Jesus's statements are taken from Matthew 23:9 and Luke 18:19.
43 "Rabbiner och mystiker" [Rabbis and mystic], *Svenska Dagbladet*, 5 January 1932.
44 "Helige och hjältar," *Dagens Nyheter*, 4 January 1932.
45 *Judisk Tidskrift*, January–February 1928.
46 *Judisk Tidskrift*, November 1932.
47 *Judisk Tidskrift*, January–February 1931.

48 *Judisk Tidskrift*, January–February 1931.

49 Simon Aberstén, "En liberals randanmärkningar" [Peripheral remarks of a liberal], *Judisk Tidskrift*, March 1931.

50 *Judisk Tidskrift*, March 1931.

51 Ehrenpreis, *Mitt liv*, p 390.

52 Quoted in *Dagens Nyheter*, 22 September 1935.

53 Ehrenpreis, *Mitt liv*, p 383.

54 Ingeborg, princess of Denmark and Sweden (1879–1958), daughter of Frederick VIII of Denmark and Louise, daughter of Charles XV. Ingeborg was married to Prince Carl, son of Oscar II.

55 "En judisk apologet" [A Jewish apologist], *Svenska Dagbladet*, 8 December 1933.

56 "Israel förr och nu" [Israel then and now], *Dagens Nyheter*, 29 November 1933.

57 *Ord och Bild*, Vol. 45, 1936.

58 *Ord och Bild*, Vol. 45, 1936.

59 *Judisk Tidskrift*, August–September 1929.

60 "Dr. Ehrenpreis and Israel's World Plans," *Nationen*, 1 May 1932.

61 Ehrenpreis, *Mitt Liv*, p 400.

62 The libel trial in Basel ended in June 1936, in the shadow of the Bern judgment of the previous year, with a settlement. *Judisk Tidskridt*, June 1936.

63 *Dagens Nyheter*, 17 November 1934.

64 Ehrenpreis, *Mitt liv*, pp 404–405. Apion (30–20 BCE to 45–48 CE) actively contributed to the outbreak of the violent anti-Jewish pogroms in Alexandria around 38 CE, and he led the anti-Jewish delegation to Caligula in Rome. Johannes Pfefferkorn (1469–1523) was a Jewish convert to Christianity who, among other things, called for the burning of all Jewish books. Johann Andreas Eisenmenger (1654–1704) was the author of the book *Entdecktes Judenthum* [Judaism revealed], whose anti-Jewish interpretations of and quotations from the Talmud became a main source of antisemitic propaganda.

65 *Dagens Nyheter*, 17 November 1934.

66 *Judisk Tidskrift*, May 1935.

67 Emmy Moor, "Chaim Weizmann, Israel's First President, a Political Memory," *Jewish Journal*, June 1948, p 198. *Berner Tagwacht*, 3 June 1948.

68 "Who Is Marcus Ehrenpreis?" *Nationen*, 1 August 1933.

69 *Israels möten med folken*, pp 193–194.
70 Ehrenpreis, *Talmud, fariseism, urkristendom*, pp 115, 150–151.

6. AN UNREQUITED LOVE

1 Hugo Valentin, "Ehrenpreis 60 år" [Ehrenpreis 60 years], *Judisk Tidskrift*, jubilee booklet, June 1929, p 3.
2 Ragnar Josephson, "The Swedish Writer Marcus Ehrenpreis," *Judisk Tidskrift*, jubilee booklet, June 1929, pp 10–11.
3 Paul Goodman: "An Interpreter Between East and West," *Judisk Tidskrift*, jubilee booklet, June 1929.
4 Hugo Valentin, "Ehrenpreis 60 år" [Ehrenpreis 60 years], *Judisk Tidskrift*, jubilee booklet, June 1929.
5 Dr. Sch. Riwkin, "A Silent Cultural Achievement," *Jewish Journal*, anniversary booklet, June 1929. Shalom Schender Riwkin was the father of the photographer Anna Riwkin-Brick and the writer and journalist Eugénie Riwkin-Söderberg.
6 *Judisk Tidskrift*, June 1929.
7 Anders Jarlert, *Emanuel Linderholm som kyrkohistoriker* [Emanuel Linderholm as church historian], Lund University Press, 1987, p 169.
8 Lars Gunnarsson, *Kyrkan, nazismen och demokratin* [The church, Nazism, and democracy], Stockholm: Almqvist & Wiksell International, 1995, p 126.
9 Speech by Emanuel Linderholm to Dr. Marcus Ehrenpreis at a dinner in Uppsala, 5 October 1925. Manuscript in private hands.
10 David Nirenberg, *Anti-Judaism. The Western Tradition*, New York: Norton, 2013, pp 114–115. John Chrysostom (347–407), canonized archbishop of Constantinople, one of the three holy hierarchs of the Eastern Orthodox Church.
11 Nirenberg, *Anti-Judaism*, p 119.
12 Paula Fredriksen, *Augustine and the Jews. A Christian Defense of Jews and Judaism*, New York: Doubleday, 2008.
13 Nirenberg, *Anti-Judaism*, pp 358–359.
14 "Die Euthanasie des Judentums ist die reine moralische Religion, mit der Verlassung aller Satzungslehren, deren einige doch im Christentum (als messianischen Glauben) noch zurück behalten bleiben müssen." Immanuel Kant, *Der Streit der Fakultäten*, 1798.

15 Johann Gottlieb Fichte, *Beitrag zur Berichtigung der Urtheile des Publicums über die Französische Revolution*, cited in Micha Brumlik, *Deutscher Geist unden Judenhaß*, Munich: Luchterhand, 2002, p 90.

16 Fichte, *Politische Fragmente* [Political fragments]. Cited in Brumlik, *Deutscher Geist*, p 118.

17 Fichte, *Reden an die Deutsche Nation* [Speeches to the German nation]. Cited in Brumlik, *Deutscher Geist*, p 122.

18 Friedrich Schleiermacher, *Über die Religion: Reden an die Gebildeten unter ihren Verächtern* [On religion: speeches to the educated among its despisers], 1799. Cited in Brumlik, *Deutscher Geist*, p 149.

19 "Ja, ein judaisierendes Christentum das wäre die rechte Krankheit, die wir uns inokulieren sollten!" Cited in Jacob Katz, *Out of the Ghetto, the Social Background of Jewish Emancipation 1770–1870*, New York: Random House, 1988, p 242.

20 Helle Klein, "Gottlieb Klein—rabbinen, forskaren och folkbildaren" [Gottlieb Klein–rabbi, scholar and educator], in Susanne Olsson, ed., *Sällskapet. Tro och vetande i 1900-talets Sverige.* Stockholm: Molin & Sorgenfrei Akademiska, 2013, p 133.

21 Gottlieb Klein, *Religion och moral. Föredrag hållet vid religionskongressen i Stockholm 1897* [Religion and morality. Lecture given at the Congress of Religion in Stockholm 1897], Stockholm: Gullberg & Hallbergs boktryckeri, 1898, p 24.

22 Letter from Nathan Söderblom to the editorial staff of *Judisk Tidskrift*. In private hands.

23 "Nathan Söderblom on the Jewish Question," *Judisk Tidskrift*, November 1931, pp 238–239.

24 "Nathan Söderblom on German anti-Semitism," *Judisk Tidskrift*, November 1931, p 206.

25 Ehrenpreis, *Talmud, fariseism, urkristendom*, pp 87–88.

26 Gerhard Kittel, *Die Judenfrage* [The Jewish question]. Stuttgart, Berlin: W. Kohlhammer, 1934. p 14. *Die gewaltsame Ausrottung des Judentums kommt für eine ernsthafte Betrachtung nicht in Frage: wenn sie den Systemen der spanischen Inquisition oder den russischen Pogromen nicht gelungen ist, wird sie für das 20. Jahrhundert erst recht nicht möglich sein.* "The violent extermination of Judaism cannot be seriously considered: if the systems of the Spanish Inquisition or the Russian pogroms did not succeed in doing so, it will be certainly not be possible for the twentieth century."

27 Ehrenpreis, *Mitt liv*, p 284.
28 *Judisk Tidskrift*, April–May 1931.
29 It was not until 1951 that a professorship in Yiddish was established at the Hebrew University of Jerusalem.
30 Josef Klausner and Marcus Ehrenpreis, "Har judendomen en 'mission'? Ett tankeutbyte" [Does Judaism have a "mission"? An exchange of ideas], *Judisk Tidskrift*, April–May 1931.
31 Marcus Ehrenpreis, "The Stranger in the Bible," *Jewish Journal*, June 1939, p 180. Also in Marcus Ehrenpreis, *The Question Mark of Israel*, Stockholm: Albert Bonniers Förlag, 1948, p 42.
32 "Die Vernichtung der jüdischen Rasse in Europa." Adolf Hitler's speech in the German Reichstag on 30 January 1939.

7. THE TRUE FACE OF JUDAISM

1 Efraim Briem, *Antisemitismen genom tiderna, orsaker och historia* [Antisemitism through the ages, causes and history], Stockholm: Natur och Kultur, 1940.
2 Mark 12:28. Also Luke 10:27.
3 Matthew 22:40.
4 Marcus Ehrenpreis, "Bibelns aktualitet" [The relevance of the Bible], *Judisk Tidskrift*, January 1939.
5 Marcus Ehrenpreis, "Religion och Lag," [Religion and law], *Judisk Tidskrift*, March 1937. The invoked interpretation is from *Pirkei Avot*, VI:2, a collection of ethical maxims in the seminal part of the rabbinic interpretive tradition known as the Mishnah.
6 Ehrenpreis, *Profeter och gudsmän* [Prophets and sages], p 52.
7 Efraim Briem, *Antisemitismen genom tiderna*, p 136.
8 Marcus Ehrenpreis, "Judisk 'partikularism'" [Jewish "particularism"], *Judisk Tidskrift*, July 1940.
9 Ehrenpreis, "Judisk 'partikularism.'"
10 Briem, *Antisemitismen genom tiderna*, p 324.
11 Briem, *Antisemitismen genom tiderna*, p 124.
12 Briem, *Antisemitismen genom tiderna*, p 338.
13 Leviticus 20:22.
14 Amos 3:2.
15 Ehrenpreis, *Profeter och gudsmän* [Prophets and sages], p 50.

16 *Judisk Tidskrift*, December 1939.
17 Ehrenpreis, *Talmud, fariseism, urkristendom* [Talmud, Phariseeism, early Christianity], pp 24–25.
18 Marcus Ehrenpreis, "När Esra grundade judendomen," [When Ezra founded Judaism], *Judisk Tidskrift*, January–February 1929.
19 Ehrenpreis, *Profeter och gudsmän* [Prophets and sages], pp 207–208.
20 Ezra 9:2, 9:4, 9:11, and 10:3.
21 Marcus Ehrenpreis, "Har judendomen en mission?" [Does Judaism have a mission?], *Judisk Tidskrift*, April–May 1931. *Profeter och gudsmän* [Prophets and sages], p 217.
22 Marcus Ehrenpreis, "Till Skandinaviens judiska ungdom" [To the Jewish youth of Scandinavia], *Judisk Tidskrift*, December 1931.
23 Briem, p 338.
24 Marcus Ehrenpreis, *Helige och hjältar som byggt Israel* [Saints and heroes who built Israel], p 141, p 147.
25 Marcus Ehrenpreis, "Meeting between two generations. Speech at the 40th Anniversary of the Zionist Congress in Basel," *Judisk Tidskrift*, September 1937.
26 "Palestine life or death for the Jews? The Zionist Congress and the division of Palestine," *Svenska Dagbladet*, 21 August 1937.
27 "Vad jag tror på" [What I believe in]. Radio address, 8 August 1948.
28 Maimonides (1135–1204), *Mishne Torah*, chapters 11 and 12.
29 Marcus Ehrenpreis, "The Bible's Message of Freedom," *Jewish Journal*, April 1940, p 104.
30 Ehrenpreis, "The Bible's Message of Freedom," pp 104, 110.
31 *Theodor Herzl, Valda skrifter, utgivna och inledda av Marcus Ehrenpreis* [Theodor Herzl, selected writings, edited and introduced by Marcus Ehrenpreis], Stockholm: Förlags A.-B. Herzlia, 1944, p 15.
32 Marcus Ehrenpreis, "Gud i historien" [God in history], *Judisk Tidskrift*, November 1939, sermon in Stockholm Synagogue, 5 November 1939.
33 Ehrenpreis, "Gud i historien" [God in history].
34 Ehrenpreis, "Gud i historien."
35 Ehrenpreis, "Gud i historien."
36 Franz Rosenzweig, *Der Mensch und sein Werk. Gesammelte Schriften I. Briefe und Tagebücher, I, 1900–1918* [Man and his work. Collected writings I. Letters and Diaries, I, 1900–1918], Rachel Rosenzweig and Edith Rosenzweig-Scheinmann (eds.), The Hague: Martinus Nijhoff, 1979, p 345. My translation.

37 Franz Rosenzweig, *Der Stern der Erlösung*, Frankfurt: Suhrkamp, 1988, p 250. My translation.
38 *Judisk Tidskrift*, May 1940.
39 *Judisk Tidskrift*, December 1937.

8. MALACHI'S CALL TO THE WORLD

1 Marcus Ehrenpreis, *Malachis rop till tiden* [Malachi's call to the times], Albert Bonniers Förlag, Stockholm 1933.
2 Ehrenpreis, *Mitt liv*, p 380.
3 Ehrenpreis, *Mitt liv*, p 380.
4 *Judisk Tidskrift*, April 1933.
5 Vilhelm Lundström, "En judisk påskpredikan" [A Jewish Passover sermon], *Judisk Tidskrift*, May–June 1933.
6 Marcus Ehrenpreis, "Genmäle till Vilhelm Lundström" [A response to Vilhelm Lundström], *Judisk Tidskrift*, May–June 1933.
7 Ehrenpreis, "Genmäle till Vilhelm Lundström" [A response to Vilhelm Lundström].
8 Fredrik Böök, "Antisemitism och antigermanism" [Antisemitism and anti-Germanism], *Svenska Dagbladet* 3 June 1933.
9 Fredrik Böök, "Midnattsbålet" [The Midnight Bonfire], *Svenska Dagbladet*, 22 June 1933.
10 Fredrik Böök, *Hitlers Tyskland* [Hitler's Germany], Stockholm: Norstedt & Söner, 1933.
11 Simon Aberstén, "Professor Böök och det Tredje Riket" [Professor Böök and the Third Reich], *Judisk Tidskrift*, July–August 1933.
12 Ehrenpreis, *Mitt liv*, p 414.
13 "Swedish Aid for Intellectuals Exiled from Germany," *Judisk Tidskrift*, October 1933,
14 Prince Carl, "From the Secret Archives of the Red Cross," *Our Red Cross*, No. 6, 1946, p 168.
15 Prince Carl, "From the Secret Archives of the Red Cross," p 168.
16 Ehrenpreis, *Mitt liv*, p 454.
17 Ehrenpreis, *Mitt liv*, p 458.
18 Ehrenpreis, *Mitt liv*, p 456.
19 Ehrenpreis, *Mitt liv*, p 473.
20 Ehrenpreis, *Mitt liv*, p 429.

21 Ehrenpreis, *Mitt liv*, p 429.

22 Marcus Ehrenpreis, "Intryck från zionistkongressen" [Impressions from the Zionist Congress], *Judisk Tidskrift*, September 1935.

23 Esther Ehrenpreis, "Palestina 1935, ur en resedagbok" [Palestine 1935, from a travel diary], *Judisk Tidskrift*, January 1936.

24 Esther Ehrenpreis, "Palestina 1935, ur en resedagbok" [Palestine 1935, from a travel diary], p 1.

25 "Ett rop från världens judar" [A cry from the Jews of the world], *Judisk Tidskrift*, October 1938. "Bön för Tysklands judar och deras förföljare" [A prayer for Germany's Jews and their persecutors], *Dagens Nyheter*, 7 October 1935.

26 Jewish Congregation Archives, Ehrenpreis, National Archives.

27 *Judisk Tidskrift*, August 1938.

28 Marcus Ehrenpreis, "Främlingen i Bibeln" [The stranger in the Bible], *Judisk Tidskrift*, June 1939.

29 Ehrenpreis, "Främlingen i Bibeln" [The stranger in the Bible].

30 Jewish Congregation Archives, Ehrenpreis, National Archives.

31 Jewish Congregation Archives, Ehrenpreis, National Archives.

32 Jewish Congregation Archives, Ehrenpreis, National Archives.

33 Jewish Congregation Archives, Ehrenpreis, National Archives.

34 Jewish Congregation Archives, Ehrenpreis, National Archives.

35 Jewish Congregation Archives, Ehrenpreis, National Archives.

36 Marcus Ehrenpreis, "Efter Nürnberglagarna" [After the Nuremberg Laws], *Judisk Tidskrift*, July 1935.

37 Government Bill 1927:198, "proposing a law on the right of foreigners to reside in the country."

38 Karin Kvist Geverts, *Ett främmande element i nationen* [A foreign element in the nation], Uppsala: Studia Historica Upsaliensis, 2008, p 74.

39 Kvist Geverts, *Ett främmande element i nationen* [A foreign element in the nation], p 245.

40 Interview with the Jewish Telegraph Agency, an American-Jewish news agency whose Berlin office closed a week later. Reprinted in M. Ehrenpreis, "The Crisis of Judaism," *Judisk Tidskrift*, July–August 1933, pp 197, 198.

41 Interview with the Jewish Telegraph Agency.

42 Two leading British-Jewish representatives, Neville Laski and Norman Bentwich, met with Jewish leaders throughout Europe in June 1933 and reported great agreement on the potentially negative

effects of a World Congress. Rudberg, *The Swedish Jews and the Victims of Nazi Terror, 1933–1945*, Acta Upsaliensis, 2015, p 60.

43 "Appeal to the Jews of Sweden," *Judisk Tidskrift*, May–June 1933.

44 *Judisk Tidskrift*, November 1933.

45 Until Germany's annexation of Austria in March 1938, Sweden had received fewer than 2,000 Jewish "involuntary emigrants"; when the war broke out in September 1939, there were still no more than 4,000. Rudberg, *The Swedish Jews and the Holocaust*, p 173.

46 Memorandum from the National Board of Health and Welfare to the Ministry of Foreign Affairs, 23 November 1938. Rudberg, *The Swedish Jews and the Holocaust*, p 97.

47 "Petition to the State Authorities on the Refugee Question," *Församlingsblad för Mosaiska församlingen i Stockholm*, December 1940. "The Refugee Question before the State Authorities," *Församlingsblad för Mosaiska församlingen i Stockholm*, March 1941.

48 Anders Jarlert, *Judisk 'ras' som äktenskapshinder. Effekten av Nürnberglagarna i Svenska kyrkans statliga funktion som lysningsförrättare 1935–1945* [Jewish "race" as a hindrance to marriage. The effect of the Nuremberg Laws on the state function of the Swedish Church], Malmö: Sekel Bokförlag, 2006, pp 56–57.

49 Rudberg, *The Swedish Jews and the Holocaust*, p 57.

50 Hansson, *Flykt och överlevnad. Flyktingverksamheten i Mosaiska församlingen i Stockholm 1933–1950* [Flight and survival. Refugee activities in the Mosaic Congregation in Stockholm], p 90.

51 Inga Gottfarb, *Den livsfarliga glömskan* [The dangerous oblivion], Stockholm: Langenskiöld, 2006, p 96.

52 Rudberg, *The Swedish Jews and the Victims of Nazi Terror*, p 87.

53 "World Jewish Conference in London. From a Lecture by M. Ehrenpreis," *Jewish Journal*, January 1934, p 6.

54 "World Jewish Conference in London," *Jewish Journal*, January 1934, p 6.

55 Marcus Ehrenpreis, "Watchmen, what suffers the night? Words of admonition at the confirmation on 7 May 1933," *Judisk Tidskrift*, May–June 1933, p 152.

56 "Farewell Letter of James McDonald," *Judisk Tidskrift*, January 1936. The original text is available at https://dl.wdl.org/11604/service/11604.pdf.

57 *Judisk Tidskrift*, September 1935. Among Ehrenpreis's papers in the Jewish Congregation's archives: a copy of a letter dated 25 July 1935

from Masaryk's office to Dr. Zollschan in Karlsbad concerning plans to bring Germany's racial laws before the League of Nations. Most likely Ehrenpreis had met Zollschan in Karlsbad and received a copy of the letter. Although Masaryk feared that Germany's influence on the members of the league would be too great, he nevertheless supported the project.

58 Ragnar Josephson, *Den dubbla lojaliteten* [The dual loyalty], Stockholm: Albert Bonniers Förlag, 1936, pp 12–13.

59 Josephson, *Den dubbla lojaliteten*, p 14.

60 Letter from Marcus Ehrenpreis to Ragnar Josephson, 7 May 1936. Jewish Congregation Archives, Ehrenpreis, National Archives.

61 Letter from Ragnar Josephson to Marcus Ehrenpreis, undated. Jewish Congregation Archives, Ehrenpreis, National Archives.

62 Marcus Ehrenpreis, "För Israels ära" [For the honor of Israel]. Speech in the synagogue on the first day of Rosh Hashanah, *Jewish Journal*, October 1935, pp 304–307.

63 Ehrenpreis, "För Israels ära."

64 Ehrenpreis, "För Israels ära."

9. THE END OF THE WORD

1 Letter from Benjamin Murmelstein to Marcus Ehrenpreis. Jewish Congregation Archives, Ehrenpreis, National Archives.

2 "The resettlement of the German Jews in progress. Transports from Vienna to Poland every week," *Svenska Dagbladet*, 12 November 1939.

3 Letter from Benjamin Murmelstein to Marcus Ehrenpreis, 26 May 1945. Jewish Congregation Archives, Ehrenpreis, National Archives.

4 Letter from Murmelstein to Ehrenpreis, 26 May 1945.

5 Letter from Leo Baeck to Marcus Ehrenpreis, 26 May 1945. Jewish Congregation Archives, Ehrenpreis, National Archives.

6 By November 1941, 128,000 Jews were able to leave Austria through Murmelstein's "collaboration" with Eichmann. Doron Rabinovici, *Eichmann's Jews. The Jewish Administration of Holocaust Vienna, 1938–1945*, Cambridge: Polity Press 2011, p 76.

7 Rabinovici, *Eichmann's Jews*, p 203. Claude Lanzmann's 2013 film *The Last of the Unjust*, based on interviews that Lanzmann conducted with Benjamin Murmelstein in Rome in 1975, has contributed to

a more nuanced understanding of Murmelstein and the role of the Jewish Councils.

8 Hannah Arendt, *Eichmann in Jerusalem: A Report on the Banality of Evil*, New York: Viking Press, 1963.

9 Klas Åmark, *Att bo granne med ondskan. Sveriges förhållande till nazismen, Nazityskland och Förintelsen* [Living next door to evil. Sweden's relationship with Nazism, Nazi Germany, and the Holocaust], Stockholm: Albert Bonniers Förlag, 2011, p 509.

10 Geverts, *Ett främmande element i nationen* [A Foreign Element in the Nation], p 163.

11 Åmark, *Att bo granne med ondskan* [Living next door to evil], p 508.

12 *Riksdagstrycket, Första Kammaren*, No. 4, 18 January 1945, p 11, italics mine.

13 Mikael Byström, "En talande tystnad? Ett antisemitiskt bakgrundsbrus i riksdagsdebatterna 1942–1947" [A telling silence? Antisemitic background noise in parliamentary debates 1942–1947], in Lars M. Andersson and Karin Kvist Geverts (eds.), *En problematisk relation? Flyktingpolitik och judiska flyktingar i Sverige 1920–1950*, Uppsala: Opuscula Historica Upsaliensia, 2008, p 129.

14 Paul A. Levine, *From Indifference to Activism: Swedish Diplomacy and The Holocaust, 1938–44*, Uppsala: Studia Historica Uppsaliensis, 1998, pp 116–119.

15 Rudberg, *The Swedish Jews and the Holocaust*, p 186.

16 Rudberg, *The Swedish Jews and the Holocaust*, p 186.

17 Parliamentary Commission of Inquiry into Refugee Affairs and the Security Service. Report on the treatment of refugees, SOU 1946:36, pp 326–335.

18 Parliamentary Commission of Inquiry into Refugee Affairs and the Security Service, Report on the treatment of refugees, p 328.

19 Parliamentary Commission of Inquiry into Refugee Affairs and the Security Service, Report on the treatment of refugees, p 325.

20 Gunnar Josephson, "Mosaiska församlingen och flyktingpolitiken" [The Mosaic Congregation and the refugee policy], *Svenska Dagbladet*, 26 January 1945. *Församlingsblad för Mosaiska församlingen i Stockholm*, February 1945.

21 Rudberg, *The Swedish Jews and the Holocaust*, p 101.

22 *Stockholms-Tidningen*, 20 February 1939.

23 *Stockholms-Tidningen*, 23 February 1939.

24 Among the sympathizers of the Deutsche Christen in Sweden was the bishop of Växjö, Samuel Stadener (1872–1937). The Nazi-affiliated church was also supported by the organ of the General Association of Priests, *Svensk Kyrkotidning.* Lars Gunnarsson, *Kyrkan, nazismen och demokratin* [The church, Nazism, and democracy], Stockholm: Almqvist & Wiksell International, 1995, p 118.

25 Marcus Ehrenpreis, "Martin Luther as the crown witness of anti-Semitism," *Judisk Tidskrift,* January 1943

26 *Judisk Tidskrift,* May 1936.

27 *Judisk Tidskrift,* February 1940. In May 1939 the British government for all practical purposes closed the borders of Palestine to fleeing Jews.

28 *Judisk Tidskrift,* June 1945.

10. SERVING THE COMMUNITY

1 Ehrenpreis, *Mitt liv,* p 453.

2 "Vädjan till Sveriges judar," [Appeal to the Jews of Sweden], *Judisk Tidskrift,* June 1933.

3 Rudberg, *The Swedish Jews and the Holocaust,* p 115.

4 Rudberg, *The Swedish Jews and the Holocaust,* p 126.

5 Rudberg, *The Swedish Jews and the Holocaust,* p 161.

6 Marcus Ehrenpreis, "Om Polens judenhet" [On Poland's Jews], *Judisk Tidskrift,* November 1940.

7 "Fundraising for the Jews of Poland," *Judisk Tidskrift,* October 1941.

8 "Fundraising for the Jews of Poland," *Judisk Tidskrift.*

9 Leon Lapidus, "Report on the work of the Swedish section of the Relief and Rehabilitation Department delivered at the constituent meeting of the World Jewish Congress in Stockholm," 27 May 1945. Jewish Congregation Archives, Ehrenpreis, National Archives. Rudberg, *The Swedish Jews and the Holocaust,* p 231. "Relief work for the Jews of Poland," *Judisk Tidskrift,* February 1942.

10 Marcus Ehrenpreis, "Det lyser i mörkret" [Shine in the darkness], *Judisk Tidskrift,* December 1942.

11 *Judisk Tidskrift,* January 1943.

12 Marcus Ehrenpreis, "Saving our children. Speech at the Opera Soiree, 15 March 1943," *Judisk Tidskrift,* March 1943, p 67.

13 Letter from Marcus Ehrenpreis to the board of Save the Children, 15 September 1943. Jewish Congregation Archives, Ehrenpreis, National Archives.

14 *Judisk krönika*, October 1942.

15 The telegram exchange between Richert and Kumlin regarding Ehrenpreis's request is reproduced in full in Steven Koblik, *The Stones Cry Out, Sweden's Response to the persecution of the Jews. 1933–1945*, New York: Holocaust Library, 1988, pp 200–202.

16 Rudberg, *The Swedish Jews and the Holocaust*, p 194.

17 Rudberg, *The Swedish Jews and the Holocaust*, p 194.

18 During several visits to Sweden and Stockholm in September–October 1942, Arvid Richert had the opportunity to pass on von Otter's information to the Ministry of Foreign Affairs, but he chose not to do so. Richert seems to have been opposed to information of this kind being passed on to the Western powers, "and had he been asked about the matter—as he was in November—he would certainly have strongly advised against such a thing," writes Klas Åmark in *Främlingar på tåg*, Stockholm: Kaunitz-Olsson, 2021, pp 107–108.

19 "Den holländska judenhetens martyrium" [The martyrdom of Dutch Jewry], *Judisk Tidskrift*, August 1942.

20 Rudberg, *The Swedish Jews and the Holocaust*, p 208.

21 Rumyana Marinova-Christidi, "From Salvation to Alya: the Bulgarian Jews and Bulgarian-Israeli Relations (1948–1990)," *Southeast European and Black Sea Studies*, 2017, Vol. 17, No. 2, p 226.

22 Transcript of telegram from Marcus Ehrenpreis to Metropolitan Stefan in Sofia, 21 June 1943. Jewish Congregation Archives, Ehrenpreis, National Archives.

23 Copy of a letter from the Legation of Sweden in Sofia to "His Excellency the Prime Minister and the head of the Royal Foreign Office," 2 July 1943. Jewish Community Archives, Ehrenpreis, National Archives.

24 Copy of a letter from the Legation of Sweden in Sofia to "His Excellency the Prime Minister and the head of the Royal Foreign Office," 2 July 1943.

25 Transcript of telegram from Metropolitan Stefan to the Foreign Office, 14 August 1943. Forwarded to Ehrenpreis on September 8, 1943. Jewish Congregation Archives, Ehrenpreis, National Archives.

26 Marinova-Christidi, "From Salvation to Alya," p 229.

27 "Bulgaria breaks with the Nuremberg Laws," *Dagens Nyheter*, 31 August 1944.

28 Rudberg, *The Swedish Jews and the Holocaust*, p 245.

29 Letters from Marcus Ehrenpreis to Erling Eidem, 27 November 1942 and 28 April 1944. Jewish Congregation Archives, Ehrenpreis, National Archives.

30 "The Swedish bishops," *Judisk Tidskrift*, December 1942.

31 Letter from Envoy Wollmar Boström to Foreign Minister Christian Günther, 18 November 1943. Archives of the Jewish Congregation, Ehrenpreis, National Archives.

32 "Appeal for help to the Jews of Denmark." *Judisk Tidskrift*, October 1943.

33 Jenö Lévai, *Raoul Wallenberg: His Remarkable Life, Heroic Battles and the Secret of His Mysterious Disappearance*, Melbourne: WhiteAnt Occasional Publications, 1989, p 34. Original in Hungarian, 1948.

34 Rudberg, *The Swedish Jews and the Holocaust*, p 216. *A Diplomatic Failure: the Case of Raoul Wallenberg and the Swedish Foreign Service*, Official Government Report, SOU 2003:18, p 160–161.

35 *A Diplomatic Failure*, SOU 2003:18, p 97.

36 Similar appeals to Horthy were made by Pope Pius XII and President Franklin Roosevelt.

37 *Judisk Tidskrift*, August 1944.

38 *Judisk Tidskrift*, August 1944.

39 Letter from Norbert Masur to Marcus Ehrenpreis, 18 April 1944. Jewish Congregation Archives, Ehrenpreis, National Archives. *A Diplomatic Failure*, SOU 2003:18, p 105.

40 Letter from Marcus Ehrenpreis to Hugo Cedergren, 4 May 1944. Jewish Congregation Archives, Ehrenpreis, National Archives.

41 Letter from Marcus Ehrenpreis to Hugo Cedergren, 4 May 1944, handwritten note, probably by Inga Gottfarb, Ehrenpreis's secretary.

42 *A Diplomatic Failure*, SOU 2003:18, p 106. Harvey Rosenfeld, *Raoul Wallenberg*, New York: Holmes & Meier, 1995, p 26. Lena Einhorn, *Handelsresande i liv* [A traveling salesman in life], Stockholm: Prisma, 1999, p 171–174.

43 Ehrenpreis's daughter Miriam Ehrenpreis, who was at home when Raoul Wallenberg came to visit, recalled long afterward that her father had told her "that he wasn't quite sure that Wallenberg wanted to do this out of conviction. [...] Dad thought it might have been more about adventurism." Einhorn, *Handelsresande i liv*, p 174.

44 Bengt Jangfeldt, *Raoul Wallenberg, en biografi* [Raoul Wallenberg, a biography], Stockholm: Wahlström & Widstrand, 2012, p 219.
45 Letter from Raoul Wallenberg to Marcus Ehrenpreis, 3 June 1944. Jewish Congregation Archives, Ehrenpreis, National Archives. See also Jangfeldt, *Raoul Wallenberg, en biografi*, p 219.
46 Letter from Kálman Lauer to Jacob Wallenberg, 20 April 1945. *A Diplomatic Failure*, SOU 2003:18, p 108.
47 *A Diplomatic Failure*, SOU 2003:18, p 108.
48 *A Diplomatic Failure*, SOU 2003:18, p 109. Harvey Rosenfeld, *Raoul Wallenberg*, p 27.
49 Rosenfeld, *Raoul Wallenberg*, p 28.
50 Rosenfeld, *Raoul Wallenberg*, p 28. Rudberg, *The Swedish Jews and the Holocaust*, p 217.
51 Marcus Ehrenpreis, "Raoul Wallenberg, a letter," *Judisk Tidskrift*, January 1948.
52 Letter from Louis De Geer, Swedish Foreign Ministry, to Marcus Ehrenpreis, 16 August 1944. Jewish Congregation Archives, Ehrenpreis, National Archives.
53 Undated copy of a letter from Inga Gottfarb on behalf of Marcus Ehrenpreis to the Royal Foreign Office, Legal Department. Jewish Congregation Archives, Ehrenpreis, National Archives.
54 *Svenska Dagbladet*, 12 January 1948.
55 Marcus Ehrenpreis, "Raoul Wallenberg, a Letter," *Jewish Journal*, January 1948, p 1.
56 Torsten Ysander, "Marcus Ehrenpreis," *Judisk Tidskrift*, 27 June 1944.
57 Einhorn, *Handelsresande i liv*, p 125.
58 *Judisk Tidskrift*, 27 June 1944.
59 *Judisk Tidskrift*, 27 June 1944.
60 *Judisk Tidskrift*, 27 June 1944.
61 From the poem "Be'ir Haharega" [In the city of murder] (1904).
62 Marcus Ehrenpreis, "Vägen uppåt" [The way up], *Judisk Tidskrift*, October 1944.
63 Marcus Ehrenpreis, "Predikans uppgift" [The task of the sermon], *Judisk Tidskrift*, January 1937.
64 Margareta Suber, *Vänd ditt ansikte till mig* [Turn your face to me], Stockholm: Norstedt & Söner, 1942, pp 261–264.
65 Letter from Marcus Ehrenpreis to the Mosaic Congregation in Stockholm, 27 June 1944. Jewish Congregation Archives, Ehrenpreis, National Archives.

66 Ehrenpreis, *Mitt liv*, p 439 ff.
67 "En överrabbins memoarer" [Memories of a chief rabbi], *Dagens Nyheter*, 4 March 1946.

11. THE VERDICT OF THE FUTURE

1 Walter Benjamin, *Theses on the Philosophy of History*, 1940.
2 Göran Rosenberg, *A Brief Stop on the Road from Auschwitz*, New York: Other Press, 2015.
3 Pontus Rudberg, "'A Record of Infamy': The Use and Abuse of the Image of the Swedish Jewish Response to the Holocaust," *Scandinavian Journal of History*, 36:5, 2011, p 540. Rudberg, *The Swedish Jews and the Holocaust*, p 226.
4 Paul Levine, *From Indifference to Activism: Swedish Diplomacy and the Holocaust, 1938–44*, Uppsala: Acta Universitatis Upsaliensis, 1996, p 200. "From the first he appears in the record until the end of the war Storch generated many ideas on how to help, and alienated many of those whose assistance he required."
5 Rudberg, "A Record of Infamy," p 542.
6 Einhorn, *Handelsresande i liv*, p 254.
7 Einhorn, *Handelsresande i liv*, p 264.
8 Rudberg, *The Swedish Jews and the Holocaust*, pp 238–239.
9 Export license notification from the State Trade Commission to Marcus Ehrenpreis, 20 September 1944. Jewish Congregation Archives, Ehrenpreis, National Archives.
10 Postcard from Leo Baeck to Marcus Ehrenpreis, 12 December 1943. Jewish Congregation Archives, Ehrenpreis, National Archives.
11 Einhorn, *Handelsresande i liv*, p 246.
12 Einhorn, *Handelsresande i liv*, p 247.
13 Einhorn, *Handelsresande i liv*, p 247.
14 Marcus Ehrenpreis, "Till våra räddade" [To our rescued], *Judisk Tidskrift*, July 1945. "Zu di geratewete fun 1945" [To the rescued of 1945], *Exodus*, 17 July 1945, No 1.
15 *Exodus*, 10 August 1945, No. 2.
16 *Via Suecia*, 4 September 1945, Vol. 1, No. 1.
17 *Via Suecia*, 16 October 1945, Vol. 1, No. 4. "An Euch, die das neue Haus bauen" was published in 1947 in the collection of poems *In*

den Wohnungen des Todes. Translated into Swedish by Margaretha Holmqvist as "I dödens boningar" [In the dwellings of death], Nelly Sachs, *Dikter*, Stockholm: Bokförlaget Faethon, 2020, p 30.

18 Maurice L. Perlzweig, "Salute to Sweden," *Judisk Tidskrift*, August 1946. *Jewish Frontier* was a Zionist labor journal close to the American-Jewish labor movement, and thus, one may assume, also to the Swedish one.

19 *Der Tog*, 29 January 1946. Cited in Rudberg, "A Record of Infamy," p 544.

20 *Der Tog*, 29 January 1946. Cited in Rudberg, "A Record of Infamy," p 544.

21 Telegram from the *Jewish Daily Forward* to "Professor Marcus Ehrenpreis, Grevmagnigatan 6, Stockholm," 1 February 1946. Jewish Congregation Archives, Ehrenpreis, National Archives.

22 Letter from Per Nyström to Marcus Ehrenpreis, 6 February 1946. Jewish Congregation Archives, Ehrenpreis, National Archives.

23 Telegram from Samuel Margoshes to Marcus Ehrenpreis, 21 December 1945. Jewish Congregation Archives, Ehrenpreis, National Archives.

24 Marcus Ehrenpreis and Gunnar Josephson, reply to article in *Der Tog*. Jewish Congregation Archives, Ehrenpreis, National Archives. The reply was also sent to *The Jewish Daily Forward*, *Aufbau*, *Judische Welt*, and *Israelitisches Wochenblatt*, as well as to the World Jewish Congress (WJC) and the Joint Distribution Committee (JDC). Rudberg, "A Record of Infamy," note 66, p 551.

25 Svante Hansson, *Flykt och överlevnad* [Flight and survival], Stockholm: Hillelförlaget, 2004, pp 360–361.

26 *The Jewish Agency's Digest of Press and Events*, 19 January 1947.

27 Hansson, *Flykt och överlevnad*, pp 362–363.

28 Hansson, *Flykt och överlevnad*, p 363.

29 Letter (in Hebrew) from the head of the Press and Information Department of *Ha'vaad Ha'leumi*, Mr. Shragai, to the Chief Rabbi of Stockholm, Dr. M. Ehrenpreis, October 19, 1945. Jewish Congregation Archives, Ehrenpreis, National Archives.

30 "Rebuttal to an untrue attack," *Församlingsblad för Mosaiska församlingen i Stockholm*, August 1947, pp 78–80.

31 Letter (in Hebrew) from the Information Department of the Jewish Agency in Jerusalem to Professor Ehrenpreis in Stockholm, February 20, 1947. Jewish Congregation Archives, Ehrenpreis, National Archives.

32 "Sweden. Jewish Community Again Taken to Task," *The Jewish Agency Digest*, 4 May 1947. Rudberg, "A Record of Infamy," p 546.

33 Rudberg, "A Record of Infamy," p 546. Gunnar Josephson, "Swedish Jewry," *The Jewish Agency's Digest*, 3 August 1947. Gunnar Josephson, "Swedish Jews Refute Charges," *The Jewish Chronicle* (London), 15 August 1947. The eighty-one-year-old Simon Dubnow was murdered in a massacre in Riga on 9 December 1941.

34 Rudberg, "A Record of Infamy," p 546.

35 Hugo Valentin, "Swedish Jewry and Refugees. A Refutation," *The Jewish Chronicle*, 25 July 1947.

36 Hugo Valentin, "Rescue and Relief Activities on Behalf of Jewish Victims of Nazism in Scandinavia," *YIVO Annual of Jewish Social Science, Vol. III*, New York: Yiddish Scientific Institute, YIVO, 1954, p 224.

37 Hansson, *Flykt och överlevnad* [Flight and survival], p 78.

38 Hansson, *Flykt och överlevnad*, p 152.

39 Hansson, *Flykt och överlevnad*, p 119.

40 Hansson, *Flykt och överlevnad*, p 190. Ralph Hermanns, *Tänk på de dagar* [Think of those days], Stockholm: Legenda, 1984.

41 Hansson, *Flykt och överlevnad*, p 79. "Flykting från 1938" [Refugee from 1938], *Judisk krönika*, June 1987.

42 "Flykting från 1938," *Judisk krönika*, June 1987.

43 "Lärdom från 40-talets flyktingpolitik," [Lessons from the refugee policy of the 1940s], *Judisk krönika*, April 1987.

44 Steven Koblik, *The Stones Cry Out, Sweden's Response to the Persecution of the Jews 1933–1945*, New York: Holocaust Library, 1988, p 50.

45 Ragnar Gottfarb, "Församlingen gjorde vad den kunde" [The congregation did what it could], *Judisk krönika*, June 1987.

46 Rudberg, "A Record of Infamy," p 547.

47 *Församlingsblad för Mosaiska församlingen i Stockholm*, August 1947, p 19.

48 Per Agne Erkelius, *Hotel Galicja*. Stockholm: Norstedts, 2009, p 60.

49 Hansson, *Flykt och överlevnad* [Flight and survival], p 123.

50 Radio lecture, 8 August 1948. Olof Molander (ed.), *Vad jag tror på: radioföredrag 1948* [What I believe in: radio broadcast, 1948]. Stockholm: Radiotjänst, 1948. Also in *Judisk Tidskrift*, August 1948.

51 Ehrenpreis, *Frågetecknet Israel* [The question of Israel], pp 197, 199.

52 Ehrenpreis, *Frågetecknet Israel*, pp 197, 199.

12. THE QUESTION OF ISRAEL. AN EPILOGUE

1 Hannah Arendt, "The Jew as Pariah: A Hidden Tradition," *Jewish Social Studies*, Vol. 6, No. 2, April 1944.

2 Chaim Weizmann, *Trial and Error.* New York: Harper & Brothers, 1949.

3 *Judisk Tidskrift*, October 1949.

4 *Judisk Tidskrift*, May 1949.

GÖRAN ROSENBERG was born in 1948 in Sweden. In 1970 he left academia to work as a journalist for Swedish television, radio, and print. He is the author of several books, including the highly acclaimed *Det Förlorade landet* [The lost land: A personal history of Zionism, messianism, and the state of Israel] and *A Brief Stop on the Road from Auschwitz* (Other Press, 2015).